TURBULENT TIMES

JOHN ROBERT ALLEN

authorHOUSE°

AuthorHouse™
1663 Liberty Drive
Bloomington, IN 47403
www.authorhouse.com
Phone: 1 (800) 839-8640

Published by AuthorHouse 07/07/2016

ISBN: 978-1-5246-1798-1 (sc)
ISBN: 978-1-5246-1797-4 (e)

CHAPTER 1

The property at 825 Michigan Avenue, Miami Beach had remained untouched since the disappearance of Eveline Paine. The Miami Herald featured an article about the whereabouts of the famed Eveline Paine who had been the recipient of a multimillion dollar estate from her deceased husband, Wallace. It had become overgrown and an eyesore to the neighborhood since Eveline was last seen in Miami. Her yellow Buick convertible remained in the parking lot, and had not been driven. The top had rotted. The only new item seen on the property was a notice posted on the front gate from the Internal Revenue Service. As a passersby looked at the notice, they would see that the government had been attempting to contact Mrs. Eveline Paine. As part of Roosevelt's New Deal, the United States Congress passed the Revenue Act of 1934 which President Franklin Roosevelt had signed into law on May 10. It stated that because of the severity of the Depression, the government had passed this law raising individual income tax rates on the highest incomes. It was hoped that receiving higher taxes from the wealthy might assist in the recovery of the economy.

The Spaulding Tropical Gardens in Coral Gables had been suffering also from a low visitor attendance as a result of the deepening Depression. The American public could not afford to travel as they once had. Winston and Jason, the owners of the gardens, and friends of Eveline's, had been visited by the Internal Revenue Service to inquire of Eveline's whereabouts. The first time they came to the Tropical Gardens, Winston thought he was delinquent with taxes. They soon found that because he and Jason's names appeared on the list of property owners of 825, they were questioned about the disappearance of Mrs. Paine. The visit did not satisfy the Internal Revenue investigators therefore they went to West Point to question Patrick and Andrew Paine about their mother's whereabouts. They also had not heard from her. Jonathon Bingham, who was still a member of the Miami Police Department, would be next to be contacted about Eveline's whereabouts.

Since the 21st Amendment to the Constitution became law on December 5, 1933, repealing Prohibition, the types of crime had changed. Some speculated that the economy would improve with this law. It became clear that the legalizing of alcohol only changed the types of crimes committed. The country was now free to indulge in alcoholic beverages; there was no more need to go underground for spirits. There had been so much smuggling of alcohol in Eveline's deceased husband's businesses, people thought she may have been murdered as a result of the uncovering of illegal conspiracies. With the Depression deepening throughout the country, people were starving in the streets and businesses were forced to close. Winston, one of the lucky owners, did not owe any one for his property. He and Jason were debt free, unlike many of the businesses in Miami. The questions remained, where was Eveline, and why was the government looking for her?

During this time of excessive wealth and extreme poverty, newspapers would often have coverage of what the wealthy were doing during the Depression. William Randolph Hearst had been reported as having lavish parties in California. The columnist, Loretta Parsons had apologized to her readers whenever a photo was shown of the extravagant parties and entertainment Hearst had been known to have. There had been a photo of a party held on New Year's Eve that featured women dressed in the highest style. When the photo appeared in the Miami Herald, Winston was convinced he had recognized Eveline in the crowd toasting with Mr. Hearst. Winston made a call to the Miami Police Department reporting what he had suspected from seeing the newspaper. He made an appointment at the headquarters, and was told not to get involved because that was not Mrs. Paine. Winston knew better and wondered about the secrecy. When he inquired about Detective Bingham, Winston was shown to the door with no thanks from the lieutenant for his concern.

When Winston left the headquarters, he drove to 825 Michigan Avenue to check the property. When he arrived, the notification had been removed and a chain had been placed on both front and rear gates. There was no way for anyone to enter the property. As Winston looked at the property, he envisioned what a good place it might be to develop an establishment for travelers. Renting a room would be more reasonable than staying in a hotel and would offer a more private homelike environment. However, who would be in charge of its operation? Now would be the time to open a business of this sort while money was tight for people. There were still travelers able to afford such a place for a vacation offering a private environment.

CHAPTER 2

Having been suspicious of the treatment Winston had received at the Miami Police Department, he discussed it with Jason, his partner. Jason told Winston that it was probably not worth the time it might take to investigate his suspicions. Winston was certain that Eveline was in California and that Jonathon Bingham may have had other reasons for befriending her, in addition to the uncovering of the kidnapping of her children. Jason was not convinced and told Winston that he would have nothing to do with any of his strange notions. Winston still felt that he needed to satisfy his suspicions.

Winston went to the Miami Public library to find out more about William Randolph Hearst. He hoped to find a clue as to why Eveline might have become involved with Hearst. While he was reading older copies of the Miami Herald, he found that Hearst had been in politics and was a Democrat who served as a senator. Hearst was now an American newspaper tycoon. His father established large newspaper companies which William took over upon his father's death. William soon became the creator of "yellow journalism" which presents little or no legitimate research, but was intended to sell large numbers of newspapers using "sensationalism". The American public had become addicted to such news reporting. Hearst continued on his road to excessive wealth because of his newspapers that used exaggerations, scandals, and jokes. Winston found examples of Hearst's tactical use of journalism especially when it came to the wealthy. Maybe that is how Eveline managed to become involved in California. Winston wondered how Jonathon was involved. He continued to investigate the Hearst empire and found information about the huge property that was owned by the Hearst family on the central coast of California called San Simeone about 250 miles from Los Angeles. He learned that a huge castle called "La Cuesta Encantada" had been constructed for the purpose of entertaining movie stars and politicians, including Franklin and Eleanor Roosevelt, along with other wealthy patrons. Winston knew that somehow Eveline may have managed to maneuver herself into the "Hearst circle of friends".

While Winston worked on the whereabouts of Eveline, Jason had returned to his construction work on Miami Beach until tourism improved at the Tropical Gardens. Winston gave Jeffrey, their office manager, full responsibility to run the gardens whenever tourist might arrive for a visit. Jeffrey had been employed by Winston ever since he left the Biltmore Hotel. After being on duty for more than two years, Jeffrey had become like family to Winston and Jason. As part of his employment, Jason had been required to be available for anything Winston and Jason may require, which was often to be a slave boy. Jeffrey had turned into an obedient personal employee and loved the position he maintained for both men. While Winston investigated more about Eveline and the possible California connection to her whereabouts, he thought about how to best utilize 825 Michigan Avenue. If he and Jason were to develop a guest facility, Jeffrey might serve well as the manager. He wondered what the clientele might be like and what type of services might be offered. These ideas came to Winston while he read about the Hearst Castle that had 56 bedrooms and 61 bathrooms with a magnificent pool overlooking the valley. The property had been named, "The Enchanted Hill". The property at 825 Michigan Avenue could never be that elaborate, but it could become a haven for the discrete traveler. Just as Winston had been finishing one of the more recent articles in a newspaper, he came upon an article about Eleanor Roosevelt. It reported about her visit with Franklin to The Enchanted Hill. Winston's eye saw the word Eveline in the middle of the article. He had found out that Franklin and Eleanor had been invited to the castle. Another picture showed that Eleanor had been speaking to a woman that was the mother of the two young men that Franklin and she had sponsored at West Point. The woman's face was not clear in the picture but the name Eveline Paine had been included in the article. When

Winston read the article, he wondered how and why the two women met there. Winston could not wait to show Jason that his suspicions had been verified. While he drove to the Spaulding Tropical Gardens, he thought about what his next steps should be. It seemed obvious to him that the lieutenant of the Miami Police Department had not been interested in what he thought. What was the reason for the dismissive behavior he had been given last week when he met the lieutenant?

When Winston arrived home, Jason had been waiting for him. Winston was full of excitement as he explained what he had discovered. Jason listened with only half an ear about the California story, but was more attentive when Winston told him his idea about utilizing 825 Michigan Avenue. When Jason realized that it was an intriguing possibility, they decided to discuss the idea with Jeffery, since he was to be an important part of the plan. Jeffrey's head was full of possibilities when he heard about the plan.

CHAPTER 3

The Depression continued to affect millions of people throughout the United States. A drought had been ravaging the mid-west forcing an evacuation westward. "The Dust Bowl", as it had been named, made farmers lose their crops for a number of years. "Black Blizzards" of dust would occur that would destroy what few crops were growing and eventually there became a mass exodus to the West. This affected millions of people that were reliant on the farmer's crops for food and their economic well-being. As thousands of people migrated westward in hopes of a better life, conditions were different and sometimes worse. There had been many tent communities established that often were destroyed by weather. If people were lucky enough to find employment, it was usually at the hands of owners of large citrus and vegetable farms. The pay was nearly nothing, with overpriced food, making survival extreme. Many people died from disease and starvation everywhere in the United States.

Since there had been very little money for pleasure, the radio had become a means for people to be entertained. The "Amos and Andy" radio show had been a favorite, as folks sat in their homes listening and looking at the radio. Another favorite pastime was going to the movies for a penny. It was a means to escape their life outside of the movie theater. Unless a person was wealthy, people were not traveling and dining out as they once had. Whenever Winston went to Miami Beach to see Jason at work, the stores and shops on Lincoln Road had maintained a better level of business because Miami Beach was still considered a "Playground for the Rich". Burdines Department store opened its doors on Meridian Avenue and Lincoln Road. The store was committed to their motto as a store for "Sunshine Fashions" that helped make the area a place to shop and be entertained. Lincoln Road did not appear to be suffering from the Depression. The Miami Herald compared Miami and their beaches to Southern California. Its focus was to show that there were places not as affected by the Depression as many thought. When Winston read the article he thought about Eveline and Jonathon. He wondered how he was going to find out what had happened to them. The next day he contacted the Internal Revenue Department. The main office was near the Miami Police Department on Brickell Avenue. Jason was irritated by Winston's obsession about Eveline and told him that he was crazy for worrying so much about her.

Winston went for the appointment and was greeted by a robust gentleman who appeared to be interested in Winston's inquiry. After Winston explained that he saw the notice on the gate at 825 Michigan Avenue and that the gates were chained, he told the man that he and his friend were listed on the deed to the property. The man knew this information and explained that Eveline Paine had never paid federal income taxes. She was being sought after for tax evasion. Winston explained his relationship to Eveline and that he had been to the police department with no help from them. The man told Winston that the government was determined to collect back taxes from the wealthy. As he put it, "The wealthy have a way of hiding their money." The robust man continued to tell Winston that in some cases a private detective had been sent out to find and investigate the background of excessive tax evaders. Jonathon Bingham had been hired by the government to become involved with the life of wealthy people, with Eveline Paine being one of them. Detective Bingham was to keep track of how and where tax evaders spend and cover up their money. While Winston listened, he tried to think of all that had been happening to Eveline since Jonathon came into the picture. Not only because of Patrick and Andrew and all the criminals involved around Eveline's past, but maybe she had been an accomplice in some of the crimes surrounding her past. The man told Winston that Jonathon's assignment had become more complicated with additional criminal activities connected to Mrs. Eveline Paine. Winston knew then not to divulge any information; he would allow the man to tell the story. After a few minutes of listening to the man's version of why Jonathon had been delayed in his work, the man told Winston that Jonathon had found Eveline Paine. Winston listened to this new information. Detective Bingham and Eveline Paine were in Southern California. Jonathon had requested a leave of absence from his duties at the police department. His superiors agreed to the arrangements and would not give any information about Jonathon's whereabouts. Jonathon was now paid by the government, not the police. When Winston heard this he knew why the appointment with the lieutenant had been useless.

Winston left the tax office after he found out what the plan for Eveline had been. The tax man explained that Jonathon had befriended Mrs. Paine and was gathering information as to the whereabouts of her money. Since Winston was an owner of 825 Michigan Avenue, the man was more generous with information. During his meeting, Winston was handed a tax bill for the property. He did not expect this but agreed to pay the bill. Now, he and Jason could move forward with their plan for the business at 825. Winston asked when Jonathon would be bringing Eveline back to Florida. The man explained it would be awhile because Eveline had become involved with the very wealthy of California. Winston shook his head when he heard this information. The man asked if Winston had any idea as to why Mrs. Paine behaved the way Jonathon had explained it to him; a flighty and impulsive woman. Winston told the man that Eveline was an unusual individual. She had many experiences with underhanded people, who had manipulated her businesses after her husband's death, many years ago. The man listened in surprise as Winston explained how Eveline unraveled the criminal activities. He wanted to know what Winston thought about the hundreds of thousands of dollars she owed the government. Winston had been unaware of these things and told him how generous Eveline had been in the past. The man laughed and said, "Somehow, she did not know enough to cover her tracks with the taxes." Winston replied, "Knowing Eveline, she was too busy taking care of herself. That is why so many people took advantage of her." Winston continued to discuss Eveline's personality. The man seemed aware of her tendencies. He told Winston that Jonathon had fully briefed the police and the tax office of her past hospitalizations and recent lapse of memory and her erratic behavior when she traveled to California in disguise. Now, Winston wondered if Eveline had ever been ill or had this been a tactic to avoid things. The man agreed that this was a possibility based on what he had been told about Eveline's behavior. He ended the meeting with no promises for any further information. Winston thought this was strange but he paid the taxes for 825 Michigan Avenue and was free to proceed with his plan. The man gave Winston a key to the locks for the chains at each gate.

CHAPTER 4

T he news of Eveline's whereabouts came as a shock to Jason when Winston revealed what he had found out from the Internal Revenue Office. Jason was satisfied to learn that 825 Michigan Avenue was without debt and that the business they had planned for was able to be established. Winston explained how Jonathon had become involved with Eveline. The circumstances had changed; the tax evasion issue had become secondary to the investigations of gangland threats, the supposed kidnapping of Patrick and Andrew, ransom letters, and corruption from Eveline's late husband, Wallace. After Winston's news, Jason agreed to be in charge of applying for the proper permits and licenses for the operation of a vacation rental property. The plan for its opening would be by the end of 1934. It would be called Bohemia 825.

After thinking about his visit to the tax office, Winston made an appointment with the lieutenant at the Miami Police Department. This time he would go with specific information and not ask for the lieutenant's side of the story. When he telephoned, he was told that the lieutenant had expected a return inquiry from him. Winston wondered about the change in attitude. All this was becoming more complicated and the reasons for Jonathon's involvement seemed to have double responsibilities. He thought that all this was a ploy on Jonathon's part to get into her thinking and behavior. Winston had a feeling that being a detective required having a dual personality.

When Winston entered the lobby of the Police Department, he was met by a security guard who ushered him to a different department. The lieutenant met Winston with a different attitude. Winston wondered why the change and what he was about to hear. The lieutenant apologized to Winston for his previous behavior. He admitted that he thought that Winston was coming to discuss Eveline Paine and to attempt to sidetrack the tax evasion investigation. Winston said nothing. The conversation was directed toward how Winston could assist the lieutenant in having more communication with Mrs. Paine. Winston had not been clear about the lieutenant's request because he had been told why Jonathon had been hired by both departments. After Winston had listened to the lieutenant, he asked, "Why do you want me to be involved?" The lieutenant paused and replied, "Because you hold more information than even Jonathon can figure out." Winston asked what that might be. The lieutenant wanted Winston to be in communication with Jonathon since he and Eveline were in the Los Angeles area. According to the recent communication from Jonathon, Eveline had rented accommodations at the Beverly Hills Hotel. Winston shook his head and said, "She loves to live in the best places." The lieutenant agreed, but told Winston that she was living on money that she owed the government. Winston was told that Jonathon had been with Eveline since he had tracked her down on the train going to California. According to the report, Eveline had faked having what was supposed to be a Fugue State. Winston asked what that was. He was told it was a temporary state of amnesia. Winston looked confused but began to think about Eveline's supposed condition years earlier at Willard State Hospital. Winston asked if Eveline might have been planning these events and not been mentally ill. The lieutenant agreed and stated that Jonathon suggested the same thing. Winston was asked to be available for a telephone conversation with Jonathon.

The next afternoon, Winston had arranged for the conversation with Jonathon. It would be early in the morning in California because Eveline had been in the habit of taking tennis lessons at the clubhouse. Winston and the lieutenant were in an office with two telephones connected to the office at the Los Angeles Police Department. After the operator connected the call, Jonathon sounded as he usually did and was glad to speak with Winston. After explaining the complications of his work, Winston asked how Eveline was. Jonathon explained that she was, as usual, taking very good care of herself. He admitted that he had found Eveline to be the most interesting and fun woman he had ever met and had fallen for her. The lieutenant made a face and reminded Jonathon that he had been hired to do a job. Jonathon asked Winston what he knew about Eveline's young life, when she first came to Rochester from Canada. Winston explained that he was jealous of her at first because he had a strong affection for Wallace, who became her husband. Winston continued explaining about her unusual acceptance of Wallace's intimate behavior toward men. The lieutenant listened and took notes while shaking his head. Jonathon wanted to know if Winston thought there was any question about Eveline's mother. Winston knew that Jonathon was aware of the criminal activity and the ransom and kidnapping a few years prior to this. Jonathon asked Winston if he knew of any unusual behavior towards Eveline by her mother. Winston told Jonathon that her mother hated Eveline and the feeling was mutual. Her father was the one who protected Eveline, usually from her mother's hatred and wrath. Jonathon explained Eveline's condition after she left Miami Beach with only her personal belongings. He explained that Eveline had suffered from a Fugue State, or so he thought, but now felt there was a deeper reason for her erratic behavior. When Winston heard this, he told Jonathon of Eveline's outbursts and unpredictable behavior in buying and traveling without purpose. He explained that everyone thought it was because, her husband, Wallace was too involved in his businesses and that she was bored and needed entertainment. Things were beginning to fall into place as Jonathon listened.

Before the conversation ended, Jonathon explained what he needed Winston to do. Since Winston was Eveline's lifelong friend, knew her well, and she trusted him, Jonathon suggested Winston, Eveline, and he go to Canada to visit Catherine Lounsberry, Eveline's mother. Jonathon said that there may have been some type of unusual treatment Eveline was exposed to that may have created these different behaviors in her. Jonathon explained how many times Eveline had acted differently and never appeared to remember the events. He explained how she acted as if she never remembered why she was in Miami and that when he found her on the train; she acted as if they had been friends from the beginning of time. She had not mentioned a word about her life in Miami or the property on Miami Beach. Winston was flabbergasted when he heard this information. How could she not remember everything that happened while she was living at the Biltmore and at 825 Michigan Avenue? Then Winston remembered the incident when she hit her head during the hurricane and her lapse of memory, or was it a lapse of memory? The conversation ended with them making plans for the trip to Canada. Winston left the police department more confused than ever about Eveline.

CHAPTER 5

Miami Beach had continued to be a destination for the warm weather seekers. The railroad companies had been offering special deals for individuals traveling from northern regions. For one price, the "American Plan", offered a ticket entitling the traveler to railroad transportation to Miami, a hotel room, meals, and entertainment for the week. There was a monthly rate available for those who wished to remain in the warm climate longer; especially during the winter months. For many people, this was a reasonable way to travel. Because of the Depression, many individuals could not afford an automobile, so traveling to Florida on the "American Plan" offered an economical way for a vacation. Entertainment had changed because of the Depression with not as much money available for frivolous spending and going to the movies for a penny offered a diversion from the doldrums of the real world. Many of the movies were silly but made people laugh. People were also attracted to ballroom dancing. There were "big bands" conducted by Benny Goodman and Fletcher Henderson that played swing music, foxtrots, and line dancing, all to help people forget their troubles and "dance the night away". Newspapers everywhere were advertising these plans and activities in hopes to stimulate the American public. Unfortunately, this type of life only attracted the wealthy. The majority of the population had been near starvation, unemployed, and on soup lines for survival. The differences were dramatic. President Roosevelt had not seen the success he had hoped for in the "New Deal" which was designed to offer welfare programs to the unemployed. He and the government were working on a "Second New Deal" designed to provide the United States work force with federally funded jobs which would stimulate the economy.

Winston and Jason had seen an increase in tourism at the Tropical Gardens in Coral Gables. There had been enough revenue to pay the bills and begin the restructuring of the Bohemia 825 guesthouse. While they worked on redesigning the property to offer various accommodations, Jeffrey ran the operation at the Tropical Gardens and had become an integral part in the business. This left Winston and Jason time to devote to the guesthouse. Since the construction of the building at 825 Michigan Avenue, there had been little done to maintain the vegetation and upkeep of the building. Eveline never found it necessary to worry about such responsibilities. As a result of the lack of care, Winston and Jason had to clean out the overgrowth, much like what had to be done to the Tropical Gardens. It was back breaking work in the summer heat and had continual interruptions because of the torrential rains of the summer.

In addition to the news of the Depression, Europe had been reported as having uneasy developments. Adolf Hitler had taken over power of the Nazi party in Germany and shortly after, the Nuremberg Laws were put into effect. Nazism, the National Socialist German Workers' Party, which was a form of fascism, had become an official ideology incorporating anti-Semitism as a form of scientific racism. The German legislation directed at the Jews, Gypsies, Negroes, and Homosexuals were banned from civil service and included a ban on sexual relations and marriages between persons classified as "Aryan" and "non-Aryan". The rise of Adolf Hitler and his determination to cleanse and maintain an Aryan population left concern for the future of Europe. Since there was so much economic strife in the United States, Franklin Roosevelt chose a path of "isolationism" whenever Nazi affairs were reported. Some felt it was as if the development of Hitler's plan for a superior race was not happening. The newspapers speculated that the attitude for intervention was ignored because the United States had not been repaid from Germany's World War I debt. The United States hoped to recover the money and leaving Hitler alone might help Germany repay their debt.

While Winston and Jason worked on 825 Michigan Avenue, they became more familiar with Miami Beach. Having never spent much time on the beach, they did not have a reason to take part in the social atmosphere of the area. As a break, they would walk to Lincoln Road. It was one of the fashionable streets on Miami Beach. Many of the finer stores had opened shops there. Burdines had opened a large store one block off Lincoln Road on Meridian Avenue. All the finery could be purchased anywhere on the street. As well as shopping, there was dining of all types. One day while Winston and Jason took a stroll for lunch, they encountered a crowd of people around a restaurant designed for quick service. As they approached the mob of people, they heard the announcement that there was a new type of lunch for sale. After the crowd calmed down, the owner of the restaurant explained that a beef lunch sandwich had been created called a "cheeseburger". It had its beginning when customers no longer wanted sausage or hot dogs; they wanted something new to eat. The sandwich would be made of a ground beef patty that would be grilled with cheese melted on a bun. Potatoes cut in strips and deep fried were called "French Fries". These were added to the plate. Winston and Jason lined up for their first taste of a cheeseburger and fries. They liked the taste of the sandwich and fries dipped in ketchup. They sat and observed thousands of tourists stroll along the street. Winston had an idea. He would have an advertisement made to be placed on the board in the middle of the sidewalk that would feature a trip to the Tropical Gardens. It would be another way for tourists to know where to go for a day trip. He told Jason that they could have a tour bus deliver the guests to the gardens. Jason thought it was a good idea but wondered who would be in charge of the trip. Winston explained that since he had worked on the beach and most of his contracting had been completed, he could be in charge of that part of the operation. Jason thought about it and agreed. While they discussed the new advertising campaign, the thought came to them that they may have too many things going on at once and may not have enough people helping them.

As they walked back to 825 Michigan Avenue, they saw various things happening on the street. Jason commented on how quiet it was at the Tropical Gardens in Coral Gables compared to Miami Beach. Winston reminded him this was a busy place with thousands of tourist coming and going every day. They noticed a poster describing a new organization that was being established. It had its roots in the need to assist people who had taken too much advantage of the repeal of Prohibition. The group was to be called "Alcoholics Anonymous". It was a 12 step program designed to help a person who was addicted to alcohol to learn to live alcohol free. It was a national program developed because so many people had indulged in alcohol to the point that they could not function. No one was required to admit to joining, it was confidential and the announcement was for information as to where the first meetings were to be held. Winston told Jason, it reminded him of the syphilis study Olitha had taken part in a few years ago. After they discussed the meetings, Winston asked Jason if he had any thought about offering either Sable or Olitha a job as a housekeeper at the guesthouse. Jason thought about it and said, "One of them might do well as an employee at Bohemia 825, but not both."

An economic reform to the waning United States unemployed situation, was the enactment of the Social Security Administration program. It was designed to offer the unemployed financial assistance until times improved. The reform would also have a retirement fund that workers would contribute to for a pension upon retirement. Part of the program offered financial assistance for the disabled that would provide food, shelter, and health services for the less fortunate. There was speculation as to its effectiveness when workers had to contribute a percentage of their income to Social Security. It was mandatory, so no matter what the individual thought, the required contribution was deducted from their pay check. There were great hopes for the return of a strong economy in the United States and as the newspaper stated, "The rich get richer and the poor get poorer." There was much unrest in the government over such a welfare and recovery program.

CHAPTER 6

W inston received a letter from Jonathon Bingham explaining the plan that had been finalized by the police department and the Internal Revenue Service. Instead of traveling to Canada, it was decided that it might make more sense in Eveline's eyes, if Winston and Jason came to California to visit. Eveline might not get suspicious about such extensive travels to see her mother who was in prison. All expenses were included and Jason would stay for a few days, then Winston, Jonathon, and Eveline would go to Canada. They would call it a business trip to inform Eveline of the changes that had been made in Miami Beach. According to Jonathon, Eveline had made no mention of ever being involved with the construction of 825 Michigan Avenue. She had discussed briefly the vacation she had been on at the Biltmore. When Winston read the letter to Jason, the story seemed like another person had been living this life, not Eveline. Winston said, "So, everywhere Eveline has lived has been a vacation in her mind with no responsibilities to life, expenses, or family." Jason nodded his head in agreement. Jonathon requested that Winston telephone him to discuss the dates and details of the trip to California.

While Winston pondered the reasons for going to California, he began to rethink Eveline's financial background. He never discussed her money or how things had been paid. She never discussed money, only when she was out to demolish the underhanded businesses while living in Geneva. Money had never been an issue because of Wallace's wealth. Jonathon remarked to Winston, while on the phone, that when he found Eveline on the train to California, all she said was, "Now we can live it up on Wallace's millions." Now, it appeared she may never have known about the finances and the supposed wealth. Winston could not discuss any of this with Jason because he had not been around for these things because all this happened years ago. Jonathon said there was an exorbitant amount of back taxes due for her late husband's affairs. All Winston could remember was that Mr. Keyes had been in charge of the legalities and overseeing the accounts after Wallace's death. Maybe there had been some connection to Thaddeus Cooper, the illegitimate detective, and his interest in helping Eveline with her financial affairs, or was he working with Mr. Keyes to swindle funds from her accounts? Eveline never cared about where the money came from and always assumed it would be available.

The next day, Winston made a telephone call to speak with Jonathon. When the call was connected, Jonathon was pleased to hear from Winston and decided that they would travel to California to make it appear as a vacation to see Eveline. Jonathon told Winston that he had discussed the possibility with Eveline of a visit from he and Jason. Eveline did not understand why they even needed to see her. Jonathon explained that Winston missed her and that he and Jason needed a vacation away from Florida. Jonathon explained that the only thing Eveline made reference to was living at the Biltmore and never mentioned the trauma of the supposed kidnapping and eventual reuniting of her children, Patrick and Andrew. Winston was speechless when he heard this story.

Before the telephone call ended, Winston explained what he had been thinking regarding Eveline's financial affairs. Under the pretense of helping to monitor her supposed wealth, was Mr. Keyes swindling money from Eveline? When Jonathon heard about the possibilities of underhanded financial dealings many years before he was involved, he knew there was much more work to be done. Eveline had been deceived, not only by her parents, but possibly by her financial manager. When the men concluded the telephone call, both were equally as confused. How could one person be manipulated by so many people?

Jason had been listening to the conversation and watched Winston's expressions while speaking with Jonathon. When he finished, Jason told Winston that they needed to get their affairs in order in Miami before the California trip. The renovation of the guesthouse could not be put on hold and work would need to continue. Jason would hire some of his co-workers that helped build places in Miami Beach to work on 825. Jeffrey would be left to operate the Tropical Gardens. Olitha, Eveline's former domestic servant, continued to work at the gardens. The idea of the tourists taking a day trip from Miami Beach to visit the gardens in Coral Gables had worked and was fully operating. Olitha had agreed to be the driver of the bus from Miami Beach to Coral Gables for the tourist's visit. Winston hoped all would work out in their absence. So much was happening and without either of them in town, so many things could go wrong.

CHAPTER 7

Eveline had been "living it up" at the Beverly Hills Hotel. There had been times she would catch sight of a movie celebrity and would make every effort to converse with them, usually with no luck. She had been taking tennis lessons from a handsome young instructor, one who might be considered a catch for a wealthy woman. Jonathon had been observing her behaviors and knew she had an eye for her instructor. Where did Jonathon stand in all of Eveline's behavior? Since they arrived in California, Eveline had not been as infatuated with Jonathon as she had once been in Miami. There had been a discussion about such matters and where Jonathon and she stood on their relationship. Eveline was certain she liked "all of Jonathon" but liked the idea that her instructor was young and firm. She suggested, in a flip way, that the three of them could investigate what a ménage a triose would be like. Jonathon asked, "How would you know about the young man's abilities?" Eveline told Jonathon that she gets massages after her lessons. Jonathon knew then that Eveline was on the move to yet another sexual adventure, never learning from her past affairs. Jonathon realized that was why Eveline was so uncertain about getting more involved with him when she lived in Miami. What caused her to have such a changeable personality and do so many outlandish things with no remorse? Jonathon began to feel as if he should begin treating Eveline's situation like any other work activity. He reminded himself that business and pleasure did not mix. He wondered why she found someone her son's age to be involved with.

One day during one of Eveline's tennis lessons, her instructor told Eveline about a movie that was being made in town. The movie stars were residing at the Beverly Hills Hotel. When Eveline heard about this, she asked who the stars were and what the name of the movie was. All the instructor knew was that two of the main characters were already working on a movie and had been in the hotel for some time. "The Talkies", moving pictures with sound, had come into popularity throughout the country and were a welcome relief to the unfortunate lives of many Americans who were suffering from the Depression. After Eveline's tennis lesson, she learned that her instructor had been giving lessons to the female star of the movie he had mentioned. Eveline, being miffed, pretended not to be interested in all she had heard. Her massage had to be cancelled and rescheduled around the movie star. Eveline was not used to being put off when she wanted something. Instead of having the massage, Eveline decided to spend time around the lobby hoping to see who the movie stars might be.

When Eveline saw Jonathon, she told him about the changes in her schedule with her instructor. Jonathon appeared sympathetic but thought it served her right for assuming such relationships might happen between the instructor, Eveline, and himself. While she was elaborating on the movie production and the stars in the hotel, Eveline asked Jonathon if they could have lunch in the hotel restaurant. He agreed under one condition, that she would not create a scene if any movie people were in the restaurant. They went to the lobby to make a reservation for lunch and saw the headlines of the Los Angeles Times detailing the newest movie being produced in Hollywood. It was to star Claudette Colbert and Clark Gable in "It Happened One Night". The synopsis of the movie explained that it was to be a comedy about how the heroine regrets her wealthy lifestyle when she meets a handsome man that is not of her caliber. The situations in the movie were a comical calamity that would have light hearted sex appeal where love triumphs over her wealth as Claudette Colbert falls in love with Clark Gable. As Eveline was reading the article to Jonathon she said, "This movie sounds like you and me." Jonathon asked what she meant by such a remark. Eveline told Jonathon that she came from wealth and he did not, but he had sex appeal and love had taken over. When he listened to her, he wondered if this was the same person who recently wanted a ménage a triose. He thought better of questioning any of her intent. It was all too difficult to figure out.

The entertainment page of the newspaper listed some of the notable movie stars who had been making films. Some were short films and others full length features. Carole Lombard, William Powell, Bette Davis, and Vivian Leigh were all reported as being in the process of making movies. Another highlight for Los Angeles was the introduction of a way to see a movie outside of a theater. The "Drive In" was a place to park your automobile in a large lot and watch the film in the comfort of your own surroundings. When Eveline heard this she gave Jonathon the eye and said, "Too bad my Buick is not here, we could see a movie and practice some of our moves on each other in the front seat." Jonathon agreed that might be fun. He was getting confusing messages from Eveline every day. Lunch was pleasant, so Jonathon decided to pursue the upcoming visit from Winston and Jason. While he was telling Eveline about them coming to have a vacation away for Florida, Eveline wanted to know if there was any other reason for their coming to California. Jonathon told her that they wanted to see her and discuss the businesses and the formation of a guesthouse. They wanted to finalize some information about her intent in Miami and what her plans were for the future. Jonathon conveniently mentioned the past taxes that were due on 825 Michigan Avenue and asked if she was fully aware of her financial status. Eveline was matter of fact when she said, "I know my status, and it's wealthy. Mr. Keyes has been in charge of my legal affairs as well as my investments and incomes. All he does is have money available in my account in Miami as he did in Geneva. That reminds me that I need to tell him to establish an account here in Los Angeles." At that moment Jonathon knew Winston might have been correct about Mr. Keyes' ethics and honesty with Eveline's business affairs. Jonathon did not discuss anything regarding her mother in Canada. There seemed to be many dimensions to Eveline and what she still did not realize about herself and those around her from the past to the present. Jonathon hoped for success in unraveling many issues with Eveline. With all of her quirks, Jonathon fought being in love with Eveline.

CHAPTER 8

After the discussion about wealth and Eveline's involvement with Jonathon, she asked how Winston and Jason were getting to California. Jonathon could not divulge the information about the financing of the trip. The government was paying for the men to come and assist in finding out about Eveline's past life and her lack of financial structure. Jonathon asked why Eveline was interested. She had been thinking about her Buick that had been left behind when she took off to California. Jonathon thought it strange she could remember the automobile when the only things she had with her were a few of her belongings. If she suffered from a Fugue State, she might have been able to remember items that were important to her. She had not mentioned anything about 825, her children, or any of the other situations that had occurred. Eveline said, "I think you need to suggest that Winston and Jason drive to California. Then, I will have my cherished yellow Buick to sport around in Los Angeles. After all, movie stars are everywhere and they might take more notice of me and my style." Jonathon cleared his throat and told her that might be a good idea that Winston and Jason drive, but it might take a week for them to travel across the country. Eveline did not think that would be a problem. She never thought anything was a problem. Eveline told Jonathon that he should offer to pay them to bring the Buick. Jonathon knew he could not tell her the truth about the reason for their coming or that their travel had been arranged for them. He told her that he would find out if her idea was possible. Eveline became suspicious when Jonathon told her he would make the arrangements. Eveline said, "Winston has been my friend for a long time. Why can't I tell him what I want them to do?" Jonathon explained, in a diplomatic way, that the men should be in charge of such minute details. When Eveline heard it put that way, she appeared satisfied but had a feeling something about the story was

25

not accurate. Before the conversation ended, the question became, how would they return to Miami?

The next day, Jonathon contacted Winston to explain Eveline's newest request. After Jonathon explained about the drive to California in the Buick, Winston agreed that might be a good idea. Jonathon would have funds transferred to Winston's account to cover transportation costs, food, and lodging. Winston knew that he was most likely not to return with Jason to Miami. Jonathon had decided the night before to send Jason back on an American Airlines flight. There had been commercial flights started between Miami, Chicago, and Los Angeles and it would take less time to return to Miami than by train. Winston was shocked that Jason was being treated so well. He was jealous that Jason would be the first to experience such a flight. Jonathon did not mention that he had been planning to take Eveline, Winston, and himself to Canada as they would be going to confront Catherine Lounsberry, Eveline's mother, about things of the past. After Jonathon had made the arrangements for the trip to California, he told Eveline the details. She seemed to be returning to her former self before her attack of temporary amnesia, or so it seemed.

Before Winston and Jason were to leave for California, there was much to organize so that progress on the guesthouse could continue in their absence. The newest undertaking of the trolley to the Tropical Gardens from Lincoln Road was being overseen by Olitha who reported to Jeffrey, manager of the gardens, for scheduling. During the week before their departure for the west coast, both Sable and Olitha had agreed to be housekeepers for the guesthouse. They made it a point to remind Winston that it seemed like old times when they ran the properties in Geneva and at the Biltmore for Miss Eveline. Winston agreed it was similar, only Eveline would not be in charge, he would. They would share the responsibilities of food preparation and maintaining a clean and spotless environment for the guests. Sable spoke up and said, "Nothing much different than when we worked for Miss Eveline." Since the women were living in Overton, Sable had learned to drive. Her husband bought her an old jalopy so she could get to work. The question remained as to who would take Sable and Olitha's place at the Tropical Gardens. Jason had discussed those jobs with a few of the wives of his construction crew on Miami Beach. Sable asked, "What if Miss Eveline dun wants to come back to her home?" Winston said, "Too bad for her."

CHAPTER 9

During the week before Winston and Jason were to leave for Los Angeles, the Buick required many repairs to make it worthy of a long trip across the country. The most difficult item to repair was the tan convertible top. Since the Buick was a few years old, the top had rotted from the intensity of the Florida sun and needed to be replaced. There was only one shop in Miami that had the knowledge and know how to make a new canvas top. Winston became the "in charge person" for these duties. Jason had the job of scheduling and making sure everyone knew what was required in their absence. Sable, Olitha, and Jeffrey were most reliable as some of the newer workers were not. Many Cubans had been hired and would work very hard when Jason or Winston oversaw them. Whenever either one was absent, the Cubans were on a "siesta", until either one of them found the workers not doing their duties. Usually, the threat of less pay was enough to get them back on task. So, in Winston and Jason's absence, they made Sable the "boss lady" of the employees. She was delighted with the job and the added income. She said, "Iz gonna treat them the ways we was treated by the ship men on the way across the ocean wiz doz babies. I threaten them wiz a whippin if they doin too much "siesta" stuff." Jason was not too sure that treatment would work and suggested a record of who would get less pay, might be better. He feared, as did Winston, that the workers may quit on the spot with treatment such as a whipping.

The day before they were to leave for California, Patrick, Eveline's son, telephoned Winston. When Winston heard Patrick's deep voice, he asked, "Is everything alright?" Patrick explained that things were fine but that he and Andrew, his brother, Eveline's adopted son, were thinking about what they wanted to do with their lives. Patrick told Winston they had been thinking of leaving West Point. Winston listened. Strangely enough, both young men were considering coming to Miami. Winston, being taken back by this possibility, told Patrick that Eveline had been found in California. When Patrick heard this, there was a pause on the line. Patrick asked, "Have you spoken to her?" Winston told him he had not. The question then was, "Do you think Mother ever thinks about us?" Winston explained about what happened to their mother and how she left suddenly for California when she experienced temporary amnesia, and no one knew where she was. After some investigation, Jonathon Bingham, found Eveline on a train to California. Patrick could be heard telling Andrew the story. Winston asked, "Why have you reconsidered coming to us in Miami?" There was a pause. Patrick in a low tone said, "We want to be near you and Jason. You have been like a father to me and I always wanted to be closer to you than I could ever admit. I loved you from the minute I met you when you and Mother were living in the mansion. I always felt a sensation whenever we were together, especially swimming in the lake. Now that I am a man, and know what I want, I have a love for Andrew as you do for Jason. We have been hiding this at West Point for fear of punishment. We feel a life nearer to you and Jason would be best for us." Winston was stunned when he heard what Patrick had revealed about himself and Andrew. Winston was not sure what to say about all he had heard. He told Patrick that he and Jason were driving their mother's Buick to California to visit her and discuss what they were planning for 825 Michigan Avenue. Patrick said, "Oh, that's right you and Jason are now the owners. We did not want anything to do with it before. Why is Mother so hard to figure out? She acted like she wanted us in Miami, but now has gone off to California." Winston explained that was another reason for the visit. Before the conversation ended, Winston told Patrick that he loved him as his son and Andrew too. He asked Patrick, "Do you want me to tell your mother about your news?" Conversation could be heard on the end of the line. Patrick finally said, "Don't tell Mother about this conversation. We need to figure out when we will arrive and where

we will be living. Maybe Mother needs her sons to straighten her out."
Winston said, "Okaaaay. We will talk when we return."

The conversation with Patrick set Winston's mind in high gear. What
he had hoped and wished for had now come true. He always vowed to be
faithful and caring for Patrick after Wallace's death. Wallace was Patrick's
father and Winston's secret love and now both young men saw Winston
and Jason as role models, and wanted to part of their lives. As far as
Winston was concerned, he knew years ago that there was a feeling he had
whenever Patrick looked at him or was close to him. Winston knew he was
the type of man that Patrick might have chosen for his father. Andrew too
became as attached as did Patrick. Winston could not wait to discuss the
newest possibilities for their lives with Jason. As Winston was thinking
about the conversation, questions began coming up. Did Patrick suggest
they live with them at the Tropical Gardens? What might they be doing
for work? Did they need to confer with President Roosevelt and Mrs.
Roosevelt of their plan? After all they were the financiers for them at West
Point. This was all becoming more overwhelming than Winston needed
at this time but he was excited and happy about the news. When Jason
arrived home from his duties and preparations for the trip to California,
Winston greeted him and said, "Patrick telephoned today. He and Andrew
want to leave West Point. They have the same feelings for each other as
we do. They want to come to Miami to be closer to us. Don't you think
that is wonderful news?" Jason's eyes were wide open as was his mouth,
saying nothing.

CHAPTER 10

A fter Jason had time to think about the news, he and Winston discussed the possibilities of Patrick and Andrew living in Miami. They came to the conclusion that there were too many things happening at this time and dealing with Patrick and Andrew would have to wait. Winston agreed to discuss their moving after the California trip. Part of the evening was spent studying road maps of US Highways that were considered the best routes to use when traveling from coast to coast. Jason had read that Route 66 was a good route to use because it had the most direct route from Chicago to Los Angeles. It passed through many scenic spots, making the trip more enjoyable. It had also been a major route for travelers trying to escape the Dust Bowl in the Midwest. As Jason studied the map from Miami to Chicago, he realized that the total trip would be over 4000 miles and would take more time than a week to arrive in Los Angeles. The original plan was to spend only a week getting to the west coast. When Jason explained this to Winston, they agreed that this might not be the best way to travel. What would they do with Eveline's Buick?

Winston telephoned Jonathon and when the call was put through to the Beverly Hills Hotel, Jonathon acted as if he did not know anything about a trip to California or who Winston Spaulding was. Jonathon sounded startled that a call of this nature would be for him. He said, "Whoever you are, do not ever call here again." Winston held the receiver in shock and wondered if he should call back. What happened to create this type of response? He found Jason in the main house of the gardens and explained what had just occurred. Jason shook his head saying, "Is this whole thing worth it? I know Eveline has been a friend for many years and she is strange and now her boyfriend or whatever he is to her acts like her. Maybe we should step aside from all her turmoil." Winston wanted to agree with Jason but replied, "How can we do that? There are so many

31

things that are mingled together with her, including her two children that now want to come to us." Jason, in a disgusted tone said, with his finger pointed at Winston's face, "Do not do another thing until you hear from either Jonathon or the Police Department." Winston knew when Jason said those things with that tone that he should do as he was told.

A few days had passed with no contact from anyone. Winston did not know what to tell everyone in his employ about why they had not left yet. Sable and Olitha were the most suspicious because they had been through many of these problems in the past. Olitha said, "Maybe Mr. Jonathon is having problems with Miss Eveline." Winston agreed that may be an issue he is attempting to sort out. While they were finishing the plans for the next month, the telephone rang. Winston answered it and heard Jonathon's voice thanking the operator for connecting the call. At first Winston wanted to do the same to Jonathon as he did to him but decided against it. Jonathon began with an apology for his behavior on the telephone. Winston listened but was furious. Apparently, Eveline had been having a raging attack of wanting a ménage a triose with the tennis instructor and himself. They were in the midst of a heated discussion when Winston had called. Eveline had been insisting they invite the instructor to their apartment and as she put it, "See how things fit for all of us." Jonathon had told her that he was not interested in having an affair with another man and her at the same time. When Winston heard the part about "an affair with another man and her at the same time", he wondered if Jonathon was capable of doing such things. As he listened, Jonathon explained that he had to act like that so Eveline would not suspect who was on the telephone. Jonathon admitted he was tiring of Eveline's antics and was getting impatient with all she had gotten into, for one reason or another.

After Jonathon finished his apologies, Winston explained the problems connected to the trip across country with the Buick. Jonathon had not been aware of the time and distance the trip would take and the possible expense of so many days on the road. Winston told him that Eveline's beloved Buick was not as reliable as it once had been. He suggested that they take the new high speed rail service from Miami to Chicago on the Illinois Central Railway and the Union Pacific from Chicago to Los Angeles. The Buick could be transported on the train for less than the road trip. Jonathon agreed that the timing was the main issue, not the money, since the government was funding the investigation. The tickets would be purchased and arrangements for the Buick made in the next few days. After the travel plans were finished, Jonathon asked Winston if he had ever had to deal with Eveline in these ways of multiple sex partners. Winston paused and wondered if he should tell him how many times that very thing occurred. He said, "Yes, we had many occasions with a number of people. There were a few times, Eveline took on the role of the director." Jonathon wanted to know if that title was the same as a dominatrix and how she received that title. Winston continued, "Eveline would enjoy telling others in the group what type of action to engage in and often would be giving orders during her involvement, sometimes three men and herself. She became more demanding when she would use a whip or a hatpin or feathers to heighten sexual pleasures and aggression." Jonathon said, "Oh my God, what have I gotten myself into?" Winston, trying to relieve the tension, said in a jovial way, "Who knows she may want all of us to be involved with her at the same time." Jonathon replied, "Can we just leave her out of all of this and have our own fun? She has too many irons in her fire and I'm afraid of what we are all in for."

CHAPTER 11

Jonathon let Eveline know more details of what had been planned with Winston and Jason. He needed to be cautious about how much he divulged regarding the trip. As far as she knew, Winston and Jason wanted to have a vacation away from Miami and they would be driving her Buick to California. Since Jonathon had located her, he would let Eveline think that everyone in Miami was aware of her being in Los Angeles. Jonathon needed a time when Eveline was relatively calm and not so argumentative and demanding because she had been restless and had been centered on her need for adventure with many men. As long as he had known her, he had not seen this side of her. He thought about his training in the police academy about individuals who exhibited various facets of their personality. Jonathon had sensed some difference in her behavior in other ways during the kidnapping and conclusion of the mob investigations but never sensed her need for multiple sexual partners. He did remember how provocative she had been in his office when he first met her. After Winston had explained some of the past occasions, for such things, Jonathon was not sure if he wanted to continue with her. Now, he understood why Eveline was not so eager to have one man as her partner.

Jonathon walked around the hotel hoping to find Eveline so he could discuss the visit. As he entered the lobby, he spotted Eveline with her tennis instructor. They were in close conversation and did not see Jonathon as he came up to them. He cleared his throat to get their attention. Eveline turned and said, "Oh, why Jonathon dear, you have not been formally introduced to my instructor. Jonathon, meet Clark, my tennis instructor. He is everything a woman wants in a man." Jonathon smiled, shook his hand, and said, "She tells all men that." When Eveline heard this she sucked her teeth with a disgusted look on her face. Clark appeared surprised at her remark and excused himself, explaining he had another appointment. As he walked away, Eveline stared at his tight behind and muscular legs with lust in her eyes. Jonathon asked, "Is he as good as me?" She shook her head and said, "No one is as endowed as you, but he does as he is told." Now, Jonathon began to understand what Eveline was trying to establish with multiple partners. He changed the subject by asking Eveline to have a coffee in the café. He said, "I have good news for you." Jonathon knew that it was always better to have good news for Eveline.

They entered the café and were seated across from a group of "high society Hollywood types", as Eveline put it. To Jonathon, they appeared to be tourists dressed for a day at the pool. Eveline sipped her coffee and asked, "So, what is this good news?" Jonathon began explaining the travel plans that had to be changed because of the distance to California from Florida for Winston and Jason. Eveline understood the change because she remembered how many days it took for her to get to California by train. She did not include Jonathon in the statement even though he had also been on the train. He wondered, as he listened, if she remembered that he intercepted her traveling to California. He decided it was not important to discuss what she remembered. Eveline asked about the status of her Buick. Jonathon said, "Glad you brought that up. We decided to have it transported to California by train. It would be less expensive." Eveline did not inquire about who was financing this event. He told Eveline that Winston and Jason would be flying on an airplane from Miami to Chicago and then to Los Angeles. The Buick would arrive a few days later. Eveline was satisfied with this news. She asked where they would be staying. Jonathon asked her if she wanted them to stay at the Beverly Hills Hotel. She said that there was no reason why they should not, as long as they pay their way. Jonathon shook his head in agreement but knew the government was footing the bill. Eveline smiled and asked, "Do you think my Buick is worthy enough for this Hollywood style we live in?" Jonathon asked, "What if it isn't?" Eveline said, "I would get rid of it for a newer type of vehicle. I have seen sportier vehicles around town than the Buick." Then, to Jonathon's amazement, Eveline said, "I'm going to let Winston know that he needs to sell that old thing. He can use the money from its sale to pay some of the back taxes on 825." Jonathon did not know what to say except, "Ok." Now, he had to re-plan the trip. It seemed whenever Eveline was involved, plans needed changing.

After the discussion and coffee, Jonathon decided to let Eveline do the telephoning to Winston to discuss the Buick and the hotel accommodations. She explained that she would do that as soon as it was 10AM in Florida. She excused herself as she had an appointment in the salon for a beauty treatment. As she walked away, Jonathon watched her demeanor when she passed by people in the lobby. She had a sash shay to her walk that had most taking notice of her. Later, Jonathon contacted the Internal Revenue Office because he was required to let them know of the progress on the case. Jonathon explained what had been decided and that the first thing that needed to be cleared up was a visit to Eveline's mother in Canada. Jonathon told the man in charge that it might take some time, but he was sure the reasons for Eveline's problems would be understood after the meeting. The Internal Revenue Officer gave Jonathon another week. The government was more interested in the delinquent taxes than a trip to see Eveline's mother in Canada.

After Eveline's beauty treatment, she returned to the apartment to find Jonathon sunbathing on the terrace. When she saw him glistening in the warm sun, she went to him and rubbed her hands on his body. He appeared to be resting when she began, but soon responded to her gestures. After a few moments of tantalizing massage, Jonathon moved Eveline's hand aside and said, "Not now, I'm saving it." Eveline moved herself off the chaise in a disgusted way and said, "I'm calling Winston about their trip." Jonathon smiled after she left and thought about how much fun it was to treat her like she treated others. It felt good to be the one in control. Eveline could be heard speaking to the operator about making a telephone call to Florida. When Eveline heard Winston's voice, she screamed, "Winston honey, how are you? I hear you are coming to see me. Jonathon told me about the expense of driving so far. I hear you are flying in an airplane and transporting the car by train. I have been thinking about my Buick. It is probably out dated; so why don't you just sell it. Use the money from the sale to pay the back taxes on 825 Michigan Avenue." Winston could hardly get a word in during the conversation, only to tell her that the airplane reservation still needed to be arranged. He eliminated the facts about who was financing the trip and that he was staying after Jason returned to Miami. Eveline never asked about her sons, Sable, or Olitha. The conversation revolved around her new life in California. Eveline ended the conversation letting Winston know that she was happy and Jonathon was here for her every desire. When Jonathon listened to that remark, he reminded himself that he needed to maintain the philosophy of "business and pleasure usually do not mix". He knew that he had overstepped his bounds when they were in Miami.

CHAPTER 12

A fter the conversation with Eveline, Winston thought that selling the Buick was a better idea than taking it to California. It was over four years old and could make a good profit on its sale in Miami because there were people that would be interested in a convertible, especially during the winter months. He placed an advertisement in the Miami Herald for its sale. Jason agreed with Winston when he heard the news about the Buick. Both men were relieved not to have to arrange for an old automobile to be transported across the country. Jason thought it was interesting that Eveline suggested repaying them for the back taxes on 825 Michigan Avenue. He told Winston that he had hoped she was not going to attempt to come back to the property and claim some of it as her own. Winston did not think she would do such a thing. Jason was not as certain as Winston about that possibility with her. Jason jokingly said, "If Eveline wants to live at 825 Michigan Avenue, she can be the "Madame of Bohemia." Winston thought this was hilarious to even think she could be the operator of such an establishment for discrete travelers and their behaviors. Maybe she would enjoy the challenge of running a place where anything goes as it did in the country of Bohemia. Winston said, "She could get it all and in any form she demanded."

Jonathon had been pondering about a way to encourage Eveline to inquire about her finances, without actually telling her to do it. As they were having breakfast, Eveline read an article in the Los Angeles Times about the current financial affairs in the United States. The article discussed the New Deal that President Roosevelt had established. It had not accomplished what most politicians had hoped for. As part of the President's plan, a second New Deal was in the making. The financial climate in the country was still bleak. As Eveline read the article, she said, "Jonathon dear, I think I need to call Mr. Keyes in Geneva to have him set up an account here in California for my money and have him go over all my financial affairs." Jonathon agreed with her. She would make the call later when his office opened on the east coast.

Later that morning, Eveline made the telephone call to Mr. Keyes, her financial advisor from New York. When he heard Eveline's voice, he said, "Oh my dear Mrs. Paine, I never thought you would call me again. I had been told you were missing." Eveline stunned by the remark, asked how he found out. Mr. Keyes appeared a bit vague with his response when he mentioned that he had contacted Olitha about a question he had. Eveline frowned as she listened to his response. Something did not make sense to her, but she was too intent on her reason for the call to pry any further. He asked what he might do for her. Eveline said, "I need to have you establish an account here in Los Angeles that will have money available to me at all times. I know you handled these things for me in the past. There is a bank on the same street as the Beverly Hills Hotel that we are staying in. It is called the Hollywood Savings Bank." Mr. Keyes interrupted her and said, "My, my, Mrs. Paine, can't you go to the bank and do this on your own? I know you used to be quite good at this in Geneva." She snapped back and said, "I'm no longer in that dreadful place. Anyway, that is why I pay you to take care of my affairs." Mr. Keyes could be heard taking a deep breath as he agreed to do what she asked. Eveline then asked Mr. Keyes about her financial affairs. He paused and said that money was still coming in on the investments through Eastman Kodak Company and Ford Motor Company. Her interest on the savings and wealth management accounts had dipped. Eveline asked why. Mr. Keyes reminded her of her extravagant life style and spending while in Florida. He used the excuse he had been attempting to contact her to let her know things were not as they once had been. He reminded her that the Depression had been deepening and many businesses had gone out of operation where much of her money had been invested. When she heard this news, she asked, "Do I have enough money to maintain my current style of living?" His response was, "Maybe." "What does that mean?" Eveline asked. He was frank and said she was spending her husband's money faster than the investments could handle. He advised her to be more careful with her money, especially with the economic climate of the country. Eveline admitted that she was happiest when spending lots of money. She still did not want to believe the information Mr. Keyes had just given her. She said, "Thank you for the advice. When will my money be in California?" Mr. Keyes told her it would be wired in a day.

Jonathon had been listening to Eveline on the telephone. When she came into the room where he was, she said, "Something is not right. Mr. Keyes just lectured me on the style of spending I have been enjoying." Jonathon, with a smile on his face, said, "Why are you so surprised? You spend money like it was water." Eveline frowned and made a face of embarrassed agreement. He asked what she was going to do about his information. Eveline swirled around and said, "After the money is in the Hollywood bank, I am going to buy a new convertible with a rumble seat manufactured by Pierce Arrow Motor Company. I've been told they are the fastest in the country with 12 cylinders of power." Jonathon knew this was outlandish and asked her why she needed such a vehicle. Eveline told him that since she was in the "beauty spot" of the country, she deserved a sporty well known automobile, that only the wealthy could afford. After this conversation, Jonathon knew Eveline was headed for disaster. Not only was she mentally challenging with so many unpredictable behaviors but now she was set on a spending spree after her conversation with Mr. Keyes. What will she do when the government tracks her down with the bill for unpaid taxes that she will not be able to pay? Jonathon decided to go one step further in his investigation of Eveline's knowledge of her finances. He asked, "Have you been paying your income taxes for the past 15 or so years since you received Wallace's estate?" She looked stunned and said, "I guess so. I assumed Mr. Keyes had taken care of that little stuff." Jonathon only said with a questioning voice, "Really?"

CHAPTER 13

Jonathon made an inquiry to the American Airlines ticket offices to confirm the flights for Winston and Jason. All flights from Miami to Chicago and continued service to Los Angeles were on schedule. Jonathon verified that the tickets had been paid for by the Internal Revenue Service. All was in order, so Jonathon made a telephone call to Winston at the Tropical Gardens to let them know they would be leaving in one week. Olitha answered the telephone saying, "Spaulding Tropical Gardens, how may I help you." Jonathon in a jovial way pretended to be a prank caller and said, "Do you have any fun people working in the gardens?" Olitha in a sassy way said, "Who dat on dis phone? Dis voice sound familiar." Jonathon laughed and said, "Yes, Olitha, this is Jonathon calling from California. Is Winston there?" Olitha laughed and said, "Oh, Mr. Jonathon you are a fooler. How is dat Miss Eveline behavin?" Jonathon laughed and said, "The usual." Olitha said, "Oh Lordy, you poo boy. Iz gits Winston." Winston came on the line and was happy to hear from Jonathon. After Jonathon explained the details of the trip, he began to tell Winston about Eveline's conversation with Mr. Keyes. Winston was not surprised by the news and Eveline's reactions and behaviors. He said, "Jonathon, you may want to rethink how involved you are with her. She has been headed for trouble for many years. Ever since she came into Wallace's money upon his death, she thinks money is everywhere." Winston told him what Jason had said about Eveline wanting to come back to Miami Beach. Jonathon agreed that she was capable of that possibility. He laughed at the title "Madame of Bohemia."

The next day, Jason was at 825 Michigan Avenue supervising some tree plantings. As usual, the Cuban workers were not as energetic as Jason hoped they might be. He had threatened them with firing if they did not get over the idea that "work a little and siesta a lot" was not going to be part of their day. When he thought about Olitha's remark about "whippin them", he agreed it might work as a last resort. He knew he could never do such a thing though. While he was getting the men to dig holes and plant palm trees, the sign company arrived with the fence and sign for the front of 825. Jason was excited to see the large circular metal letters that said, "BOHEMIA" being placed over the wrought iron gates and fence. It was a thrill to finally see that the place was actually coming together. When they arrived back from California, the interior needed to be finished and they would be ready to advertise for guests. Jason hoped for a grand opening in early November.

Winston had been finalizing the lists of work items he wanted Olitha to supervise the men with. Olitha told Winston what Jonathon told her before he spoke to him, that Miss Eveline was acting up again. Winston told her that was nothing new. They laughed at all that Eveline had done since they had known her. Jonathon was in for a surprise according to Winston. Olitha agreed. The telephone had been ringing with many inquiries about the Buick. Winston had set the price to enable them to recover the back taxes on 825, as he was instructed to do by Eveline. A gentleman had inquired and seemed to be interested with the price at $4,000.00. This did not seem out of line for him. He would come to see the Buick. Winston informed him that Jason, his partner, would be at 825 Michigan Avenue. Winston telephoned Jason who was delighted that the Buick might be sold before they left for California. Jason wondered how Eveline was going to react to the finality of her Buick and the past taxes its sale would satisfy.

A few hours later, Jason saw a dapper British gentleman watching the new sign being installed. It occurred to Jason that a door bell was needed for guests to be able to ring for entrance. Jason welcomed the man who had on a panama hat and carried a walking stick. He was impressed with the property and inquired what it was to be. Jason explained that it would be a guesthouse for the discrete traveler. The man gave an interested look at Jason and asked, "How discrete?" Jason replied, "Discrete enough for travelers who want some fun and not be caught by a husband, wife or whomever. Anything that may go on here will stay here." The man asked when he could make a reservation. Jason gave him the information and told him that he could make reservations after October. The man explained he might want to rent an apartment for the season. Jason said that could be possible as he showed him the shiny yellow Buick with a new convertible top. He and Jason went for a drive; with the man in the driver's seat and Jason to his right. During the drive, Jason asked what the British man's name was. As they were turning the corner to return to the parking lot, the man said, "My name is Jerome and this car is sold." Then he slowly moved his hand on Jason's leg.

CHAPTER 14

Jason, not expecting such an advance from Jerome, moved quickly out of the passenger side of the Buick. Jerome turned off the engine and handed Jason the key. Jason did not discuss Jerome's advances as he asked when the money would be available for the transfer of the keys for the Buick. Jerome explained he would return the next day. Jason set a time and Jerome left never mentioning his suggestive advances toward Jason. Jason decided not to tell Winston what had occurred and he would have him meet Jerome the next day. After all it was Winston's friend's transaction and Jason realized he rather enjoyed the attention Jerome had initiated. Later in the day when he saw Winston he explained what had transpired with Jerome and the possibility that he may be registering as a guest at the Bohemia.

The next morning, Winston left the Tropical Gardens to meet Jerome at 825 for the transfer of the keys and paperwork for the Buick. While Winston waited, he studied the property and made a list of things that needed to be done when they returned from California. It was a warm and humid July day, so Winston decided to get into the water and rest while he waited. He never thought about the need for a doorbell. When Jerome arrived he had no way of letting anyone know he was there. Winston had lost track of time as he enjoyed the water. He thought about not wanting to go to California and deal with all of Eveline's issues again. Just as he was dozing off, a man's voice could be heard at the gate leading to the parking area. Winston, startled, jumped out of the water and went to the gate without thinking about his clothing. It was Jerome standing there with a smile on his face when he saw Winston's body coming toward the gate. Winston realized what he had done and covered himself with his hands as best he could. Jerome said, "I am Jerome. I am here to collect on my Buick". Winston cleared his throat and said, "Sorry for my appearance.

I am Winston, Jason's partner." Jerome said, "Don't be sorry for your appearance. I can't wait to stay here for the season if this is how it will be." Winston opened the gate and in came Jerome. He followed Winston and watched as he put his clothes on, with an excited look on his face. The exchange of money and keys took a few minutes and Jerome wanted to know when he could reserve an apartment for the season. Winston sensed an aggressive manner in Jerome and asked, "Why are you so eager to set up your visit? It is only July and we are not ready to take reservations." Jerome explained that he was going on a trip with his new Buick and would not be back to Miami Beach until October. This made sense to Winston as he escorted Jerome into what would soon be the office and dining room for the guests. Winston took Jerome's information and a deposit to hold an apartment. He chose an upstairs unit overlooking Michigan Avenue. He jokingly said, "I will be able to see who is on the street and who knows what might happen if I invite them in." Winston smiled and knew then that this business would never be to Eveline's liking if she ever decided to return to 825.

Winston finished his work at the guesthouse leaving a list for the workers that Olitha was to supervise in his absence. He returned to the Tropical Gardens and told Jason what happened when Jerome arrived for the Buick. It was then Jason told Winston that a door bell was needed but did not mention what happened with Jerome. Winston explained how he answered the back gate. Jason made a face and said, "You are always running around naked so why would that be any big deal." Winston thought about it and agreed that if it did not offend others, why should he care. Anyway, Jerome was delighted to be escorted into the property by an unclothed man. Jason said, "I wonder how the rest of the clientele will be?" Winston said, "It will be fun to see. Maybe we should live there and run the place and have Jeffrey do the room services. That way, we will be sure to keep Eveline away." Jason told Winston they needed to keep her out of this business. Jason feared that Eveline would probably scare the guests away. They decided that living at 825 Michigan Avenue might be a good idea. Then, Winston thought of the conversation he had had with Patrick and Andrew. He mentioned it to Jason who immediately told him not to worry about that until they returned from California. Winston already had decided that if the young men left West Point, they could live and work at the Tropical Gardens.

It was one more day before Winston and Jason were to go to California. Both were very anxious about flying in an airplane. American Airlines had recently begun using the DC3 airplane for long flights. They would be flying for most of the day with a layover in Chicago. Winston had figured this out because of the time difference and hours of flying and stopping in Chicago, they would arrive in Los Angeles at 4PM. He thought it strange that they would leave Miami at 9AM and go across the country in less than a day. This was truly a marvel to him. Jonathon telephoned to make sure all was set for the trip. While he was speaking with Winston, Eveline could be heard screaming that Jonathon should ask about the sale of the Buick. Winston told Jonathon to let her know it was sold for $4,000.00. Eveline grabbed the receiver from Jonathon and said, "So, Winston dear, how much was left after I reimbursed you for the back property taxes?" Winston cleared his throat and said, "There was $50.00 left." There was a pause and Eveline said, "Keep the change. If it were hundreds or a thousand, I would expect some back." Winston thought what a changed attitude in Eveline. Why was she so cheap, all of a sudden, especially after they made the Buick look almost new? Some friend she was turning out to be.

Jason and Winston took a taxicab to the airport with the left over money from the Buick. They laughed with the thought that her last dollars from the sale of the Buick were used to get them to the airport. They boarded the airplane and were surprised at every step of the way. They did not expect a stewardess dressed up that would serve them food and drinks. The seats were full and when the stewardess told everyone about the seat belts and safety precautions, they felt a bit panicky. As the airplane moved from slow to very fast, Winston's face turned white as did Jason's. They said to each other that maybe they should have never done this. How could anything go so fast? Before they knew it, they were above the clouds, still in shock. The stewardess told everyone to be calm when they hit turbulence. Winston and Jason did not know what to expect and when that happened, they screamed. The stewardess assured them all would be fine and she offered them a cocktail. Within three hours they were told that they would land in Chicago. When the airplane hit the runway and bounced, Winston grabbed Jason and screamed. Jason said, "Jerome should see you now wrapped around me like a baby. He would never believe a big hairy man like you would act like this. Winston looked at Jason, whose face had returned to a faint white. Both were not sure air travel was for them.

Eveline had been occupied at the bank at the same time Winston and Jason were on their way to see her and Jonathon. She wanted to surprise them with her new Pierce Arrow White Convertible with a Silver blue finish. She had been determined to take possession of it and go to the airport to greet them. Jonathon tried to slow Eveline's easy spending but was unsuccessful. He had gone with her to the Hollywood Savings Bank to watch her do business with money that was probably not hers. He was a bit uneasy with the future possibilities of her being charged with tax evasion. She might go wild when that happened, but he hoped somehow there would be an answer for her situation. Eveline moseyed into the bank with Jonathon following behind. She was greeted by the main bank officer who seemed to know about her. Jonathon wondered if Mr. Keyes had tipped him off or if it was the Internal Revenue Office checking on her accounts and spending. Eveline withdrew enough cash to cover the new vehicle. The bank officer asked what the money was being used for. She lifted her head in a haughty way and said, "It's for my Pierce Arrow Convertible." The man's eyebrows went up and he told her she only had another thousand dollars available in the bank. Eveline left the bank in a fury and asked Jonathon if he knew anything about the money issues. He only told her that maybe she was spending too much without knowing if there was enough money coming into her accounts. She pretended not to hear what he had said.

Eveline hailed a taxicab outside the bank and went with Jonathon to the Pierce Arrow Auto Dealership. Jonathon wanted to know how she knew about the place. Eveline explained that she had visited it a few days ago and put a hold on the Pierce Arrow she wanted. Jonathon shook his head as they entered the showroom. It was lavishly decorated for the well to do customer. Jonathon found it hard to believe that folks were spending in these expensive places when there were millions of people starving because of the Depression. The sales person greeted Eveline with utmost formality, which Eveline soaked up. He knew why she was there and escorted her to an office. Jonathon was invited after Eveline approved. He felt inferior in the atmosphere of such an establishment.

Eveline signed the necessary paperwork and waited for the automobile to be driven to the front door. When it turned the corner, she remembered how Wallace reacted to his new black Ford many years ago in Rochester. She also remembered how confused she was about how he could afford such a vehicle. Now, she was doing the very thing she could never understand. She shook her head and told herself that she had just paid cash for it, so there was no problem. It was a dream of a ride, like being in a cloud in the sky, as Jonathon put it. Eveline loved the remarks as she drove around Hollywood and twice on Hollywood Boulevard hoping to be seen. Jonathon reminded her about the time and the arrival of the airplane at 4PM. She needed to go to the hotel to freshen up before going to the airport. She parked as she had at the Biltmore in Miami, at the front door. She instructed the valet not to move it. She explained that she had to be at the airport and would be leaving soon. Jonathon waited in the front seat. The valet asked him if she always acted that way. Jonathon nodded his head. When Eveline entered the apartment, she saw an envelope that had been slid under the door. She had a flashback of the troubles that a note under the door had given her in Miami when she was living at the Biltmore. All she could think of was another ransom letter about her children. Funny, it had occurred to her that she had not inquired about Patrick and Andrew in a long while. As she looked at the envelope, she had a strange sense about her two young men. The envelope had her name in fancy writing on it. She opened it and discovered an invitation to the Hearst Castle. William Randolph Hearst had invited her and guests to a lavish affair in two weeks. President and Mrs. Roosevelt would be the honored guests. An RSVP would be in order, as the invitation stated.

CHAPTER 15

Eveline hurried from the hotel and left the parking area in a rush because she had spent too much time thinking about the invitation and what she was going to wear to the airport. Jonathon asked her if she realized how far the airport was from the hotel. When he asked her that, she put the pedal to the floor and said, "This baby has power. Watch me get to the airport in half the time." Jonathon's eyes went up as they raced through the streets of Los Angeles. As she pulled up to the American Airlines terminal, there at the curbside was Winston and Jason. They did not recognize the new car or Eveline until she raced up, slammed on the brakes and yelled, "Get in." Winston laughed at the tone she used as they sat in the rumble seat for the ride of their lives. Eveline was giddy and talked about everything she had been doing. While she sped back to the hotel, she mentioned the invitation to the Hearst Castle. Jonathon had not known about this either, so all were surprised. While Eveline detailed the party invitation that the Roosevelt's were to be honored guests, Jason told her that he was only in California for 4 days. Eveline wanted to know why. He used the excuse that he had too much work to accomplish in Miami. Eveline accepted the reason and was sorry he could not join them.

While Eveline was elaborating on the party that Randolph Hearst had invited them to, Jonathon thought this would be a good time for them to go further north to Canada. The Hearst Castle was located a few hundred miles north of Hollywood along the ocean. Jonathon hoped to convince Eveline that a trip to visit her mother would continue after the party as long as they were headed north. He had been informed by the Miami Police Detective Bureau that Catherine Lounsberry, Eveline's mother, had been placed in a prison near Vancouver, Canada, not far from the United States border. There was train service from Los Angeles to Vancouver, so they could either start in Hollywood or go to San Francisco to meet the train. Now, Jonathon and Winston's job was to convince Eveline to agree to see her mother.

When they arrived at the hotel, Eveline instructed the valet to take extra care in parking her Pierce Arrow. He was polite to Eveline, but it was obvious to others that he resented her condescending attitude. Winston and Jason checked in to a traditional style room. Eveline made no effort to offer accommodations closer to her apartment. Little did she know that the government was paying for this trip. After they had time to freshen up and unpack, they agreed to meet in the lobby. Winston told Jason that there was something very different about Eveline's behavior, especially toward him, who had been her friend the longest. He mentioned this to Jonathon also and he explained that she was different. He had a notion that Eveline's behaviors were a result of a condition that started in infancy, because of her mother's behavior toward her. He explained briefly that through his training of personality and behaviors of people, most of their adult issues can be a result of early childhood treatment by the mother. That was the reason Jonathon wanted Eveline to have a meeting with her mother for this discussion. Jonathon was to contact the prison so that a psychologist could assist with this meeting. If all went as it usually did, they might need a few sessions to complete this meeting. It was Jonathon's hope that Eveline might better understand her past and why she reacted as she did with such radical behaviors. Part of the temperament is also attached to spending and taking no responsibility for anything but keeping herself happy by surrounding herself with luxury. When Winston and Jason listened, they knew this was a gamble until Jason said, "I may be able to convince Eveline of the importance of a meeting of this nature." Winston, with a surprised look, asked why. Jason had never told him about his childhood. It was, as he put it, horrific. His mother had controlled him and kept him in hiding from others until the school investigated. They found her to be sexually abusive and neglectful. Jason had been finally taken away from his parents. His father had turned a blind eye to the torture. After being away from his mother, Jason went back to question her. She was not apologetic and admitted she wanted Jason as a play thing, to torture and belittle, whenever she felt the need. He explained how she overfed him so he would get fat, so no girl would want a "fatso" as she put it. Then, to her liking, she would starve him and have relations with him. Winston and Jonathon were shocked at such a story. Jason explained that he was saved by a foster mother who cared for him and gave him all things his mother had not. He had been in counseling for many years, his mother ended up in prison. Jason went to visit her in prison, as they were hoping for Eveline to do with her mother. Jason explained how angry he was to make the visit but it cleared up his anger and his mother explained things that he never knew as a child. After all of this, Jason left and moved to Miami, never planning to be close to anyone again. He feared that he was not manly enough or had the ability to love anyone so avoided getting close to anyone. Winston had been the first person that Jason allowed himself to get to know. Winston had never heard these things but thought about his alcoholic father who ended up in the poorhouse and his mother who had deserted the family, never to be heard from again. Maybe that is why they are so good for each other. They had never discussed the past but somehow knew they were safe for one another.

After Jason finished his story, Jonathon told him that he was correct and that he might be able to convince Eveline of this meeting. He agreed to do it before he went back to Florida. Now, they had to figure out when. Just as they were finishing their conversation, Eveline walked up to them in the lobby and said, "Are you boys having fun talking about me? I'm sure you have loads of good stories about me and my ways. You know I have a method to my madness." No one said another word as they got up to go for a ride around Beverly Hills. While they were speeding up and down the streets looking at movie star's homes, both Winston and Jason were thinking the same thing, maybe Eveline does know what she is doing after what she just said.

CHAPTER 16

During the four days before Jason had to return to Miami, they took a tour of a movie studio and they had lunch at a fancy restaurant that catered to the movie stars and producers in Hollywood. Eveline nearly fainted when Clark Gable was seen in the restaurant. Jonathon and Winston were seated on either side of her so she was not able to get out of the booth to go after Mr. Gable and she began to pout. Jason watched her turn into a person who was used to getting what she wanted. He asked, "Eveline did you get that behavior from your mother?" She looked surprised and said, "Probably, my mother did many things that affected me well into my adulthood." Jonathon and Winston listened while the two discussed the remark. Jason said, "My mother was a terrible woman. She did things to me that left me with feelings of shame, fear, insecurity about myself, and ruined my physical development at a young age." Eveline listened as if something was registering in her mind. Jason continued to explain about his father's absence and avoiding any conflict with his mother regarding the horrific treatment she was administering. Eveline asked, "What kind of treatment were you given?" Jason took a deep breath and explained the sexual activities, the colonic cleansing that was administered when his mother thought he was too fat, then starvation to make him thin. Jonathon interrupted, "Jason, how did you get away from this?" He told them that the school had intervened and he was placed in foster care. He loved the woman who acted as a mother should. His mother and father were convicted of abuse, neglect, and physical danger. While Eveline listened, she thought that her life was much like that but did not admit it to them. Jason ended the conversation when he told Eveline that he never felt he was man enough to be in love. She looked at him in a quizzical way and said, "You are such a man. I can't believe you felt that way." Jason said that he explained to Winston that he needed a buddy and would be happy to get to know him. That was the first time in Jason's life that he dared to take that chance. Winston spoke up and said, "And what a great buddy he has been. I'm glad he spoke up to you Eveline and admitted this publicly."

While dessert was being served, Jonathon commented on Jason's story. He asked Jason how all this was resolved and how he was able to go on with his life. Jason knew then that the conversation about Eveline's visit to see her mother was taking place without even a plan. He decided that may be the best way, now that the discussion had started. Jason told everyone that his counselor suggested a visit with his mother in prison. Eveline looked suspicious when she heard this. Jason explained it was the best way to get rid of feelings and behaviors that affect your life. This would enable him to understand everything and let it go. Jason went on to discuss the meeting which took two sessions. He heard things from his mother that allowed him to forgive her for her torturous ways and was glad to have escaped his mother's wrath. He was not surprised when he heard his mother admit she did not have the nerve to get away from her husband. The counselor explained that it was an attachment issue and the mother especially could not let go of her son. She wanted her child to herself no matter what it took. Jason's mother admitted to the things she had done to make Jason unlikeable to anyone. His father ignored the entire thing by staying away because of work. Jason said that there was much more done to him, but this was why he went through the visit and has never regretted it or looked back.

After Jason's troubling story, everyone took a walk instead of a ride since the weather was breezy and warm. While they were strolling on the street, Eveline told Jonathon that Jason's story made her begin to think back on her childhood. Jonathon was delighted to hear this and hoped she might want to meet her mother and not have to be convinced that she needed to do this. Jonathon asked her if she knew where her mother was imprisoned. To Jonathon's surprise, Eveline knew she was in Vancouver, Canada. When Eveline said this, Jonathon wondered if during Eveline's Fugue State she had told the conductor she was Catherine Lounsberry, her mother, and was subconsciously planning to go to her. Jonathon had a feeling Eveline had no notion of those possibilities. She was mixing up her hope to get her mother in more trouble by doing what she had but could have possibly been on her way to Canada, by way of California. Jonathon asked, "So, Eveline do you want to do the same thing Jason did many years ago?" Eveline paused and said, "I think I may need to do that to see if what I think is true." Jonathon explained that he could arrange the meeting and it could take place sooner than she thought. Eveline made sure to remind Jonathon and Winston that they were going to the Hearst Castle and to make sure the meeting was after that. Jonathon told her that they could go by train from San Francisco to Vancouver after the party. Eveline appeared satisfied and ready for such an encounter with her past.

During the evening, Winston felt a need to talk to Jason about all he had heard about his childhood. Winston and he spent private time having dinner. Winston listened to Jason explain what a chance he took the day he told Eveline that he liked him. Winston explained about his life as a teenager living with his alcoholic father who never had work or money, but always found money for booze. He explained about Alice Paine, Wallace's mother, who let him live with the family. He and Wallace shared a bedroom and Winston admitted that Wallace was his secret lover. Wallace's father, Frank, hated Wallace for what he accomplished and his unique personality. Alice had been their advocate and he would never forget her for that. Jason asked if Eveline knew about Wallace's interest in both men and women. Winston explained that it never was an issue and that Eveline encouraged them to be involved with one another. Jason shook his head and said, "It will be interesting to see what the visit to Eveline's mother creates." They admitted they had come from backgrounds that were similar and were satisfied with the way it turned out. Jason reminded Winston that he was the only person in his life. Winston told him he had all of his friends back in Miami. Jason laughed and said, "I wonder what Olitha has done to the workers?" Winston said, "Maybe the workers did away with her and there will only be Sable and Eveline."

CHAPTER 17

J ason had been preparing to return to Miami. He had enjoyed his time in California but felt a need to leave. He was glad to have been in Hollywood for four days but he told Winston he liked Miami better because of the temperament of the people and the way they lived. Winston agreed that Miami was home for him too. Eveline had been acting strangely after hearing Jason's story. Jonathon was concerned that she might decide not go to Vancouver for the meeting with her mother. Jonathon had told her that the arrangements were made for the three of them to go from San Francisco to Vancouver the day after the Hearst party. Eveline was satisfied with the arrangements and Winston reassured her that he would be with her as well as Jonathon. Eveline made a remark about fearing the encounter with her mother. She did not explain why she had that fear only that she was afraid of what she might find out. She admitted she had begun to remember things that she thought could never be true. No one ever helped her to resolve those thoughts. She told Winston that being in Willard State Hospital some 20 years ago gave her time to better understand things on her own. She had been made to feel like she had gone crazy or was that the idea others wanted her to believe. Winston, having been the only person left to know anything about her condition then, after Patrick's birth and attempted murder, knew she was not as crazy as they made her out to be. He had always thought it was a plan to eliminate her by committing her permanently to the mental institution. Eveline turned out to be much stronger than expected and made her way out of such an environment. He told Eveline that it appeared to be a good plan by going to find out about her childhood.

The next day, Eveline called for her Pierce Arrow to be parked in the front of the hotel. She, Winston, and Jonathon were taking Jason to the airport. He was fearing the flight to Chicago and on to Miami, especially

56

by himself. He told Winston as he embraced him that he wished he could come home with him. Winston felt bad and explained he felt the same way. Eveline drove at a more civilized manner and they thanked her for that. She smiled and said, "I am hoping to turn a new leaf on my life. My driving will be the easiest to change." Jonathon was surprised at this remark and said, "Who knows you may really understand everything and really like me too." Eveline turned and winked at him.

It was evening after they returned from the airport. Eveline decided she wanted to have a little dinner party in the apartment, not in the restaurant. Winston thought this was something Eveline might have concocted years ago for a holiday or to have an encounter with someone she needed to know better. Eveline told Jonathon of her intentions as Winston stood by listening. He watched Jonathon while Eveline told him how she wanted him to dress and that the three of them could enjoy some private time. She said, "I want to celebrate my upcoming events at the Hearst party and in Vancouver. Jonathon thought that was unnecessary but Eveline explained the bill was on her. Eveline knew that both men were about the same in stature and she had gone wild in the past for their manhood. Winston had a feeling that she might be up to one of her past parties that Jonathon had never experienced. Winston decided to go along with her because he wondered what she might really do. Winston knew that she had fond feelings for Jonathon and wondered why she kept placing him in uncomfortable situations.

The dinner party was to be at 9PM. Eveline had ordered the meal and all the fixings and drinks. Both Winston and Jonathon had worn open shirts. Winston laughed when he saw the grey hair on his chest instead of dark brown. Age had a way of making him look like an attractive middle aged man. Eveline wore one of her gowns she was noted for while entertaining. Winston decided that it might be fun to be with Jonathon and her. He remembered having done the exact thing with Rudolph and Thaddeus, not to mention Wallace, Rudolph and himself in Geneva. They sat and had a drink of vodka and Eveline talked about how she used to do these things while living in Geneva. Winston kept waiting to see where she was going with this plan. After they had a second cocktail, Eveline told them how appealing they both looked to her. Jonathon was happiest to hear this since Eveline had been treating him badly as of late. Winston said, "Jonathon, you have had good training with your body and you should be proud of all you have." Eveline spoke up and asked Jonathon if he was still as excited about having sex with her as he was in Miami. She reminded him of their sexual activities in the ocean and the back yard at 825 Michigan Avenue. He blushed and smiled and said he was still ready for her. Eveline had loosened her top pretending to cool her bosom. She told Winston that it had been awhile since the two of them had enjoyed each other's body. She laughed and said, "At least this time we are not trying to find out about that criminal, Thaddeus Cooper. Remember that tire swing we put him in?" They laughed at such a scheme. Eveline asked if the two guys could take off their shirts so she could admire them. They made a face but did what they were asked. Eveline began her moves on them. First she went for Jonathon and massaged him to a point of madness. Winston watched and was next, enjoying the attention. Then Eveline said, "Now it is your turn to work on each other while I watch you and get ready. I haven't done this in a long while. I love having two men at the same time." Jonathon was surprised that he enjoyed the tension she created between Winston and himself. She had a way of making things happen without much work. Eveline appeared in her black cape that she had used while in Atlantic City years ago. Winston remembered what she had done to Rudolph with the gag, hat pins, and a feather. Was she trying to replay that evening? It was almost as if she liked the idea of torturing people she seemed to care about. Jonathon, being overwhelmed by her behavior, let her do as she pleased with him. She used the feather on both of them in places that aroused the senses. While she was twisting and pinching them in erotic places, they grew more aggressive. She said, "This is how I like it. I like to be in control, now we will take turns on one another." Jonathon and Winston went along with her demands, but both knew this was one of the reasons they were going to Vancouver. After an hour of sexual activities on everyone's part, they finished.

The next morning, Mr. Keyes made a person to person call to Eveline. When she answered the telephone, Mr. Keyes sounded upset and unlike his usual self. It was only 9AM in Hollywood, so it was 6AM in the east. Eveline asked what the matter was. Mr. Keyes began by explaining that because of the Depression many small businesses had to close, some were Eveline's investments. He explained that he had tried to maneuver funds so her accounts would stay high enough to maintain her style of living. Eveline had a feeling there was more to this issue and asked, "What else is wrong for you to get in touch with me so early in the morning?" He paused and began to explain that she may need to sell her Ford Motor Company stocks. They were at the highest they could possibly be for such economic conditions. Eveline knew this could not be the whole story. She wanted to know why the need to sell a million and half dollars in stocks. Mr. Keyes could be heard shuffling papers and spoke in a nervous tone when he told Eveline he had been avoiding making tax payments. Suddenly, Eveline remembered Jonathon's question about her financial affairs. She demanded an answer. Mr. Keyes changed the subject to explain that because of President Roosevelt's Second New Deal, part of it included the Wagner Act of 1934 or more commonly known as the Wealth Tax Act. Eveline said, "So how does this involve me? You have been in charge of my money for a long while. What has happened to create this huge need to sell off my stocks?" Mr. Keyes went on to explain that the wealthy in the United States had not been affected by the Depression. They had maintained their level of wealth while many were destitute. Eveline said that she still wanted to know what happened in her individual financial house. Mr. Keyes explained the wealthy would be taxed at a rate of 79% of income over 5-million-dollars. So far, according to Mr. Keyes, the only person in that category was John D. Rockefeller. There would be a lower percentage on incomes below the 5-million-dollar level. Mr. Keyes continued to explain that because he had not paid her income taxes for many years, the federal government notified him that they were attempting to find her and have the courts determine what needed to be done. Eveline screamed, "So, you have made me a criminal. What am I supposed to do about all this?" Just as she screamed, Jonathon came in the apartment and heard her question. He listened but Eveline did not know he was there. Mr. Keyes explained that was the major reason to sell as much as she could to satisfy the government. They were tracking many wealthy people in the same situation as she. Along with delinquent taxes, there were huge fines for nonpayment.

After some conversation about the possibilities for and against full payments of back taxes, Eveline asked how much would remain for her after all was satisfied. Mr. Keyes told her that she could maintain half of Eastman Kodak Company stocks and have a small investment that yielded a fair amount of money for her monthly expenses. He said, "That was why I tried to discourage you from transferring so much money to a Hollywood Bank. Everything is overpriced there." When Eveline heard it put that way she thought of how much she spent on her Pierce Arrow. No wonder the bank officer told her she had nearly nothing left after her withdrawal for her purchase. Eveline told Mr. Keyes to wait until she contacted him before he took any action. She needed time to figure out what needed to be done. Mr. Keyes said, "You do not have much choice unless you want to go to prison." Eveline ended the conversation with her demand to have him wait. She had in the back of her mind that she was going to see President and Eleanor Roosevelt soon and maybe something could be worked out.

Eveline was furious when she finished the call. She felt like firing Mr. Keyes but knew that would do no good. Jonathon walked into the room as if he had just arrived. He saw Eveline's state and asked her what was the matter. She explained the story to him. He listened but knew what the story was all about. He was surprised that Mr. Keyes knew. Jonathon had not yet thought how he was going to explain that this was one of the reasons he had been hired to find and bring Eveline back, to face the charges of tax evasion. Maybe, he might not need to be part of the investigation now that her accountant and Eveline knew the government was looking for her and the money. Mr. Keyes could be held in the case for not submitting tax extensions or making some type of payment to satisfy the government. There would be much less tension on their relationship if he could back away and only work with Eveline on the meeting with her mother in Vancouver. Eveline asked Jonathon what she should do. He said the same thing Mr. Keyes had, "You need to pay up or possibly go to prison." Jonathon knew that Mr. Keyes had attempted to blame Eveline for the situation but in reality, the government would investigate Mr. Keyes' business practices as well. He too could be heavily fined or jailed.

Eveline decided she needed to have a tennis lesson from her instructor, Clark. She decided to maintain her way of living until she was told it was over. When she was leaving the apartment, she asked Jonathon if he would like her to invite Clark to the apartment to have some fun. She said, "I have had a chance to see him nearly naked and I'm sure he would be fun for us." Jonathon refused the invitation and told Eveline he needed to get ready to go to the Hearst party and Vancouver. Eveline looked disappointed but agreed she needed to do that too. When she left, Jonathon thought that maybe Eveline was the type of person that liked lots of variety and needed more than one person to satisfy her insatiable need for sex. While Eveline was playing tennis, Jonathon made a call to the Miami Income Tax Office to discuss what he had found out. The man who had assisted Jonathon with the plan and arrangements was happy that the case was coming to a head. He told Jonathon that his office had found Mr. Keyes who was the financial person in charge of Mrs. Paine's affairs. Jonathon listened and hoped he would be released from that part of his investigation of Eveline. Jonathon was finished with locating her and getting the tax issues out in the open, but he was told to make sure he got her back to Miami. That was his responsibility to the government. Jonathon attempted to explain to the tax man about the trip to Vancouver but he did not seem to be interested. Jonathon was told that getting the huge sums of money from Mrs. Paine was the most important item. The government did not want to imprison her because the money would still be owed. The man thanked Jonathon for finding Eveline and reminded him of the importance of her return to Miami. As Jonathon ended the conversation he thought that was all everyone needed was to have Eveline back in Miami.

CHAPTER 18

onathon finished his calls to Florida, having spoken with the chief of police in Miami to give him an update on his work. The chief gave Jonathon another week to conclude his work on Mrs. Paine. Jonathon had been on this investigation for quite some time and was told it was time to return or he may not have a job. He knew he had to work quickly to get this case solved and Eveline's past debts dealt with. He was packed and ready to go along with Winston when Eveline walked in with Clark. Jonathon said, "I thought I told you we needed to go when you returned." Eveline looked at Jonathon as if she had never heard that. She sucked her teeth and told Clark, "I tried, but we need to get to a party at the Hearst Castle." Clark's eyes went up and he turned and left. Eveline hurried around throwing things in a suitcase. It was a sight to see her move so quickly and have herself ready within a few minutes. She freshened up and away they went. She was driving the Pierce Arrow as she used to. Winston asked her, "I thought you were turning a new leaf on your driving." She replied, "Not today, we need to get there so we can dress up. We can't go to a party looking like this." The Hearst Estate Castle was on the Central Coast of California in the San Simeone region about 250 miles from Hollywood and had been nicknamed "La Cuesta Encantada", "The Enchanted Hill" or "The Ranch". The party was scheduled for 8PM. Eveline figured they would arrive midafternoon. Away she sped at 100 miles per hour. Jonathon and Winston sat in a frozen position as Eveline swerved in and around traffic on her way north. Jonathon reminded her that they needed to move on to San Francisco in the morning in order to be on the train to Vancouver, so getting arrested for speeding would not be a good idea.

Around noon, they stopped to have some lunch. It was advertised as a fun restaurant that featured movie star lunches. Eveline wanted all the lunches if the star came with the lunch. Jonathon told her not get too excited because they were quite far from Hollywood. Winston made a crack when he said, "Eveline, you would probably get some beat up old cowboy, not a William Powell." She made a face as the men laughed. During the meal, Winston said that he had been thinking about Jason and hoped he arrived in Miami safely. Eveline said, "Oh Winston your boy will be fine. He managed to live quite well before he met you." Jonathon thought this was a strange remark especially after his story and traumas. She told Winston that he worried too much. Winston wondered what he would do if Jason was not around. They finished a lunch that never lived up to the billboard advertisement on the road. Eveline being disappointed, allowed Jonathon to drive with Winston in the rumble seat. During this time, she had been massaging Jonathon's legs and was having fun bringing him to the point of climax. She told Winston that she used to do that when Rudolph would be driving to Rochester. Winston reminded her that she had done that to him. She said, "I love to tantalize my boyfriends." Jonathon attempted to move her hands away just before they swerved to avoid another slower moving vehicle. Eveline thought that was fun and a thrill. Neither man was as thrilled as she and told her they would put her in the rumble seat tied to the frame. She looked at them with interest and told them that might be fun.

When they were about a mile from the Hearst Castle, there were iron fences and guards stationed everywhere. Jonathon thought it may be secret service agents because of the President and Mrs. Roosevelt. Eveline began to show too much excitement and Jonathon told her to calm down and not create a scene. She did as she was told for a change. Jonathon was surprised that she listened to him. They approached the large iron gates as the guard asked for identification and the invitation. Jonathon remembered the invitation as Eveline had not, he had taken it and did not tell her. Jonathon showed his Miami Police Department papers and when the guard asked for the invitation, Eveline panicked and said, "Oh my God, I left it in Hollywood." The guard told her that she could not be admitted into the castle without it. Jonathon played along while Winston sat and watched Eveline wither into the seat. Just before the guard was to turn them away, Jonathon presented the invitation. He smiled at the guard and said, "I was trying to teach her a lesson. She was too busy with her tennis instructor to remember the important items." The guard opened the iron gates and smiled at Jonathon as they drove through a tree lined road to the castle. When they arrived they saw an enormous building decorated with American flags and roses everywhere. The valet took the Pierce Arrow and Eveline did not even give instructions for its care because she was too overwhelmed by the environment. When they entered the lobby, they were escorted to a gentleman assigning accommodations. They were to be in separate rooms next to one another. The lobby was the old style with ornate decorations and huge palm trees that swayed in the breeze. Eveline knew then that she was inappropriately dressed because she looked like she came from a tennis match. Jonathon reminded her that she should not have spent the time with Clark. She made a face and walked toward the elevator with Winston and Jonathon following behind.

According to the diagram in the rooms, there were 61 bathrooms, 56 bedrooms, four swimming pools, and two restaurants. This was not a hotel, but a private estate that William Randolph Hearst had built from his millions that he made on the newspaper business. A social gathering was to take place before the dinner party that evening. In Eveline's room, there was a special note for her to be sure to see Mrs. Roosevelt. Eveline wondered what that could be about. Jonathon and Winston were sharing a room next to Eveline, but thankfully there was no door between them. Winston told Jonathon that he did not want to entertain Eveline again. Jonathon was sure he did not want to be involved that evening with her either.

They took a walk around the estate after they had unpacked. There was an enormous swimming pool that made the Biltmore pool in Miami look small. There were waiters offering drinks and sandwiches as the guests strolled around the grounds. The view from the castle was spectacular since it was on top of a mountain giving panoramic views in all directions. Eveline said, "I feel like we are in heaven. Some ranch this is." The men agreed and said it was too bad that they were only there for that day and had to be on their way to San Francisco. There were at least 300 guests on the estate from what Winston had heard from one of the waiters. Such a lavish environment, one would never know there were people starving and without work because of the Depression. When Eveline heard these remarks, she thought about her financial state and wondered if she might be headed in that direction. Maybe something would change all that for her.

The evening social gathering was a formal event. Eveline wore a gown that had sequins with the front of the gown cut in the center to just above the navel. Jonathon and Winston were surprised that she had so much to show on the top. Since they knew her, Winston asked, "So, Eveline where did you get all that chest?" She made a face and said, "Wouldn't you like to know?" Winston turned and said to Jonathon, "Do we really care?" They agreed that now was not the time. They watched her maneuver through the crowd toward Eleanor Roosevelt. She was dressed in a formal, but as one might say, a dowdy outfit. Eleanor had not been noted to be a fashion conscious person. President Roosevelt was in a formal suit greeting and speaking about the countries current affairs. He was running for a second term and part of this affair was to get sponsors for his upcoming campaign. He spoke about the Second New Deal that was to focus on improving the nation's roads, schools, hospitals, arts, and entertainment venues. Eveline heard him discuss the WPA, Works Progress Association and Wagner Act, which were to equalize taxes, especially relative to the wealthy. He wanted to promote labor unions so workers could bargain collectively for benefits. When Eveline heard the Wagner Act mentioned, she froze thinking of what was about to happen to her.

Eveline made her way to where Eleanor Roosevelt was standing chatting to people. When she saw Eveline she excused herself and went to Eveline and extended her hand to shake it. Eveline did the same. When

Eleanor asked Eveline what brought her to California, Eveline could not remember why she was in California. Eleanor looked surprised when there was no response. Finally, Eveline said that she had always wanted to see Hollywood and was on her way to Vancouver. Eleanor asked, "What takes you to Vancouver?" Eveline paused and did not want to admit she was going to see her mother in prison. She made it appear to be a vacation to the other side of Canada since she was born near Toronto and had never seen what it was like in Vancouver. Eleanor smiled and told her it was a nice country. Mrs. Roosevelt began to tell Eveline that she had heard from her sons, Patrick and Andrew. Just as she was speaking, Winston and Jonathon joined the conversation. Eveline introduced them to Mrs. Roosevelt. She had remembered them from the investigations and the letters to sponsor her boys at West Point. All of a sudden, Eveline drew a blank and had difficulty remembering all that had happened then. Jonathon spoke up and reminded Eveline that Patrick and Andrew had been in West Point for some time. Eleanor said, "As a matter of fact, I received a letter from both Patrick and Andrew." Now, Winston's ears perked up because he had a conversation with them about leaving West Point. They had gone ahead and contacted President and Mrs. Roosevelt about the possibility of leaving and moving to Miami. Eleanor explained how successful they had been from all the reports she receives from their superiors. Eveline was feeling left out of the conversation because she had not contacted them in a long while. Mrs. Roosevelt told Eveline that Patrick and Andrew were resigning and wanted to be released from their duties at West Point. She asked Eveline why they might want to do such a thing. Eveline was not able to give a reason because she did not know any of this information. It was like she had abandoned them. Eleanor did ask how often she spoke to her sons. Eveline said that she had been busy and every time she tried to call they were in training. Mrs. Roosevelt had a suspicious look on her face and her tone changed as she said, "If your sons want to leave West Point and move to Miami, Franklin and I will settle up the expenses and allow them to end their career as officers." Eveline had not one word to say because she did not know any of this. Winston stood in silence as he watched Eveline be taken down by Eleanor Roosevelt.

After this encounter, Eveline's attitude was reduced to nearly nothing. Winston knew this might happen, but Jason was the one to suggest Winston wait until they returned from California to discuss Patrick and Andrew's moving to Miami and the reasons why. He was not about to let on that he knew this might occur. Never did he think the Roosevelt's would know before Eveline. This did not look good in their eyes about supporting a woman's children who had been admitted to West Point under such conditions many years ago and without the mother's knowledge of any of it. Mrs. Roosevelt excused herself in a lady like fashion, leaving Eveline to wonder what had happened to her life.

CHAPTER 19

The next morning, an elaborate brunch was served to the hundreds of guests who were at the Hearst party. Eveline was not sure she should make an appearance after the previous evening and what Eleanor Roosevelt and she had discussed. Winston and Jonathon were hungry, so they went without Eveline. When they left the room, they took a bet on how long it would take Eveline to change her mind. Before long, Eveline appeared in a casual and sporty outfit suitable for a morning affair. She acted as if nothing had occurred the evening before when she saw President and Mrs. Roosevelt. She moved near to where they were seated and spoke to them. At first, they were not very receptive, but after Eveline apologized for her lack of understanding last evening, they conversed about other things. Eleanor discussed her writing of "My Day", a daily radio program and writing that focused on current events and her work to help the less fortunate. She suggested that Eveline listen to it and let her know what she thought. Eveline left the conversation feeling better about her relationship with Mrs. Roosevelt. She thought back on the lavish luncheon she had at the Biltmore a few years ago with Mrs. Roosevelt. Eveline realized that she needed to get herself back in touch with her world and now knew she had to change the way she was living.

After the brunch, they left the Hearst Castle feeling like it had been a dream. The only thing they did was attend a party and get ready to go on to San Francisco which was a few hours north. Eveline told Jonathon that she was too worn out emotionally to drive and asked if he could get them to where the train would be. He agreed and was satisfied to be in charge of driving at a more sensible speed. Eveline wore a kerchief tied under her chin with her white sunglasses. Winston remarked, in a joking way, that she looked like a movie star after a hard night. Eveline did not find his remark as amusing as the men laughed. Jonathon quizzed Eveline on what else was discussed with Mrs. Roosevelt. She explained how embarrassed she had been when she had no knowledge that Patrick and Andrew sent a letter telling them they wanted to resign from West Point. Winston spoke up and reminded Eveline that she had been too busy with her life and had ignored many people and things surrounding her life. She turned and glared at Winston but he was not about to let her off so easily. He said, "Don't try that stuff on me. I have known you a long time and your manipulative ways and your life needs to change." She said nothing. Eveline continued speaking about the conversation the night before and told Jonathon, "I decided not to discuss my financial situation with the Roosevelts. I did not want to put them on the spot about giving me some leniency." Jonathon gripped the steering wheel when he heard such a preposterous idea. Why would a President give any one such leniency when so many taxes were due to an ailing country? He chose not to say a word.

As they neared San Francisco, they were in awe of the terrain along the Pacific Ocean. Much of the road was near the edge of high cliffs down to the water. Jonathon commented, "It is a good thing Eveline was not driving. We might be in the ocean by now with the way she would be taking these turns on this road." Winston thanked him for his good driving because many times it looked as if the road went out of sight with the water below. Eveline smirked at Jonathon's remark. Soon they arrived at the train station that was near the center of San Francisco. They were surprised the climate was cooler than they expected for California and that the city had been built on rolling hills. When they parked the Pierce Arrow in a secure area, they saw Alcatraz Penitentiary in the San Francisco Bay. Eveline stared at it and Jonathon asked, "Are you worried you might end up there?" She shook her head and said, "I wondered if that was what type of place my mother is in. I hope it looks more inviting than the one in the bay."

The train going north to Canada was due to leave in an hour. Jonathon was happy they had arrived as they had, with very little time to spare. He suggested they go to Fisherman's Wharf to see what type of food they might find. Winston was agreeable but Eveline found the odor of fish to be disgusting. Winston told her that was why it was called Fisherman's Wharf; there were all types of fresh fish available. She followed the men as they found a restaurant that served a variety of fish. The meal was fantastic and Eveline was the first to finish and want a second serving. After the meal, they went to the train and found their seats. It would be an overnight trip and a berth was provided for them. Eveline said, "This is a funny way to have two men in bed with me, bouncing on a train." They informed her that she had one for herself and they were to share a larger berth. Eveline smiled and told them to have a good time. Jonathon thought that she never stopped thinking of what people might do to one another.

The trip to Vancouver was uneventful since most of it occurred during the nighttime. Sleeping in a berth was not comfortable. There was very little privacy when people walked by speaking and smoking. This was definitely not like traveling on a ship. The train bounced along and the clatter of the wheels moving over the rails became hypnotic, but did not help with getting much rest. Eveline changed into a sleeping gown, but Winston and Jonathon removed their clothes and put them in the corner of the berth. Winston said it reminded him of camping. Jonathon had never been camping but asked if they had to go swimming in a lake to get clean in the morning. Winston thought that might be fun.

When morning arrived, the train named the Zephyr was a few hours from the Canadian border. Eveline had found a facility for washing and cleaning herself for the day. This was the lowest form of travel she had been familiar with. When she eyed Jonathon coming out of the berth with his turgid manhood she said, "Oh Jonathon, why don't you come in my berth and let me help you with that thing." Just then Winston jumped out in the same condition. Eveline shook her head inviting him too. They took her up on her offer and had breakfast two hours later. Just as they had finished their meal, the conductor walked through the train announcing that in another hour they would be in Vancouver, Canada. Jonathon checked his information about how to get from the train to the

Vancouver Island Correctional Center. There was taxicab service that would take them to the Wilkinson Road entrance. He showed Eveline and Winston the details he had been given when the appointment had been made. As they walked from the train to the taxicab area, Eveline said, "I hope it does not look like Alcatraz. When you said island all I thought of was the one in San Francisco." Winston tried to be supportive and said, "I'm sure your mother has been well cared for." Eveline took a deep breath as they sat waiting to go.

CHAPTER 20

The taxicab driver knew exactly where to take Jonathon, Winston, and Eveline. He told them that many people came to visit inmates and most of his work was driving back and forth from the train station to the Correctional Center. As the taxicab came closer to the prison, a Medieval Castle came into view. The grounds surrounding the prison were manicured and offered an inviting atmosphere. Eveline told Winston that it reminded her of Willard State Hospital. He told her that this was a prison for criminals, not an asylum. The driver corrected Winston and explained that it was built in 1913 to be a psychiatric hospital and soon was converted to a correctional facility. While the others conversed, Jonathon worried about how this meeting was to be. The taxicab pulled to the front entrance where a portly man dressed in a grey uniform greeted them. He said in a gruff tone, "Are you the group that is to meet with a Catherine Lounsberry?" When Eveline heard it put this way, she could not believe she was actually there to see her mother. She feared she might have heard something like, are you here to see the prisoner from Toronto? Jonathon took her hand as they entered the main office to wait for the person in charge of the meeting. The officer took their names and told them to sit on the bench. It was not very comfortable and Winston said, "This sure isn't the "Enchanted Hill" we just came from.

A man approached them and introduced himself as the counselor who would be conducting the meeting. He explained that Catherine had been rather negative about seeing her daughter but had extensive counseling to prepare her for the meeting. Eveline looked at Jonathon who had explained his position and that he was the investigative detective in the case that ultimately put Catherine in prison. The counselor led them into an office with chairs in a circle. He explained that the circular arrangement was most beneficial to a meeting of this type. Before Catherine was to be part of the group, the counselor asked why a meeting of this nature was requested. Jonathon began with the history of turbulent relationships and criminal behavior by many people that were mainly targeted at attempting to drive Eveline crazy, in the hopes she might commit suicide. The counselor had no expression on his face as he watched Eveline as Jonathon spoke. Winston sat wondering how he had ever gotten into so many things since he had known Eveline.

During the introductory conversation, Eveline was asked what she hoped to accomplish from the meeting. She nervously explained how she had thought for many years that there were situations and personality conflicts surrounding her parents and no one had ever taken the time to investigate these things. The counselor asked her if this uncertainty or confusion had affected her adult life. Jonathon moved in his chair while Eveline adjusted her outfit and tried to fix her hair. The counselor thought this type of response indicated unresolved issues. The counselor asked Eveline if she was okay. She told him she was feeling confused and not sure what was important to ask or find out. The counselor looked at Jonathon and asked why he felt this meeting was important to have and why Winston was involved. Jonathon reviewed the reasons he came into Eveline's life through a possible kidnapping and ransom situation with her children a few years ago. He continued to speak about the underworld gangs that had been menacing Eveline. All of this stemmed from her late husband's business dealings about 30 years earlier. Jonathon discussed the human transfer program, the rum running activities during Prohibition, and her late husband's general underhandedness in business. Winston spoke up and explained that he had been a friend of Eveline's late husband since early childhood. They became close friends and shared many things in life. Eveline frowned at Winston with a strange look when he said this. The counselor picked up on this and asked him for further information. Eveline cleared her throat and Winston said, "I was his secret lover." The counselor said nothing. Jonathon continued with the outcome of the criminal cases that sent many people to prison. The counselor looked intrigued and asked, "Were all these situations connected to Eveline and her family?" Eveline spoke up and said that her parents had been in the underworld activities when they still lived near Toronto. She explained that about15 years ago, after her husband's death; she had been through investigations while living in Geneva, New York that involved her husband's unlawful business practices. She explained that she thought everyone had been apprehended and put in prison and all the problems had been solved. Soon after, her children were supposedly kidnapped on their way to Florida where she had been living. People began to appear in different ways. The counselor asked what this meant. Eveline discussed how one man, Rudolph Williams, had supposedly hung himself in Rochester, New York, and appeared in Miami as Randolph Wilson. He had changed his appearance and talents. He had been involved with the underworld crime rings and was out to hopefully drive her crazy and undercut her wealth. That was when Jonathon Bingham came into the investigation as the detective who solved the intertwined criminal activities in Miami. The counselor wanted to know if that had been true. When Eveline heard this remark, she wondered if he thought she was crazy, as others tried to make her out to be. Jonathon spoke up and said, "That was all part of the plan to drive Eveline crazy. The man she referred to was never dead because the detective at the time lied to her about the man's hanging himself in a hotel in Rochester."

The counselor was not satisfied with Eveline's responses when she had been questioned about why this meeting would be so helpful. Jonathon spoke up again and explained that Mrs. Paine had been in Willard State Hospital near Geneva, New York around 1916. The counselor looked at Evellne and asked her why she had been placed there. She explained that she had attempted to strangle her newborn son, or so she had been led to believe. Eveline told the counselor that she did feel a sense of confusion at the time because her son was born with brown skin which came as a shock to everyone. The counselor's eyes went up. The counselor, hoping to ease Eveline's tension said, "You sure have had an interesting life." Eveline agreed with him and continued on about the elixirs she was given and about being committed for nearly 2 years in Willard. She explained that while in Willard State Hospital, she had time to think about people in her life and how they had affected her. Winston spoke up to defend Eveline saying, "I never thought she did that to her son. I always thought she was put in Willard as a way to get rid of her." Eveline agreed and spoke about her feeling of not remembering things. The counselor wanted to know about situations when she felt forgetful. Eveline explained that it seemed to happen under stress or when things were not going well. She said, "I always hear my mother telling me that she hated me and wanted to see me dead. I do not know why my mother has hated me so." The counselor told her that maybe she would find that out during the meeting. Jonathon asked her if she understood why she went on spending sprees and moved to far ends of the country. The counselor agreed this was an interesting question. Eveline, with no hesitation, said, "Because I deserve to do as I please. I have always been left alone to my own devices and spending money is what I have control over. My parents left me alone, as did my husband Wallace. He was too busy making millions on corrupt businesses and selling children into servitude or worse. No one knew he was so malicious because he was a sociopath." The counselor smiled when he heard her comment about a sociopath. Winston spoke up for Eveline and explained, "Wallace was a master at having everyone do the dirty work as he stood by getting all the credit with no dirt on his hands." The counselor appeared fascinated with these stories. He asked Eveline if she ever loved her late husband or her parents. Eveline paused and said, "No, I never knew what love was. I thought I loved my father, but he must have been controlled by my mother because I overheard them fighting years ago when I was very young. She told my father to never let me know about love because I did not deserve it. As for Wallace, I wanted to love him but he was always too busy working or being with his boyfriends. I decided to play it for all it was worth. That is why I told Jonathon when he found me in California, that we were going to live it up on Wallace's millions."

The counselor wanted to know about Jonathon finding her in California. Jonathon stared as Eveline struggled to explain that she wanted to get away and took her mother's name as she traveled in disguise from Miami to Hollywood. She had no problem telling the counselor that she hoped she could get her mother in more trouble by doing this, even though she was already in prison. Jonathon spoke up and told the counselor that she had suffered from a Fugue State. The counselor seemed impressed with his knowledge of behaviors. Jonathon explained that Agatha Christie had suffered from that too. He was in training when that occurred and her situation was part of his training to understand what people did under those conditions. He said it was usually brought on by a high stress situation. Eveline sat without a word being spoken.

CHAPTER 21

The counselor suggested a break from the conversations. There was a solarium for guests to rest in until the next session. It had been an hour for the introductory meeting. Before they left the room, the counselor asked Eveline to think of as many situations that might have been connected to her mother and her effect on her life from childhood. They would discuss those things to see if Catherine remembered any of those times or if it had been Eveline's perception. Jonathon and Winston were asked to reserve comment during the next sessions on whatever Eveline might say. The counselor requested individual meetings with Winston, then Jonathon, while Eveline was thinking about her past life.

Winston was invited to speak with the counselor first. He asked him to explain some of what he had revealed in the first meeting. Winston explained that he had come from an alcoholic family with a father who ended up in the poorhouse and a mother who had deserted him. Wallace's mother, Alice, was kind enough to have taken him in and raise him. That was how he and Wallace became so close. Winston explained that Wallace was always very distant and made him feel less important. According to Winston, Wallace did that to everyone. He explained the relationship between Wallace's father, Frank, which was jealousy because Wallace advanced in many ways that Frank never did. Winston discussed his dislike of Eveline when she came into the picture. Winston was certain that the only reason Wallace married was to make it look good. Wallace never showed love to Eveline; just let her do what she pleased. There had never been a good relationship with Eveline's mother and father much less any love. Winston admitted he loved Wallace and pledged to care for his children after his death. Winston discussed how Eveline was generous with her money when it came to herself and people she cared about. The counselor wanted to know if Winston had ever thought of marrying Eveline. The answer was a quick "no" even though they had lived together with separate life styles. The counselor told Winston that he found Eveline's attitude about her late husband's sexual activities acceptable. Winston explained that Eveline would sometimes want to watch and give instructions during sexual contacts. The counselor said nothing as Winston left the session.

Jonathon was the next to have a conversation about his opinions of Eveline. He explained how he came into the situation and found that the detective Eveline had been involved with in New York, was never a detective. He posed as one and was part of the underworld gang system during Prohibition. He was a master of disguise and helped set up what the supposed dead man was intending to do by driving Eveline crazy. Jonathon discussed how Eveline had been easily taken advantage of many times because of her generosity. She had many dimensions, according to Jonathon, when it came to being smart about her relationships, especially when she was told to beware of people. He explained that she could be difficult and determined to do as she pleased no matter what the consequences might be. Jonathon added the issue of her financial state of affairs and her determination to live well beyond her means. The counselor said, "That goes along with what she told us earlier about her spending sprees." Jonathon admitted that he had fallen for Eveline and cared very much for her. The counselor, appearing surprised, asked why. Jonathon said he knew that it was not good to get involved with clients, but it happened. The counselor asked if Eveline cared about him as much as he did for her. Jonathon explained how romantic she could be and at a moment's notice be very distant and act as if she did not care. The counselor wanted to know if Jonathon had any idea why this occurred. Jonathon told him about his personal reason for never getting involved with a woman, until he met Eveline. The counselor lowered his eyelid and asked, "How come?" Jonathon blushed when he explained that there had never been another woman who could receive him sexually. He said, "Eveline is an amazing woman in bed." The counselor smiled and told him that all men should be so well endowed and to feel lucky to find someone so accommodating.

Eveline had been thinking of things from the past about her mother. Most of her recollection was of a distant person who had little to do with her. She remembered the day she was taken away from their home by a strange man and placed in a private girl's school in Toronto. It was rare for her parent's to visit her. Eveline remembered the conversation when she wanted to place Patrick, her son, in a private school at such a young age. She thought nothing of it because that was what had happened to her. As she thought about past things, she realized much of her behavior was much like her mother's. Her mother hated her and she hated her mother. How could that be, when behaviors are similar, there was constant hatred occurring. There must be a deeper reason for so many things to have happened, especially when Eveline found out that her parents had been part of the underworld crime system, long before she married Wallace. After some thought, Eveline was beginning to look forward to whatever she might hear when she met her mother in a controlled environment where no one could overpower the conversation. The counselor came to see how Eveline was doing. She smiled and said, "You know, I am looking forward to this. I have a feeling much of my behaviors and habits, whether they be good or bad, will be better understood after the meeting. I hope to change my life." The counselor smiled and said, "That is our hope for people such as you. Your mother will probably not change nor can she start over. She is here for the rest of her life. You, on the other hand, have new possibilities and can change things for the better. With some counseling and awareness, you will be able to move on."

CHAPTER 22

I n the solarium, while waiting for the session to begin, Eveline thought about many situations surrounding her parents and how those times had affected her life. While these things were happening, Eveline had not been aware or old enough to understand, how her behavior had been conditioned to either ignore the atmosphere or learn to accommodate it and become like her mother. She found herself understanding why she had reacted to situations such as the spending and extravagant lifestyle which was a means to cover up her anxiety and loneliness. She tried to justify all those thoughts by telling herself that she had been generous and caring for the people she associated with. When she thought of the words "associated with", she asked herself if she ever really cared for or loved anyone. As she pondered that thought, Jonathon came to her mind. He was the first person she felt differently about. Why was she so cruel and heartless with him at times? Maybe her attitude toward others, spending, and her excessive sexual behaviors were a result of something from her childhood. She had been around wealth and never understood poverty; she thought everyone lived well, except hired help and laborers. Now that the Depression had ravaged the country, she saw more destitute people than ever before. She still blamed it on them for not knowing how to keep a job. Jonathon asked her what she was in such deep thought over. She told him she had been trying to put things of the past in better order and wanted to be ready for the next session.

The counselor appeared from the office where they had the first meeting. He explained that Catherine was in the office and had been given the guidelines for the meeting. He explained the rules to Eveline, Jonathon, and Winston. The first would be to listen, with only one person speaking at a time. There would be no arguing or threatening statements. Belittling or pointing the finger at another person would not be tolerated. There would be a time for questioning one another. He asked Eveline if she had anything to say before they entered the room. She shook her head and admitted she was very nervous about seeing and speaking with her mother. The counselor explained that Catherine Lounsberry had changed since she arrived at the Vancouver Island Correctional Center. Eveline asked how. The counselor said, "You can be the judge of that."

The counselor led the way as the three followed. Catherine was standing by a chair that was in a circular setting. Eveline saw her mother for the first time in many years. She remembered the day of the trial in Rochester, New York when she told her mother she hoped she rotted in hell, now it looked like she had. Eveline tried not to appear surprised by her mother's appearance. She was shrunk and stood hunched over. Her hair had always been well cared for and stylish, now it was pulled into a bun and greasy looking. Her hands and arms had withered and become bony and her legs were no longer shapely. The dress she wore was a typical wrap around with a tie at the waist, with no style. Eveline had a difficult time with the initial shock of seeing her mother in this condition. Winston had known Catherine for many years and could not believe it was the same person. Jonathon stood quietly because he had never met Catherine Lounsberry. He had only heard of her. It was an eerie atmosphere for the two women, who for many years were at odds with one another and had not seen one another. Now, Eveline thought about how could she expect a conversation about issues of the past when she saw her mother. This person did not even look like the mother she remembered. It seemed hard to understand this had been the woman who belittled her, made her feel unworthy of love, and hated her. The counselor invited everyone to have a seat. He reviewed the guidelines for the session. He encouraged the women to try to be honest but not argumentative. He asked that Winston and Jonathon only speak if a question was directed to them. Winston thought, how did I get myself involved with so much drama? Jonathon studied the reactions of Eveline and her mother. Eveline wrung her hands and had twisted a handkerchief into what looked like a rope. Her mother sat quietly, with her hands folded, staring at Eveline. The atmosphere had become tense; the time had come for the most important meeting of Eveline's life.

CHAPTER 23

———————⟨∞⟩———————

The counselor asked if they were ready to pursue a conversation about life in the past. Catherine's eyes moved around the room and focused on the light that was hanging above Eveline's head. Jonathon watched as Eveline fidgeted in her seat. This was not the usual behavior for her. The counselor looked at Catherine and asked, "How was your life as a young person before you married your husband?" Catherine hesitated then said, "It was like any other person's life. I wanted to be married and my parents were not the type to meddle in my affairs. I was pretty much on my own and led a life of promiscuity and fun. I never thought I would marry the man I did. He ended up being a good provider. Since he was from a well to do family in Canada I lived better than most." The counselor asked more about her life as a young person. Catherine said, "I wanted to be with as many men as I could find. I had excessive sexual desires." Jonathon and Winston thought Catherine was describing Eveline. Catherine said, "I never spoke of this to any one until now, but I had an affair with a black man. He was everything I needed and wanted, without the threat of marriage. He was like me, couldn't get enough." While Eveline listened, she thought about herself and realized how her mother's story sounded cheesy and cheap. Is that what people thought of her? Eveline raised her hand to ask a question. The counselor acknowledged her and she asked, "Mother, is that why we used to argue and fight about my behavior, because you saw yourself in me?" Catherine's eyes focused on Eveline like there was a fire in them. She said, "Yes, I saw you in me and I hated it and I still hate you." The counselor reminded Catherine of the guidelines for the session. Catherine continued, "Furthermore, I had to marry your father because of you. I didn't want to, but I had no choice because women then were put away if they were unmarried and pregnant. Since I was pregnant with my Negro boyfriend's child, who only wanted a good time with no strings attached and knew that we could never be together, I tricked your father into marrying me." Eveline began to think of Alice, her late husband's mother. She never knew who her father was and Eveline now realized that she did not know her real father either. Catherine's story of her life sounded similar to Alice's. Catherine took a deep breath and said, "Your father always assumed you were his child and he tried to love you in a way I could not. I hated the idea that you were illegitimate. I nearly died during your birth and was never able to have children again. Then, when you figured out our businesses both connected in Canada and the United States during Prohibition, the court deported us to Canada and made us sell everything and all our money went to orphan kids which I also hated." The counselor had no expression on his face and Eveline wondered if he heard stories like this all the time.

The counselor told Catherine to relax because he had some questions for Eveline. He asked if she could elaborate on her view of her childhood as far back as she was able to remember. Eveline took a deep breath and began, "I remember feeling unhappy most of the time. Mother, you never hugged me or touched me. You only hit me and made me cry. Daddy was the one who protected me from you. I remember when you were beating me when he came home and found you trying to choke me. It was then that he told you that if things did not change, he was leaving and putting me in a boarding school. You were hysterical and screamed that you wanted to kill me, and that he better get rid of me or you would." Catherine looked at Eveline and said, "That's right. I should have killed you with arsenic instead of choking you." Jonathon and Winston sat and watched the two women and wondered how all these things had happened. There seemed to be so many people that they knew who had suffered from such abuses. The counselor directed his question to Catherine asking, "Why did you hate your only daughter?" Catherine said, "Because she is too smart and no one can ever get anything by her. She could uncover things that most never could and point the finger and ask why. I never wanted to have anything to do with her because of what her father was, a Negro! Eveline was a reminder of what a good time I had with him. I was strapped with you because of that. I saw you as a punishment for my young life. Your father was too busy working the underworld gangster businesses and let everyone think he had a big job. He had a big job alright. He connected himself with other criminals in the United States; one was your fancy husband that took you for a ride. You were too busy running around with Women's Rights Movement and all your spending and lavish life that you never cared what he was up to." The counselor directed his next question to Eveline, "Why did you try so hard to keep the families together after you had your son Patrick?" Eveline made a face and said, "I did not try to do very much until after I was released from Willard State Hospital. It was only after that I found out Patrick was alive and being cared for by two Negro women in Geneva. Doctor Haynes had made those arrangements unbeknown to anyone. It had been after Wallace's death that I attempted to unite with what was left of the family. After being at Willard, I was finally released. I found out later that most everyone hoped I would never get out." The counselor asked Catherine to speak about that period of time. She said sarcastically, "Most of us wanted to see her commit suicide or go crazy in a place like Willard State Hospital and die there. When we visited her, Eveline lit into me about how much she hated me, right in front of the whole room. On the way back to 380 Washington Street that day, Wallace was not as upset as he had let many folks believe, because he also wanted to be alone. He knew you would someday find out about his private business affairs. When you found out, luckily he was dead, because otherwise he knew you would persecute him, as you did us. That fancy friend Rudolph hated you too as did many people, but they let you think they liked you. Your friend Rosie Haynes, as her business friends called her, worked you just the way she wanted to along with my friend Lucille Preston. We were all in business to transfer humans, sell them, and place the Negro women, as domestic servants, after they were surrogates for the children transfers from the Orient." Eveline looked overwhelmed. The counselor suggested a break.

During the break, Eveline told Winston and Jonathon that she felt as if she were reliving all that happened before she moved to Florida. Jonathon said he now saw why she wanted to leave the north and move to the south. Winston was as disturbed because he had lived through more than even Eveline had. He had his early years before Eveline, to remember things that Wallace was noted for. Eveline admitted that she found all types of sexual relationships intriguing and that was why she thought it was okay for the men to get together, even in her home. Jonathon wondered if that was what men did, because even as young boys his friends would play around with one another. Eveline told them she was going to ask more about the sexual part of the conversation with her mother.

The counselor let Eveline begin after the break. She asked, "Mother could you tell us about some of the things you did with me when I was young and before I was sent away." Catherine said, "I always thought it was fun to make you experience things that most girls might not. I used to be with your father, and sometimes another person, in the bedroom, with you in the room. Your father never wanted you to see such things. I told him that you needed to know at a young age what life was all about. I threatened your father with the law about his business corruption if he made me stop having you experience all the things adults do to one another. It was probably a good idea you went off to a school." Now Eveline began to understand why she had such an aggressive sexual thirst. She saw it as normal behavior. Jonathon had been watching the reactions of others in the room and felt the sorriest for Eveline. He became more aware of why she had been suffering from such anxieties, not just her sexual life, her financial life, and family life. She had come from an abusive environment and was trained to think what she saw was normal. Catherine continued, "When that brown skin kid of yours was born, that was the worst. I had hoped you did kill him because then there would never be a question about anyone's past. I thought that would leave me off the hook and I might never need to divulge my past life. Whenever I saw you, it was a constant reminder of the mistake I made so long ago. If I had been sent away and you had been born a Negro, you would have been taken away. My life would still be ruined no matter what. So, I decided to watch you struggle and hoped you would be driven crazy and commit suicide. We almost accomplished our goal until you moved to Miami and hired this detective. I guess this man you call Jonathon is the one." The counselor asked if Eveline or Jonathon had any questions. Eveline had no questions except a remark. She said, "Now all this becomes clear to me. I understand that my issues stem from a vindictive and unhealthy upbringing. I know why I was always high strung and anxious. I have felt a sense of hysteria that I had learned to overcome with my lavish style of living by surrounding myself with people and expensive things. I have been lonely because the important people that I thought I loved were against me. I know I have excessive emotional and attention-seeking behaviors, especially when I feel scared and alone. Winston has seen me in highly excitable situations and I love doing sexually inappropriate things. I did not think any of this was wrong, thanks to you Mother."

The counselor explained that many people had suffered from similar circumstances. The hysteria had been associated with women more than men. He explained that some studies had claimed that hysteria came from a monthly female cycle. For some, it gets worse as they get older because of hormonal fluctuations. He discussed the difference between Eveline's upbringing to that of a normal life. He said, "A normal upbringing is not discussed as readily as the unfortunate ones such as Eveline's. You, Catherine, deceived your husband, threatened him, and exposed your daughter to a lifelong curse." Catherine smiled and said, "That's what I had hoped for every time I belittled her or did something to her. I accomplished my goal." Eveline spoke up and said, "Remember what I told you in the court room in Rochester, I hope you rot in hell." Winston and Jonathon each took her hand when she said this. They felt terrible that a mother would be so vicious even after all these years. Catherine's final remark was, "Go away from here and have a good life, what's left of it, with your Negro and orphaned children. They are a living example of what I have had to endure for my entire life because of you." The counselor called for a guard to take Catherine away. Eveline, Jonathon, and Winston went to the solarium to rest before the counselor had a concluding conversation with them.

Eveline was furious when she sat down and had a moment to think of all that she had learned. Jonathon and Winston tried to calm her, but all she could say was, "Now I know why things are the way they have turned out. I can't change her or what Wallace had done, or others connected to the past." She looked at Jonathon and apologized for her behaviors. She admitted much of what she had done, by running away, moving, and spending, were all a way to try to escape her life. Jonathon told her that he would be there to help her straighten things out. Winston agreed and reminded her that he had known her since a teenager. She thanked them and then asked about what would happen next. The counselor came in and explained that Catherine was a very ill person and a criminal. Eveline nodded her head in agreement. He recommended that Eveline and her friends go back to Southern California and let time take care of all that had been discussed. Eveline told him that she did not regret this visit. She found out more than she expected. The counselor said, "That is the case often times. Now, you need to change your thinking and deal with your future."

CHAPTER 24

While they were waiting for the taxicab to take them to the train station, Jonathon asked Eveline if she remembered her journey across country. Eveline admitted that she did recollect parts of it. Jonathon explained that she had suffered from what was called a Fugue State or temporary amnesia. Eveline talked about her attempt to change her name to her mother's, in hopes she might get her in more trouble. Jonathon told her that was delusional thinking, because her mother had been in prison for quite some time. He suggested that Eveline find a counselor when they return to Miami. She acted surprised that she was being expected to go back to Miami. Jonathon said, "What were you planning to do? Your money has nearly been depleted. What are you going to survive on?" Eveline shrugged her shoulders. Jonathon reminded Eveline that she needed to deal with Mr. Keyes and the tax office when she returned. She thought he meant to Hollywood, not Miami. Jonathon took a harder stand and told her that the government had given him another week to get her back to Miami, otherwise she could be considered a tax evader, making her eligible for prison. He told her that he had been on the case that landed Al Capone in prison for tax evasion. Eveline acted as if she could never end up like her mother, appearing to dismiss this idea. Jonathon told her that he would be on her side, but she needed to return to Miami to deal with the issues at hand.

The train ride was more uncomfortable than before because there were no berths available for rest. The train had been overcrowded and most passengers slept in their seat. "What a terrible way to have to travel so far", Eveline said. As they neared San Francisco, Alcatraz came into view. Winston asked Eveline if she felt anything more about the prison her mother was in and how she felt about the news. Eveline looked out the window and said, "I never want to see a place like that again. I want my life to be simpler and happier." Winston agreed that would be best for all of them. He told Eveline and Jonathon that he had been concerned about Jason and his return on the airplane from Hollywood to Miami. Eveline told him that Jason was probably alright and was back at work. Jonathon assured Winston that all was fine.

When the train arrived in San Francisco, they decided to drive through to Hollywood. They agreed to take turns driving so there would be no need to stop. They laughed when they went by the Hollywood Restaurant where they had eaten on the way to San Francisco. They passed it by and stopped in a more realistic restaurant which only served diner type food, with no movie star possibilities. Eveline admitted she was too worn out to go after any stars; all she wanted to do was get back to Hollywood. Jonathon agreed and said they needed to make arrangements to transport the Pierce Arrow and settle up the hotel charges before they left for Miami. Winston was to go back a day before Eveline and Jonathon; his ticket had been predated and he had no choice but to travel alone. He still thought about Jason but did not talk about his concern.

The ride to Hollywood was long and tedious. They did not have a party to stop at as they had on the way to San Francisco. When they went by the area of the Hearst Castle, Eveline thought of her interaction with Eleanor Roosevelt. She knew she had given a poor representation of herself that evening. This was another example of why Eveline must be more alert to her surroundings and family. Eleanor Roosevelt had done her a favor with Patrick and Andrew and the way Eveline responded to her was disgraceful and unappreciative. Eveline thought she might have to do something for the Roosevelts for their generous gifting to Patrick and Andrew. There was very little conversation between the three of them, most of the time each person was deep in thought about their own issues. Jonathon thought about what he was going to do with Eveline when she returned to Miami. She had no place to go, since 825 Michigan Avenue was no longer hers. Winston had Jason heavy on his mind and was not sure why. Eveline worried about getting her life back with her children, her few friends, and her financial entanglements.

When Jonathon approached Hollywood, Eveline was asleep. Winston had been staring out the window and Jonathon was glad to be back from the long journey. He pulled the Pierce Arrow into the valet area of the hotel. He woke Eveline and told her they had arrived. She did not seem to care and only wanted to go to bed. Winston helped with the luggage while Jonathon tipped the valet. As they entered the lobby, the hotel clerk ran to Winston. He handed him a message. Winston looked at it. Olitha had called the day they left for Vancouver. The message said, "Call immediately". Winston looked at Jonathon and Eveline and knew he had been correct, something had happened. He went to the hotel telephone and had the operator connect him to the Tropical Gardens. He did not realize that it was 11PM in Hollywood, making it 2AM in Miami. The operator could be heard connecting the calls; Winston, impatient, stared at the others. Olitha could be heard on the other end, not saying the usual Tropical Gardens. Winston said nothing as Olitha screamed, "Oh my God Winston. Jason he be killed in the airplane. It crashed goin over the Rocky Mountains. I tried to call you but you left to go to Canada. He be dead for 3 days. What we gonna do?" Winston dropped the receiver and screamed, "Jason is dead!" Olitha could be heard screaming and crying on the other end of the line. Jonathon was stunned as Eveline went to Winston and held him as he wept.

CHAPTER 25

Winston ended the call when he told Olitha he was coming to Miami in the morning with Jonathon and Eveline. He was more interested in the details of what happened to the airplane. He called the operator who connected him to the American Airlines number. After he waited for what seemed like forever, he was connected to the office that had information concerning the tragedy. Winston was told that the DC 3 had run into a violent, early winter storm going over the Rocky Mountains, that had caused the plane to ice up and crash into one of the highest peaks of the mountain range. There were no survivors and because of the area of the crash, no one had been found. Winston was told that it may take until springtime before crews could venture into the rough terrain. Winston hung up the telephone and wept saying, "What am I going to do without him. He was the first person I was allowed to love and we had planned a life together. After what he told us last week about his family life, I did not have time to talk with him about it." Eveline and Jonathon held Winston as they went to the apartment. Eveline said, "Living in California has done nothing but create tragedy and heartache. I think we need to get out of here as fast as we can." Jonathon agreed and Winston went to his room to be alone. Everyone felt a sense of loss from all that had been discussed about everyone's family, and now the news of Jason. Winston's true and only love had suffered a tragic death.

Jonathon asked Winston if he would rather travel with them in two days instead of alone the next morning. Winston said he would rather travel with them, but he could not change his ticket. Jonathon told him that he would work that out for him. He telephoned the office in Miami that had arranged the tickets and was able to get Winston's changed for travel with Eveline and Jonathon. The next day everything was difficult to understand. The airline tragedy had not seemed real but having no known survivors, made it harder to comprehend. What was Winston to do when he returned to Miami? There would be no Jason. Eveline telephoned Olitha to find out if there was more information. When Olitha answered the telephone it was not in her usual tone. When she heard Eveline's voice, she perked up a bit and said, "Oh Miss Eveline, Iz so upset and don't know whats to think." Eveline told her that she was returning to Miami with Winston and Jonathon because she had had enough of the California lifestyle. Olitha was happy to hear this. She asked Eveline if there was anything that could be done with a funeral or something for Jason. Eveline did not know anything either and explained that there would probably be a service of some type. Olitha told Eveline that Sable had been more upset than she had been over Jason because he had become part of the family. Olitha said, "Wez had too many peoples dies on us. Wallace first, now Jason, what wez gonna do?" Eveline had no answer for that except that she would see her soon. Before the call ended Olitha asked, "Miss Eveline wheres you gonna live? 825 been turned into a hotel for discrete travelers, whatevers that means." Eveline told her she had no idea but would work something out. She too was confused about a hotel for discrete travelers.

Jonathon confirmed the arrangements for both Eveline and him to go with Winston on the next day's flight to Florida. Winston had been in his room since he found out about Jason's death. Eveline had been too upset with the news of her own affairs that no one had much to discuss. While they were arranging for their travel, Eveline and Jonathon went to the front desk to get the bill for the apartment. When the clerk handed Eveline the bill, her face turned red. Jonathon asked to see the bill. Eveline accused the clerk of doubling her charges. He begrudgingly went over the bill item by item and it was correct. Eveline had only enough money in her account to pay for half. She said to Jonathon, "What am I going to do?" Jonathon told her that she might consider selling the Pierce Arrow. Eveline eyes went up when she heard this suggestion. He asked, "If you don't sell it what are you going to pay the hotel bill with?" She thought for a moment and agreed that she might as well try to get her money back because she could not afford to ship the automobile to Miami. Eveline explained to the clerk that she needed to go to the bank and would return later to pay. While they waited to have the Pierce Arrow brought to the front of the hotel, Eveline told Jonathon than she had reached the end of her patience with Mr. Keyes. She would telephone him when they returned from the dealer and find out exactly what was left in her accounts and ask if he had notified the office in Miami to settle her financial commitments. Jonathon knew that there would be more involved than what Eveline thought, but he needed to get her back to Miami first.

Eveline drove the Pierce Arrow to the dealer and the same salesperson met her. She had only owned the vehicle for a month. The man asked if there was something the matter with the vehicle. Eveline explained that she would be moving back to Miami and was interested in selling the automobile and not transporting it back to Miami. It must have been Eveline's lucky moment because there had been a gentleman interested in buying her Pierce Arrow. He had seen her driving it around town and wanted one just like it. He had inquired about it the previous day and luckily the salesman had taken the gentleman's name and number. Jonathon and Eveline were invited to be seated while the call was made. Eveline said to Jonathon, "This would be a lucky thing if I could sell the automobile today." Jonathon agreed she would be very lucky. The salesman returned with the news Eveline had hoped for. The gentleman was on his way to make the deal. The salesman suggested that because it had only been out of the dealer for a month, it would be considered new. Eveline explained that they had taken it to San Francisco. The salesman said, "A powerful vehicle such as that is not nearly broken in with over a thousand miles on it. That will not be an issue." The gentleman arrived and was satisfied with the deal that the salesperson had suggested. Eveline agreed to sell the Pierce Arrow for a thousand dollars less than she had purchased it for. The transaction was completed; Eveline left the dealership with cash in her hand. As they waited for a taxicab to take them back to the hotel,

Jonathon said, "You amaze me. When the chips are down, something happens to bring you up." Eveline smiled and said, "This time I'm doing things on my own. I think I've used up Wallace's millions."

When Eveline went to pay her charges for the hotel, the clerk asked what had happened to the beautiful blue Pierce Arrow. Eveline casually said, "Oh, I just bought it to sport around in while I was here in California. I sold it back to the dealership. I am going back to Miami in the morning." After she settled her charges, she had a thousand dollars left. Jonathon stood and waited to see what she might be up to next. She turned to Jonathon and said, "I need to go to the Hollywood Savings Bank and close my account. Would you like to come along?" Jonathon agreed to go because he thought it might be a good idea to be with her when money was involved. She had been using up her big accounts and did not realize the severity of that yet. Eveline returned to her flashy way as she did whenever she would go into the bank in Geneva, many years ago. She wore a large brimmed hat, had her cigarette holder in hand and sashayed through the lobby to the bank manager, with Jonathon following. The tellers watched as Eveline strolled through the bank. She said to Jonathon, "I've had a lot of practice in banks, watch me." Jonathon was astounded that Eveline had made a complete turnaround of attitude and behaviors since returning from Vancouver. It had begun to make sense to him, whenever Eveline was in an uncomfortable situation; she would bring herself up and make it a success or run away attempting to forget everything. Eveline sat down, crossed her legs, exposing most of her leg, and told the manager that she was there to close her account. The bank manager explained that there would be a penalty for closing an account before one year. Eveline puffed smoke toward the manager and said, "Take your penalty and you know what you can do with it. I'll take the rest." The bank manager appeared startled to have been told such a thing, especially from a woman. Eveline sarcastically said, "Make it snappy. I've got things to do." She sat while the account was being closed, puffing smoke throughout the office. The manager handed Eveline a paper for her signature to verify the closure of the account. She signed it and was handed a check for only $475.00. She showed Jonathon the check on the way out of the bank. He said, "You better keep it. You may need all the money you can get your hands on for the taxes." She made a face as her upper lip twitched.

CHAPTER 26

⎯⎯⎯⎯ ⬦ ⎯⎯⎯⎯

When Eveline returned from the bank, she had the operator connect her to Mr. Keyes' office in Geneva. A woman with a stern voice answered the telephone; a surprise to Eveline; explaining that Mr. Keyes was no longer conducting legal or accounting businesses. Eveline asked what had happened. The woman informed Eveline that she had been hired by the federal government, along with an investigator, to follow up on the accountants and lawyers who had been representing wealthy individuals. Eveline began to feel overwhelmed when she listened to the woman explain that the Revenue Act of 1934 had provisions for such hiring of inspectors to follow up and retrieve unpaid taxes for the federal government. Eveline asked how she was to find out the status of her accounts and how much she owed the government. The woman told Eveline that she would be receiving a statement of amounts due for the last 15 years. Eveline asked where the statements would be sent. Without hesitation and a sarcastic tone, the woman said, "Florida, 825 Michigan Avenue in Miami Beach." Eveline was told that an investigation had revealed that wealthy people did not worry about their finances; they had hired a person such as she had, Mr. Keyes. The woman said, "To the surprise of wealthy individuals, the supposed honest accountant had been embezzling huge sums of money by avoiding tax payments for their clients. They were masters at putting off the payments or paying very little" Eveline sighed and said, "So; I have been one of those lucky people. Is there any way you can assist me in determining the value of whatever is left of my investments?" The woman explained that she had been working on the records that had been found in the file and a detailed list and values of those remaining investments would be sent to her. The woman said, "By the way Eveline, the government has placed a hold on all your transactions involving the accounts and investments. The mailing will be sent to the office of taxation in Miami first, and then a copy sent to you."

Eveline put the receiver down and stood in shock of what she had just heard. Jonathon came into the room and thought she had gone into one of her mental states. He yelled, "Eveline, are you there?" She whirled around and said, "Oh, I am here. I just found out that my dear and entrusted friend Mr. Keyes has been arrested and the government has secured all accounts dealing with me, a supposed wealthy person. What do you think of that?" Jonathon knew he needed to appear surprised because he knew this was the way the government had been handling tax evaders. He said, "That is terrible. What did you find out about your taxes and money?" She screamed, "Nothing, they are sending me a statement of expenses and what is left after the taxes and penalties are satisfied. The government has placed a hold on all of my accounts. I am surprised I was able to close the account at the Hollywood bank." Jonathon explained that the news may not be as bad as she thought. Eveline wanted to know how that could be. Jonathon said, "At least this way, you probably have enough money to pay your back taxes and penalties. If that is true, then there is no possibility of going to a judge or jail." Eveline made a face and said, "Furthermore, they are mailing me the financial statements to 825 Michigan Avenue, a place I gave away. I don't even have a place to live when I return to Miami." Jonathon told her that she could work that out because there were enough people she knew that would help find a place for her to live. Eveline smiled slyly asking, "Can I go back to the Biltmore?" Jonathon shook his head as Eveline went to pack for the trip back to Miami.

Jonathon had thought about Eveline's predicament. As he packed, he wondered if he should invite her to stay with him. Was that the smartest thing he could do? He liked her and she was great for sexual fun. What would she do with her time? Whether she realized it or not, she had little money left and would need to get a job. He rethought the idea of an invitation to live with him and hoped she might be able to stay with Winston at the Tropical Gardens. There had been so much that had happened and now there was to be new situations to get used to in Miami. Jonathon tried to forget the possibilities and wanted to get back to Miami and begin a new investigation. This one involving Eveline had gone from one thing to the next and he was tired of the drama and heartache this had created for all involved. Had she not run off to California, Jonathon would not have had to track her down, and Jason would still be alive, and Winston would not have had to go to California to help with Eveline's childhood issues in Vancouver. Jonathon had hoped that Winston would not blame Eveline for any of the things that had happened because of her California episode.

It was time to go to the airport. Winston looked as bad as he did the time Wallace had died. Eveline had to help pack his luggage. While she was doing this, she told Winston how he looked and that it reminded her of the time of Wallace's death. Winston had not thought of that until she mentioned it. He said, "You know, this is the second time in my life I have lost someone I cared about. I have had a sad life. You and Alice are the only ones left that have been on my side. I am not sure what I am going to do or how I will survive." Eveline attempted to console him, but with no success. Stories of the past did not make a difference in Winston's suffering. She hoped he would recover and move on and wondered how Patrick and Andrew might help in this situation when they came to Miami. Maybe, they would take over some of Winston's responsibilities, leaving him time to do new things.

When they arrived at the American Airlines terminal, Winston panicked and refused to get on the airplane. Jonathon tried to convince him that the airplane would be okay. He explained that the reason the airplane crashed was not the fault of the airplane, but the terrible weather. All predictions were for good flying weather; no storms had been in the forecast. Winston hesitated until the very end when he was the last person to go to the plane. He realized that if he did not go, he would be left in California by himself. This was not what he wanted. He knew he needed his friends, what few he had left. The flight to Chicago had been uneventful and calm. Winston relaxed and looked out the window when the airplane went over the Rocky Mountains. He felt a deep sense of sorrow and loss for the friend he had in Jason. Now, Jason was somewhere in the treacherous terrain below.

The flight from Chicago to Miami went as planned, arriving on time, and Jonathon was the happiest to be back in Miami. When they got off the airplane, the warm moist Florida air and tropical breeze reminded Jonathon how much he missed Miami. Winston had very little to say except that he wanted to get back to his gardens to see Olitha, Sable, and Jeffrey. He said, "At least they are alive and familiar to me." Eveline stood wondering where she was to go. Jonathon had decided not to suggest his place. He realized that he needed to distance himself from her as difficult as it might be. While they were waiting for a taxicab, Winston handed a key to Eveline for the front gate of 825. He said, "You can stay there for a few weeks. The guesthouse is not scheduled to open for another month. You can use one of the apartments." Eveline felt like she didn't recognize the property when she heard Winston speak about it. She had been the one who had it designed and built. Eveline did realize that she messed things up when she gave the property away and left leaving everything behind, including her life. The taxicab pulled up in front of 825. Eveline got out and stood staring at the silver sign above the gate that read "BOHEMIA". She wondered what would become of this property when it welcomed discrete travelers. She had heard about the atmosphere in the country of Bohemia, was this to be like that?

CHAPTER 27

For the first week, Eveline took time to re-orient herself to being back in Miami. She spent time thinking about what she had done in California and what the visit to see her mother had accomplished. She decided that Alice, Wallace's mother, should be told about her mother's affair with a Negro. It might help satisfy more questions of why Patrick was a brown skinned person. She knew it would make no difference about who had affairs with whom, but at least Alice would not keep thinking it came from her side of the family. Now, no one would ever be able to know for sure. She had the operator connect the call to Rochester, New York. The operator had a difficult time finding a number for an Alice Paine. The number Eveline had given the operator had been disconnected. The only other number the operator had for Alice was a nursing facility. Eveline had the operator connect her to that number. While she waited, all she could visualize was Alice, who had been so full of life, sitting in a chair staring at the wall. When the call had been completed, a voice could be heard that sounded like Alice's, saying "Good Morning, Rest Haven, what can I do for you." Eveline said, "Is that you Alice?" Alice asked who was calling. Eveline said, "It's me Alice, Eveline." Alice said, "Oh my God, Honey, how are you? I haven't heard from you in years." Eveline apologized for not being in better contact. Alice asked how she had been. Eveline left out the parts about her wandering off from Miami and going to California. She did explain about her visit to see her mother at the Vancouver Correctional Facility. Alice asked if she went by herself. She explained that her police investigator went along with Winston and his friend Jason. Alice wanted to know about Eveline's mother. Eveline explained how she looked and that the reason for the visit was to get a better understanding of her life as a young girl. Alice listened. Eveline left out parts about the behaviors her parents had exposed her to. Eveline said, "I thought you might be interested in what my mother told me about her life before I was born. She told me that she had to get married to my father to make him think that her pregnancy had been his doing. However, my mother was a sexually wild person and had an affair with a Negro man." Alice said, "Oh this is good to know that both sides of the family had affairs with Negroes. Your mother always belittled me and you about Patrick's color. Now, she sits in prison and you finally learn the truth." Eveline agreed that it was upsetting, but she had found out many other things that had helped her understand her childhood upbringing. Alice explained that she had left her apartment and took a job in the nursing home and had a room of her own. She told Eveline it was like being home with all the old people. Alice laughed and said, "I'm the youngest one here and I don't need any help. I get paid to work here." Eveline told her she was happy she was okay and suggested that Alice come to Miami for a vacation. She mentioned that Patrick and Andrew may be in Miami too. She did not mention their newest intent.

Life in Miami had changed more than Eveline expected. She had not seen Jonathon since their return from California. She took a taxicab to see Winston at the Tropical Gardens. While on the way, Eveline thought of her many fast trips in her Lincoln and Buick. Now all she had was a taxicab to go places in. When she arrived at the Tropical Gardens, Olitha came running out of the office yelling, "Oh Miss Eveline, you lookin so different. Iz so happy to see you no matter what you looks like. Poor, Winston still stays alone all days. He not eatin my good cookin. When Iz go home, Jeffrey try to have some fun wit him. Winston do not want anything. Wez worried about him." Eveline wondered how bad she, herself, looked after Olitha's remark. She thought she had been holding up well considering her latest news from her mother and the government. She did feel different, that was true, and she had very little cash, only enough to get back to 825 in the taxicab. She could never admit to anyone that she was almost penniless.

Eveline went upstairs to Winston and Jason's apartment. When she entered the room, she found him unshaven, unbathed, unclothed, and staring at Jason's clothing. Eveline had not expected such a sight. Winston had been noted for his rough and manly odor, but this had gone beyond appealing. She went to him and said, "Winston, I came to see how you have been doing since we got back from California." He looked at her, expressionless, and said, "It was because of you and your problems, Jason died a tragic death. If we did not go to California, there would not have been any need to fly in an airplane. This is all your fault." Eveline stood in shock saying, "I am sorry about what happened to Jason. It was not my fault the weather went bad during his airplane ride." Winston made no eye contact with her and said, "I want you to leave now!" Eveline, feeling a sense of rejection, told Winston again that she was sorry and left. Olitha and Jeffrey were in the office when Eveline returned. They knew what had been said because Jeffrey and Olitha and even Sable were told to leave Winston alone. Sable had made a special effort to speak about a service for Jason. Winston did not think that was needed. No one knew what to do. Jeffrey asked if Jonathon Bingham might be of some help. Eveline had not spoken to him, but agreed to telephone him when she returned to 825. Jeffrey asked Eveline what she thought of the new 825. She made a face and said, "I should have never given it away. Now, I am a temporary guest in a place I built and once owned." Sable said, "Oh Miss Eveline, my sugar and mes gots a room in the back building you could lives in. You been good to me and we duz not want any money for it." Eveline thanked her for the offer, wondering what the room must look like in the back of a building in Overton, a Negro neighborhood.

Eveline returned to 825, upset and now scared, because she had only a dollar in her purse after paying the taxicab fare. She kept reminding herself that everything would work out, but this was getting close to the end for her. She had never been without money and an automobile. Instead of worrying, she telephoned Jonathon in the hopes of a better conversation than she had just come from. Jonathon answered, he was happy to hear her voice, asking how she had been doing. Eveline explained about her visit to see Winston and finding him such a state of depression. Jonathon listened to the suggestion that he should visit Winston. Eveline told him that it might be good because Jonathon and Winston had shared time together, on the trip to Vancouver. Without making a commitment to visit Winston, he asked what Eveline was planning to do about a place to live. She hesitated and said, "Sable offered a room for me in the back of her building in Overton." Jonathon's eyes went up when he heard that. He knew what type of neighborhood Overton could be. He could not see Eveline living in a Negro neighborhood. He wanted to ask her to live with him but before he thought more about it, Eveline asked, "Jonathon dear, do you think I could stay with you? You have such a nice apartment. We have so much fun together and I miss making you feel like a fulfilled man." Jonathon had to make a decision in that moment. He said, "Eveline, I don't think we should do that. I have realized I did more with you than I should have. I should not have mixed business and pleasure. Yes, you were the first and probably the only woman to accept me. Sex cannot be the reason to live together. I have other issues and preferences that I realize I need to fulfill. I'm sorry, but living here cannot happen." He ended the subject and asked Eveline if a memorial service had been planned. Eveline had felt yet another rejection from Jonathon and said, "Don't ask me about a service. I need to find a place to live and it won't be on the streets of Overton."

CHAPTER 28

A few days after Eveline's visit to see Winston, her situation had not improved. She had not heard from the tax office about her financial situation and if there were any funds that might be turned over to her after all was settled. She decided to telephone Mr. Keyes' office to inquire about his whereabouts and hoped she could find out about her delinquent tax payments. The operator placed the call and the same woman answered. Eveline identified herself and the woman remembered her. She was more civil to Eveline than the first time they spoke. The woman explained that her affairs had been investigated and all the items had been sent to Miami. Eveline asked if there was to be any remaining stocks or funds for her. The woman said, "I'm sorry Mrs. Paine, but I am not at liberty to divulge that information. I do not want to get your hopes up. You will be receiving further information from the Miami Internal Revenue Office." Eveline knew this but did not push for further answers. She asked, "What happened to Mr. Keyes?" The woman cleared her throat and said, "I'm not supposed to tell you this but he admitted he had been working with a man named Thaddeus Cooper. Mr. Keyes attempted to cover his tracks after Mr. Cooper had been sentenced to prison for various crimes." Eveline, shocked, said, "Oh I have had many encounters with him. He was a crook for sure." The woman continued, "When Mr. Cooper was tracked down and sent to prison, Mr. Keyes became jittery and claimed he was having a nervous breakdown with all the financial unrest of the Depression. He did not realize we had already begun investigating him, finding that not only you had been swindled, but many others. He has been committed to Willard State Hospital for observations." When Eveline heard this, her eyes went up, remembering what it had been like years earlier in a mental institution. She thought that it seemed like many people she knew ended up in either a prison or a mental institution. The woman

105

asked if Eveline had other concerns. She said that all of her questions had been answered. Before they hung up, the woman said, "Mrs. Paine, you are a very lucky woman not to have been arrested and imprisoned for owing so much money to the government. Al Capone went to Alcatraz for the same amount of money that you owe but because Mr. Keyes had manipulated you and your money, the fault was placed on him, but you still have to pay taxes. Many people in your position have been victims of embezzlers." Eveline thanked the woman and hung up.

Eveline paced around the apartment after hearing from the woman in Mr. Keyes' office. She began thinking about how far back these situations had occurred. She thought everything had been solved and life might be less complicated. Shaking her head, she thought that she needed to get a job and wondered what she could do. She had never worked a day since being a secretary in Rochester 40 years ago, before she married Wallace. While she was thinking, she flipped through a newspaper that had been in the apartment. She saw the Burdines advertisements and knew a job there might be what she needed. While she thought about a job in a department store, she hoped it might be in cosmetics, dresses, or accessories. She reminded herself that she was nearly penniless and any employment would be welcome.

The next day Eveline dressed in her best outfit. She was at least able to look great and in style. She had her wardrobe and would make the most of it. When the taxicab stopped in front of Burdines in downtown Miami, Eveline thought about having shopped there and having grand luncheons with the woman of Miami. She wondered about some of those high class women seeing her working behind a counter. Eveline decided that it did not matter. Her survival only mattered at this period of her life. She knew she had overcome many obstacles in the past, so why not this time. She put her best foot forward and went to the sixth floor employment office. She was greeted by a fashionable woman who explained that there were fewer positions available because of the Depression. Eveline felt like she had been told no before she even applied for a job. The woman sensed something about Eveline's anxiety and said, "My dear, there is a position open in the cosmetics department. It is temporary. Would you be interested? You may start tomorrow. The woman you will be replacing just left town, with her husband, with no notice." Eveline accepted, she would make enough money to at least survive until something else happened.

Upon arriving back to 825, Eveline was greeted by Jonathon. She was not expecting him, but he was delivering a registered letter from the tax office. He explained to her that because he had been involved with her in California and Vancouver, part of his responsibilities was to deliver official mail. He told Eveline that he had found a counselor for her at Jackson Memorial Hospital. Eveline had not expected any of this information, much less to see Jonathon. She invited him in to the apartment. She explained about her new job at Burdines. He was surprised she had acted so fast and found employment. Jonathon said, "You amaze me. When your chips are down, you rise and make everything work out." She smiled and said, "You know what a life I've had and I felt I needed to take care of myself." While she spoke to Jonathon, she studied his trousers and wanted to go for him in the worst way. She had not been with him in a very long time. She knew part of her problem with sexual activities stemmed from her childhood and her impulsivity to overcome her insecurities. Jonathon handed Eveline an envelope. She signed her name and opened it. The letter informed her that all delinquent taxes had been paid. The hold on her investments and bank accounts had been lifted. When Eveline read this she screamed, "My accounts have been released." As she read further, the letter gave the totals of debts paid. The next section listed the remainders of her accounts. There was a total of $500.00 that would be sent to her when receipt of this letter had been sent to the tax office. All of her investments had been confiscated by the government and sold for nearly nothing just to recover money for taxes. Jonathon watched Eveline as she fell into the chair saying, "This is all I have to show for my many years of putting up with everyone else's bad behavior. I thought I would be rich for the rest of my life." Jonathon said nothing. Eveline decided at that moment that she was going to make something of herself with no one's help. After some chit chat Jonathon excused himself because of other business. He handed her the name of the counselor at the hospital. He said, "Eveline, do yourself a favor and go meet the doctor."

After Jonathon left, Eveline thought about what her life had become. Going from a wealthy widow to an almost penniless person, she now faced a new type of life. Could she be successful at the cosmetic counter selling perfumes and makeup, when not long ago she was buying those expensive items. She hoped a good attitude might make the job easier. She remembered how demanding she had been to saleswomen in the past. Now, she was going to be one of them. How would she treat an uppity shopper? The telephone rang, taking Eveline's mind off her worries about her new job. Sable could be heard speaking loudly, "Miss Eveline, wez got bad news here at the Tropical Gardens. Jeffrey he leavin us. He goin back to Key West. He do not want to work for Winston no mo. He says he not happy that Winston is so mean and depress. What we gonna do here? Who gonna bring dat boy Winston out of his depress mind?" Eveline told Sable to let Jeffrey go. She told Sable that she had asked Jonathon to speak to Winston. Sable asked, "When he comin? Wes can't take dis no mo. There no business and no one to works the office now." Eveline assured Sable that things might change soon. She told Sable about her new job at Burdines. Sable said, "Oh my lords, now you like us, workin for the rich peoples." After Eveline hung up the receiver, she thought that she did not like the sound of working for rich people, when she had been one herself.

CHAPTER 29

The oppressive summer heat and humidity had begun to lessen in South Florida. Radio announcers had been telling the listeners about a possibility of a hurricane. The Miami Herald reported that the storm had been gaining strength as it moved across the warm ocean waters. It was not certain of the pathway the storm might take. There had been photos of other hurricanes. Eveline read about the hurricane that devastated Miami Beach just before she had contracted to have 825 Michigan Avenue built. The newspaper suggested that all residents of Miami and the Keys should prepare for the worst. Eveline telephoned Sable at the Tropical Gardens to see if they had begun to prepare for the storm. Olitha answered the telephone only saying, "Hello." Eveline clearing her throat said, "Excuse me, is this Olitha? When did you stop answering the telephone with the correct greeting?" Olitha apologized but told her that Winston demanded that no more business should be taken at the Gardens because he did not want anyone around. Olitha said, "He just told Sable and me to get out and not to come back. Jeffrey, he left because of the storm. He never say nuttin. Winston lookin worse every day and getting skinny. Wez gonna go home to our husbands and not comes back. Wez be fired." Eveline had called to speak with Jeffrey, but Olitha said he did not give an address in Key West. Eveline told Olitha that she would try to get Jonathon over to see Winston as soon as she could.

Eveline had learned to economize since she had lost her financial empire. She even learned the bus route from Miami Beach to Burdines. The first time she waited for the bus, she felt as if the whole world knew she had been reduced to such transportation. She hated that she no longer had a snappy vehicle to drive around town in. How could such things have happened in so short a time? Riding the bus became a time for Eveline to think about things and she found herself figuring out what she needed to do with her life. She looked at the doctor's name that Jonathon had given her for counseling. When the bus went by Jackson Memorial Hospital, she knew she needed to make that appointment. How would she pay for such sessions? Why did Jonathon find her the doctor? Why had he stayed away from her when they had a love for one another? The questions had nagged her day and night. Eveline was afraid she may be going into another state of confusion and might do something crazy. She decided to make an appointment but wondered what she might say to him if she could not pay.

While thinking about Winston, she remembered the conversation and realized Jonathon had never told her he would go to see Winston. Why was he being so evasive? Should she call him again? Her mind kept telling her things to do but she did not know if these were the right things to do. After tormenting herself with the questions that had no answers, she decided it was time to get in touch with Patrick and Andrew. Since she had been embarrassed to have found out of their plans of leaving West Point from Eleanor Roosevelt, it might be time to find what was happening. She telephoned the operator to connect her to West Point. The call went to the main number and Eveline was told that a message would be given to her sons. She felt a sense of helplessness because every way she turned did not give her the help she needed.

Days passed with no response from West Point. Eveline had been enjoying her job at Burdines and felt a sense of worth seeing and speaking with customers. She enjoyed demonstrating various ways to use makeup and how to purchase the correct fragrance for special occasions. Her supervisor complimented Eveline on what a good job she had been doing. Women began asking for Mrs. Paine because she had the reputation as the best saleslady in Burdines. Eveline, for the first time since her involvement with the Women's Rights Movement, felt like a valuable woman who contributed to making customers happy.

The forecast worsened and stores were closing to prepare for the hurricane. Eveline arrived at 825 just before the wind began and torrential rains poured down. The radio had announced that the storm had been approaching the Florida Keys. Eveline wondered if Jeffrey had made it to Key West. The next day was Labor Day, September 2, the hurricane had turned and hit the Middle Keys with winds of over 150 miles per hour. Eveline had been listening to the radio until the power went out. The next morning, the news reported that Miami had not been in the path of the hurricane. It had been the worst storm in history and had destroyed Henry Flagler's dream railroad from Miami to Key West. Eveline reminisced about the trip she and Jonathon had taken a few years ago on that very train to Key West. That was when they fell in love! She shook her head in mourning of days gone by. The longer it went that Jonathon had not been in contact with her, she suspected it had to do with what had been discussed in Vancouver.

After the storm had passed, businesses resumed their operations and Miami had been spared from destruction. Eveline returned to work, where the cosmetic counter was located in the front of the store. Eveline had her head turned when she heard a deep voice say, "Hello Mother, you look great. We thought we would come to see you working." Eveline knew it had to be Patrick with such a voice. She whirled around and saw both Patrick and Andrew, not in military uniform, but in sporty shorts, high socks and tropical shirts. They looked handsome and grown up. She came from around the counter; each son took turns lifting her up, kissing and swirling her around. Customers had stopped and stared. It was unusual for such things to occur at the front door of Burdines. Eveline, being surprised, asked why they were there. They explained that they had resigned from West Point and intended to live in Miami. Eveline knew of their intent because of Eleanor Roosevelt, but did not expect them so soon. Patrick explained that Mr. Bingham had contacted them about Jason's unfortunate death and Winston's state of mind. He suggested they see Winston because he had been like a father to them when they were children. Eveline did not know what to say as she kissed them and pinched their cheeks. She stopped when she realized they were no longer her little children. They were now handsome men. Andrew said, "You know Mother that we are in love."

Eveline said, "No, I did not know this." Patrick explained he had telephone Winston about their leaving West Point and moving to Miami. They told her that since they had a relationship with one another that West Point would not support, they had resigned. Patrick explained that Winston had promised to discuss this with Jason after they returned from California. Then, we heard of Jason's death. Mr. Bingham called us at West Point and told us that you had asked him to go see Winston. Instead, Mr. Bingham suggested that we may be able to support Winston and help him because we had been like family. Eveline's mind was now in a whirl of thought about all that had been happening and she had not known any of it.

CHAPTER 30

—————

Being perplexed over many situations, Eveline telephoned Jackson Memorial Hospital to make the appointment with the counselor Jonathon had recommended. When the operator directed the call to the office, Eveline wanted to hang up because she felt the appointment might be a waste of her time. She thought about all that had been happening in her absence and felt she needed to attend to family matters, as well as the reasons for her behaviors. Just as she was about to put the receiver down, a man's voice could be heard saying, "Good morning, how may I help you?" Eveline was surprised that a man answered and said, "I am Eveline Paine and I need to make an appointment to see a counselor." The man thanked Eveline and said, "I'm Doctor Kane, when can we schedule a meeting?" Eveline explained that she worked at Burdines and could be at the hospital in the afternoon. The appointment was made for the next day at 4PM.

After Eveline hung up the receiver, she thought how pleasant the doctor seemed. She liked the tone of his voice and hoped she would have a good relationship with him and gain a better understanding of herself. While Eveline worked at the cosmetic counter she thought about Patrick and Andrew's life together and what that might mean for their future. Not many men would admit that they had a love relationship, especially in a military institution. They had been smart to realize the need to leave such an environment, but how would they be received in Miami? She hoped that when they saw Winston, things might get better and Patrick and Andrew could take his mind off the loss of Jason. Now that Jeffrey had abandoned Winston and Olitha and Sable had been fired, a new beginning might be what was needed. Eveline still wondered why Jonathon had so much involvement in her affairs, but had not made an effort to see her. She needed to discuss these thoughts with the doctor.

Patrick and Andrew had been staying at the Flamingo Hotel in Miami. It was luxurious and fun. They enjoyed swimming in the salty water and playing in the sun which had a way of making frolicking in the water more fun. Patrick had been the aggressive one since an early age, so he edged Andrew on to remove his bathing trunks. Men these days had given up wearing the big underwear looking bathing suits. Andrew loved dropping his trunks while Patrick and he manhandled one another under the water. Patrick always seemed to be the winner and have his way as they wrestled in the warm salty water. They had been living it up at the Flamingo Hotel and Andrew reminded Patrick that their mother had lived it up at the Biltmore. They agreed that she had not been living it up any more and they did not understand what had happened and had no answer for her less than luxurious life now.

Eveline's appointment with Doctor Kane was in the afternoon. She had not told anyone about it. She arrived at the hospital early and was greeted by a receptionist. Eveline had to fill out a form with questions about her health, family and illnesses of anyone related to her. While she worked on the questionnaire, she observed people coming out of the office. They appeared normal to Eveline. She thought about what their issues might be. Did she appear normal? Just as she was thinking of all these things, she was invited into the office. Her legs felt as if they were giving out from underneath her as she entered the room. It must be fear of the unknown, she thought. When she saw the doctor, she wanted to turn and leave. He was tall and handsome. Eveline reminded herself that she had not come to have an affair with this gorgeous man. He was the one to hopefully help her out of the problems she had. He extended his hand and shook Eveline's hand saying, "I'm Doctor Kane, please take a seat." Eveline's mind had been in such a whirl, she held the doctor's hand longer than the usual. The doctor released the shake with a smile as Eveline lowered herself in the seat. He knew what had just happened because that was the usual reaction when meeting a new patient.

Dr. Kane reviewed the file that Eveline filled out. He studied it for the longest time, and then said, "Tell me why you are here." Eveline, confused, said, "I'm not sure where to begin." The doctor said, "Tell me about your present life." Eveline explained about her late husband and his early death, leaving her with uncovered business dealings. She explained the financial crisis she had recently been a victim of. She spoke about the underworld crime groups that attempted to drive her crazy. The doctor shook his head as she discussed the supposed kidnapping and ransom of her two sons. Eveline mentioned how her life had been when she was married to Wallace, her late husband. The doctor wanted to know what that life had been like. Eveline said, "It was lonely. I had everything I wanted. I had been instrumental in the Women's Rights Movement in New York State. I advocated and demonstrated for the right for women to vote. I traveled with groups for those causes. Wallace had always been too busy working and being a criminal at the expense of others. He was a sociopath, you know. I had my domestic servants that followed me from New York State to Miami and still are employed at the Spaulding Tropical Gardens. They have become like family to me."

Doctor Kane looked at Eveline as she elaborated on situations and people surrounding her life and said, "You have explained about many people that have been with you. How was your husband as a lover?" Eveline had never been asked such a question. She thought for a moment and said, "He was not much of one except to get me pregnant once. He had other sexual interests in life. He liked to jump the fence with his boyfriends. One of them is living in Miami and is a longtime friend of mine. He has been like a father to my children." Doctor Kane picked up on the idea of more than one son. He asked, "How many sons do you have?" Eveline laughed when she heard his question and said, "I have two, one through birth and another through adoption. Andrew was adopted after his mother and father were murdered in a speakeasy in New York City. Little did I know, at the time, that my late husband had been the mastermind in the crime world with rum running and human trafficking. My son Patrick had been in Manlius Pebble School near Syracuse, New York, and Andrew and he had been roommates. I adopted him when he was five."

The next question the doctor asked was about her childhood. Eveline explained that had been the reason a friend of hers suggested she seek counseling because of what she had been told by her mother about her early years. Doctor Kane asked about her friend who made the suggestion to meet for counseling. Eveline said, "His name is Jonathon Bingham, he is a Miami Police Department Detective. He helped to solve the kidnapping, crime rings, and the underworld activity surrounding my late husband's business affairs. He also tracked me down when I took off to California from Miami. He claimed I had been in a Fugue State. He compared me to Agatha Christie and said that she had suffered from that too." The doctor's eyes were wide open as he listened to these stories. He asked, "Do you have any understanding why you took off to California?" Eveline explained, "I was weary and confused. I just left everything and ran away. Jonathon tracked me down and found me claiming to be my mother, Catherine Lounsberry. She had been the reason for my childhood terrors. I never understood the impact she had on me and found she made my father hate me too. When we arrived in California, I was seeing Jonathon and we had begun a relationship. Jonathon admitted he liked the relationship because I had been the only person to be able to accept his manhood. He claimed everyone else said it was too big." The doctor blinked as Eveline explained the details of their sexual activities. She was beginning to enjoy telling the story of her involvement with Jonathon.

Doctor Kane tried to refocus his questions away for the sexual activity that Eveline had been having fun discussing. He asked, "What did you think you were accomplishing from running from your home and family?" With no hesitation Eveline said, "I always do that when things get confusing and hard for me to accept. I learned to do that when I was young. I trained myself to become someone else so I did not need to deal with the treatment I had been receiving." Doctor Kane then realized that Eveline had developed the ability to get rid of one personality and live like another to get away from painful experiences. He asked Eveline to describe her mother and father. Eveline began, "My mother is the blame for all of this. She had an affair with a Negro and hated me because I reminded her of that affair, which she claimed had been terrific. Then, she had to marry my father to cover up her behavior. When I gave birth to Patrick, a brown skin baby, my mother badgered and continually criticized me, telling me I had been a whore. She has hated me since the day I was born. I found out these things when I went to Vancouver Correctional Facility to see my mother about my past. Jonathon and Winston were with me when we had the meeting. It was after that, the counselor in Vancouver suggested I seek out counseling here in Miami." The doctor wanted to know about her father. Eveline said, "He was probably a good man but my mother forced him to have sexual relations with more than one person, with me present. He was told never to tell or my mother would report him for his criminal behavior in Canada, where we lived, and then in Rochester, New York. He ended up being murdered by the Black Hand during Prohibition because he never paid his debts to them. He must have been a coward not to have reported my mother for her abusive treatment of me. She would do things to me in the bathroom, after over feeding me and then starving me. She would give me enemas and threaten me if I could not hold them. She always had hat pins ready to stick them in places on me that hurt. She told me that she needed to punish me for being alive. She told me she wanted me dead."

Doctor Kane asked Eveline how she managed to survive this horrific treatment. Eveline explained, "I learned to shut off Eveline and behave like someone else who could take the treatments my mother had been giving. My father finally was told by my mother to send me to a boarding school near Toronto. If he did not, I would be dead. When I was a teenager, we moved to Rochester, New York, and little did anyone know, it was to be nearer the crime world my husband had been part of." After some conversation about life in Rochester, which seemed to be better because Eveline had been working, the doctor ended the appointment. He gave

Eveline some things to think about for the next session. He explained that there had been advancements in the mental health areas. Up to this point, woman in particular, had been considered insane when stories of this type were told. Recently, women that suffered hormonal episodes were often committed to institutions, being diagnosed as crazy. Doctor Kane explained that a form of therapy had been tested on patients with mental traumas. He did not think that Eveline was a candidate for the shock treatment that might adjust the brain patterns for suffering individuals. When the doctor mentioned institutions, she told him about her time at Willard State Hospital which she had not mentioned on the questionnaire. She explained that she had been admitted for rest, because she attempted to strangle Patrick when he was born. Eveline explained she had been tired and confused about having a Negro baby. The doctor and Wallace decided she needed to be committed to Willard State Hospital. According to others, they wanted to get rid of her and hoped she might commit suicide. Doctor Kane shook his head as he listened to Eveline's story.

For the next meeting, Eveline had been given the task of trying to figure out why she behaved the way she did when she was overwhelmed and scared. Doctor Kane told Eveline that she had given him good information and their job was to figure out how to avoid the traps she falls into. He explained that he hoped she would think about what had been discussed and attempt to see patterns in her behavior that were a direct connection to her childhood experiences and treatments. He said, "Often we do things because we were trained in ways that we thought were correct. Most of our behaviors and thoughts are set before the age of five." Eveline left the hospital beginning to realize why she had been living the life she had. Either it was to run away, punish, or torture people the way she had been treated by her mother and father.

CHAPTER 31

Eveline arrived for the next appointment with Doctor Kane; he reviewed what had been discussed in the previous session. Eveline listened and asked if she could add a few remarks connected to things she had thought about. The doctor asked what those things had been. Eveline said, "I gave a lot of thought to why I learned to change my personality based on treatments I had been receiving. I think I recognize three different people I can escape to. You know it is good to be able to get away and be someone else for a while. People accused me of being crazy but they did not know I am able to survive things that threaten me by being a different person. When I went to California, I went as my mother, Catherine, hoping she would get in more trouble. I really wanted to be like her at that time and get back at people by treating them badly. That is why I have a collection of long hat pins that I have used on some men when they have tried to cross me. I learned that from my mother." Doctor Kane sighed saying, "So, what I hear you saying is that you have two different types of personality traits based on the situation you are experiencing." Eveline shook her head saying, "Actually, I think there may be another person in me. Her name is Trixie. I remembered that name many years ago when my late husband had a New Year's Eve party in a hotel in Rochester. It was a burlesque show and one of the entertainers had been named Trixie Will Do. I enjoyed her suggestive actions and took that name for myself to use while I'm engaged in sexual activities." Doctor Kane had been attempting to focus his questions away from the sexual aspect of Eveline's personality, he had been unsuccessful. He had decided that more discussion was necessary about her lust for sex.

Eveline felt a sense of relief after admitting and speaking about the three personalities she had been aware of. Thanks to her mother, she had to unwind and retrain herself in a healthier way. Doctor Kane asked more about Trixie Will Do. Eveline laughed and said, "I loved that name from the minute I heard it because I love sex and the more "tricks" I can have the better. Now I understand why I like to have sex with more than one person and be the center of all the action, no matter whom or what it may be. I like to be the dominate one. I get a thrill out of telling two men what to do to one another or while I'm in the middle. I saw my parents like that and my mother was in charge." The doctor wanted to know if these multiple partner affairs still occur. Eveline smiled and said, "Not lately. I have been so in love with Jonathon, and he with me, that all that other stuff does not matter. Until then, I had been sexual with many men in Miami, like Winston and some others who are now either dead or in prison." Without seeming critical, Doctor Kane asked, "Do you understand why you have behaved the way you have described? If so, what can you do to avoid such actions?" Eveline responded, "I love sex. That is not wrong, is it? I guess I need to stay calm and remind myself that those other actions are my mother coming out and I am trying to get rid of her when I am in that situation. Usually, I act that way when I sense someone is trying to hurt or be bad to me." Doctor Kane explained that much of people's actions can be related to something that makes the brain respond in a protective way. When a person is not bombarded, they respond in a calm and intelligent fashion.

The doctor asked if they could discuss her relationship with Jonathon Bingham. Eveline went over how they met and what had happened as they got to know each other. Doctor Kane wanted to know how Eveline felt when she was in his company. Eveline explained that she had never felt like that with anyone else, even Wallace. She said, "I think Wallace only married me to cover up because men needed to be married back them if you were in business. Jonathon, on the other hand, is kind and a gentleman. He pays attention to me, not like Wallace, who only bought my affections. Jonathon appreciated me, not because of sex but because we had fun together. I still wonder why he has gone off." Doctor Kane suggested that he might have felt he was enabling her and not making her get the help she needed. Eveline agreed saying, "He told me that he had mixed business and pleasure and that was not a good thing to do. Even while we were in California, and on the way to Vancouver, he and Winston had a little something to do with each other. I tried to excite Jonathon one day and he told me he was saving himself." While the doctor had been listening to Eveline's life and her many stories, he kept thinking that Eveline would be an interesting study in human behaviors. She might be a candidate for a psychological study at the University of Miami. He had written in his journal that she had been through more traumas than ten people may have in a lifetime. He said, "If you feel you have understood and learned to deal with these reasons for your erratic behavior, do you think Jonathon might come back to you?" Eveline told him she would like that very much. Eveline still wondered how Jonathon knew about the counselor, so she asked him about that. Doctor Kane hesitated and said, "Somethings I cannot tell you. Things that are discussed in here must stay here. All I will tell you is that Jonathon Bingham and I have been long time acquaintances. I did not know you had been referred to me by him."

The next appointment had been scheduled in a week. Eveline's work was to think about Eveline, Catherine, and Trixie and to figure out when they arrive in her life and why. After that, Eveline needed to think about a different way to deal with such temptations. Doctor Kane told Eveline that he had seen improvement in her. According to him, most people could never recognize different personalities and why they came and went in a person's life. Eveline had begun to feel like she had a better understanding of her life. By telling the doctor all that she had been through, made a huge difference in her outlook. She now began to feel like she was not guilty but had been the victim of sick people. She reminded herself that she had been strong for many years and now felt stronger against the tempting personalities that had driven her mad. Before she left Doctor Kane's office, Eveline said, "Doctor, I have a problem." The doctor smiled as if to say, really? She said, "I would like to know how much these office visits cost? I have come into hard times and may not be able to continue because I have very little money." The doctor waved his hand and said, "Don't worry; it has been taken care of. All your visits will be covered." Eveline left the hospital wondering who had been financing her time at Doctor Kane's office.

CHAPTER 32

———◇———

Having been intrigued with Eveline's life story, Doctor Kane investigated a person who had been notable in his theory of amnesic states. He went to the University of Miami Medical Research Library and located information about Pierre Janet. He had been born in Paris, France in 1859. Doctor Kane's analysis of Eveline coincided with what Janet supported. Pierre Janet's patients had been nervous, had suffered from hysteria, had been confused, had experienced amnesia, and Fugue States. Doctor Kane learned that a person in a Fugue State does not remember everything that happened during their temporary amnesia and can behave as the person they want to be. This was an interesting fact Doctor Kane had not known and gave him the reason why Eveline wanted to pretend to be her mother, on the way to California. He had wondered, as he read, if a person in a Fugue State needed to be another person. All the references pointed to the idea that the Fugue State gave the person a means to get away from themselves and become someone else for whatever the reason may be. Doctor Kane had thought it humorous to discover that Pierre Janet had been nicknamed, "Doctor Pencil," and still in his current work wrote every word that his patient said during a session. It had been a way for the doctor to refer to what had been revealed when a patient might have been in a different state of mind. According to Janet, "It was a way to prove to a patient what had been said if there had been any denial of the information." Doctor Kane liked the idea, even though he had maintained a journal, but now would begin recording everything that he and Eveline spoke of in the next sessions. According to what Doctor Kane concluded from Janet's theories, Eveline suffered from unresolved traumatic memories stemming from her childhood.

Before leaving the research library, Doctor Kane found more information about how a dissociative person can transform themselves into a different personality. For some in a Fugue State, a person would dress and appear as a man, when they were a woman, and can remember doing all the things a woman might have done looking like a man. That example gave Doctor Kane the rationale as to why Eveline had been able to act as Trixie, Catherine, or herself and remember and know exactly why and what had gone on. After finishing his afternoon in the library, he knew Eveline was a perfect example of all he had read about. How would he go about helping her to put these personalities in order so they would not continue to disturb her?

During the next session, Doctor Kane explained what he had learned about Pierre Janet's theory. Eveline listened and thought, why is he telling me these things that I already know? When he finished, he said, "Our job is to help you understand why you choose to change from one personality to another and what to do when it begins to occur." Eveline looked at the doctor and asked, "What happens if I like the personality I am going into?" Doctor Kane looked at Eveline and said, "Some of these occasions are not good for you and could be dangerous to your life." Eveline had not thought of that in those extremes. She said, 'Mainly, I like Trixie because she allows me to have all the sexual activity I want and not be committed to anyone." Doctor Kane knew he had a good response to her statement. He responded, "What if Jonathon comes back to you, what will you do with Trixie? You told me you never felt like "Trixie" when he was with you." Eveline hesitated and said, "You are right. Jonathon was the only person in my life where Trixie did not torment me. What will I do if he does not come back to me?" Doctor Kane asked, "What are some things you might think about?" Eveline thought that she would need to have a way of getting rid of Trixie. She told the doctor she could be with friends or remind herself that these dangerous ways could kill her. Doctor Kane had Eveline write down what she had just said so she could remind herself of the dangers Trixie unleashed. Eveline's reaction gave Doctor Kane the feeling that he had begun to readjust Eveline's thinking. He did make a point of saying, "Eveline, you must remember that only you can control Trixie. No one will be around to do this work for you."

While on the bus to Burdines, Eveline thought about what she had learned and reread what she needed to do when she felt like Trixie. She laughed to herself about all those years; she never understood the difference between a caring romance and crude dangerous sexually reckless actions. As she walked up to the cosmetic counter and began working, Patrick and Andrew stopped to see how she had been doing. They had been in Miami for a while and had decided it was time to see Winston. Eveline said, "I hope you men can help him out of his situation. You might be the only ones for that job."

CHAPTER 33

T he next day, Patrick and Andrew set out to visit Winston at the Tropical Gardens. While they were on their way, they reminisced about the time Winston had invited them to live in Miami to help set up the Tropical Gardens. At that time, they had little interest in living in Miami, which had been a disappointment to their mother. Andrew told Patrick that it had been too bad they were not able to stay at West Point, but their life style would never be tolerated. They admitted that having been away from West Point had helped them realize how confining their lives had been. Leaving West Point was the right decision which allowed them to admit to their lifestyle.

As the taxicab pulled up to the main gate, neither man could believe the condition of the property. It had returned to what it had been like when Winston took possession of it years ago. What would it take to restore what now looked like an overgrown and abandoned ruins? Patrick said, "If I did not know better, I might think this was an old deserted plantation." Andrew agreed, it looked scary. The taxicab driver asked if they wanted him to stay. Andrew told him that would not be necessary because there was a man living on the property that they were there to visit. The taxi driver shook his head and said, "Ok. Be careful of the ghosts that might be there. No one has been to this property in months. They say the owner is inside trying to starve himself. His boyfriend was killed in an airplane crash and is haunting the owner to death." They got out of the taxicab and watched it leave the entrance. They stood looking at an over grown entanglement of vines and underbrush. The entrance was camouflaged with dense growth that covered the walkway. The vines and huge spider webs hung over the front door, making it scary and impassable. They were not sure if they should knock or walk inside. When they attempted to open the door, they found it had been bolted closed. They began to bang on the door, with no response or sound of life.

After trying to get into the main house where Winston's apartment had been located, they could not find a way to enter inside. The windows had bars over them. They had yelled Winston's name but there had been no answer. Even though it was late autumn, it was hot and humid, making everything look and feel damp and moldy. The building had begun to turn green from moss and dampness growing on its walls. Animals could be heard and birds could be seen flying in and out of some open windows. Andrew told Patrick that they might want to call the police for help in entering the building and have them look for Winston. Patrick had worked up a sweat and appeared to be very warm as he said, "No way are we involving the police. Winston is in there and we will find a way to get to him. I only hope he is not dead." They thought the same thing and about what the driver told them about Winston being haunted to death.

After all attempts had been made to enter the building, Andrew found a heavy pipe lying in the weeds. They knew that Sable and Olitha had been fired, but did they take the keys or were they told to leave with Winston locking himself inside? Now was not the time to get Sable or Olitha involved, they needed to use the pipe and attempt to pry open the door or the bars on the windows. Prying open the front door had been futile because it was made of thick wood with iron latches. The pipe did not do a thing against the thickness of the door. They worked on prying the bars on a window and were able to make an opening just large enough for Andrew to crawl inside. When Andrew hit the floor, he yelled as if he had seen a ghost. He had fallen on the remains of an animal that had been trapped inside. Andrew went to the front door and opened it letting in light to a dark, damp, and eerie place.

Once inside the main floor, they found the place to be worse than an abandoned property. There were vines growing through the windows and on the floor. Small lizards and croaking frogs had made their home in damp and dark places. The front desk had cobwebs crisscrossing it where so much business had been done. It had been difficult to imagine that this once had been so lush. They passed by the once lavish gift shop and found price tags on items that now had become a place for moss to hang from. Patrick looked at one tag with a price of $1.00; it had been an orchid that had been engulfed with moss and a vine growing through the window. They wondered how anyone could survive in a place like this. If they had known things were as bad as they found, they would have come much sooner.

Patrick and Andrew went upstairs where Winston and Jason's apartment had been. They felt sure they might see Winston, but there was no sign of him. It made no sense that Winston was nowhere to be found. They decided to walk around the grounds to see if there were any other places Winston might have gone off to. If he had not eaten or had water, he may be dead somewhere. Supposedly, no one had been to the property for quite a few weeks. How could anyone survive that long without food or water? They walked on the trails that had once been carefully trimmed and saw vegetation that had not been maintained. "Could this place ever look good again?", Andrew asked Patrick. Neither one had an answer for this and only hoped to find Winston.

They hiked around the grounds with no luck. After an hour, they came upon what appeared to be an old gardener's shed. The roof had broken open from branches that had fallen through from windstorms. The door was half off the hinges but when they pushed it open, they found an emaciated Winston. They hardly recognized him. The last time they saw him was when they spent Christmas together with Eveline at the Biltmore. If they had not known better, he was not the same person they had once known. Patrick went to Winston who was slumped in a corner with a container in his hand. He appeared unconscious and must have been without food or water for many days. He had only a ragged shirt on and held the container near his chest. Patrick said, "Winston, it is Patrick. We came to see what you were doing. Mother asked us to come to you." Winston, in a groggy way, looked at Patrick as if he did not recognize him. Andrew spoke up and said, "Winston, this is Andrew. We want to help you." Winston had no recollection of them. Andrew went to get some water but had to run to the main house in hopes of finding something to drink. He found a trickling stream, on the way, that felt cool to the touch. He wondered if it was okay to drink, but decided he had nothing to lose. Andrew returned and offered Winston the water. He took some and began to come around. He looked dazed and his eyes had sunken into his head, showing he had lost weight. Patrick thought how different Winston appeared. He remembered him to be the strong one, that took care of them. Now it was their turn to take over. It took some time to get Winston to be able to show signs of being able to move. He said nothing to them and did not answer any questions they might have had. After some time, Patrick was able to help Winston get up and Andrew and he carried him to the main house. Winston never let the jar go. What could it be? Was it grain or meal for him to eat? If so, he had not done that, it was full. They arrived at the main house and found a flat surface for Winston to lie on.

There was no sign of food to offer and Patrick told Andrew to go to the main road and find someone that could help. Now, they wished they had told the taxi driver to stay. While Andrew was gone, Patrick tried to clean Winston's face and arms. The odor had been so intense from poor hygiene that Patrick nearly vomited. All the while, he could not believe this had been the man who loved and cared for him for so many years. After what seemed like forever, Andrew returned with a woman who claimed she was a distant neighbor. When she saw Winston she screamed saying, "He is the one who is being haunted by his dead boyfriend. Everyone thought he was dead." Patrick asked her if she had any food for Winston. She said, "You know it is the Depression and no one has much to eat." Patrick knew this was true but everyone he knew had been living quite well. Then he thought about why his mother had to go to work at Burdines. Being at West Point did not allow for a poor diet or inadequate life style. Andrew gave Winston some of the soup and small pieces of bread that she brought. After eating,

Winston seemed to be more coherent but never let the container out of his grip. The woman acted uneasy and fidgeted about being in the midst of a naked man and the environment that was haunted by his boyfriend. She asked if she could leave. They thanked her, never getting her name. Winston's eyes met hers when she got up. This seemed strange to Patrick. Andrew had been too busy trying to feed Winston to have noticed any eye contact.

Winston began to show signs of being aware of his surroundings. Patrick stayed by him while Andrew looked for some clothing. Patrick asked, "Winston, how long have you been here alone?" He mumbled that he could not remember. He said he wanted to be alone to die and be with Jason. Patrick told him that he knew what had happened and that he and Andrew had resigned from West Point to be in Miami. After hearing this Winston said, "Oh, I'm sorry I never spoke with Jason about the time you called me about moving closer to us." Patrick and Andrew both told him that had not been a problem. Winston became more talkative and asked why they wanted to live in Miami. Andrew spoke up before Patrick and said, "We are in love and wanted to be nearer to you. West Point would never allow us to live together. We would be abused and who knows what else might happen." Patrick said, "We wanted to be like a family with you because you had been like the father we never had. Mother had always hoped this might happen. It is too bad things have turned out this way." Winston shook his head and told them how much he missed Jason. Andrew and Patrick wanted to cry as they listened to a sobbing Winston. Andrew asked, 'Winston what is in the container?" Winston looked down at it saying, "This is what is left of my Jason. Everyone, including your mother, kept bothering me about a memorial service. I had a container for his ashes so no one would question me." Patrick wanted to know what he planned to do. Winston said, "I am going to be with Jason soon. You know that woman that came with Andrew. She is the angel that is helping me get to Jason." Patrick looked at Andrew suspiciously. Andrew asked, "Do you know her name?" Winston shook his head and said the name did not matter. She is giving me potions to get me home to Jason."

After an hour, Winston appeared more coherent but refused to let go of the container that supposedly held Jason's ashes. He refused to go with Patrick and Andrew to Miami either to his property at 825 Michigan Avenue or the Flamingo Hotel. He told them that he blamed their mother for Jason's death. They asked why. Winston said, "If it had not been for your mother's crazy ideas about running away, claiming she had a Fugue State and then going to visit her mother in Vancouver Prison, we would never have gone to California, much less on an airplane. Jason left days earlier, after your mother's attention getting behavior, and went down in the airplane crash over the Rocky Mountains." Andrew spoke up and told him that might seem true in his mind, but Eveline never intended for the accident. Winston looked at him and said, "That's easy for you to say with Patrick standing next to you. I have never had anyone as good as Jason, not even Patrick's father, Wallace. He was too self-centered and only used me." No one said anything to this remark. Patrick asked what they could do to help Winston. He told them to leave him alone. He explained that his angel would be done with her work soon. He asked them to leave, never thanking them for coming.

The telephone service had been disconnected; there was no way to get a taxicab back to Miami. Winston overheard them discussing their dilemma and told them to use their mother's old Lincoln that she had donated to the gardens. It had not been driven in a long time. He said, "Get rid of it. There is gasoline in the tank and it might take some work to get it started. Why don't you take it to 825 and let your mother pretend everything is alright." Patrick thanked Winston. They found the Lincoln covered up and looking good, considering it had not been driven in some time. After getting it started, Andrew wanted to drive it but neither one had a license to drive, so being careful not to be caught, became a game to get to Miami. While driving, Patrick discussed the "angel" Winston referred to. They agreed something was not right about the story. Andrew suggested they get in touch with Mr. Bingham to look into what the woman was all about. It seemed as if she might be poisoning Winston and making him think he was going to Jason. They agreed to not tell their mother the details of what they suspected. They would tell her that Winston needed their help and hoped he would get better.

CHAPTER 34

nstead of taking the Lincoln to 825, Patrick decided to keep it at the Flamingo Hotel where they had been staying. If they parked it at 825, Eveline might get suspicious and question them about Winston and what they had found when they visited him. Andrew asked Patrick how long they should stay as guests at the hotel. He told Patrick that they might want to move into 825 Michigan Avenue, since Winston owned it and only their mother occupied one of the apartments. Patrick told Andrew that would be a good idea after Winston had improved and was able to decide what he wanted to do with 825. Neither of them knew that there had been plans and construction done to convert the property into a residence for travelers. Until they could have a logical discussion with Winston, they would stay at the Flamingo. Andrew said, "How could anyone want to leave such a plush environment when people were barely able to live in these desperate economic times?"

Andrew and Patrick debated about calling Jonathon Bingham. They did not want to alarm anyone, but there had been something very strange with the "angel woman" who appeared when they visited Winston. What had she been doing to Winston to create such a situation with him? They decided to go to the police department instead of making the call. They left the hotel driving the Lincoln, feeling strange, driving their mother's former vehicle, and her not knowing a thing about what was happening. They entered the Miami Police Department and were escorted to Mr. Bingham's office. He was surprised to see them. When they stood at attention in the front of him, Jonathon said, "You guys sure look great. How are you doing and where are you staying?" Andrew told him they were at the Flamingo. Jonathon looked surprised when he heard this. Patrick explained about their visit to Winston and the conditions they had found. He spoke about the "angel woman" that came to give bread and soup to Winston. Jonathon looked surprised at the story. He asked, "What do you think the woman's intentions are?" Andrew mentioned the jar with something in it and that Winston had told them he was going to Jason because the "angel woman" was helping him get there. Jonathon asked more about the jar. Patrick said that it was Jason's ashes and that Winston had him cremated, with no one knowing about it. Jonathon looked suspicious with that story saying, "Jason's body was not found in the Rocky Mountains." Andrew wanted to know if Jonathon had any idea what the woman could be trying to accomplish by doing this to Winston. Jonathon had no definite answer but he would investigate what she might be up to. Jonathon requested that they not discuss any of this with their mother. Patrick and Andrew agreed not to tell, but wanted to know why. Jonathon said, "Your mother and I are not together. That was a mistake I made mixing business and pleasure. She is going through her own problems and needs to work those out before she can deal with anyone else."

While Patrick and Andrew drove back to the Flamingo Hotel, they discussed their confusion about what Jonathon had told them about their mother. They had not been aware of any problems Eveline had, but they had little interaction with her. Maybe what Winston referred to about their mother's attention getting behaviors was what he had been referring to. They had not listened carefully enough when he mentioned her, but maybe he knew more than he said. When they arrived at the hotel, Jonathon had left a message, "Am going to find the "angel woman" and see Winston. I hope to have some answers for you. I found out that Jason's body had never been found after the airplane crash. The contents in the jar are not his ashes."

Jonathon set out for the Tropical Gardens. He found the supposed "angel woman" and questioned her when he ran into her leaving the property. She had been certain that Jonathon had been sent by those young men to help her get Winston to Jason. Jonathon spoke as a friend to her which made her more talkative. She explained how she met Winston after his boyfriend's death. She had been envious of such a property so near to her run down home, that she could not afford anymore. Jonathon inquired about the other people who used to work and stay at the gardens. She made a nasty face and said, "They were either Negroes or fancy ass boys. The customers did not know what type of place they were coming to. I made it my business to discourage people before they entered the property. Winston told me that after he went to be with Jason, I could have the gardens all to myself. So, I started telling him that I was his angel sent to get him to Jason." Jonathon asked about the container that Winston had. She continued, "I told him the ashes were Jason's but they are really only sawdust. Winston probably forgot he had him cremated after living through the shock of his death. I waited a few weeks after everyone had been fired or told to never come back before I told him all that." Jonathon asked her about the potion Winston mentioned. She said, "It was a remedy I used on my husband that made him slowly lose his mind and it helped with some arsenic as I am doing with Winston. I know this property will be mine in a few days." Jonathon invited the woman to walk with him through the gardens to visit Winston. She was glad to be escorted and while they were walking, she explained her plan. She said, "You seem to be different than those other men and woman that came to see Winston. That one woman that he threw out because she was the reason for Jason's death, acted like she might have been his wife. Winston never had a wife with a boyfriend too. I hated both of them for what they were, but when Winston befriended me, I took advantage of his bad luck. Now, I'll be the owner of this dump. I'll try to sell it to the city so I can afford my place."

They came upon Winston in the main house, still lying where he had been left a day ago. When Winston saw the "angel woman" he begged for more of the stuff she had given him so he could get to Jason. Jonathon realized that Winston had been delirious from drugs and lack of food. The woman told Winston that he would have his biggest dose in a few days. She told him that she had to make sure he was ready to go to Jason. In front of Jonathon, as if he was not present, she handed Winston a paper to sign that would release the property to her upon his death. She looked at Jonathon and said to Winston, "This nice man came to be a witness for your signature." Jonathon thought that he had investigated many situations, but this had to be the most bizarre one yet. Not only had this woman killed her husband but was now convinced she could do this to Winston. Jonathon asked if he could see the potion she had been giving Winston. She pulled out a small bottle, which had a skull and cross bones on it, and the word arsenic written over it.

Jonathon spoke to Winston; he had no recognition of Jonathon, even though they had recently returned from the trip to California and Vancouver. When Winston was questioned about the trip, the woman interrupted, telling Jonathon that Winston had been trained to block that out. She claimed it made Winston too upset. Jonathon found it difficult to believe that Winston had been the man he and Eveline had traveled with on the West Coast. Jonathon asked the woman, "How could a person change so quickly?" She told him that Winston wanted to lose as much weight as he could so when she had him cremated he and Jason could fit in the same container. Jonathon knew then that this woman had been behaving just as a serial killer might. He told Winston, who was in and out of consciousness, that he and the "angel woman" needed to go outside. She was easily led outside and delighted to go, forgetting about the signature. Once outside, Jonathon pulled out the handcuffs and said, "You "angel woman" are under arrest for the murder of your husband and the premeditated murder of Winston Spaulding." He put her in the back of the police vehicle, cuffed her leg to the iron ring on the floor and drove off to the police station.

As Jonathon drove, the woman began singing a song about being the angel of death with her wings that flew folks to heaven. Jonathon wondered, as he listened to this woman, how many more crazy people he could handle in his line of work. When they arrived at the police department, Jonathon ordered the woman to be placed in a solitary cell and await a judge's decision. He made a telephone call to Jackson Memorial Hospital requesting an ambulance be sent to the Spaulding Tropical Gardens.

Jonathon explained that he would be there to assist the attendants with Winston. He did not want to go back to such an eerie environment, but knew he had no choice. If it had been anyone else, he would have sent another officer. Jonathon had been heavily involved with this group and could not abandon them at this time.

CHAPTER 35

The ambulance met Jonathon at the Tropical Gardens just as they had found Winston crawling out of the main house. He had been screaming about Jason and wanting more potions from the "angel woman". Winston had no recognition of where he was or who Jonathon was. The ambulance attendants had a difficult time getting Winston into the ambulance. One of the attendants had to tackle Winston in order to fasten him to the stretcher. As the ambulance turned to leave, all that could be heard was Winston screaming, as if he were being murdered and yelling Jason's name. Jonathon followed as the ambulance headed for the hospital.

After Winston had been admitted and examined, Jonathon left to go to tell Patrick and Andrew what had happened. He went to the Flamingo Hotel and inquired about where Patrick and Andrew were staying. The clerk explained the hotel's policy of not telling guest's room numbers to strangers. Jonathon pulled out his Miami Police Department identification and the clerk asked, "Are those men in trouble?" Jonathon replied, "Now, it's my turn not to tell anything. Where are they?" The now nervous young man told Jonathon they were at the hotel pool having massages. Jonathon thanked the clerk and went to the pool, thinking after what he had just experienced, maybe he needed a massage. He found both men being massaged, under the shade of palm trees. The masseuse asked Jonathon if he could help him. When Andrew and Patrick heard the voice, they knew something had happened to have Jonathon come to them so unexpectedly.

Jonathon told them he would wait until they had finished but neither one of them were willing to wait because something must be wrong. They wrapped a towel around themselves and sat down to listen to Jonathon. He explained that Winston had been admitted to Jackson Memorial Hospital to revive him from what was suspected to be murder, by slowly administering arsenic and a potion that made Winston delirious. Jonathon explained about the "angel woman" who had murdered her husband in the same fashion. Both guys sat astonished at such a scheme. After Jonathon finished with his news of what had happened to Winston, and the crazy woman, Jonathon suggested they needed to tell their mother. He explained that he preferred not to mingle with their mother. As he put it, "Not enough time has passed for us to see one another." He did tell them to be careful how they presented the news because their mother had been in a temperamental frame of mind. He recommended they only focus on Winston's condition and nothing else. Both Patrick and Andrew still did not understand what had gone on while they were at West Point.

The next morning Patrick and Andrew went to the hospital to see Winston. As they approached the desk to inquire of Winston's whereabouts, Eveline walked in and spotted them. They had their backs to her as she came up to them and said, "Coming to spy on your mother? Why else would you be here?" Surprised to hear Eveline's voice, they turned and said, "We are here to see Winston. We were going to tell you but we have not had time." Eveline by now had her hands on her hips and said, "Don't you think it is time someone begins to tell me what has been going on. It seems I am the only one who is in the dark." By this time, Eveline had elevated her tone of voice to a pitch for most to hear. An attendant came to offer assistance. Eveline, with a smirk on her face said, "I don't need any assistance with my children. They need to start talking to me about what has been going on." Patrick took her arm and led her to the seating area and they sat down to explain about Winston. When Eveline heard of what had happened, she said, "Winston threw me out because he blamed me for Jason's death and fired Olitha and Sable. I'm surprised you even got to him." Andrew explained about the "angel woman", Eveline shook her head and said, "It seems like we are still being haunted; now it was Winston. When will this all stop?"

Patrick explained that they were there to see Winston and he was expected to recover from the arsenic poisoning. Eveline said, "This sounds like Wallace's grandmother who went back to Canada and killed herself with arsenic. Why is everything so confusing?" When they heard Eveline say this, they questioned her on why she was at the hospital. When she heard this question she panicked and ran to the elevator. Patrick ran after her and stopped her before the elevator arrived. She told him, "Patrick honey, I am seeing a counselor to try to unravel my life. I am trying to figure out why I behave the way I do." By now Andrew was with her and they hugged her and said, "You are the best mother ever." She turned and entered the elevator saying, "Most everyone else does not think so." They stood even more confused than ever about Eveline.

Patrick and Andrew discussed what their mother had told them on the way to Winston's room. They needed to find out more about what she had referred to. Who would be able to know or tell them? Jonathon seemed to be the only person that had contact with her. Winston might know, but was in no condition to discuss anything, much less their mother's past life. As they stood outside Winston's room, they overheard a doctor explaining to a nurse what the remedy was for a person exposed to arsenic. Patrick and Andrew knocked on the door and looked inside. Winston saw them and motioned for them to come in. The doctor asked who they were and how they were related to Mr. Spaulding. They explained their long time relationship with Winston and explained that he had been like the father they never knew. Winston looked at them like he understood but he was only able to mumble words. Patrick attempted to explain to the doctor what had happened to Winston and his friend Jason. The more he tried to explain things, the more unlikely it sounded. The doctor interrupted and told them that Detective Bingham had informed him of what had happened to Mr. Spaulding. He explained that he understood the relationship of the deceased Mr. Hess to Mr. Spaulding. All seemed okay with the doctor. They were told that they could visit for a short time, but Mr. Spaulding needed to rest and drink as much water as possible. He suffered from Arsenic Toxicity and fortunately had not yet received high enough doses to cause his death. The doctor explained that Detective

Bingham told him that the woman who had been administering this had increased the daily dose and admitted that the last and deadliest dose would be cyanide that would cause an immediate death. Andrew asked why arsenic had been used. The woman wanted to watch Winston suffer from arsenic's effect which causes confusion, delirium, loss of appetite, and bloody diarrhea. According to the doctor, Mr. Spaulding had been strong enough to survive, but if it had been any longer, he would have been dead.

CHAPTER 36

E veline appeared at Doctor Kane's office in a frantic state of mind. She paced around his office talking in what appeared to be riddles. She carried on about being confused about her life and about everyone around her knowing about situations and not telling her. Doctor Kane convinced Eveline to sit in a chair and relax and asked her to give him some examples of what she had felt. She said, "I never knew that my sons had resigned from West Point until Eleanor Roosevelt told me at a party put on by Randolph Hearst. Then, I had to find out that my longtime friend Winston had been trapped and tortured by an "angel woman" and is in this hospital and I just ran into my sons who were on the way to see Winston. Jonathon has been involved with all of this and has made no effort to see me or let me know about these things. My life is a mess and now I feel alone as I often have throughout my life." Doctor Kane had been impressed with the fact that Eveline had been in the company of Eleanor Roosevelt. He said, "How do you get to know so many interesting people and have so many experiences?" Eveline sat and thought before she said, "I'm beginning to think because I can change from one personality to another that all these situations are involving all three of my people." Doctor Kane picked up on the "my people" part and asked what that meant. Eveline said disgustedly, "I have explained all this to you. They are the ones that come and go whenever I get in certain moods. I thought we were going to talk about the worst one today, Catherine."

After a brief break, Doctor Kane observed that Eveline still had been in a belligerent attitude. He saw the personality that Eveline had described in previous sessions and wondered if she was going to behave like her mother, Catherine. What would he need to do to make this happen? As he observed Eveline's movements, he asked her if she had felt this way whenever her mother said or did something to her. Eveline said, "You mean like a punishment." Doctor Kane nodded his head in agreement. Eveline thought for a moment and then mimicked her mother's tone and facial mannerisms. Doctor Kane watched Eveline act and respond like he had never seen before. She got out of the chair and moved around the room lecturing about how things were not her business and how she dared to try to interfere and cause more trouble. Before Eveline sat down she screamed, "You are a rotten and hateful girl. You need to be dead." Doctor Kane sat quietly as Eveline came to a calmer state and appeared exhausted and said nothing. She had perspired so much that her makeup had run and her hair was stringy from wetness. Doctor Kane offered her some tissues. She attempted to put herself together and act as if nothing had happened.

While Eveline sat in a pensive way, Doctor Kane offered her some water. He spoke about the episode he had just witnessed and asked how she felt about it. Eveline said, "Now I understand what a hold Catherine has had on me. I hate when this happens. I do nasty things to myself and sometimes others. I need to tell myself to stop. These actions are not me, but my wicked mother. I hate her as much as she hated me. I need to confront people with things that I feel are bombarding me and stop before I become Catherine." Doctor Kane agreed that calmness was better than letting things get out of control and could be more beneficial than waiting for an explosion. He recommended that Eveline have conversations with the people that bothered her and to change the things she had control of but to realize that not everything could be her way. He reminded Eveline that Catherine was no longer in charge of her and to let her go. Eveline sighed after she listened to the doctor. Her next session would focus on herself and no other people that have been tormenting her. Doctor Kane asked if she understood that she was the only one in control of her behavior. She shook her head as she left the office.

While on the elevator, Eveline thought about Winston and went to visit him. She remembered what he had said to her when he threw her out. The receptionist handed Eveline Winston's room number. She looked into the room and saw a person she hardly recognized. He had lost weight and his face had not been shaved in days. He looked like a little old man. Eveline took a deep breath and went to his bedside. She said, "Winston, I came when I heard what happened to you." Winston opened his eyes and stared at her. He acted like he had no idea it was Eveline. She touched his arm that felt bony. She wanted to cry but reminded herself that might not help. Winston mumbled, "Where's Jason?" Eveline told him that Jason had died. He looked at her and shook his head and tried to say, "Only one I loved." She did not know what to say or do. She thought this may not have been a good idea. She turned and walked away. As Eveline left the hospital she wondered if life would ever get better.

CHAPTER 37

Burdines had been advertising an early winter fashion show. Eveline had observed new fashions and trends for the upcoming season. Even though the United States had been in the grip of the Depression, women had been purchasing clothing as if there had been no financial problems. She had been wearing many of the outfits from years past, since she had no money to spend on her wardrobe. She had been able to rework her clothing to make it appear new. Her boss admired her style and asked if she might like to help plan the fashion show. It was to be a "strolling throughout the store show". Eveline would be announcing the fashions as the models began strolling from the front entrance. She accepted and was ecstatic to think that she had been chosen for such a position. She had been requested to go to the fashion office to meet the person in charge of store promotions. While Eveline was on the way to the office, she felt that this might be the beginning of something new. She hoped this might bring her out of the economic situation she had been living in. When she entered the fashion office, much to her surprise, there was a gentleman dressed in an up to the minute suit, wore an ascot, and wore shoes made of patent leather. Eveline thought she had mistakenly gone to the men's fashion office and turned to leave. The gentleman said, "My dear Mrs. Paine, please come in." He took hold of her hand and stroked it. Eveline recognized the fragrance of an expensive men's cologne that she had sold only to wealthy men. She had no idea of what to do or think as she stared at the dapper man, in charge of the women's fashion office.

After Eveline had calmed down, the gentleman introduced himself saying, "I am Mr. Berman. Your reaction was just like all women who enter this office for the first time. They think this job should be handled by a woman. The owner of the store hired me to replace a woman that held this position. When I had interviewed for the position, I explained that some men who understand fashion and what women like, are best for this job. I can make a woman feel "FAAABULOUS" and they will spend any amount of money for that feeling." Eveline listened and watched Mr. Berman move around the office with a sway to his movements. She wondered, as she watched, who else he could make look good and feel fabulous. No matter, Eveline wanted this position and would do anything to get ahead. He offered her a cigarette as they sat and began discussing the fashion show. Mr. Berman told Eveline that he had been observing her and knew she had come from a good background because of her style and mannerisms. He had intended to promote her to the office, when the time was right, where she could make a fashion show be better than ever.

They discussed the length of the show and how it was to be executed. Because it was a strolling show, it would begin by the front entrance and end in the restaurant. Eveline's job was to introduce the models and the type of clothing being shown. Mr. Berman explained that he would be on the men's floor when the models passed through to the restaurant. Eveline asked why. Mr. Berman explained that her job was to encourage the woman to buy and his job was to make sure men purchased the fashions for their wives. As a bonus, Burdines would include a gourmet lunch for customers purchasing clothing shown in the show. Eveline crossed her legs and smoked her cigarette in a subdued way, not like she might have with her cigarette holder. Mr. Berman held his cigarette daintily. Eveline thought he held it like a woman might. She found him fascinating, but refreshing, after what she had been through in the last few months. Eveline remembered that at one time, she had been a preferred customer of Burdines. While she spoke to Mr. Berman about her job, he had his legs and arms crossed appearing refined. Eveline realized why Mr. Berman had been given a job such as this; he was a ladies' man. Maybe not in bed though, she thought.

On the way home, Eveline's mind raced at the possibilities of what her new work might become. She gave thought to her sessions with Doctor

Kane and reminded herself of what she needed to overcome to move ahead. While she sat on the bus, it occurred to her that all of her misfortune of late might be a blessing in disguise. Never had she had to survive on her own. She had been taken care of by others, only to keep her out of their way. Because of that life, she had been able to be generous and cared for everyone she knew, in hopes they would like and love her. Now, she saw things from a different angle. Her spending and generosity had been to buy others affection and company. For the first time, she enjoyed doing things on her own. Maybe this is what Jonathon saw and understood the importance of taking charge of herself.

When she arrived at 825, her next job had to be a discussion with her sons. Eveline telephoned the Flamingo Hotel and was connected to Patrick and Andrew's room. Andrew answered and was delighted to hear her voice. Eveline asked if it might be possible for them to come to visit her. Andrew could be heard telling Patrick this as he replied in the background, "For sure, I thought she would never ask. I was beginning to think she did not like us." When she heard this, she was surprised and thought, maybe she had overreacted to them. Now the time had come to work out the past.

Patrick and Andrew left the hotel driving the Lincoln to 825 Michigan Avenue. They discussed what might happen when their mother saw the Lincoln she had given to Winston. After some conversation, they stopped worrying about her reaction and reminded themselves that she had also given 825 to Winston and Jason. They could not understand why their mother did such crazy things. She was always kind and generous but never seemed happy. Why did Eveline want to see them? She had not bothered for many years when they had been away. The last time they had a good time was at the Biltmore, quite a few Christmases ago. Andrew drove the Lincoln to the parking lot behind the property. It looked much different than when it had been first built. The vegetation had matured and not been trimmed. It had the appearance of a tropical fantasyland that had been hidden from the street. When they waited for Eveline to come to the gate, they wondered what the property had now become. Eveline hurried from the front doors and rushed to open the gate, then hugged and kissed them like she had when they were younger. They did not have the heart to tell her to stop. Eveline appeared to be on a high tone this evening.

They went into the apartment where Eveline was staying since her return from California. She explained that Winston had allowed her to reside there until she could find a place of her own. Patrick asked what had happened to create this living arrangement. Eveline explained about what Mr. Keyes had done with her inheritance from Wallace. Never knowing the facts, Eveline admitted she had overspent and had huge sums of delinquent taxes to pay the government. After everything had been liquidated, she had enough to pay her debts, but nearly nothing left for herself. That was the reason for the job at Burdines. Eveline explained that after her fiasco in California and having met their grandmother in a Vancouver prison, the counselor there, suggested she seek a doctor when returning to Miami. Jonathon Bingham knew a doctor that he had recommended. Patrick and Andrew sat and listened to Eveline give the details of her life in a few short minutes. It seemed like she was attempting to explain it all and get it over with. They asked what the reasons had been for counseling. She explained that for most of her life, she experienced various ways of behaving that affected her ability to feel happy. Until recently, she had felt that everything that happened had been her fault and she was always scared of being punished in severe ways. After having weeks of counseling, Doctor Kane helped uncover the reasons for her feelings and behaviors. Andrew wanted to know why she had been unhappy; he always thought she was the happiest and greatest mother. Eveline smiled and thanked him saying, "My mother and father were wicked people that exposed me to things a child should never have to experience. My mother hated me and accused me of having ruined her life and wanted me dead. Finally, I was sent to a boarding school for girls near Toronto. My parents were criminals just as your father had been. They all should have been imprisoned, but some died before that." Patrick asked if that was the reason he had been enrolled in Manlius. She admitted that often times a person did to their children the same things that happened to them. She made sure they understood that she loved them and never hated or wanted them dead as her mother had. Andrew asked what else the doctor helped her with. Eveline hesitated and said, "Because of the childhood abuse, I created different personalities to help protect myself when under tormenting conditions. This has continued still. I have three personalities; Catherine, your grandmother, Trixie, my sexually promiscuous personality, and myself, the ordinary Eveline." Patrick laughed and said, "You are so far from ordinary, that isn't even funny." Eveline blushed and admitted she had had quite an eventful and extraordinary life.

Eveline told Patrick and Andrew about the situations that had lead Winston, Jason, and Detective Bingham to go to California to be with her. She explained the Fugue State, which led her to California in a state of temporary amnesia. She explained that while she had been in California, she met Randolph Hearst and had been invited to a party he had given. While there, President and Eleanor Roosevelt had been the celebrated guests of honor. During the evening, Eleanor had a conversation with her and told her of their resignation from West Point. Eveline asked, "Why did I have to hear such things at a party? Why didn't you boys telephone me about this? Then, I find out that you are in love and want to be nearer to Winston." Patrick explained he had telephoned Winston before the trip to California to discuss the idea of resigning and moving closer to him. Winston told him then that Jason and he needed to discuss it after they had returned from the trip. Then, Jason died and now Winston had been under the influences of a crazy woman who tried to kill him for ownership of the Tropical Gardens. Eveline reminded them that the Roosevelt's had been the financial sponsors for their training at West Point and they had expressed dissatisfaction at the resignations. They admitted that the timing had not been good but had left because of the possibilities of what might happen when they admitted their lifestyle. Eveline shook her head and said, "I am sorry you boys had to leave for such reasons. It seems that we have been the target for lots of bad behavior."

Eveline told Patrick and Andrew about her promotion at Burdines. They congratulated her and offered to take her out for dinner. When they went to the parking lot, Eveline stared at her old Lincoln. Andrew asked, "Are you alright Mother?" Eveline continued to stare at the Lincoln saying, "I'm great. This Lincoln was three vehicles ago. This vehicle represented a time when no one knew where you boys were and I thought life had been all about my supposed wealth. All that is over and I don't care, let's just go to dinner." Patrick said, "That's a great way to look at it Mother."

While enjoying dinner along Miami Beach, Eveline asked what type of work they had considered. Patrick explained that they had thought of helping at the Tropical Gardens. After what had just happened to Winston, that did not seem too likely. Eveline listened and wondered if Winston would be able to resume the operations. Andrew said, "Maybe when Winston has recovered, he will ask Olitha and Sable to return and we might help out too." Patrick asked, "What is to become of 825? You cannot stay there forever." Eveline explained that she had hoped to find a different place because Winston and Jason had remodeled 825 to make it into a vacation property for discrete travelers. Patrick inquired what discrete travelers meant. Eveline shook her head saying, "I have no idea. Maybe, it will be for government officials, or movie stars, or people on vacation hiding from other people." Andrew said, "Sounds like an intriguing business. Maybe Patrick and I can operate it for Winston." Eveline shrugged her shoulders saying nothing.

CHAPTER 38

The next counseling session Eveline and Doctor Kane had scheduled would focus on herself, as the third personality that dominated her life. While Eveline waited in the office, she thought about how recent events had helped her with a better feeling about her future. She studied the patients that came and went from the office; all women. Eveline thought she would ask why the clientele consisted of women and not men. She thought about the doctor's knowledge of Pierre Janet and that he specialized in women's hysteria and dissociative behaviors. Eveline had a smile on her face when she was shown into the doctor's office. When Doctor Kane saw Eveline's smiling face he said, "You look great with a smile; it shows you have a pleasant outlook today." Eveline nodded as she took a seat across from the doctor. He asked if she had any ideas about the things they had spoken about in the last sessions. Eveline shook her head, still with a smile on her face, and said, "I have lots of good news but I have a question for you." The doctor blushed asking what she had on her mind. Eveline asked, "Why is your office always occupied with women patients?" Doctor Kane smiled and said, "I wondered how long it might take for you to notice that. You have noticed more than most of my clients. My practice has developed from my interest in Pierre Janet's work in Paris and I have been instrumental in developing sessions for women who suffer from hysteria and dissociative issues." Eveline wanted to know if men had had issues like the women. Doctor Kane explained that men usually do not suffer from that because men do not have the same chemical makeup as women. They do not suffer from a monthly female cycle.

Doctor Kane inquired how Eveline's week had been since their previous meeting. She, in a perky way, explained about her promotion at Burdines. The doctor asked what that had been. Eveline told him that she had been moved to the fashion office and would be assisting with the store promotions. She told him about the upcoming show for the early winter fashions. They laughed at the thought of a winter fashion show in a place where the sun shines and it is 80 degrees most of the winter. Eveline asked him if he had ever been to the fur floor at Burdines. He looked surprised and admitted he had not. Eveline described how the entire floor had been devoted to winter garments, mostly furs. She shook her head as she told him that the store kept the temperature on that floor at a cold 65 degrees to convince women to buy a fur or outerwear. The doctor watched Eveline giggle at how surprised the women were when they "hit the heat" wearing a fur.

Doctor Kane said, "Eveline, you are in a fine mood. This is very helpful for our conversation about your third personality. Have you given thought about yourself and why you move in and out of Eveline?" She looked off to the right, taking some time to respond. She said, "Because of all the information I have received from my mother, and our conversations, I understand how I had been able to develop three ways of dealing with my anxieties. I'm learning how to avoid Catherine and Trixie. Having lost my wealth has been a blessing in disguise. I, for the first time, have been able to rely on myself and to survive on my own. I also realized that I have been overly generous to people around me, in hopes they would love or like me. I have been buying their attentions and being a maven with most of them taking advantage of me." Doctor Kane had been nodding his head while he watched and listened to Eveline be so clear about her issues and their resolutions. He said, "Eveline, you are an amazing woman. You came to me in a state of panic. You had no understanding of why you had been behaving in all these ways for much of your life. Now, you seem to be able to deal with Catherine and Trixie, who have been haunting you for most of your life. You have emerged as a middle-aged woman with potential for a happy future." Eveline listened as she tried to keep the tears back; it did not work as Doctor Kane handed her tissues. He asked if she had any other issues to discuss. Eveline shook her head as Doctor Kane hoped she would not expose any other issue that might be tormenting her.

Eveline sat up in the chair, looked to the right, and told Doctor Kane that the only thing she hoped for was the return of Jonathon Bingham. She explained how she missed him and that he had been the first and only man she had truly loved. Doctor Kane asked about her late husband. Eveline shook her head with a disgusted look and said, "He was like all the rest who tormented me while they went off on their merry way." Doctor Kane interrupted Eveline and asked, "Do you know why you always turn your head to the right when speaking to me?" Eveline looked surprised and admitted she had not realized she had done that. She wanted to know if there had been a reason for that behavior. The doctor asked if she remembered doing that anywhere else. Eveline said, "Yes, whenever I had to make a decision or have a conflict, while in a conversation. I used to do that with Wallace, Rudolph, and anyone who attempted to make me feel inferior." Doctor Kane smiled and told her that was common because it was easier to deal with an issue, rather than look the other person in the face. He suggested that since she was aware of this that she needed to start looking people straight in the eye. This would make the other person know you mean business. Eveline explained how many things she had learned in the last months during her sessions and thanked the doctor. He made certain Eveline understood that she should come back for a session if she felt herself returning to her tormenting personalities. There would be no more reasons for continued meetings.

While Eveline was on her way to Burdines, she thought about the thing that she would need to work on, which were her strong desires for sexual satisfaction. Even though she understood what made her behave sexually, how would she deal with it without getting into trouble? Maybe she needed to get rid of her hat pins black cape, and restraints that she had kept in her closet. She thought of Jonathon, who never made her feel like she was being a sexual deviant. She had little hope that he would come back to her. Should she let him know that she had completed the counseling that he had recommended and paid for? Eveline was not sure of what to do, so she decided to wait and see and try to satisfy herself.

CHAPTER 39

Winston had been in Jackson Memorial Hospital for a few weeks and had shown signs of recovering. His doctor suggested that he might do well being cared for at home. Winston had been speaking with Patrick and Andrew about the possibility of having them stay at the Tropical Gardens instead of the Flamingo Hotel and agreed to this suggestion. After speaking with the doctor, Winston would be released under Patrick and Andrew's care. The only restriction Winston had been advised about was the limitation of heavy work. Patrick and Andrew confirmed that he would not be doing much of anything but walking and resting in the sun. After the doctor left, Andrew said, "Now it is our turn to teach you a few new tricks like you did when we were young.

When Winston arrived home, he was aghast at what his property had turned into. He had little recognition of what had happened; only knowing that Jason had died. Anything afterward had been blocked from his memory. Patrick asked Winston if he remembered when the "angel woman" appeared. He remembered that she came shortly after everyone had left after the trip to California. Winston remembered arriving at the gardens alone and upset. It was the next day the woman appeared with something for Winston to drink. After that, he remembered only feeling like he was dying. Winston admitted that it must have been the potion that he had been given. He now understood Jason's death and realized it had not been their mother's fault as he had vaguely remembered accusing her of. Andrew asked about Olitha and Sable. Winston remembered firing them after he had learned that Jeffrey left for Key West. Patrick asked if it might be possible for Winston to rehire them. He said, "Winston, they are like your family. They are probably upset and do not know what to do." Winston nodded his head in agreement, all these things needed to be dealt with even though he missed Jason.

The first thing Andrew did after they moved from the Flamingo was to clean the apartment. Patrick organized the main floor, where the gift shop had become overgrown and cleaned and set up the guest entrances. Winston made a call to both Olitha and Sable. When Olitha heard Winston's voice she said, "Oh Winston, you be a sick man. You acted crazy and mean to me. You told me to get out before you killed me." Winston listened in horror of what he had said to the only people that he had as his family. Olitha agreed to return on one condition, she said, "You gonna listen to what I says or I never comin back no matters what." Then, Winston made his call to Sable, fearing what she might say. She had always been the tough one. When Sable heard who had called, she screamed, "Winston, you be so messed up and ugly, I'm not sure that I won't slap you silly when I sees you." Winston's face cringed as he listened to Sable. She went on, "Don't you go sayin mean things to me like you did when you threaten me. My husband says I should have whooped your ass the day you fired me." Winston had never heard such things from Sable. After she finished yelling at him, she agreed to return to her job as long as Olitha and she could be in charge. After what Winston had just heard, he said, "After what you just told me, you will be in charge. Patrick and Andrew will be here helping too." Sable laughed and said, "They's nice boys. It no wonders they turned out the way they did. Our Miss Eveline and you dun something right. They is still our favorites. We gonna make big chocolate cookies for them." Winston hung up the receiver and told the guys what he had just heard. Patrick and Andrew laughed and agreed that those women had not changed a bit.

Winston made a call to the company he had employed to trim and maintain the grounds. He could not remember if he had fired them too. When Winston spoke to the foreman of the Cuban worker group, he was told that the Negro boss lady whipped his men if they took too many siestas. Winston laughed when he heard how Sable and Olitha had joked about doing such things; never did he think they would do it. Winston apologized for them and the foreman agreed to be back to work the next day. Winston explained to Patrick and Andrew about the treatment the workers had received from Sable and Olitha. Patrick laughed and said, "Don't they know slavery has been abolished?" Andrew said, "What makes it funnier is that the men were Cubans not Negroes like Sable and Olitha." Patrick suggested that a new advertisement should be featured in the Miami Herald welcoming tourists to the Spaulding Tropical Gardens. January, 1936 was just around the corner and time to hope for some visitors. Winston set up the advertisement to be in the newspaper. He found out when he spoke to the newspaper office that the Miami Herald had made reciprocal arrangements for coverage in the New York Times.

The next day, Sable and Olitha arrived. Winston had been relaxing on the veranda when they came up to the main house. Sable had her hands on her hips and said, "Well if it ain't our boy Winston. He takin life easy. Who doin the work around here?" Winston made a face at them and told them to sit down. He told them what he had found out about what they had done to the Cuban workers. Olitha laughed and said, "Oh Winston, you should saw how we made doz lazy boys jump. I swished that whip back and forth and they did jump. I chased them around and they worked. They bez afraid to stop. Sable used a whistle too. We got so much done it amazing. They never came back tho." Winston told them that he had rehired them and there was no need for whipping. Sable shook her head and said, "You crazy. These Cuban boys all wants a siesta and do little work. Now, they knows the whip." Winston smiled and shook his head. When Patrick and Andrew appeared, the two women jumped up and took hold of them with hugs that took their breath away. Andrew said, "You still got the strength to show us who the boss is." Both women smiled and Sable asked if they were there to stay. Winston spoke up saying, "Yes, they are here to stay. They resigned from West Point because they are in love." Olitha screamed, "Oh my Gods, you boys in love. What dat means?" Andrew told them that they had always admired Winston and had felt a strange feeling toward him, even when they were little kids. He explained that if they admitted this at West Point, bad things might happen because they would not understand our love for each other. Sable raised her hands and said, "Thank you Jesus, we gots it all here." Then, the question was what their mother thought of this. Patrick explained that their mother was happy that they were in Miami.

Sable asked Winston if he had seen Miss Eveline. He had not and Sable told him, "You best get you ass to the telephone and invite her here to talk." Winston knew he needed to do that. Patrick explained to Sable and Olitha that their mother had fallen on hard times as many folks had in the United States. They were shocked at what Mr. Keyes had done with her money. Winston told them that Mr. Keyes had been wrapped up with Wallace and his underhanded business dealings for many years. Eveline had not suspected anything, as many wealthy people did when they trusted their financial advisor.

CHAPTER 40

Winston made the telephone call to Eveline inviting her for lunch on Sunday. While they conversed, Eveline explained that she had been promoted. She was working in the fashion office and assisting in the store's promotions. Winston was impressed that Eveline had again survived events that could have easily thrown her into one of her wild behaviors. He had not known much about the counseling that had been suggested when they were in Vancouver. Eveline asked if her sons would be present for lunch. Winston said, "Absolutely, we are a family, as we always have been; now we are truly together." Eveline had been pleased to hear this and thought how quickly things had changed.

While at work, Eveline had a better chance to get to know Mr. Berman. He explained that he had moved from New York when he came upon hard times. When Eveline listened to this, she wondered if his hard times had been like hers. She asked, "Mr. Berman, what type of hard times did you encounter?" He waved his hands and swirled around the office while saying, "It was not like many folks who lost their financial empire. Mine was a loss of a love relationship. He died a tragic death. He jumped off a building the day the stock market crashed in 1929." Eveline picked up on the "he" part and now understood the story more clearly. She asked Mr. Berman how he was. Mr. Berman thought she meant the dead person. Eveline laughed and said, "I mean you. I have a friend that recently lost his partner in an airplane crash over the Rocky Mountains. He was the love of Winston's life. Maybe he and you could meet one another." Mr. Berman's eyes went up with a sparkle that had been obvious to Eveline. Eveline asked, "Would you like me to see if you can come to the Tropical Gardens for lunch on Sunday? I do need to know your first name though." Mr. Berman giggled and covered his mouth saying, "Rex."

Eveline could hardly wait to telephone Winston to ask if she could bring her boss to lunch. When she found time during her break, she telephoned the gardens with Olitha answering. When Olitha heard who was on the end of the line she said, "Oh Miss Eveline you sound real goods. Who you wants to talk to, you boys or Winston?" Eveline told her Winston. Winston could be heard asking who was on the telephone and some noise could be heard in the background. When he heard Eveline he said, "Sorry about the racket. The Cuban boys are here cleaning up this place. I took the whip and whistle away from Sable and Olitha. How are you?" Eveline told him that she had been fine and that he sounded like he had returned to his old self. Eveline asked if she could bring her boss for lunch. Winston asked why. She said, "My boss is a perfect gentleman and he lost his partner in 1929. I think you and he are about the same age." Winston had not been sure of what to say, he did not think he could ever meet anyone to replace Jason. After what seemed like forever, Eveline said, "Well, can he come along? I don't think he bites." Winston laughed and said, "Why not. You never know, the next best person could be right around the corner." Eveline said, "That's my Winston. You still have it in you. Thank you and we will see you on Sunday." After she finished the call, Eveline thought that she and Winston had not discussed his behavior the day he threw her out and blamed her for Jason's death. She decided it might be better to leave the past alone. Eveline had been pleased that her sons had come to Miami to be closer to Winston; the man who treated them like the father they had never known.

Eveline had given a lot of thought to her life, in greater ways than she ever had, before her counseling. She had been able to enjoy what her life had become with less opulence. Eveline had not given up with the hope of Jonathon and her reuniting. Maybe he had reconsidered his future after she had heard he had been tired of the type of work he had to do at the police department. Every night she went to bed thinking and wishing Jonathon could be at her side, enjoying the pleasures of love. Eveline had never felt this way about any other man in her life.

Mr. Berman had been surprised that Winston agreed to include him for lunch. Eveline explained Winston's past and his recent recovery. Mr. Berman appeared nervous and flushed as she spoke about the invitation. Eveline told him, "Don't worry, Winston is a man's man, tough but a love and fun to be with." Eveline continued to address him as Mr. Berman while at work. He thanked her for that and agreed he would address her as "Miss Eveline". He told Eveline that he thought the name sounded like a woman who operated a fashion shop of higher style. Eveline had returned to her glory when she heard what Mr. Berman said. They had finished the plans for the fashion extravaganza that would be in one week. Eveline had been instructed by Mr. Berman to be fitted for one of the newest style dresses Burdines would be showing in the store for the winter. She would be wearing it for the show and it would become hers. Mr. Berman explained, "When you work in the fashion office, you get to wear the newest styles." Eveline wondered how she got so lucky. She hoped it was because of her new outlook on life. She still hoped every day that Jonathon would appear.

Sunday arrived and Mr. Berman had offered to pick Eveline up. Eveline waited outside the gates for her ride. She spotted a sporty convertible approaching, it was Mr. Berman. Eveline eyes went up when he pulled up. He asked, "Do you own this lovely property? It looks intriguing." Eveline shook her head explaining that she had owned it but gave it to Winston and his deceased partner, before she went to California. She could feel a tension rise when she spoke of that trip. Mr. Berman did not question any further and Eveline worked at convincing herself not to be trapped by her other situations. She had learned to not think of her personalities but label then as other situations. That had been her way to stay calm. Eveline told Mr. Berman that 825 was to become a residence for discrete travelers. When Mr. Berman heard this his eyes went up. He made no comment. Eveline spoke about how Winston had acquired the Spaulding Tropical Gardens, as a gift from her. Mr. Berman listened to the story and wondered how far back the relationship went between Eveline and Winston. He made up his mind that he might end up getting to know someone he had never planned on.

When they pulled up to the main house, Winston appeared in a panama hat, Bermuda shorts, and a tropical shirt open to the waist. He looked more than appealing when Eveline said, "Rex, I'd like you to meet my longtime friend, Winston Spaulding." Mr. Berman had on trousers, which had been tailored perfectly to his body and a white shirt. He wore a straw fedora and black and white saddle shoes. Every bit of him was in style. Eveline called for Sable and Olitha who came running from the kitchen. They looked like they had not changed and hugged Eveline while looking Rex up and down saying, "Oh Miss Eveline you sure does pick the good ones. Is he for Winston or us?" Laughter broke out as Patrick and Andrew appeared. At first, they thought the laughter had been directed toward them until they realized what had just been said. Both guys wore sporty trousers and casual shirts, no hats. Eveline introduced them saying, "This is Rex Berman." They shook hands as Patrick and Andrew introduced themselves to Rex. Eveline sensed confusion with Rex when he saw a mulatto and a white man in front of him. Winston spoke up and said in his husky voice, "Rex, they are a long story. Maybe I can tell you about it sometime." Andrew spoke and said, "This woman saved my life when Patrick and I were roommates at Manlius Pebble School." Eveline stood blushing and listened to the story of her life being told in a new way. She soaked up the new feelings. Rex had already studied what a man Winston appeared to be. Winston had been thinking about what Rex might be like if he got to know him better.

CHAPTER 41

The Burdines Fashion extravaganza had been scheduled for the week after the New Year. 1936 was sure to be a good year for Eveline, or so she hoped. She and Mr. Berman had much to do during the holiday season which began the day after Thanksgiving and ended a few days before the New Year celebrations. For some reason, that no one understood, customers had been shopping more this year than before. Despite the Depression, Burdines had higher sales than in the last years. Eveline had contributed much to the fashion office by introducing the idea of multiple ways to utilize fewer outfits. In this way, accessories sold faster than entire outfits. Eveline had been given any accessory she desired so she could be seen wearing what she had developed for the store. The men who had wives that shopped at Burdines were pleased that the costs seemed lower because fewer outfits needed to be purchased. The women found it hilarious that their husbands did not catch on to the accessory part. They only asked about the amount for an outfit. The women loved Eveline's ideas and soon the branch stores were following the main store's ideas. She had been the founder of the "Mix and Match Era". Mr. Berman could not have been more pleased that this came from his fashion office.

One day, Eveline took a chance and asked if Winston and Mr. Berman had seen one another since the luncheon. It had been over a month since their meeting. Mr. Berman blushed when he said, "Oh Miss Eveline, Winston is every bit of a man that I can't get enough of. He has invited me to his property many times. I even had him to my apartment on Meridian Avenue." Eveline had been surprised that Rex lived so near to 825 Michigan Avenue. He told her that he had watched 825 develop into a beautiful home a few years ago and then it seemed to be abandoned. Eveline knew she had to explain the details of what she had just heard from Mr. Berman.

She said, "I had the property designed by Henry Hohauser and was the financier to it. I wanted to leave Geneva, New York, after living there with my late husband. I remained for a few years until I had concluded the investigations of his underhanded business dealings. That was when I left New York and lived at the Biltmore Hotel until the property was completed. After moving into 825, everyone I knew had left and I found myself alone. I did have Jonathon Bingham, the detective, who conducted investigations about my supposed kidnapped children. He and I became madly in love. I suffered from psychological issues and ran off to California and Jonathon tracked me down. In the midst of my spending spree in California, I was informed that my accountant in New York had not paid my taxes to the government and all of my assets had to be liquidated. This left me with very little money. I never thought I would live any other way except the life of a wealthy widow. I found out differently. After returning to Miami from California, I spent many months with a counselor at Jackson Memorial Hospital that helped me unravel my past. If I had not had this conversation about the past, it would have thrown me into another mental downfall. Thankfully, I now understand my past and how to deal with threatening situations." Mr. Berman told Eveline that Winston had explained his recent misfortunes with the death of his partner, Jason, and what the "angel woman" had done to him. Eveline agreed that Winston had been through many unfortunate times. She explained how they first met as young adults in Rochester. She told him about how Winston had been secretly in love with Wallace and that Winston had been more of a father to her children than her husband. She looked at Mr. Berman and said, "I am so glad all that is over. Those years seemed good, but now I know looking back, they were hell." Mr. Berman agreed that the future and 1936 looked better than the past.

Mr. Berman told Eveline that he had been invited to Winston's for a New Year's Eve dinner. Eveline had wondered if that might happen. She knew her celebration would be much different, alone. She knew she would not be spending her holiday as she had in past years. Eveline realized that this was another example of how her life had changed. She knew she could not rely on her sons to entertain her that evening either. Mr. Berman asked what she had planned for the last day of 1935. Eveline told him she was not sure, but knew something would come up. He admitted that he had spent many a holiday alone. Because of Winston, this was the first year he had a reason to celebrate. Eveline felt sad for herself wishing she had a plan to look forward to.

When Eveline spoke to Patrick, she inquired about what they had planned for Thanksgiving, Christmas, and New Year's Eve. He explained that Winston had invited them to help with the Thanksgiving preparations and that she was to be included. As for Christmas, they had no plans. Eveline thought it strange that she had been invited in such a casual way. She remembered how much effort she had put into holidays, even at the Biltmore. She accepted the invitation for Thanksgiving, not asking questions. She hoped something might be decided for Christmas during Thanksgiving dinner. She felt like an outsider but could not figure out why. She had been thinking that life had changed for everyone, even her, now that she understood her past. She had not found an apartment she could afford, still rode the bus to work, had no love in her life, but was highly successful at Burdines. Maybe that should be her focus in life, not the people of her past. She made up her mind that she would find something new and exciting to do on the last day of 1935.

Miami had record breaking temperatures on Thanksgiving Day. Everyone dressed in cool casual attire since it was 90 degrees in the shade. Rex offered to pick Eveline up to go to Winston's. During the ride to the Tropical Gardens in Coral Gables, Eveline asked about the remainder of the holidays, knowing she had already discussed this with Rex. She hoped he might invite her for something. Rex explained that he was going home for Christmas and when he returned, he and Winston were having a dinner to celebrate their meeting and the New Year. He asked what Eveline had planned. So far, there had been no mention of including Eveline in any celebrations. Rex explained that Winston told him that Patrick and

Andrew had met other men and had been invited to a New Year's Eve party on Miami Beach. When Eveline heard this she knew that there would be no women at that party. Now, she began to better understand why her sons wanted to be in South Florida, not necessarily to be closer to Winston.

Sable and Olitha had prepared a traditional Thanksgiving meal. They made a shoofly, pecan, and pumpkin pie. Everyone was amused by such a name for a pie, much less the type. Olitha spoke up saying, "You best enjoy this pie. I made it from scratch." Andrew laughed saying, "It looks like you scratched around and killed some flies for it." Eveline, Winston, and Rex sat staring not sure what might happen next. Olitha left the table while Andrew and Patrick knew they had crossed the line and had offended Olitha instead of being funny. Olitha came back and said with hands on her hips, "My shoofly pie is famous, which ones of use want the first piece." Eveline wanted to laugh when she saw what was about to happen. Rex was stunned because he had not been familiar with the relationship the domestic servants had had with the family. Andrew's hand went up first as he got up from the table. Olitha followed him saying, "My shoofly pie is famous, now make you mind up. Do you want me whoopin your ass or eatin my pie?" Before everyone knew it, it had turned into a comedy. Olitha went to Winston and said, "This is what I shoulda did to you when you threw me out. I shoulda beat your ass for being so mean to me but you might have enjoyed it too much." No one was sure if they should laugh or be quiet. Finally, Rex said, "There are some folks at Burdines that might benefit from Olitha's form of training." Everyone burst into laughter.

During the ride back to Miami Beach, Rex discussed what had happened at the dinner table. Eveline admitted that she had never been to a Thanksgiving quite like that before. She asked Rex if he thought Winston was the person for him. Rex had no idea because they had been very proper with each other but seemed to have a genuine interest in one another. Eveline thought about the times she and Winston had sexual encounters with others. She knew Winston liked to be the dominant male as she had liked to be the dominant female. She decided not to delve into the past because that was an area that Trixie had control over. Before Eveline got out of the automobile, she thanked Rex and said, "Whatever you do with Winston, remember he is a rough one to tame." Rex laughed saying, "I've trained many that have been rougher than Winston." Eveline watched as Rex drove toward Meridian Avenue, thinking about what everyone had turned into. She thought she may be seeing the world differently now, and no one had changed; only her.

CHAPTER 42

The holiday season in a department store was full of excitement. Eveline found herself enjoying her work more than ever before. Whenever children came into the store with their mothers, the atmosphere reminded Eveline of days gone by when she had Christmas celebrations in her home. She reminisced about the lavish decorations and gifts she had for everyone when she lived in the Geneva mansion. It all seemed like a distant memory now that everyone had been living a different life and had grown apart. The best part of her work day was watching Santa Claus greet the children and promise them anything they wished for. Mr. Berman and she assisted with the costumes and fashions that women would buy for their homes and celebrations. Burdines sold more Christmas ties and hats. The women bought a special dress for the holidays. The store had been decorated as if it were in New York City or Chicago, not Miami in the heat.

Mr. Berman left the office early on Christmas Eve, wanting to get to his destination. He told Eveline that she had full control of the office until New Year's Eve. He wished her a happy holiday and thanked her for introducing him to Winston. After he left, Eveline thought about how she had always been a social maven when getting folks together, now she was alone and no one had offered for her to meet anyone or go anywhere. Eveline had to remind herself that this was the time she would be most tempted by Catherine and Trixie. The holidays were the most difficult time of the year for people who had suffered from psychological issues. She reminded herself of what Doctor Kane had told her about more people suffering from depression and suicide during the holidays. She knew she would not allow herself to fall into that trap. She must rely on herself and her wit to make the most of these lonely times. Eveline decided that she was not going to call and appear needy for an invitation either from her sons or Winston. She thought about Sable and Olitha who used to have her as family in the past, who were now married and worked for Winston. She had never expected them to include her for holidays because she did not fit into the way the Negroes celebrated. While she was thinking of these things, she remembered when Olitha offered her a room in the back of her building in Overton. She shook her head when she thought of such a life. That to her, would be worse than what she had to accept, since losing her supposed wealth.

Eveline purchased a copy of the Miami Herald that featured a section on holiday happenings. While she rode the bus home, she read articles about decorating and places to dine, nothing appealed to her. She spotted an article about ballroom dancing parties for the New Year. Swing Dancing had become the newest form of ballroom dancing. Eveline thought about the name and remembered when she did the Charleston in her Flapper days. The article gave information as to where parties were being held throughout Miami, one was at the Biltmore on New Year's Eve. The prices were for couples and now a singles rate had been available. Eveline knew this was for her. No matter what it cost, she was going. The evening included a five course dinner, champagne, and set ups for midnight and was $25. The article explained that single people could come and have fun, learn to Swing Dance, and maybe meet someone new. The Biltmore offered this idea to attract single men and women, while most hotels did not do this. Eveline had not felt such a thrill in a long time about the possibilities of going out by herself. This might be the start of something new along with the other new things in her life. She made up her mind that she needed to distance herself from people of her past and not feel like they should protect her. Since she had been in such deep thought about her life and the idea of going out by herself, she had missed the bus stop for the 825 Michigan Avenue area. She had to spend another half hour going back, but enjoyed thinking of all the possibilities that were ahead.

Burdines closed early on Christmas Eve. Eveline had been invited to have dinner with Winston, Patrick, and Andrew for the holiday. Since

Eveline had no way to get to the Tropical Gardens, Andrew agreed to pick her up. She felt uneasy that he would have to get her and take her home, but it would be too expensive to hire a taxicab. Andrew drove to the beach to get Eveline and they discussed how their work had been going. Eveline was careful not to ask too many questions about their plans. Andrew did not ask what she was doing either. Everything discussed seemed to be like speaking with a casual friend, not family. Before dinner, gifts were exchanged; many were of minimal cost because of the Depression and the gifts did not seem to be the focal point of the holiday. Winston told everyone at dinner that he was grateful for each of them, especially Eveline because she had kept the family together. When she heard this she wanted to cry but reminded herself how things had changed. Patrick and Andrew agreed that she was the best mother ever. Eveline felt like she had missed something, because she had not been around for so long. She wondered if this is what happened when people grew up and moved on.

After dinner, Winston asked about New Year's Eve. Patrick and Andrew explained about the party they had been invited to on Miami Beach. Eveline listened and Winston watched them be uneasy. Andrew said, in a squeamish way, that it was a party where everyone needed to dress up as someone else. Eveline smiled and wondered what they were planning for costumes. Patrick said, "We decided to go as Mr. and Mrs. Paine." Eveline's eyes went up and she said, "Oh my God, who will be the man and who will be the woman? That is so not legal." Patrick said, "That's the point, we want to show that a mulatto and white man can be in love. I will be the man and Andrew will try to look like a woman." Everyone burst into laughter with the thought of the two of them appearing that way. Then, they admitted this was to be a "drag show party", and that those were usually the most fun. After hearing about their evening, Eveline wondered what they would think about her plans at the Biltmore. She said, "Well, I can't beat that, but I am going to the Biltmore for a party and learn to Swing Dance. They have reservations for singles this year. Maybe I'll meet someone and have some fun." Everyone congratulated her on her nerve to do such a thing at her age. Eveline was not sure she understood the significance of the term "at her age", but did not question the intent. It became obvious that everyone at the table had a new life. Eveline felt good that she had stepped up and did it for herself. Patrick and Andrew said she was a cool mother to do such a daring thing. Eveline then knew that everyone was on the right track with their lives, no matter what their ages might be.

CHAPTER 43

————— ❦ —————

"Now Year's Eve 1935, the end of another year of Depression, how was 1936 to be?" Eveline read these headlines in the newspaper as she was contemplating what the New Year might be like. She hoped it would be better than 1935. As she thought about the last year, she realized that many good things had happened as well as difficult times. She appreciated what her misfortune had trained her to do, make it on her own. Her counseling with Doctor Kane had unleashed her from the torments of Catherine, Trixie, and herself, when under their psychological temptations. The position at Burdines fashion office had been a boost for her ego and helped her understand what it meant to "earn a living". The thing that had not been good was her loneliness over losing Jonathon Bingham.

While Eveline prepared herself for the evening at the Biltmore, she thought about the years she had lived there before 825 Michigan Avenue had been completed. It was in Eveline's mind half good and half not so good. The living conditions had never been better. The situations surrounding her children's supposed kidnapping and all that had been connected to that event made life at the Biltmore uncertain and at times scary. These thoughts still revolved around Eveline's sadness over Jonathon's leaving her because he had witnessed and investigated all that occurred at the Biltmore. While she put on the last of her outfit, she decided to get out of the apartment, get a taxicab, and see how the evening would be at the Biltmore. Eveline coached herself the entire time the taxicab took her to the hotel. She kept telling herself that no one would meet her if she stayed at home sulking about her past love.

Eveline had very little cash for the evening. After paying the taxicab driver, she placed the same amount of money in her brassiere for the return ride to 825 Michigan Avenue. She knew that would be the last place anyone would go to find money, and if she got lucky, the brassiere would be one of the last things to come off. She made sure not to spend money on a cocktail and only to drink the champagne that had been part of the price for the evening. She hated the idea of being penniless, but this was better than being alone for the holiday. As she entered the lobby, a feeling of her previous life came over her as she thought about how many times she had gone through the lobby in a much higher style of life. While Eveline maneuvered herself through the crowds to the ballroom, she passed the front desk remembering the times and situations that had occurred there. Maybe this had not been a good idea to return to old places that reminded her of bad times even though it now seemed like it had never happened. Eveline reminded herself again that this had been the only place in Miami that offered a singles reservation, so she put her best foot forward, raised her head, had her cigarette holder lit, and sashayed herself into the ballroom as if she were royalty. At least she had not lost her style.

As Eveline moved around the ballroom, she looked at the table arrangements. The hotel, in order to ease the discomfort for the singles, mixed them with others who had not come as a couple. Eveline found her name at a table for eight people. She looked at the names and found that most were women's names. Being a bit confused, Eveline moved around to see how other tables had been set. To her surprise, more than half of the tables had been set for singles. She thought it strange that there had been so many people coming alone. She felt better knowing she was part of the largest group at the party. Not sure what to do with herself, Eveline stood on the side and observed the crowd. After seeing how folks had dressed, she looked at herself and realized she had dressed better than most. She had worn one of the expensive outfits from Burdines. Eveline thought how lucky she had been to have a job that dressed her in the finest outfits.

Patrick and Andrew had been preparing themselves for the evening of "Drag". They had more fun getting Andrew dressed to look like a woman; he was supposed to be like Eveline Paine, their mother. They became hysterical when they looked at themselves in the mirror. Andrew looked a bit better than a street woman waiting for her next trick. Patrick looked as dapper as his father might have looked, only Patrick had dark beautifully toned skin and looked like Andrew's pimp. After the hysteria calmed down, they had all they could do to talk about what their mother would think of how they appeared. They agreed that Eveline would probably have had a better time with them than going to the Biltmore by herself. The most difficult thing for Andrew to do was to walk on high heels. Laughter erupted when he tried to walk. Patrick had to hold Andrew's shoulders as he wobbled down the street, appearing intoxicated as he stumbled off the shoes. When they entered the Acey Doucey Club, the party had just begun and they were introduced as "the couple who defy all rules". They began dancing around the floor as if they had been professional dancers. Andrew said, "Just put a pair of high heels on a man and once he gets used to them, he turns into a woman." "The Madame of the Night", had been hired to be the Mistress of Ceremonies. She turned out to be the hairiest and most muscular man when someone dared to ask if she was really a woman. "The Madame" having been challenged by the dare, undid herself showing that she was a real man, especially when she lifted her dress to verify the gender. When the crowd saw what had been tucked into "The Madame's" girdle, they went wild with desire to have the chance to dance with her. Patrick and Andrew were the hit of the party too because they dared to cross boundaries and prove that all things were possible, including the love of a mulatto and white person, no matter what they looked like or did.

At midnight, the party moved to higher temptations. The music had been such that it intoxicated the crowds. "The Madame of the Night" dared the crowds to show what they had been hiding under their outfits. Some came in loin cloths or bathing suits and others were more conservative, coming as gangsters, police officers, or business people. During the midnight celebrations, "The Madame" demanded attention while she pointed to people and invited them to the stage. She would instruct them to follow her demands or else! Most people could not wait for their turn because "The Madame" wanted a show. While this was happening, Andrew said, "Mother should have that job. She has always been good at giving directions." Patrick's eyes went up and he smiled as they were told to come forward. By this time, "The Madame" had become more demanding and wanted them to demonstrate what it looked like when a man and woman were in lust. At first they thought she meant love, but were corrected, the word was lust; and "The Madame" demanded they give a show, no matter what it was. The crowds had been cheering and wanted them to show what it was like in the bedroom. "The Madame" said, "Only if I can be in the middle. I know how these mulattos are and I want him." The crowd went wilder as Patrick seduced "The Madame", as a man might, and Andrew pretended to be the jealous wife, tearing at "The Madame's" dress. The crowd had been screaming for more as "The Madame" let loose on Patrick taking him to the floor and throwing her dress off for Patrick's pleasures. Andrew maneuvered himself doing the same thing following "The Madame's" demands for a time of pleasure on the stage. By this time, the crowd had been dancing and throwing costumes everywhere exposing that half of the crowd had been women having the same fun as the men were having. "The Madame" told Patrick and Andrew, while in the heat of excitement, that this was a good way to welcome in the New Year.

CHAPTER 44

Winston anxiously awaited Rex's return from his family holiday. He had Sable prepare her famous dinner of fried Southern Chicken, sweet potatoes, corn, and collard greens. She joked with Winston that she had made a shoofly pie for the dessert. Winston was not sure if she had been telling the truth until she showed him a pecan pie. He thanked her for not having a shoofly pie because he did not want another demonstration like they had at Thanksgiving. During the time after Sable left and Rex had arrived, Winston became sentimental when he thought of Jason. It had not been very long since his death and Winston wondered if he had become involved with Rex too soon. He convinced himself that Jason and he had a good life, but he was still alive and needing companionship. Just as he stopped burdening himself about his past, the bell rang.

Winston went to the main door. Rex stood at attention with a bouquet of flowers in his hand. He wore casual attire, not like his usual well-tailored outfits. Winston had on a shirt and shorts; it still felt like summer that evening. Rex handed the flowers to Winston and patted Winston on the behind as they went to the kitchen for a vase. Winston had not expected the flowers or Rex's obvious advances. He had been the one who usually took over. Winston wondered if Rex had a different personality in the heat of passion than the image he portrayed when he was well tailored and in high style.

During cocktail time, they discussed Rex's week in New York City and Winston listened to Rex's escapades in some of the darker places in the underground of the city. Winston, being baffled now, had serious questions about what Rex might really be all about. He asked, "Do you take part in all you have told me or do you just observe others for fun?" Rex hesitated with a smile on his face saying, "I love to administer treatments that take my victims to the height of arousal. However, I am very good at giving directions. As you know, my job is to please people and give them as much pleasure and feeling as they want." Winston had never been in such a spot and in a conversation with so much detail of underground pleasure palaces in New York City. He asked Rex if he knew of any places like that in Miami. Rex's eyes lit up as he said, "Absolutely, my apartment is one of those places where one can come for anything they desire. I have a collection of apparatus to help make the most extreme treatments pleasurable." Winston's next question was, "Do you allow those kinds of treatments to be administered to you?" Rex nodded his head. As uncertain and scary as a place of this type made Winston feel, he was at the height of intrigue and felt a sense of excitement thinking about all he had heard. Rex sensed Winston's confusion and asked if he could entertain him at his apartment. Winston hesitated but knew he wanted to find out in the worst way.

During dinner, Winston had difficulty thinking of things to talk about. He felt like anything he might bring up might bore Rex, after what he had heard earlier. Most of his worry eased up when Rex treated the evening as if he had been invited to a royal occasion. Winston calmed down. Everything had been moving along until Rex stood up, took off his outer layer of clothing, exposing a provocative outfit of leather pants with openings in various places leaving nothing to the imagination. In the bag that he came in with, contained apparatus for restraining and training. With a seductive smile on Rex's face, he asked, "Winston can I offer you another level of pleasure?" While Winston attempted to be calm, Rex had already put on a rubber glove and had leather straps for Winston's hands and ankles. Rex reassured him that once he learned his lesson, he would want many more. Winston felt like he had just moved into a world he had never expected.

The Biltmore ballroom had an overflow of guests for the Swing Dance party. Eveline had been enjoying the company of everyone at her table. She thought how easy it had been to attend an evening on her own. The folks at the table were the same age as she and had lost partners through death or separation. Some were women who had lost their girlfriends. Most admitted they had come to the party in hopes of meeting a new friend. During the conversations, Eveline thought about all the sexual partners she had experienced. She never had been in the company of or been approached, or had experiences with a female. She wondered what the attraction might be all about. When the dance instructor began, most of the woman found another woman to be partners with. Eveline, still confused, wondered if this party had been designed for women and the idea of finding a man may not be as possible as Eveline had hoped for. Eveline, looking like a socialite, had many offers from men of the same caliber to dance. During the course of the evening and before midnight, some of the women began to feel the effects of too many cocktails. A few attractive women approached Eveline and attempted to have a conversation. Eveline enjoyed the interaction until she had been touched in places that she thought a man should be doing. Another woman approached Eveline because she knew her from Burdines and was determined that Eveline and she should get together. It was a strange combination of guests. Eveline had danced and felt like this had been a good idea but had not met a man that intrigued her. During the height of the occasion, an argument occurred among a group of less than social acting women. After the management failed in calming the situation down, they called for police assistance. One of the women threatened another woman because she had allegedly approached her girlfriend. Eveline thought that the evening had not been what she had expected but found the party to be the most unusual social event she had ever attended. She had never been to such an occasion where people fought physically. This reminded her of the days during the "Women's Rights Movement", only the men were the culprits. She began to enjoy the action and a side of society she never knew existed. Getting out in the world was much different than the life she had been familiar with.

Shortly after the police had been called, a group of officers appeared. Eveline had taken her seat to watch how the police attempted to break up the situation. Never had Eveline experienced a scene of tearing clothing, pulling hair, and scratching skin. One woman took a nail file and threated to use it on an officer if he did not let her loose. He wasted no time in handcuffing her. Hoping this would not escalate into a larger problem, Eveline wondered if she should call a taxicab and leave. She realized this had turned into a less than elegant evening where singles might meet. As she gathered her belongings and fought off the woman from Burdines, she managed to get to a telephone. The lobby had been in a state of near panic as the hotel had not been used to such behavior in a place as opulent as the Biltmore. While Eveline waited to speak to the taxicab company, she had her hand on her hip, holding the receiver, and tapping her foot. Just as Eveline had arranged for the taxicab, a man came up to her from behind. As he moved past her he said, "Hey baby, how are you? I heard you are better now that you took my advice." Eveline turned and saw Jonathon Bingham. She dropped the receiver to the floor and stared at Jonathon, not able to say a word.

CHAPTER 45

After Eveline composed herself, she picked up the receiver and attempted to act casual. Jonathon stood watching Eveline return to her "in charge" attitude. She could not believe she had run into Jonathon. He smiled and asked in a jovial way, "Do you always attend such rowdy parties?" Attempting to minimize on what had been happening in the ballroom, Eveline said, "I wanted to go out tonight and the Biltmore was the only place I found that offered a singles dance and dinner. This is not what I had hoped for." When she heard herself say that, she worried Jonathon might take it the wrong way and think she was not happy to see him. Eveline had to do a mental reminder not to fall into old traps. Jonathon did not make an effort to do much more than have a quick conversation. He said, "Eveline, I am working and cannot spend time with you. I need to get inside to attend to the problem." Eveline shook her head trying to understand what was happening. She tried to stay composed, but was having trouble, because this is what she had hoped for. Jonathon walked away; Eveline went to the waiting taxicab. While riding to 825, Eveline sobbed. The driver asked if she needed help. She told him that the help she needed had gone off to work. The taxicab driver shook his head saying, "I hear many stories. This is the newest one." Eveline sucked her teeth, never thanking the man, as she handed him the money.

New Year's Day, 1936, Eveline cried most of the morning. At noon, the telephone rang, it was Patrick. He asked how her evening turned out. Eveline made the answer brief saying, "It was alright." Patrick had called to invite her to come to the Tropical Gardens for a late lunch. Rex would pick her up. At first Eveline hesitated and Patrick asked why. Eveline made an excuse that she had some work to do to get ready for the fashion show. Patrick said, "Mother, it can wait. The store does not open until Tuesday." Eveline realized how ridiculous she sounded and told him she would be ready. Patrick told her to be out in the front of 825 in an hour. Eveline decided to step it up, dress herself up, and ring in the New Year. She stood at the gate as she watched Rex pull up in his convertible. The day was about 80 degrees, hard to believe it was January. Rex treated Eveline like he was chauffeuring her. He opened the door and she got into the car. The ride was pleasant but Rex admitted he had a very late night with Winston. Eveline asked no questions.

When they arrived, Patrick, Andrew, and Winston were lounging in hammocks. Winston had purchased a number of them for guests to relax and spend the day in the shade of Kapok trees. Rex and Eveline were greeted by Olitha. Sable had been busy in the kitchen. Their newest arrangement was that during holidays, they prepare the food and go home to their husbands. Olitha told them that they were going to an Overton New Year's Day street dance. When Eveline heard this, she felt like telling them that she had attended one last night. She thought better of this remark. Rex found a hammock while Eveline stood wondering if she should try to get into one of them. She had on a fancy dress, a wide brimmed hat, and high heels. How would that look for her to attempt a hammock? The men made no effort to offer assistance, so Eveline called Sable and Olitha to come help her. They lifted Eveline up and nearly threw her on the hammock. Eveline screamed as her hat fell off. Sable and Olitha both said, "Oh girl, you so funny with you dress over you head and hat hangin by the string. You sure looks comfortable. Who gonna help you get out a dat thing?" By this time there was laughter and the men waved their hands while Winston said, "She's a big girl. She can help herself." Eveline felt like everyone must be thinking like that lately. Maybe it was time to go back to Doctor Kane before she did something more drastic.

During lunch, the conversations were about what everyone did for New Year's Eve fun. Andrew took over telling about "The Madame of the Night" and that they had been dressed like Mr. and Mrs. Paine. Eveline stared, thinking of what a show they must have created. Patrick said, "Mother you should have been with us. You could have been the MC instead of a man in drag." Eveline shook her head wondering what had come over everyone. After the description of the events at the Acey Doucey Club, Andrew announced that they were going to be in a show with "The Madame". Winston asked what they were doing in the show. Patrick said, "I am Mr. Paine who seduces "The Madame" and Andrew joins in to entertain the audience." Eveline spoke up, "Now, I need to know if you are doing sexual things on stage?" They shook their heads while Rex and Winston were waiting to discuss their evening. Eveline said, "Oh my God, what kind of job is that." Andrew said, "Mother, you need to come for our opening night." Eveline only shook her head.

Winston took a deep breath and said, "I experienced things last night that I never knew could happen. All eyes were on Rex and Winston when the explanations began. Winston explained that Rex appears to be a refined and well put together man. Eveline said, "I hope so since he works in a fashion office." Winston continues, "That is what is surprising about him." Rex sat motionless. Winston explained about the dinner and flowers that Rex gave him. He explained that he usually is the dominant one. Rex interrupted saying, "He is not that way anymore." Eveline's eyes opened wider and Patrick and Andrew sat staring at them. Winston told about the underground pleasure palaces that Rex went to in New York City. Eveline was now wondering what on earth had happened. She thought she had experienced many diversions, what more could she learn? Winston admitted he never knew about places where people went to be disciplined, manipulated and held down, while allowing themselves to be used for whatever the pleasure may be. Patrick asked, "Rex, do you administer these activities or do you allow people to do these things to you?" Rex smiled saying, "Both." Now everyone's question, that no one dared to ask, was finally attempted by Eveline. She asked, "Winston tell us what Rex did to you that you have never experienced. I thought you were a master at all that stuff." Rex interrupted saying, "He's a submissive with me. He's had his first lesson and now wants more." Patrick and Andrew appeared stunned, as Eveline shook her head.

Eveline sighed and said, "After hearing about all of your escapades last night, my evening seems boring to speak about. Patrick coaxed his mother to tell about her evening. Eveline explained that the event had been advertised as an evening at the Biltmore to learn to Swing Dance. There were singles rates and she went. She explained how she dressed compared to most women. The music and dancing was fun because she had been asked to dance by many men that were there by themselves. So far, Eveline described the evening as pretty ordinary. Winston asked, "Did you have any excitement or do something new?" Eveline laughed and admitted she did experience new things. She said, "I had never seen groups of women go after one another in ways most women do not do. There were some very pleasant women that came to me. I had never thought of what that type of relationship might be like. While I was trying to understand all this, some of the less fashionable women had an argument that led to a need to call the police. I watched the action and most of the people I was with were not involved. As a matter of fact, a woman who works at Burdines wanted to get to know me better. She is as stylish as me." Andrew told Eveline that it was good for her to see how others live. He explained that half of the crowd at the Acey Doucey Club were women. Patrick interrupted and said, "Mother, you really need to come to our show. You might see some of the same people there." Rex laughed and looked at both Winston and Eveline and said, "You both have not seen the real world as it is and might be ready to go deeper in pleasures." Eveline wanted to jump up and run away. All she wanted was to have Jonathon come back to her, not get involved in dark demonic activities.

After hearing such things from her family and friends, Eveline felt more alone than ever. She wondered if she should divulge what else happened to her. While she was contemplating the discussion, the men were all chattering about working at the Acey Doucey Club. Rex explained about his apartment and that selected people, even women, were allowed to visit. Eveline felt a little scared thinking of what Rex, her boss, must really be like. Rex mentioned another club that offered activities such as he had in his apartment. Mona's Tropical Bar was frequented by groups and individuals that enjoy deep pleasures. Rex said the name was a clue for the sounds that come from the place. It was around the block from the Acey Doucey Club on Miami Beach.

Eveline stood up and said, "I have had enough of this deviant conversation. You can all do what you want to one another but I saw Jonathon Bingham last night." The conversations ended as they watched Eveline express deep concern over what had happened. They knew how devastated she had been that Jonathon had left her, after all she had been through. Eveline explained how it happened that Jonathon and other officers had been called to the Biltmore to settle the women's dispute. She told them that she had been calling a taxicab when he came up behind her telling her that he was happy she was better. The men watched Eveline sob, using her handkerchief and wiping her eyes saying, "All he told me was that he was working and left me standing there." Patrick went to her and attempted to calm her down, but she asked for someone to take here back to 825. She admitted she was nearing her limit of being alone. She said, "It seems like everyone is crazy or perverted and I do not want to be involved."

CHAPTER 46

E veline spent the next few days feeling depressed. She hoped to have heard from Jonathon, or was that her fantasy? Why would he make such an effort to speak to her that night at the Biltmore? He could have avoided her. Eveline's mind filled with question after question, leaving her at her wits end, feeling more confused than ever. She felt uncomfortable about going back to the fashion office and seeing Rex, after what she learned about his private life. She needed the job and had been successful and wanted to continue with her work. Eveline felt a sense of worry about Rex's dual personality and that Winston appeared to be taken by it. Her sons had surprised her by the type of entertainment they had come to enjoy. Eveline had no answers to any of her questions. She decided it might be best to make an appointment with Doctor Kane. When she telephoned, she was able to have an appointment that afternoon. While Eveline made her way to Jackson Memorial Hospital, she realized she had no money to pay for the appointment. She decided to go back to 825 to avoid embarrassing herself.

When Eveline sat in the apartment she felt old temptations coming back and began to panic. While she franticly paced around, the telephone rang. It startled her, but when she answered it, Doctor Kane was on the other end of the line. He asked, "Eveline are you okay?" There was no sound from her and Doctor Kane asked, "Are you on the line?" Eveline said, "Yes." He asked why she had missed the appointment. She paused then said, "I cannot afford to pay you." Doctor Kane said, "You come immediately and we can work out the payment arrangements for the appointment. Your health is more important." Eveline thanked him and left for the hospital.

When Eveline entered the doctor's office, she felt like she had been on the verge of collapse. She sat in the chair facing the doctor's desk. As the doctor entered, Eveline did not turn to him. When he saw her face and condition he knew she had had a relapse. She acted as if all of her old personalities had been tormenting her. The minute she saw Doctor Kane, she became hysterical. He convinced her to calm down and asked why everything had unraveled for her. Eveline explained about Thanksgiving and the behaviors of her sons and friends. She said, "They all seem to have changed." The doctor listened and observed Eveline. He had a notion it might be Catherine and Trixie attacking her, making her react to her friends and family, just as she thought Catherine and Trixie had done in the past. Doctor Kane listened to what happened to everyone during the New Year's Eve activities. This time, Eveline had transferred the issues to blaming herself for what her sons had taken part in. She blamed herself for not being better to Winston. She had worked out, in her mind, that Winston had gone for Rex's behavior and treatments because he had lost so many people and this was his last attempt at a relationship. Rex had convinced Winston to be submissive because he saw him as a lonely victim. Eveline was convinced that Winston had lost his mind. Doctor Kane asked if there had been anything else that may have triggered this mental event. Eveline looked at the doctor with a strange look of confusion. She asked him why. The doctor said, "It seems to me that Catherine and Trixie have been nagging you and blaming you for being alone and wondering about your friends and family. Are you aware of this possibility?" Eveline looked off to the side and said, "I had thought this might be happening. I have tried to get rid of those two demons. Another thing happened to me on New Year's Eve." Eveline explained about the party at the Biltmore. She described her feelings as she went through the lobby and what had happened during the evening and admitted she hoped to meet someone. Doctor Kane asked, "Were you disappointed when that did not happen?" Eveline made a face and said, "I was not disappointed. I felt stunned and confused when Jonathon Bingham came up to me telling me he was happy I was better and he could not talk because he was working."

After Eveline had explained her feelings, Doctor Kane asked if she had any ideas of how to move on after these troubling times. Eveline made a gesture of not knowing the answer to the question. He reminded her of their sessions about what holidays create for people. He asked, "Eveline, do you believe that any of what has upset you had been your fault?" Eveline said, "I think my sons are experimenting with their new life style in Miami. I am disappointed that Winston has fallen for such deviant behavior and I have to work with Rex. I'm not sure how to behave around him. I continue to mourn over Jonathon and after seeing him I am even more unhappy and lonely. I still believe he loves me." Doctor Kane told Eveline that she had avoided answering his question. Eveline looked away saying, "I guess none of what I have felt about others was my fault. My demonic personalities are telling me that." The doctor said, "No mother wants their children to be harmed. They will decide what is best for themselves. They may be just having fun as young men do. Sounds like they want you to be part of their fun instead of you judging what they tell you. This might be the time for you to be supportive of them. How would you feel if they never told you? After all, they came back to you after you left everyone and went to California." Eveline listened with no expression. Doctor Kane continued, "As far as Winston and Rex, what they do is not your business or your fault. Winston has made his mind up, at least for now. Do you understand?" Eveline shook her head saying, "I felt bad when I stormed out of the New Year's Day luncheon telling everyone I did not want any part of them or their demonic behaviors." Eveline stopped speaking and thought. The doctor watched her processing information. She continued, "I think I know why I have been so judgmental. I have experienced many of the things my friends and sons are talking about and I felt I should try to help them by convincing them to stop. I now realize, after meeting with you, I could not stop and did not understand what had driven me to be so deviant." Doctor Kane looked with a slight smile on his face. He wondered how long Eveline would take to understand most of her judgements were coming from old habits and mental torments.

Doctor Kane could not let Eveline leave the office until he asked about Eveline's mourning over Jonathon Bingham. Eveline explained that she felt like a part of her had died when he left her. She had a sense of mourning for her past life that had ended, in so many ways, in the last years. The doctor listened and told Eveline he felt the use of the word "mourn" was interesting. He said, "Many people never recognize that they mourn situations or losses in their lives. Most people think of mourning only over a death." Eveline said, "I feel like a part of my life has died. When I think of Jonathon, I feel my life with him died." The doctor knew that the situation with Jonathon and Eveline had come too close for him to counsel her on. He said, "Eveline, you understand that Jonathon and I are close friends?" Eveline shook her head. He continued, "I cannot discuss him with you, only to let you know he has been very busy and has traveled for federal investigations. So when he told you he was working, he told you the truth. He had been instrumental in the case of Giuseppe Zangara who went to prison for 80 years after attempting to assassinate President Roosevelt in Miami." Eveline left the office having a better understanding of herself, but was still unhappy over Jonathon.

CHAPTER 47

———— ∞ ————

A few days after the New Year, Winston had a meeting with Patrick and Andrew to discuss the future of 825 Michigan Avenue. He asked them if they were still interested in operating the vacation rental business. They agreed they wanted to take over the property and run it as a guesthouse for the discrete traveler. Winston asked them if they understood what that type of operation entailed. Both of them thought that it meant that whoever stayed would want privacy from the outside world. Winston explained that it might be more than that. Andrew wanted to know what else they needed to understand about the operation. The property had been designed for guests to experience whatever they wanted in the privacy of a secluded tropical environment. Since the weather was warm most of the year, guests would be free to do as they pleased inside and out. Winston had set up employment for a masseuse to be on duty for the guests and available for private room services. During the conversation, Patrick thought it might be time for him to present the idea that he and Andrew purchase 825. Patrick said, "Winston, have you considered selling 825 to us? Since the plans you had for the property have changed since Jason's death would you to consider selling it to us?" Winston had a surprised look saying, "I had thought about that too. I gave up on the idea when you seemed satisfied working at the Tropical Gardens. When you told your mother about your plans to work at the Acey Doucey Club, I decided not to give it another thought." Andrew spoke up cutting off Patrick saying, "That was his idea to be doing things like that in public. I thought we should have discussed buying 825 Michigan Avenue from you instead." Patrick sat speechless and appeared embarrassed when he listened to the reality of such work at the Acey Doucey Club.

After the decision to sell the property to Patrick and Andrew, Winston agreed to have the paperwork drawn up for the purchase of 825 Michigan Avenue. Winston reminded them that they had the chance, a few years ago, to be the owners. They had forgotten that their mother wanted to transfer the property to them before she took off to California. Winston told them that he would sell the property for $98,000.00 because that is what Eveline paid for it. A mortgage would need to be applied for, but with the Depression gripping the economics of the United States, securing a loan might be difficult. Andrew spoke up, "Winston is there any way you could give us the mortgage? You set the conditions and we will pay you instead of a bank." Winston thought for a moment and said, "Since your mother gave me the property before she took off, I suppose all I really want is to have the property operating as Jason and I had planned. If you pay the transfers, taxes, and legal fees, I'll give 825 to you. I'm sure your mother will be happy with this since she wanted you to have it in the beginning." Winston told them he had one condition, that he oversees the property. He mentioned the idea of bringing Rex for the weekend so they could experience pleasures in the out of doors instead of a dungeon. Patrick asked, "Will that be instead of Mona's Tropical Bar on Miami Beach?" Winston smiled and shook his head.

Patrick and Andrew agreed that they needed to tell Eveline about the transfer of ownership of 825. Patrick telephoned Eveline, there was no answer. He telephoned the fashion office at Burdines and Rex answered. Eveline came to the telephone and asked, "What is the matter? You have never called me at work." Patrick laughed and said, "Mother, you will never guess what is happening with Andrew and me." Eveline wondered what could possibly top what she had heard about their stage performances. He said, "Remember when you asked Andrew and me if we wanted 825 and we told you no. Things have changed. Winston has offered the property to us. We agreed to take it as long as the property is maintained as Winston and Jason had planned." Eveline could not believe what she had just heard. She asked, "What does this mean for your work with "The Madame of the

Night?" Patrick explained that after considering the type of work that it would entail, they decided owning and operating a guesthouse would be a better choice. Eveline sighed and said, "Oh thank God, I worried about that type of activity and where it might have taken you. I am elated." Patrick left out the part that Winston was planning to bring Rex to the guesthouse for a weekend. He thought better of discussing Winston's ideas. Eveline asked, "When is the guesthouse opening for business?" Patrick told her in November.

Burdines had been advertising the fashion show every evening in the Miami Herald since the New Year began. It had been scheduled for the first Saturday in January. Fashions for winter and the upcoming spring and summer seasons would be featured. Eveline had been in charge of the female models and Mr. Berman had been fitting the outfits for the male models. The store had been decorated with the theme of "The Tropics on a Balmy Evening". Eveline reminisced, as she set the schedule, about the many warm balmy evenings she had spent with Jonathon. She tried to get her mind off him, but something nagged at her. Having just been to Doctor Kane, she wondered if another demon was pulling at her. She convinced herself that it was okay to remember good things. She still hoped she could be with Jonathon, which weighed heavy on her mind. While Eveline finished her day's work, she wondered when she might have to leave the apartment at 825. Where would she move? There was still little money for an apartment. While she rode the bus to the 825 block on Miami Beach, she convinced herself that something would happen to make everything work out. Eveline reminded herself that even when her luck had been at its lowest, she had always managed to survive.

Saturday, January 4, 1936, was the day of the fashion show at Burdines. Eveline felt like she had to prove to herself and Mr. Berman that she had done a good job. Even after what she knew about his personal activities, Eveline had no problem working with Mr. Berman, as she had feared she might. Both were anxious to have the show be a hit, especially since people had less money to spend on clothing, much less on high fashions. Eveline dressed in her latest ensemble from Burdines. She would be announcing the models and their outfits as they entered the fashion runway. Mr. Berman would do the same for the men on the second floor. After the introductions, the models would stroll throughout the store so shoppers could see the fashions up close. The strolling would end in the restaurant where a luncheon would be served for everyone who purchased items at the show, compliments of Burdines.

Eveline had hired an orchestra to provide music during show. Just before the show began, men arrived acting like they were there to protect someone. Eveline, being at the main floor entrance, was asked where Mrs. Eveline Paine might be. Eveline's heart began racing, not knowing what this was all about. She said, "I am Mrs. Paine and have done nothing wrong." As the men moved aside, Eleanor Roosevelt appeared. She said, "Hello, Mrs. Paine. I read in the Miami Herald that you had been instrumental in organizing this fashion show. Franklin and I had been scheduled in Miami and I wanted to see you. How have you been since we met in California?" Eveline, stunned, tried to compose herself. Not only did she have to do a job, but now had to speak to Mrs. Roosevelt. All she could think of was the last time they met at the Hearst party in California and she had been scolded by the First Lady. Eveline said, "I have been fine. Many things have changed in my life since we last met." Eleanor said, "Yes, I know and have been meaning to contact you because we have unfinished business to discuss. We are only in Miami until noon, but I will be sending you a letter soon. Would you be so kind as to give me your current address?" Eveline, even more confused, told her 825 Michigan Avenue.

Mrs. Roosevelt moved through the store with her entourage of men who stayed close by the First Lady. Eveline began the fashion show as the models entered. The orchestra could be heard throughout the store, making it a perfect environment for a fashion wonderland. Eveline kept her eye on the models and wondered during the show what Mrs. Roosevelt wanted. As the show ended on the main floor, the customers went to the upper floors where more models had been positioned showing men's outfits. As Eveline went to the second floor on the elevator, she had a strange feeling come over her. She steadied herself as the doors opened and the elevator attendant assisted the folks out. She strolled around looking for Mr. Berman. He was nowhere to be found. While she stood listening to the customer's comments, a voice said from behind, "You are looking beautiful." Eveline turned but there was no one that looked familiar. She heard the voice again, only this time she thought it came from a model that had been hired to be a human manikin. She looked again at the manikin and no sound could be heard. Human manikins were hired to model the outfits, not to speak. Eveline felt weary and confused, as she turned the corner to the men's summer suit department. There were so many shoppers; it was difficult to see too far ahead. As she stood, a voice said, "Hey baby, you look terrific. Can we go out sometime?" Eveline's heart sank and thought the voice was Jonathon's. She turned and noticed the manikin's lips were sealed. Eveline wanted to scream when she realized she had been consumed with the thoughts of Jonathon ever since New Year's Eve. The model could have been Jonathon's twin, handsome with a muscular stature, a tanned face wearing a white suit and white fedora. Eveline remembered that Jonathon owned a suit just like that.

CHAPTER 48

A fter the fashion show had ended, Eveline, still upset about hearing voices, asked Mr. Berman if he had seen Mrs. Roosevelt. He said that he had and that she autographed introductory samples of her latest works entitled, *My Day*. It was her plan to write a daily story about her life's philosophy and work. Its focus would be to give Americans hope and an understanding of what she stood for, mainly women's rights and child welfare. Mr. Berman asked if Eveline had spoken to her. Eveline said that she had, but it was about another matter that she was not certain of. While she spoke to Mr. Berman she wondered what might be in store for her when Mrs. Roosevelt sent the letter to her. As Eveline walked away from him, he said, "I think I did a superb job with the manikins. They looked so artificial that one would think they were not humans." Eveline wanted to scream when she heard this because she thought they had spoken to her. Now, she feared she may be having another breakdown. She remembered that was a question Doctor Kane had asked her, did she ever hear voices? She had feared that if she admitted to hearing voices, he may want to send her to an asylum.

The Sunday edition of the Miami Herald featured a special section on Burdines extravaganza of fashions. Eveline's name was mentioned as the "mastermind" of the show. When she read this, she remembered that was what Wallace had been called in all of his businesses. She delighted in the newspapers accolades of the show and her work, but the word "mastermind" took her back to unpleasant places in her past. Mrs. Roosevelt had been mentioned as a surprise guest to Burdines. She was now being referred to as "The First Lady of the World" because of her involvement with people throughout the world. Her daily writing of *My Day* had been the main reason for her travels to Miami, according to the newspaper article. Eveline thought, as she read, that there had to be another reason for her being at

Burdines. Things did not make sense. She wondered if Mrs. Roosevelt was there to see her or did she use her new writing as another reason for showing up at the store.

Winston telephoned Eveline to confirm that she knew about and understood the transfer of 825 Michigan Avenue to Patrick and Andrew. He explained that Bohemia 825 would be receiving guests on November 1st. During the conversation, he explained that she would need to vacate the apartment by the end of September. Eveline understood, but did not admit to her fear of having no place to live. Winston asked how she had been getting along with Rex. Eveline explained that their work relationship had not changed, he was a perfect gentleman. Winston told her that he was glad her fears had not been realized after what she had learned about the activities Rex enjoyed. Eveline wanted to hang up the receiver when she thought of what Winston had allowed Rex to do to him. Eveline asked, "Winston, are you sure you like Rex enough to be treated like a submissive slave?" Winston hesitated and said, "I like his style and his ability to be someone different at night." Eveline said, "What if he goes too far and hurts you or kills you?" Winston laughed and said, "That will never happen. I am stronger than he is." Eveline said, "Are you that desperate that you need to have affection in an abusive way?" Without responding, Winston hung up the telephone. Eveline knew she had touched on a sensitive spot with him. She sensed that something bad might happen between Rex and Winston. When she thought about her own issues and the voices, she wondered if she had any right to ask such questions of Winston.

Andrew and Patrick stopped to see Eveline. She was surprised and pleased they came to visit her. Not many people came to 825 because the other accommodations had been set up for travelers. The apartment she had occupied was to be the owner's living quarters. During the visit, her sons acted in a strange way. Eveline asked what the matter was. Patrick explained that he and Andrew were still performing Drag Shows at the Acey Doucey Club. Eveline did not give any clue about her thoughts when she heard about the shows. They had come to invite her to be their guest. When Eveline heard this she remembered what Doctor Kane had said about them wanting her to be part of their life. Eveline asked when they wanted her to be at the club. They laughed and said, "Tonight, we want you to be the Mistress of Ceremonies." Eveline shook her head and said, "Oh, am I competing with "The Madame of the Night"?" Patrick told her that "The Madame" was not able to be the Master of Ceremonies. Eveline wanted to know what she should wear and what to do on the stage. Andrew said, "One of your sexy dresses from Burdines. With your attitude and mouth, the crowds will love you." Eveline shook her head saying, "Now, I'm announcing "Drag Shows", another form of fashion shows. Maybe this will be my new calling in life, entertaining people who love to dress up." Patrick assured her that she would have the information about the entertainers, and not to worry. Andrew said, "Mother, you are going to have the greatest time. Just wait until you hear the music and laughter." Eveline's eyes went up as she left the room to prepare for yet another experience.

Patrick whispered to Andrew while Eveline was in the bedroom, "Don't let Mother know that Winston and Rex have agreed to be part of the show, only they will not be in drag. The audience will think they are in drag until Rex takes over." Andrew smiled and agreed to the plan. Andrew did ask if having Mother as the Mistress of Ceremony was such a good idea, especially with Rex's behavior. Patrick waved his hand and told Andrew to stop being a worrier. Eveline walked in to the living room and asked what they had been whispering about. Both were shocked that she could hear them and told her they were planning a surprise for their act. Eveline had dressed in one of her older outfits, not from Burdines, that made her appear more provocative than the types of dresses she wore to work. Andrew told her she looked the part. Eveline made a face wondering what that meant.

Upon arriving at the Acey Doucey Club, Eveline was surprised that it appeared like any other night club. It had been decorated in a tasteful manner. She had thought it may be like a dive in a back alley. She mentioned this to Patrick and he said, "Mother, what type of guys do you think we are? Just because we are a pair does not mean we are low class." Eveline realized what she had said and how hurtful it was, and apologized. While she read the list of entertainers, there were some that sounded like ordinary performers. She asked if all the people on stage were impersonators. She was told not everyone in the show would be in Drag. Eveline recognized Patrick and Andrew with the title "The Couple that Defies all Odds". She knew they were impersonating her and Wallace. She wondered why she needed to be reminded of what being married to Wallace had created. She wished the night was over, but knew this was what Doctor Kane had recommended.

The show began with jazzy music. Eveline appeared on the stage to a full night club. At first she felt panic. When she saw Patrick and Andrew give her the okay signal, she began speaking. She introduced herself as the substitute Mistress of Ceremony. The audience clapped and cheered. She looked into the crowd and saw men and women of all types. When she introduced Mr. and Mrs. Defy all Odds Paine, she laughed as the audience clapped for them. They waltzed on to the stage and began dancing around Eveline. Andrew had mastered the use of high heels and he no longer needed to be held up. Patrick had taken over when he grabbed Andrew and twirled him around as a man might do to a woman while dancing. Eveline stood in amazement at the response they received from the audience. She began clapping, as did the crowd. When the music stopped, Patrick announced that his wife would be leading the next dance. Eveline knew, as did the audience, that was not allowed in society. Andrew yelled, "Guess we are defiant." The music began and Andrew twirled Patrick around and picked him up and threw him over his shoulder. Andrew's dress flew up in the air exposing himself without undergarments. Eveline's eyes went up and she blushed as the audience screamed for more. Andrew put Patrick down and began shimming around him. Andrew jumped up and spun around landing on Patrick's foot digging into his toes with the high heel. Patrick limped around and Andrew threw him on the floor. Andrew told the audience that now he would have his way with Mr. Paine. Eveline was shocked that her sons were having such a good time at being out of control and defiant of society, as she watched the audience scream for more. Eveline knew that she and Wallace had never behaved this way, even in private.

While Andrew played the submissive role, which was not a normal way for a husband and wife to behave, out came Winston dressed in leather pants, exposing his bare behind, and only a vest showing his chest. He wore leather gloves and carried a bull whip. Eveline could say nothing as she then knew what the list had meant, two men fighting for the top, one needing training. She even felt that old sensation she had forgotten about as she watched her sons maneuver themselves on one another, both exposing how turgid they had become. The audience went wild when they saw how rough Winston appeared. He cracked the whip, shocking Eveline, as Rex appeared in his black leather master's outfit. Eveline stared at them as they looked down on Patrick and Andrew, who had now given the audience the climax they had yelled for. She was sure this was not what Doctor Kane had thought when he recommended that she support her sons in their work and interests. She had followed the doctor's suggestions but did not appreciate what their act involved and felt they could be arrested for public lewdness.

As the audience cheered the entertainers, Rex had begun his attack on Winston. Eveline was not sure she could stand to watch what she thought might occur. Rex tied Winston's hands behind his back, took the whip and draped it over his body. The crowd screamed for more as Winston struggled to get free. He threatened Rex with severe punishment when he broke free. Rex had been pinching and twisting Winston's chest, in sensitive spots, while pulling the hair on his chest. Winston showed a face of determination and self-control. When Winston broke free, he threw Rex to the floor and began whipping him. The audience, as well as Eveline, watched in shock as Rex begged for more. Winston tied him up and beat him with his fists. Rex seemed to enjoy the pain Winston had been administering. He kept telling Rex that he was in charge from now on. Patrick and Andrew watched and began to wonder if they were actually acting or had Winston taken over. Eveline felt like she had been invited to this club to watch Winston take charge, or was that her hope?

Before the show ended, Rex had been assaulted everywhere on his body leaving blood and bruises. The more Winston whipped and hit him, the better he enjoyed the treatment. Eveline never saw Winston act so violently. Maybe he was letting out his aggression on Rex that he should have let out on Wallace. The more she watched, the more she wished Winston would have done this to Wallace; he deserved a beating after how he treated Winston so many years ago. Eveline wondered if Winston knew this might be what made him go for Rex. At intermission, the audience raved about the show and liked the idea of defying society with Patrick and Andrew's act and Winston's treatment of a controlling man. The second half of the show featured singers either dressed as a man or woman, nothing topped the first half of the show. While the crowds were getting drinks and waiting for the second half, the lights began blinking. That was a signal that a raid was about to occur. The crowd could not leave because the door had been blocked by the Miami Police Department. There had been rumors that the city officials were attempting to close establishments that openly encouraged deviant behaviors. Eveline stood on the stage as the police entered and moved toward her. She closed her eyes trying not to panic, a voice said, "Oh my God Eveline, what are you doing in a place like this? I am here to arrest the entertainers for lewd behavior and you are as responsible as they are for this." Eveline opened her eyes as she looked at Jonathon and the other officers ushering them to the paddy wagon. While she and everyone else sat in the wagon, she said, "I should have never listened to all of you about your demonic behaviors, much less introduce all this to the public. Now look what has happened." No one said a word. As she looked at Rex and Winston she said, "I work with you and look at you. You are a sick mess. Winston, I feel like beating your ass too. You all need to go to Doctor Kane and figure out why you are all so screwed up."

The paddy wagon came to a stop. Jonathon opened the door and helped Eveline get out first. He looked at her shaking his head saying, "Is this the best you can do to get to see me? I told you I was busy and still want to get together." The rest listened and watched as Jonathon treated Eveline like she was royalty. Patrick whispered to Andrew, "Maybe this will get the two of them together so Mother can have Jonathon like she used to. She would not need to watch a show anymore. I've heard he is man enough for two."

CHAPTER 49

While the group waited in the police department, Eveline thought about what had happened and was angry she had become involved in such entertainment. She had been working hard to avoid such sexually driven behaviors. While she looked at Patrick, Andrew, Winston, and Rex, she saw men who had been through situations in their lives that caused them to behave in these ways. She had spent many hours figuring out her life and why she had been behaving in ways that she never would have realized. If it had not been for Doctor Kane, Eveline would still be acting as she once had. She snapped her fingers at Winston, who appeared to be in a trance, and said, "Listen to me! I have known you since adolescence and I have never witnessed such violent behavior or heard of such activities since you met Rex. Have you given any thought to why you have behaved and accepted his ideas and treatments? After seeing you tonight, I was at least glad you stood up to him." The others watched as Eveline told Winston that he may have had a poor life, and a friend like Wallace who treated him and everyone else like they were his slaves. Winston said, "Remember what I told you the last time we talked about this? I told you that Rex would never hurt or even kill me. I have been doing a lot of thinking about why I went for him. He reminds me a lot of Wallace. Even in his style and mannerisms. When I allowed him to do the things we have told you about, I realized that is what I had hoped Wallace would have done to me. After a while, I understood that and had reconsidered my feelings and plans for Rex. It was this evening that I had such a good feeling of punishing Rex the way I did because I wanted to punish Wallace for how he treated me for many years. That is why I had been so upset when I did not get back to Geneva to see him before he died, I never had a chance to talk about this. The sad part is that Wallace probably would not have admitted to anything, even on his death bed." Eveline said, "I had hoped you recognized why this behavior was coming out of you in a violent way because you never were given the chance to deal with it." Winston looked at Rex saying, "I was never sure why I liked you. At first, I thought we could grow to have a stable relationship. After our New Year's Eve activities, I knew something had been tearing at me. It was me reliving the time that I felt taken by Wallace's manipulative personality. I took all my aggressions from those times out on you and I never want to see you again. Tonight was the ending of many years of suppressing my anger. I now understand that you were a rebound after Jason's death. There will never be anyone like him again."

After an hour of waiting, Jonathon came from the office to the holding area. He looked the group over and said, "I'm not sure where to begin. We have arrested the owners of the Acey Doucey Club because it was their idea to develop such lewd and sexual entertainment. As for the rest of you, you will be released without any arrests, except for you Rex. I am embarrassed to say I know all of you except this man who is badly injured." Winston looked at Rex as if he were a stranger. Patrick and Andrew said nothing because they were embarrassed that they were pulled into entertainment such as this by friends who had led them astray. Andrew spoke up and said, "We should have known better than to get into such activities, but we were new in Miami and felt part of a new group that we had met." Eveline stood up and went to them with fire in her eyes saying, "I am your mother whether you like it or not. You are young men that had a future at West Point and you screwed it up because you wanted to defy society and were afraid of what the men at the academy might have done to you. I would like to let you have it too, but you are too old and will not change. I have taken care of myself and now it's your turn to grow up!" Patrick tried to apologize to Eveline but she shook her hand and pointed her finger saying, "You guys do not need to apologize, just think about your reputation." Jonathon stood motionless as he watched Eveline go after all the men in the room. He thought, as he watched, that he was happy she was not going after him. He admired her for standing up to all this crazy activity, even though it was none of her business. He knew she was worried for her children.

Jonathon warned everyone, except Eveline, about any future behaviors in public. As for Rex, no one knew why he had been arrested. Jonathon had all he could do not to laugh when he watched them leaving. Andrew's dress had been ripped to shreds and had only one high heel in his hand walking in ripped stockings. Winston's leather pants were exposing more than his behind after Rex had torn them apart. Rex was still sitting there with marks and blood all over his body. Eveline looked the best, as if nothing had happened. She remarked, "You are all a mess. I wish I had a camera to take a picture of you. The way you look, you might never dress up again. You look like you have been in a drunken brawl." Jonathon agreed and told Eveline that she should make better decisions about the men she associated with. He asked, "Can we go out for dinner and discuss all that has happened since coming back from California?" Eveline winked at Jonathon and said, "Absolutely, you name the time and I'll be ready."

On the way home from the police station, Eveline wondered about how she was going to be able to work with Rex at Burdines. After what had happened now that Winston had gotten rid of Rex, working conditions might be strained. She was not resigning because of Rex but would wait until the next work week to see how things might be. Patrick and Andrew dropped Eveline off in the front of 825 saying they would soon be living in the apartment she occupied. Eveline did not like the tone of the remark and lectured them on how to speak to her. Patrick apologized and was only trying to speak about the future, not make her feel put out. While she stood at the curb she said, "This has been a bad evening. I realize how important it has been for me get a better understanding of why people do what they do. You boys need to reconsider your attitude and actions. Your lives have been well taken care of and I tried to keep you out of the family business. I hope this event tonight will set you in the right direction." They looked like little boys being scolded, but Eveline did not care how they felt. She turned and went inside with new hopes for Jonathon and herself.

Before she went to sleep, all she could think of was how good it would be if Jonathon would make love to her as he once had. She was more than ready for all he had to offer her and her sensations were making her crazy for love. She reminded herself not to fall into the Trixie patterns she had once resorted to.

Winston telephoned Eveline to discuss all that had happened the previous evening. He apologized for being so violent in front of her. Eveline told him she was not upset. Winston explained that he had sent Rex a note reinforcing the fact that they were finished. Eveline complimented Winston on finally understanding that his feelings and anger had been hidden for many years. He agreed and asked how she would handle her job. Eveline explained that she would not let anything get in the way of her success at Burdines. Winston understood her determination to do a good job regardless of Rex. He asked if she had looked into places to live. She had not and gave him her philosophy that all things work for the best. Winston said, "You are amazing. You have lived through more than most."

The telephone rang. Eveline answered it and heard Jonathon's voice. Her heart started racing when he asked her to go to dinner. Eveline was in a flurry because this was what she had hoped for. She reminded herself of all that she and the doctor had discussed about relationships. It had been a long time since Jonathon and she had spent time together. Eveline worried about all that Jonathon had listened to and did to get her back to Miami and into counseling. Eveline felt Catherine coming after her and could hear the terrible words of "You are not worthy of such a good man." She wanted to call someone or do something but nothing seemed logical. Before she panicked, she decided to go outside and stand by the gate. Soon, Jonathon pulled up and got out and opened the door for her and looked at her legs as she sat down. He said, "You look as pretty and appealing as always." Eveline felt like she had never been treated better.

Jonathon had reserved a table in an intimate restaurant. The valet parked the sports car and they entered a classy environment where soft music could be heard. Eveline said, "Oh Jonathon I feel like we are in heaven." He smiled as he helped push her chair in. While having cocktails, they discussed the past. Jonathon explained that he had always cared for her in the deepest way. As he said, "Eveline you were the only woman who accepted me for what I am and what I do. I wanted to continue with our relationship, but realized I had overstepped professional boundaries by falling for you. I will never forget how many places we made love no matter who could see us. I had to end the affair because you were in a desperate place. That is why I stopped and paid for your counseling. I hoped you would get better and we might revive our relationship. After seeing you in the strangest places with crazy things happening and watching you react the other night, I knew you were better." Eveline sipped her cocktail feeling like she wanted to jump over the table and caress every part of Jonathon's body. Her sexual tension had not been like this in many months.

Eveline explained about her counseling and how much she had learned about her past life and childhood. She asked, "Jonathon, what is your relationship with Doctor Kane?" He told her that they had been in training school to learn about psychological patterns that people exhibit when in a crisis situation as she had experienced during her Fugue State. Jonathon referred to the study by the French psychologist that Doctor Kane had studied about and he was able to help her to understand that behaviors both good and bad come from childhood experiences. While he was explaining these things, Eveline wondered if Doctor Kane and Jonathon had a thing for one another. She asked him if that might be a possibility. Jonathon's eyes went up saying, "No way, we have been friends for a long time." Eveline explained that she seemed to attract men who like other men. She laughed saying, "At least this time, I don't have to compete with another man." Jonathon assured her that would not be a possibility.

During dinner, Jonathon inquired about her work at Burdines. Eveline explained how well she had been doing and that she liked her work. She told him how proud she was of herself for overcoming her financial disaster. Jonathon asked how she planned to deal with Rex Berman after what had happened. Eveline shrugged her shoulders saying, "That is his problem. I will continue as if nothing happened." Jonathon congratulated her on her attitude. Then, he told her that she might not need to worry about that. She asked why. Jonathon said that he had to write a report about the people who had not been arrested from the event the other night. The problem with Mr. Berman was that he had been arrested many times for brutally injuring other men. When Burdines learned of this, Mr. Berman had been put on probation. If he were to be arrested again, he would be fired from the store. Eveline shocked, said, "Who will take his place?" Jonathon was not sure but he had a hunch it might be her.

While having dessert, Jonathon discussed his job and how he felt a need to have a change. Eveline hoped this might be leading up to a plan that might involve her. Jonathon had years of experience in detective and security work and explained how tired he was of dealing with criminals. Security for high level people was what he wanted to do. Eveline sensed that he was not thinking about her being included, as much as about himself in his work. Eveline asked, "Where will you find work such as this." Jonathon said, "President and Mrs. Roosevelt have offered me the job of Head of Security for them. I received a letter from them last week and met them while they were in Miami." Eveline wondered if that had been the reason for the visit and not to see the show at the store. She now wondered what Mrs. Roosevelt meant when she told Eveline about a letter being sent to her. There must be a plan in the works that Eveline might be part of, but had not been privileged to know yet.

While returning to Miami Beach, Eveline wanted to ask more questions about Jonathon's intent to work for the President. She decided that whatever Mrs. Roosevelt meant when she spoke to her at the store would have to be dealt with later. She felt confused and anxious. Jonathon pulled up to the front of 825 and kissed Eveline good night. Eveline decided to invite him in for a night cap. As they went into the apartment, Jonathon went for Eveline in a way she had never remembered. He caressed her arms and followed up to her neck as he unzipped her dress. She began to fondle him and had forgotten how well-endowed he was as she moved herself closer to his groin. Eveline felt his hands between her legs as he lifted her into position as he had done many times. They kissed in passionate ways over their bodies. Jonathon squeezed Eveline as he moved his tongue over her. Eveline could not get enough of Jonathon as they broke into a sweat that ran down their legs. He ran his hands through Eveline's hair as she caressed, manipulated, and stroked Jonathon to a point of ecstasy. Eveline remembered how she could manipulate Jonathon and positioned herself for him. She accepted and teased him, while Jonathon kissed her admitting he had missed her. Eveline, in such a heat of passion, had a difficult time not to admit that she loved him.

CHAPTER 50

The political and economic climate had not improved as Congress and President Roosevelt had hoped it might, gripping the United States and the world. President Roosevelt introduced the Second New Deal that was instituted to improve the condition of the roads, flood zones, and public buildings. By establishing the Second New Deal, there would be more jobs available and would help to improve the economy, or so it was hoped. Bridges and damns were being built throughout the country. Hoover Dam had been completed and more dams were to be built, as part of the Tennessee Valley Authority, for flood control and developing electrical power plants from the dams. While reading about the Second New Deal in the Miami Herald, Eveline saw an article about Henry Ford. His seventy-third birthday had been on July 30, 1936. According to the report, there had been a large celebration at his summer home on Lake Superior. Eveline thought about how she had been part of Henry Ford's empire. She felt like her past was coming forward again. After thinking about all that had happened, as a result of being a major investor in his company, she decided it was not worth thinking about. She reminded herself that her life was different now and appreciated that she had come out of the financial downfall. All she hoped for was that Jonathon might ask her to become part of his new adventure in the Roosevelt administration.

During Eveline's job review at Burdines, the owner discussed Rex Berman's reputation. Eveline listened to the reasons why he had been fired from the store. Having been aware of the story, she did not divulge any knowledge about Rex. After receiving the highest review and a raise in pay, Eveline was offered Rex's job. The owner admitted that Rex had been good for the men's department, but lacked a thorough knowledge of their best customer's desires, who were women. Eveline would receive a clothing allowance for her wardrobe, a pay increase, and would be required to travel to fashion extravaganzas. As part of her responsibilities, beyond what she already did, she would oversee the buying department and offer suggestions after her travels to other merchandising companies. Burdine's philosophy would remain the same, "A Sunshine Fashion Store", but would maintain a competitive edge with all department stores in Miami. While Eveline listened to the extent of her new responsibilities, she wondered if she was capable of such a high position. As she thought about this, she heard a voice telling her to take the challenge. When the owner asked what her decision was, Eveline accepted. She knew that what she heard in her mind had been a result of her sessions with Doctor Kane, never to doubt yourself.

That evening while Eveline pondered all that had happened at work, she felt troubled about what might be happening between Jonathon and her. She had a gnawing feeling that her decision to start her new position at the store would create a difficult situation, if she were to be asked to go with Jonathon. Eveline felt that old voice nagging at her as she thought about her future. It pounded in her head telling her that she was not smart enough or capable of such responsibilities, much less the love of a man like Jonathon and she should kill herself. Eveline heard it over and over until she wanted to scream. She thought about calling Doctor Kane's office, but it was evening. She paced around the apartment wringing her hands and felt sweat on her body. The voice had never been as intense as it was for her at this time. As Eveline was in a near panic state, the telephone rang. It startled her and the voice stopped. When Eveline answered it, there was only the sound of breathing on the telephone and she slammed the receiver down. Now, Eveline panicked thinking that the voice she heard might be the same as the breathing on the telephone. She wanted to call someone but who would believe such a story? She kept reminding herself that this must be Catherine haunting her. Whenever there was a decision to be made, Eveline understood it was her mother who used to say such terrifying things to her. After she thought about what had been happening, she calmed down and rationalized the feelings. While Eveline sat attempting to rest, the telephone rang again. She wondered if she should answer it. It rang and rang and finally Eveline decided to answer it. When she said hello, she heard Jonathon's voice. He asked if she was alright. Eveline asked why. Jonathon said, "I just telephoned you and I did not recognize your voice. I thought I had the wrong number." Eveline listened and thought the voice he had heard sounded like her mother. She thought she was beginning to sound like her mother when these events happened. Eveline said, "Oh Jonathon I must have been hurrying to the telephone and sounded out of breath." Jonathon thought something was not right and said, "Are you okay?" Eveline told him she was and began explaining about her promotion at Burdines and all it entailed. Jonathon listened and congratulated her. He told Eveline that he had called to see how she was after their dinner and sexual reunion. While she listened, Eveline felt a hot flash as she had the night they made love. She sensed he might be waiting to be invited to her apartment. Jonathon said, "Just thought I would call to see what you were doing." Eveline shook her head and knew she could never tell the truth about what had just happened, no matter how much she wanted Jonathon to make love to her.

The Miami Herald featured a section about what the current events were in the world. The Depression had ravaged not only the United States but it had an effect also in Europe. The Roosevelt administration had continued a policy of isolationism with Europe and according to the newspaper, there had been Nazi takeovers. Germany never repaid the United States for their debt from World War I and Roosevelt felt by leaving Europe alone, Germany might repay the debt to the United States. The Olympics were being held in Berlin in August. According to the reports, the removal of the Jews was not obvious in Berlin. There had been no official report of any wrong doing and Berlin was preparing for the Olympics. The United States had not been planning on sending athletes because of the "Stay Out of European Business" policy. After much prodding from the athletic world, athletes were to be sent to Berlin for the Olympic Games. Reports coming from Berlin gave no cause for concern. The people appeared friendly and happy, as the city welcomed the Olympics. There was suspicion that Adolf Hitler and his Nazis were up to something that had been covered up in Berlin.

The new responsibilities at Burdines turned out to be less of an issue than Eveline had panicked about a few days earlier. During her first week she met with the buying department and planned the fall and winter fashion outlook. The term "outlook" was a new way to focus on seasonal buying. The buyers liked Eveline's approach and told her how demanding and cruel Rex Berman had been. One man in the department said, "Berman was like a crazy man who acted like he wanted to torture people if they did not do what he demanded." Eveline listened, never admitting to anything she might know. When she returned to her office, there had been a telephone call from Jonathon. The message read... Can you do lunch today? Call me at the police station. Eveline would have lunch with Jonathon no matter what she had to cancel. Eveline called and agreed to lunch. Jonathon suggested the Tropical Paradise Restaurant between Burdines and the police station.

The atmosphere of the restaurant was like being on a tropical island, not downtown Miami. Jonathon kissed Eveline when she arrived. He admired her classy outfit and her professional manner. While they were enjoying lunch, Jonathon said, "Eveline, there is something I need to discuss with you." Eveline thought he was preparing to ask her to come with him to Washington. He continued, "You know I am leaving in a few days to begin my work for the Roosevelt's." Eveline listened and wondered if she had missed something when he said, in a few days. She thought he may not be going for a while. Jonathon explained the plan had changed and he would be needed in Washington sooner than expected. Eveline admitted she thought he was staying longer. He asked if she had found an apartment yet. He knew that she needed to leave 825 by September. He asked, "Would you be interested in my apartment?" Eveline's mind went into a spin when she thought about how it might be to live in Jonathon's apartment with his furnishings and not him. Jonathon watched as Eveline tried to avoid the question. She really wanted to ask him if she could go to Washington with him. Now, she knew that was not part of the reason for the lunch date. Eveline tried to fight off the tears but was not strong enough saying, "Jonathon, how could I possibly live in your place without you. I have a hard enough time when I think about you. I would miss you so much and especially knowing how far away you will be. I may never see you again." While Eveline had been telling Jonathon these things, he realized that she had never received the letter that Mrs. Roosevelt had mentioned to Eveline. Jonathon said, "It was only a thought and I could come to see you when I get a chance." Eveline shook her head saying. "I can't agree to such an arrangement. I need more stability in my life. You know what I have been through. I would love to be with you more." Jonathon agreed that he was going to miss her but he needed to leave. Jonathon said, "The offer will be open for you. I will pay the rent for a few months to let you decide if you want to do this."

When Eveline returned to the office, she was a mess from crying. Her makeup had run and her eyes were red. She had blown her nose so much it appeared swollen. She sat at her desk thinking that she could never live in Jonathon's apartment. She would think of him and miss him more than if she moved to a new place. While she was trying to straighten up, Jonathon telephoned. He asked if she was alright. Eveline began to sob. Jonathon knew he would miss her as much as she would miss him. He told her so. Eveline said, "Then why don't you ask me to go with you?" He told her he thought she wanted to be a success in her work and would not want to leave. Eveline tried to control the sobs, but to no avail. She explained how much she cared for him. Jonathon admitted that he missed her more than she knew when they did not see one another. Jonathon explained that his offer was the best he could do, considering the situations and her new job. He invited her for dinner before he left for Washington. Eveline sobbed as she told him okay. After the conversation, Eveline was in no condition to work. She left the office and took a taxicab, instead of the bus, to 825. During the ride, she had never felt so confused and sad about someone she wanted to be with. When she entered 825 and looked at the mailbox, there was an envelope addressed to Mrs. Eveline Paine from the Office of Mrs. Eleanor Roosevelt, 1600 Pennsylvania Avenue, Washington, DC.

CHAPTER 51

————— ∞ —————

A s Eveline went to her apartment, she stared at the envelope remembering the last time she received correspondence from Mrs. Roosevelt. Eveline had been expecting this letter, but was now feeling uneasy about its contents. She opened the letter and saw that Eleanor Roosevelt had a personal seal on her stationery. The last letter she had received did not appear as formal. It read:

Dear Eveline Paine:

I hope this letter finds you well and enjoying your successes at Burdines Department Store. When we met, a few weeks ago, you were in the midst of a fashion extravaganza that was grand. I wished I could have stayed longer to see more fashion ideas. Franklin and I were on a busy schedule but I made time to see you and another person on business matters while in Miami. I have written this letter to discuss some unfinished business between you, myself, and Franklin.

As you well understand, business is business, and there is a need to discuss the resignation of your sons, Patrick and Andrew Paine, that we had sponsored at West Point. Part of the agreements we entered into with West Point were that Patrick and Andrew would complete the program and become officers for the United States Armed Services. This has not happened and we are left to retrieve the funds that we allocated for their academic training. I am not certain that Patrick or Andrew understood the ramifications of their resignations on the contractual agreement. It clearly stated that if the cadets do not become officers, all monies are to be returned to the sponsors. We have no choice but to negotiate a repayment for their termination at West Point. Since you are their mother, we felt you should be the first to know.

Franklin and I have discussed a few options for the reimbursement of funds. The first option is that Patrick and Andrew reimburse the government. The second option could be that you and they contribute to the reimbursement to the government. After doing some investigation, we were uncertain of the financial stability of your sons, so the second option may not be possible. The third option would focus on you to deal with the government. Unfortunately, the amount in question is almost a quarter of a million dollars for expenses accrued during the years Patrick and Andrew attended West Point.

If we were to entertain the third option, you would become part of my department. As you may know, I have many goals for improving our rights for women and social changes. You would be working with my staff and traveling to various places. You would not receive a salary, but would become one of my assistants, with all essentials for living taken care of. After knowing about your husband and his past criminal activities with human trafficking, especially children, I would be placing you as an advocate for children and their well-being. In addition, because you were so instrumental with the Women's Rights Movement, I would be working with you and utilizing your expertise with social reform and women's rights. These are my top priorities.

I understand this letter may come as a shock after all you have managed to overcome, but we need to settle a debt. If you choose option three, you will be working in a positive way for our troubled society. Please give this your attention and your decision within a week.

Respectfully yours,
Eleanor Roosevelt

After reading the letter, Eveline sat and thought about all that the letter had stated. While she pondered the possibilities, she began thinking about her children. They did not have the money or the ability to repay the debt to the government. She was still furious about what they had gotten into at the Acey Doucey Club and the reason for leaving West Point. The work they did for Winston did not nearly pay enough to repay the government. She thought about what type of future Patrick and Andrew would have operating Bohemia 825 and she still did not understand what type of business would be available to the discrete traveler. To Eveline it sounded suspicious. Was she ready to leave her position at Burdines that she did well with and enjoyed? She would never be able to repay the government nearly a quarter of a million dollars on what she earned. While thinking, she felt anger about all the money that had been taken from her because of the past and corrupt people. Now, she had been hit with yet another financial situation that she needed to deal with. She thought about Jonathon's behavior when he hesitated the day they had lunch by changing the subject about his going to Washington. While questions went through Eveline's mind, she realized she did not react as she once might have. Not in a desperate way, she asked herself what the best thing would be for her to do. Forgetting her job, her children, Winston, Sable and Olitha and leaving Miami, might be the best chance to survive and begin a new chapter in her life. She took a deep breath and had made her decision. It was time to let it all go and start over. The time was right; Eveline told herself that she had only herself to rely on. Now, she would no longer worry about a place to live. She did not have to give Jonathon an answer about his apartment. Her children would have to make it on their own. As far as Winston was concerned, Eveline reminded herself of how much she had helped him as he had her, but it might be time to say goodbye. The thought about working with Eleanor Roosevelt in a new place was just what Eveline knew she needed. She composed her response, it read:

Dear Mrs. Roosevelt:

Thank you so much for your letter. It came as a surprise because of situations I and others were not aware of. In regard to my sons, they are not financially able to repay the government, as you stated in your letter. My work at Burdines Department Store is wonderful, but the salary could never repay you. In light of all that, I am accepting your offer to work with your staff on your social reforms for women and children. I look forward, with excitement, to be part of your work and philosophies. I will await further directives before I resign from Burdines.

Yours truly,
Eveline Paine

CHAPTER 52

After sending her acceptance letter to Mrs. Roosevelt, Eveline wanted to announce the news of her leaving. She knew that giving her resignation to Burdines should not happen until she received confirmation and orders from Washington. She did not want to make it look like she was abandoning them and she wondered about Patrick, Andrews's, and Winston's well-being. She had been worried about Winston after he admitted his reasons for getting involved with Rex. She wondered how she would explain the recent turn of events. Working at the store would be more difficult, at this time, now that she had plans elsewhere. She had not thought of how to manage her work and still be ready to go to Washington, without letting others know.

Patrick and Andrew had not made an effort to see or be in touch with Eveline after the fiasco at the Acey Doucey Club. She, instead of telephoning them, sent a note asking what they had been doing. Hoping to get some response, she waited. In the meantime, Winston telephoned Eveline. He admitted he had been lonely and down because of what his life had turned into. Eveline said, "Why don't you make an appointment to see Doctor Kane. He will be able to help you figure out what you might want to do with your life, now that you understand you had repressed feelings about Wallace, that you took out on Rex." Winston was not sure this was what he wanted to do when he said, "That was good for you because you are a woman. Men don't get into those brain things with other men. I would not want to give him the wrong idea." Eveline, when hearing such foolishness, said, "How dare you make such remarks? You make it sound like only women have issues. Let me tell you, men are the reason for the women's issues but we are smart enough to go for counseling. How could you forget all the times we worked for equality during the Women's Rights Movement in Seneca Falls?" Winston could be heard taking a deep breath saying, "Now, that you have supposedly cured yourself of all your problems, you think everyone else needs to go to Doctor Kane." Eveline replied, "What are you afraid of?" Winston admitted that Jonathon told him when they were going to Vancouver, that Doctor Kane could be with a man or a woman. Eveline could not believe what she had just heard. She ended the conversation telling Winston that she was sorry he was so against getting help, especially after all the experiences they had over the years. She told him that Doctor Kane may be exactly what he needed, counseling not sex.

Patrick and Andrew received their mother's note and were surprised she sent a note instead of telephoning. Andrew made the call to ask Eveline about her intent. When Eveline heard Andrew's voice, she waited to hear what he might say. The conversation was tense at first. Finally, Eveline asked, "Where have you two been? I hope not getting into more trouble." Andrew said, "Mother, what is going on?" Eveline explained that she wondered why they had not contacted her. Andrew apologized, saying they had been busy getting ready to move to 825 and told his mother about how depressed Winston had been. Eveline listened and realized she had worried unnecessarily about them. She knew that some of her anxiety was because of her business and leaving Miami. She said, "Honey, I need to have a conversation with you and your brother. I have had some news that concerns us. Can you come to see me?"

Within an hour the bell rang, it was Patrick and Andrew. Eveline hugged and kissed them when she saw how concerned they were. She gave them a drink and they listened to her read the letter from Eleanor Roosevelt. Eveline saw two young men look like little boys when she read the part about their resignation from West Point and what the ramifications had been. When she read the part about the amount and the repayment issue, they looked at one another and said, "We did not know this would happen." Eveline admitted this had been a shock to her also. Patrick asked how they could ever come up with so much money. Eveline looked them in the eye and said, "I have lost everything because of your father's and Mr.

Keyes' corrupt and criminal ways. I have barely made enough money to live on. Now, we are sent a letter with a price tag of a quarter of a million dollars. How do you expect to pay this back?" Eveline had not yet told them about the third option. The boys worried about what might happen if they did not repay the money for West Point. Eveline watched them squirm. She asked, "Do you now think that your resignation was worth it for the reasons you used?" Patrick was the first to say things had not turned out as they had hoped. After the fiasco with their supposed new friends in Miami and the near arrests from the Acey Doucey Club, they admitted they may have made a mistake. Eveline decided to read the rest of the letter instead of watching her children be so upset and discouraged. She said, "There is another part of this letter you need to understand. I have been offered a job to be part of Eleanor Roosevelt's staff. Instead of repayment, I will be working on social reforms for women and children. The reason I am being assigned to child advocacy is because of my experiences with your father's human trafficking, involving children. I will be leaving Miami as soon as I receive further instructions from Mrs. Roosevelt. It is time for me to leave all of you. I have spent my life taking care of and providing for everyone, at my expense. Now that I know more about myself and have proven I can survive, I feel it is time for me to move on. I want to seek a new life and adventure." There was no response from neither Patrick nor Andrew as they stared at their mother telling them what was about to happen.

Before they left, Eveline made sure they understood the importance of why she had decided to accept Eleanor Roosevelt's offer. She admitted she would miss them and it might be time for them to be more responsible with their lives and to stay in touch with her. Eveline requested that they not tell anyone else because she needed to have confirmation from Washington before she made her announcement. Andrew told Eveline he was proud of all she had done for him, especially adopting him after his parents had been killed. Patrick admitted he had forgotten how many times she had been there for them, no matter what the circumstances. Eveline told them that they would be free to move into 825 as soon as she received her orders. Before they left, Eveline said, "You two will never be too old to hear from your mother. I will always worry about you and hope you will take good care of yourselves." They kissed and hugged Eveline as they left. After the door closed, Eveline broke down and sobbed, wishing things would have been different. She told herself that this had happened many times in her life and that she needed to take care of herself. The time had come.

CHAPTER 53

Waiting for news from Washington did not happen as quickly as hoped. Eveline continued working at Burdines and Patrick and Andrew had begun moving into 825 Michigan Avenue. Patrick told Eveline that they needed to stay at the Tropical Gardens until she left because of Winston's mental state. Jonathon had made arrangements to have dinner with Eveline before he left for Washington. Everything appeared uncertain, which made Eveline tense. She found herself being tempted by old voices. Whenever she heard what a mistake she made, coming from her mother, she wanted to scream. Eveline worked hard not to succumb to her past.

After work, Eveline called Patrick to come to 825 to get her because she wanted to visit Winston and tell Sable and Olitha about her future plans. They came to 825 with more furnishings and drove Eveline back to the Tropical Gardens. When Eveline saw Winston she said, "Are you going to start behaving like you once did after Jason's death?" Winston made a face and said, "You don't understand how lonely I am. You never loved someone as I did Jason." Eveline saw fire when she heard Winston's remark saying, "How dare you tell me I never loved anyone. Yes, you are right about Wallace. You seem to forget my last year waiting and hoping that Jonathon and I would be together. I love that man. This is the first time in my life I have felt this way. So, don't feel too sorry for yourself." Winston had never heard Eveline be as direct with him as Patrick and Andrew stood motionless, Sable and Olitha came onto the veranda. They knew something had happened because no one moved or said a word. Olitha looked at Sable and said, "There they all goes again. Look like they be fightin about sumthin." Eveline, with hands on her hips, glared at the group, Andrew spoke up, "Mother has been lecturing all of us on many topics. She has new ideas for all of us." Eveline snapped back, "I'm

221

not taking over. I am telling you that I am leaving and that you all need to learn more about taking care of yourselves." Sable said, "Oh Miss Eveline wez love you and wez already knews you were gettin out of town." Olitha nudged Sable but had been too late after hearing about Eveline's news. Winston stared at Eveline as she waltzed around the group. He said, "We knew of your intentions." Eveline, assuming Patrick and Andrew had made the announcement, pointed her finger at them saying, "I thought I told you not to mention this news." They shook their heads as Winston said, "Jonathon and I had lunch and he explained about his moving to Washington to be Mrs. Roosevelt's body guard. He also told me that you had been requested to become part of Mrs. Roosevelt's staff." Now, Eveline wondered how much Jonathon had to do with the West Point situation and her working for Mrs. Roosevelt.

Sable had prepared cool drinks and snacks after the news had been discussed. While they sat on the veranda, Winston told Eveline that he had spoken to Doctor Kane, just before she arrived. Eveline, feeling foolish for being so direct with Winston, apologized. He did not mind and said, "That's what we love about you. You have a quick tongue and tell it like it is. We will miss that." Eveline frowned, but everyone found the remark funny. After a moment, Eveline smiled and agreed that she had been telling it like it was lately. Winston asked if she had any intention of visiting or returning to Miami. She told them she had not thought about that and was only waiting for her orders from Washington. Eveline asked, "Winston, did Jonathon tell you anything else about me? Did he mention if he had any involvement with my being called to Washington?" He changed the subject saying, "I am seeing the doctor in a few days." As the rest of the group watched, Eveline asked, "Is this for sex or counseling?" Winston had no response.

While Andrew drove Eveline back to 825 Michigan Avenue, the conversation centered on the Bohemia that was scheduled to open in a few weeks. Eveline, listening with only a half an ear, wondered more about Jonathon's involvement in her moving to Washington, than the new guesthouse for discrete travelers. Andrew spoke about the guests that had made reservations for November 1. He said he had not met Jerome, but he was the British gentleman that Winston had met earlier in the year when he made his reservation. Andrew reminded his mother that Jerome had purchased her yellow Buick convertible. Eveline shook her head saying, "That seems so long ago. I guess I had forgotten about it".

The next evening, Jonathon and Eveline were to have dinner. Jonathon would pick Eveline up and they were going to return to the restaurant they had dined in a few weeks earlier. Eveline dressed in a sophisticated outfit that she recently acquired from Burdines. When Jonathon saw her, he remarked at what a knock out she was. Eveline liked the remark but had never heard such an expression used about her. While having a cocktail, Jonathon held Eveline's hand and stared at her with lust in his eyes. Eveline had a difficult time concentrating on her drink; her body tingled as she too stared at Jonathon's face. After calming down, Eveline asked Jonathon what he knew about her going to Washington. She did not want to accuse him of anything. She had a need to know if he had more to do with the situation. Jonathon explained that he had known that there would have been a penalty for not completing the officer training program. He admitted that she would have never known the stipulations because Patrick and Andrew had been placed at West Point while they were supposedly kidnapped. He explained that Franklin and Eleanor Roosevelt had discussed this unfortunate situation with him and there had been no clarification of contract, when Patrick and Andrew resigned from West Point. He said, "The bottom line with the Roosevelt's was that a debt needed to be repaid."

During dinner, Eveline asked about his position as body guard to Mrs. Roosevelt. He told her that he would be one of many men and would be discreetly near all of the First Lady's staff. Eveline wondered if he had somehow arranged this situation so he could be more involved with her. She knew Jonathon wanted to do new types of work, but wondered if he had set this up with the Roosevelt's, so she would have no choice but to go to Washington. Her mother's voice interrupted Eveline's thinking, nagging her that she was not good enough for Jonathon. Eveline wanted to scream at the voice but took a deep breath saying, "Did you set this thing up to get me to Washington, so you could have your new job and me there too?" Jonathon looked devilishly at Eveline and winked saying, "You bet baby. We are on our way." Eveline wanted to jump over the table at Jonathon because now she understood how this all came to be.

CHAPTER 54

Early the next week, Winston had his appointment to see Doctor Kane. It was a few days before Bohemia was to welcome guests to the new property. Patrick and Andrew had been working on the last details and Eveline had not yet had any word from Washington. Everything seemed to be up in the air, which made her uneasy. Whenever situations such as these happened, she felt vulnerable to regressing to her old habits and would hear the voices nagging her that she was not worthy of anything good. Jonathon was scheduled to leave for Washington at the end of the week and Eveline hoped to see him before he left. She only had a few days left to reside at 825 Michigan Avenue and she worried that she may have to live on the street, after the discreet travelers arrived.

Winston arrived at Jackson Memorial Hospital trying to find Doctor Kane's office. He ended up on the maternity floor. The nurse inquired which baby he was there to see, as Winston blushed saying, "I have never been a father and am looking for the counseling offices." The nurse smiled and gave Winston the directions. While he left, he looked at the newborns and realized he had missed something in his life. He wondered what Doctor Kane would discuss and if he was ready to be counseled. When Winston entered the office, he saw women waiting. He wondered why he was there and thought he should leave before the doctor came for him. Just as Winston stood to leave, the doctor came out to invite him into his office. As Winston entered the office and shook the doctor's hand, it was as if electricity went through their hands. Each had firm handshake and Winston felt a growing sense of excitement. Doctor Kane looked Winston up and down intensifying Winston's arousal.

Doctor Kane sat across from Winston, not behind his desk. He sat in a casual way while he introduced Winston to what counseling would possibly do for him. Winston tried to look at the doctor's face, but had become so aroused he wondered if the doctor noticed. After some discussion, Winston knew he had come to the session for the wrong reasons. Doctor Kane asked if he was okay with what was happening. Winston thought he meant with his physical state. Winston nodded saying that he was okay. Winston asked what he should call the doctor. Doctor Kane told him it would be okay to call him Mitchell. Winston thought the name matched him perfectly. Then he remembered Eveline's question about him being there for sex or counseling. Doctor Kane asked Winston if he was uneasy because he had been fidgeting. Winston knew that the doctor had noticed that he had been positioning himself to conceal his excitement. He admitted that he was not sure what his reasons were for the visit. The doctor asked, "Has anything been bothering you lately?" Winston took a deep breath and explained his story that began with his love for Wallace. He described some of the activities they had engaged in, sometimes with more than he and Wallace. The doctor listened. Winston explained that he figured out why he had reacted to his latest affair with someone who resembled Wallace and the behaviors had been similar for both men. While Winston was speaking he realized that Wallace never acted as Rex had, sexually controlling and torturous. He clarified that with the doctor. Doctor Kane asked, "What was your childhood like and how did you become involved with Wallace?" Winston explained about his father's drunkenness and how abusive he had been to him. The doctor asked about his mother. Winston told him that his mother left and was never heard from. He admitted he had been abandoned both mentally and physically by his parents. Winston told the doctor that Wallace and he had been in school together and he had been in love with him from childhood. His attraction had been heightened when Wallace's mother took him in and treated him like a son.

After a break from the discussion, Doctor Kane inquired about how it had been being in love with a man who had been married. Winston explained that Wallace's wife never seemed to mind because she had all the money she needed and was involved with the Women's Rights Movement, while living in New York State. When the doctor heard the reference to

New York State he began to wonder if Eveline was the woman Winston had been describing. Winston explained how abusive Wallace was in an indirect way. He would never admit to his feelings and died before Winston could see him. Doctor Kane asked, "Have you had any other relationships that you felt good about?" Winston felt himself becoming emotional when he spoke about Jason. He told the doctor that Jason was the only man he truly felt loved by. The doctor picked up on the remark and asked why he had felt that about Jason. Winston explained that they were perfectly matched for each other and had come from similar family backgrounds and had a deep appreciation for each other. He continued with Jason's unfortunate death while flying back from California and that he had suffered from depression as a result of his death. Finally, Doctor Kane needed to clarify his thoughts and said, "The stories you have told me sound familiar to me. I have wondered if I may have counseled or know people you have spoken about." Winston had assumed that the doctor knew all about him before the appointment. Winston said, "I am here because my friend has been to see you many times." Then, the doctor figured out the connection. He said, "Oh, you are friends with Eveline Paine." Winston nodded. Doctor Kane said, "That clears up some of my confusion. I know about all the dimensions of Eveline's life and her friends." Winston wondered what he meant by the word dimensions.

After some discussion of the personal connections they both knew of, the doctor asked Winston what he expected to accomplish during counseling. Winston explained that he finally understood why he had become involved with Rex Berman. The doctor told Winston that it was good that he understood why he reacted to Rex. It was suppressed feelings that he never had been able to conclude with Wallace. Winston explained that he has been lonely and feels that he has no reason to live. He admitted he may never find another person like Jason. Doctor Kane asked what Winston was doing to meet new people. Avoiding the question, Winston explained how all of his former partners came to be. While Winston spoke, he wondered how this conversation had affected the doctor. After he finished explaining his past, Doctor Kane told Winston that his feelings were not unusual and that there were many possibilities for the future. Winston still felt aroused even after nearly an hour looking at and listening to the doctor. He found his mind focusing on what the doctor might be like outside of his office. Doctor Kane said, "Winston, I find your situation fascinating. I have heard similar stories but I find I cannot continue seeing you for counseling. There are too many situations and people that might get in the way of good counseling sessions. As you know, Jonathon Bingham and I have been friends for many years. He has spoken about Eveline Paine, her family, and her background. I feel I could not do the best work for you because I have too much prior knowledge. There are other counselors I could recommend for you, if you wish to continue." Winston listened but had a feeling the doctor only told part of his reason for not wanting to have him as a patient. Doctor Kane asked Winston if he had any further things to discuss, otherwise, he would not be charging Winston for his visit. He said, "Maybe we could go out sometime and you could make this up to me." Winston smiled for the first time in a long time saying, "You name it, and I'm ready."

After leaving the hospital, Winston decided to stop at Burdines to see Eveline. He had the valet park the automobile and he went to the fashion office. When he walked into the office, the receptionist thought he was there to apply for a modeling job. She looked Winston over and asked what his hourly rate might be. Winston, thinking she meant he might be a hustler said, "I don't charge for my services." Just as he finished, Eveline came out of her office and went up to Winston and hugged him and gave him a kiss on the check. The receptionist looked embarrassed and apologized. Winston said, "Oh that is alright. This has been my lucky day." Eveline asked why. Winston explained about his meeting with Mitchell. She looked confused as Winston told her how his appointment went at the hospital. Eveline smirked saying, "Already on a first name basis. Is there anything left of the doctor?" Winston smiled with a twinkle in his eye, admitting they would not be in a counseling situation anymore. Eveline shook her head and laughed saying, "I knew it. You have another one on the hook."

That same evening, Eveline arrived home from work to find Patrick and Andrew, moved into the apartment she had occupied. They apologized for moving in so soon but handed her a registered letter from Washington. Eveline had forgotten how disturbed she had felt finding her apartment had been overtaken by her sons, she opened the letter and it read:

Dear Eveline,

I am sorry to have taken so long in responding to your acceptance letter. We have been busy reorganizing my offices. I am pleased to welcome you as part of my staff. As you know, Jonathon Bingham will be one of my bodyguards, along with other men covering my staff, as he will be in full charge of our security. He and you will travel to Washington on American Airlines on November 1. All expenses are covered, all you need to do is to bring your personal belongings and Jonathon and you will be greeted at the airport. Hoping and looking forward to a long association.

Respectfully yours,
Eleanor Roosevelt

Eveline read the letter to her sons and said, "This has worked out perfectly. Your business is opening on November 1 and Jonathon and I are leaving the same day. She picked up the telephone and dialed Jonathon's office. He answered and Eveline screamed into the telephone, "Jonathon, I received my orders from Eleanor Roosevelt. We are leaving on November 1. Let's celebrate." Jonathon laughed saying, "Yes, Eveline I know. I wanted you to get your orders before I mentioned it. Of course we can celebrate. Shall we start in the bedroom?" Eveline's eyes blinked as she said, "Oh baby, you bet we can start there. I need everything you have to offer and more." Patrick and Andrew stood watching their mother turn red hot with excitement.

CHAPTER 55

Things began to move quickly after receiving the letter from Eleanor Roosevelt. Before handing in her letter of resignation at Burdines, she thought about how down and out she had been when she first began working at the store. Nearly penniless and wearing outdated clothing, Eveline had proven that she could overcome the worst of odds. Thanks to Jonathon's encouraging her to go into counseling she has come to a new horizon in her life. As she walked into the personnel office, she reminded herself that she would always be able to depend on herself and that everything worked out for the right reason.

That evening, Jonathon and Eveline were to have a celebration. As promised, Jonathon appeared at 825 ready to celebrate in the bedroom, before dinner. Eveline met Jonathon at the front gate and noticed he wore a casual outfit instead of his usual attire, a suit. It was a warm evening for the day before Halloween. His shirt was unbuttoned half way. When Eveline saw this, she felt the familiar hot surge of desire. Patrick and Andrew had occupied the apartment and Eveline knew that would be uncomfortable going to bed with their belongings around. When she explained the dilemma, Jonathon smiled in a devilish way saying, "Let's do what we used to do in the backyard." Eveline's eyes went up saying, "It might be fun for old time's sake." They went to the backyard, which had become more of a jungle, tore off their clothing and began rubbing against one another. Eveline felt Jonathon against her stomach while he caressed her. Being a warm balmy evening, it reminded them of the many times they had engaged in sex in that very place. The warm humid air enhanced the sensation as they perspired on one another. Eveline, being in such heat, succumbed to Jonathon. While they were in the height of ecstasy, Eveline whispered in Jonathon's ear, "Do you think we will get away with this around Eleanor Roosevelt?"

Mitchell telephoned Winston inviting him for lunch. It had been a few days since they met at the hospital and Winston had begun to think they might never get together. Mitchell suggested they go to Miami Beach for lunch and spend the day at the beach. Winston told him they could meet at 825 Michigan Avenue. Winston arrived earlier because he wanted to see how the preparations for the grand opening of Bohemia had progressed. Patrick and Andrew showed him around the property and Winston explained how important it was that there were places for guests to have privacy to do as they pleased, inside or out. Patrick said, "Oh there are places like that everywhere. Mother and Jonathon were running around naked and having their way with one another in the backyard." They laughed and said they found it exciting to have watched them. Patrick said, "Jonathon did not know it but he gave us some new techniques and ideas." Winston shook his head and walked away.

Mitchell arrived and Winston took him for a tour of the Bohemia. Patrick and Andrew were introduced as the owners and operators of the business. Mitchell wanted to know what type of guest facility this was intended to be. Winston explained that the name came from the country of Bohemia. The type of behavior in that country had the reputation of being Bohemian, meaning that anything goes. He explained that he wanted to establish a guest facility for the discreet traveler. Mitchell asked what that meant. Winston wondered if Mitchell was playing naïve when he asked these questions. He explained that some people go on vacation for privacy, not necessarily with their partner, and some will come to play and met other discrete guests. Mitchell said, "This sounds like it could fun, especially outdoors." To see what Mitchell's reaction would be, Winston told him about the day Jerome, a British man, came to the back gate and he greeted him naked. Without any hesitation Mitchell said, "This is my kind of place." Winston knew then that they were on their way to having fun. Winston and Mitchell set out with their bathing suits and beach equipment for an afternoon of lunch, sun, and fun.

November 1 was the day to leave for Washington and the opening of Bohemia. Eveline had packed her belongings in suitcases and had a steamer trunk full of her treasured mementos. As she finished packing the trunk, she felt teary eyed about leaving. A part of her felt she had abandoned her children, friends, and a job she had enjoyed and worked hard for. Her life had been uncertain for so long that this new horizon made her feel tense, even though she looked forward to it. Why couldn't my life have been easy, with having Jonathon stay in Miami and me at Burdines, she thought. She knew this move was the best way to settle some of the past while still being challenged with her new work. She belabored these issues until a voice told her to move on. This was a new voice that she had never realized. For so many years, she only thought she heard Trixie and Catherine terrorizing her. After calming herself, Eveline took a deep breath and remembered Doctor Kane's suggestion to listen to herself and her conscience.

The taxicab had arrived at the gate, Patrick and Andrew carried the trunk and suitcases to the waiting driver. Jonathon stood to the side, waiting, as he studied Eveline's sophisticated mannerisms and stroll, as she neared the waiting taxicab. He helped her into the back seat and commented on how nice her legs looked in her stockings. Eveline said in a suggestive way, "You probably want to take them off of me I suppose." He blushed as he closed the door. As the taxicab drove off, Eveline yelled to her sons that she would be in touch when she got settled. Andrew said, "I wonder if we will ever see or hear from her again?"

CHAPTER 56

Winston and Mitchell strolled to the beach after leaving Bohemia. They chatted about insignificant things. Winston listened to Mitchell tell about his younger days before he became a counselor. He had been treated much like Winston had been in early years. That was why he studied to be a counselor after he realized he might be able to help others who had difficult backgrounds. As Winston listened to Mitchell, he could not help but think about Jason. He asked himself why was he trying to get to know another person, especially after what he learned about Rex. Winston wondered if he was going to find out more about his past when he got to know Mitchell better. Was all this even worth it, Winston thought? Mitchell asked more about Winston's past and what his plans were for the future. Winston thought that was a lead question and still felt he was in the counseling office. He thought Mitchell did not want to discuss that type of thing. Winston decided to tell about his reasons for moving to Miami, because of his close relationship to Eveline. He told Mitchell about her gift of the Tropical Gardens to him and their moving to Florida to let the past go after the complicated situations related to Wallace's businesses and behaviors. Mitchell listened, asking no more questions.

During lunch, Winston felt uneasy and could not relax as he listened to Mitchell tell about his life and how he got to know Jonathon. Something did not make sense when Mitchell explained that Jonathon and he had lived together during their training. Winston felt like he might not be smart enough for Mitchell and still wondered as he listened if he was getting involved for the wrong reasons. He did not have the same feeling of aggression as he had while in the counseling office, things did not add up for Winston. Mitchell did not act as he had when he agreed to lunch and the beach. Winston wished he never had gone to meet Mitchell. Maybe he got the wrong impression of Mitchell or was this another of his needs to have a conquest. Winston wished that counseling might have helped him to understand why he had to be the aggressor in all of his relationships. He still had no answers and wondered why Mitchell was so interested in the atmosphere at the Bohemia.

After lunch, they found a place on the beach and set up for the afternoon. The sun felt hot for a November day. They went for a swim, both going in opposite directions. Winston watched Mitchell perform swimming strokes like a professional. He went far out in the ocean without any problem. Winston waded into the water until he could barely breathe. Mitchell waved his hand for Winston to come to him. Winston tried, but found his swimming ability to be less than Mitchell's. He came to Winston, taking him by the shoulders and pulled him to the deeper water. This scared Winston because Mitchell was taking charge as Rex had done. After some treading of water, they made their way to a sandbar. They were able to sit and see to the bottom of the ocean. The sand was soft as powder and warm to the touch. Mitchell asked, "Winston, are you okay? You seem to be in deep thought." Winston told Mitchell that he had been having flashbacks of other people in his life. Mitchell seemed confused and said, "I thought we had discussed that in the office and were ready to let that go." Winston nodded his head and moved closer to Mitchell. As the waves moved them back and forth, their bodies bumped into each other. Winston remembered the time when he and Mike were in Atlantic City with Eveline. There was not the same excitement today as then. Something made Winston less aggressive now.

The water was warm, the sun hot, and the atmosphere had affected Mitchell more than Winston. Mitchell let the waves push him into Winston. He knew what might happen next as Mitchell's hands moved around to investigate his body making him feel uncomfortable. All he could think of was Jason and wished it were him. Mitchell moved in a gentle way and was smooth with his movements. Winston thought that anyone else would love to be in his position. Mitchell was every bit what

Winston would want in a partner. What was wrong? Jason had been dead a long time and Winston thought he was ready to move on. He still felt depressed, lonely, and missed Jason more than ever. Mitchell backed away, saying nothing for a few moments. As they sat, Winston began feeling aroused and had a complete turnaround. He moved toward Mitchell, grabbed his swimsuit, pulling it down. Mitchell did not resist and allowed Winston to grope wherever he pleased. While they were at the height of arousal, Mitchell said, "Now I know what you are looking for." Winston's hands moved away asking what that meant. Mitchell said, "You want to be in control all the time. If you are to be in a relationship, you need to be the top man. Relationships are not like that, at least for me. A healthy relationship does not need to have a master and slave, like Rex wanted. I like no boundaries." Winston listened and knew Mitchell had been correct. Jason and he had the perfect relationship of give and take. Winston had convinced himself that might never happen again.

As the afternoon turned into evening and they walked back to Bohemia, Winston wondered how the day would end. He remembered how interested Mitchell was when Andrew and Patrick told about their mother and Jonathon doing as they pleased in the jungle like backyard. Maybe he needed to stop comparing his past relationships and enjoy Mitchell's kind and gentle personality. As they entered the back gate, Winston asked, "Would you like to take a shower and enjoy the freedom of the outdoors?" Mitchell nodded his head as he began taking his shorts off. Winston felt as aroused as he had the first time he met Mitchell. Within seconds they were under the shower washing one another's back. While Winston was massaging the soap around Mitchell's body, both men were engaged in each other while Patrick was touring a guest around the property. When they saw Mitchell and Winston, the guest said, "No matter what the price is, I want to stay for a week."

CHAPTER 57

Eveline and Jonathon had arrived in Washington as scheduled. The American Airline flight was much better than the time they flew back from California. This time they were treated to first class seating, and it was noticeable that air travel had improved. The seats were larger and more comfortable and anything they wanted was available. Eveline had a more difficult time tantalizing Jonathon because he was further away. Every time she attempted to arouse Johnathon he smiled and said, "Too bad for you. Maybe we should take the seats in the back of the airplane, they are smaller." Eveline smirked and said, "I hope we get to be with each other when we are in the midst of the Roosevelt's company." Jonathon shrugged his shoulders knowing that he had already been briefed on his responsibilities, many of which would not be in Eveline's company, much less in bed.

When the airplane landed, a limousine awaited to take Eveline and Jonathon to a government compound. Jonathon was less surprised than Eveline as they pulled up to a building that looked like a prison. Eveline said, "This is not what I had expected. This looks like a place for immigrants." Jonathon laughed and explained that it was a stop off point for them to be checked in and to verify their identification. He told her that everyone had to be registered to be part of the White House staff. Eveline made a face saying, "It sounds like we are working as housekeepers." Jonathon shook his head and made a face. Eveline knew she had said the wrong thing. When they entered the building, there was a group present to welcome them. Jonathon was taken to the security department and Eveline was ushered to Mrs. Roosevelt's office compound. When she entered, Eveline was surprised that there were so many women working on what seemed to be many different things. The woman in charge introduced herself as Mrs. Roosevelt's assistant for operations. She verified all of Eveline papers and explained that she would be having a meeting with Mrs. Roosevelt in the morning. Until then, Eveline was given information on living accommodations, and needed to fill out a form releasing the Roosevelt's from paying Eveline a salary for her work. For the first night, Eveline would be in a hotel adjacent to the White House. She was told that Mrs. Roosevelt had special plans for her and all this would be discussed at the morning meeting.

Eveline was told to wait at the entrance and the chauffeur would take her to the hotel. She was informed that there was no more need to pay for things because an account had been established by Mrs. Roosevelt. While she waited, Eveline wondered if Jonathon had been treated the same for the introductions. While she sat, the chauffeur came to her and told her he was ready to go. When Eveline got to the limousine, the windows were dark so she could not see who else might be in the vehicle. As she got in, Jonathon sat alongside of her and explained that he was her bodyguard for the evening. Eveline asked, "Why do I need you as a body guard." Jonathon whispered in her ear that Mrs. Roosevelt wanted her to be safe from any possibility of assault. Eveline asked what that meant. Jonathon explained, "Apparently, there had been rumors of criminals still looking for people who might have knowledge of a new type of crime involving businesses that have treated employees unfairly, many of whom are homeless and without jobs. Part of Mrs. Roosevelt's work is too advocate for workers' rights, especially women and child laborers. So, since you are a woman who has lived through some of these situations, you could be at risk and Mrs. Roosevelt wants you to be guarded until tomorrow when you will be assigned to a more secure environment." Jonathon did not tell Eveline that his first directive was to guard her because she had a debt to pay the Roosevelt's. He knew better than to tell her the whole story.

The hotel had been well decorated, but not to the level of the Biltmore. Eveline made certain Jonathon understood the differences. They were to have adjoining rooms. Eveline asked, "Why can't we stay in the same room?" Jonathon reminded her that they were now employed by the

Roosevelt's and this was not a vacation. Eveline wondered if this was going to be all she thought it might be or was this a planned event to get their money back? While she thought about this, she heard a voice telling her to beware. She tried to get rid of it but it kept nagging her. Jonathon had gone to his room to unpack before they went for dinner. Eveline did not find it necessary to do much unpacking, her trunk and suitcase were not coming to the room. All she had was a large purse that contained her essentials. Jonathon had less than she and she wondered why he had to leave. Was she becoming paranoid? The voice told her to watch out because there were underhanded people very near her. Eveline felt like she had before she left 825 Michigan Avenue. She reminded herself that these were desperate times for many people and anything could happen.

While Jonathon was in his room, he was directed to telephone the security office to report the safety of Mrs. Paine. They had separate rooms, so he could carry out his security work without Eveline listening to his business. Jonathon was not at liberty to tell her everything but there had been a threat made involving the people working for Eleanor Roosevelt. Because of the tensions in Europe, there were politicians and people in high places that were against the administration's views and activities and anyone connected with them. Since Mrs. Roosevelt had instituted reforms on the behalf of workers, there had been much unrest between the owners and workers. The administration had been blamed for the slow improvement of the state of the economy. Jonathon had been given orders to organize his security staff for an upcoming trip to California. While he was speaking about this business, Eveline knocked on the door. Jonathon ended his conversation because of the top secret information. He opened the door, Eveline walked in and asked if he knew more than he had told her. She said, "I have been nagged about being careful and that danger was nearby." Jonathon looked at Eveline in a strange way saying, "Are you going to start worrying about that stuff again?" Eveline, in a defensive way, said, "Never mind. I see that your new position might be changing you." He assured her that things would calm down when they became officially part of the Roosevelt administration. Eveline continued to be bombarded by something telling her to be cautious.

During dinner, Eveline tried not to compare the hotel to the Biltmore. She knew things should get better, but this place was not top notch. She felt like she and Jonathon were in a holding tank, as she put it. Jonathon told her that was preposterous, that she would expect this place to be like the Biltmore. Eveline calmed down after she sipped her cocktail. Jonathon suggested that she contact Patrick and Andrew to let them know they had arrived safely. When Eveline heard the word "safely", she made a face saying, "Are we safe?" Jonathon assured her they were safe as he opened his jacket showing a holster with a gun. Eveline's eyes opened wide as she said, "Okay, I guess we are safe. I'm not calling anyone until I feel like I know what I am doing." Jonathon said nothing as he watched Eveline's restless behavior.

CHAPTER 58

The next morning, Jonathon woke Eveline to prepare for their meetings. Jonathon would be going to the head security office in the White House and Eveline would be meeting with Eleanor Roosevelt in her private offices. During breakfast, Jonathon explained that he and his security agents would be assigned to different people depending on their proximity to the President and First Lady. Since Eveline had been personally invited to be part of Mrs. Roosevelt's staff, she would be under close scrutiny. Eveline asked, "How dangerous will this job be? You make it sound like we will be under the gun all the time." Jonathon said, "All persons close to the President and First Lady fall under the same security and protection. So, consider yourself lucky that my staff will be close by and you may not even notice our presence. We have been trained to be discrete, making us more likely to curtail any possible mishaps." Eveline smiled and told Jonathon that she hoped they could spend some personal time when not on duty. Jonathon smiled saying, "For now we will not be able to act as we did in Miami. When things become more routine, we might resume our relationship. The Roosevelt's understand our relationship and felt it would be good for you to be nearer to me. That is one of the reasons you were invited to work with Mrs. Roosevelt." Eveline thought, while Jonathon spoke, that was not all she was needed for. Everyone knew she owed them lots of money. Eveline thought that she should have made Patrick and Andrew be responsible for their debt. She wondered if staying in Miami might have been better for her where at least she was making it on her own.

When the limousine arrived, Jonathon escorted Eveline to the waiting chauffeur. He did not get in with her only told her that he would see her later. Eveline did not expect this and felt uneasy when the chauffeur got into the limousine and told her they were going to a private entrance to the

White House. Eveline was still not sure if this was how she had anticipated her life was to be. While they rode, Eveline had flashbacks of other times in her life that she felt like she had been told where she was going, often times without her fully knowing or approving of what had been happening. She thought of the rides with Wallace and Rudolph, not knowing what was going on, always being left in the dark. Eveline thought about how much information Wallace had left out about his money and businesses, she had fallen for his smarmy ways. When the limousine stopped, the chauffeur opened the door and assisted Eveline through an entrance to a well decorated and comfortable lobby. She thought this was more like what she had expected.

The secretary greeted Eveline and gave her some papers to fill out, while she waited for Mrs. Roosevelt. She briefed her on where she was to reside while working for Mrs. Roosevelt. Eveline was surprised to find out that she would not have one place, but many, depending on where her work might send her. This part, Eveline had not expected. She thought she might have one spot as her home, but now realized that was not the case. Another fear of uncertainty came over Eveline as she realized she was not independent anymore, like she had been in Miami. There were people coming and going into various offices and whenever a door opened, Eveline expected it to be Eleanor Roosevelt. After what seemed like an hour, Eleanor appeared. She walked up to Eveline and extended her hand saying, "Hello Eveline, I'm so sorry to have kept you waiting. I have been very busy these days. I can't wait to spend time with you and explain what you and I will be doing." Eveline smiled as they shook hands and said, "Thank you for having me and I am excited about my new endeavor." When they walked into Eleanor's office, Eveline wondered what all this might entail.

Eleanor and Eveline sat across from one another in comfortable armchairs in front of her desk. Eleanor was casual in her appearance; not like she had been other times in Miami. Eveline still could not believe she was in the White House speaking to the First Lady in such a casual way.

Eleanor appeared more down to earth than Eveline had expected and began to feel more at ease as they spoke. Eleanor explained that she was an advocate for social issues and activist. She told Eveline that the job she had for her was connected to work related situations for women and children's welfare, with some who had been made to work in dangerous places. When Eleanor discussed the child labor issues, Eveline remembered those times during World War I when children were made to fill jobs that men had done before they went off to war. Eveline discussed this with Eleanor and she smiled saying, "We have done a thorough background of you and found that you were capable of handling situations that involved human trafficking, child welfare, and women's rights." I felt after meeting with Jonathon that you were a good candidate for such reforms."

While having coffee and a cigarette, Eleanor explained that Jonathon was to be her personal bodyguard. Eveline listened as she was told Jonathon would have a staff of men that would oversee the security of her staff while Franklin had his own group of agents. Eveline got the feeling that the relationship between Eleanor and President Roosevelt was not close. She remembered the lunch at the Biltmore when Eleanor discussed her lack of interest in sex and had only done it to have children. Further discussion let Eveline understand that there were many close relationships that Eleanor had with women, as well as a few men in her recent past. Eveline wondered why Eleanor was telling her these things. She asked, "Will my work be here in Washington or will it be in another location?" Eleanor laughed saying, "Funny you should ask. There is a trip we will going on with my staff and some of Franklin's staff. After the trip my staff will be going to the Hudson River area. I had a cottage built near the Hyde Park estate called Val-Kill. As I explained to you when we had lunch at the Biltmore, Franklin's mother and I do not see eye to eye. Franklin is a "Momma's boy" believe it or not and is a President. So, in order that we are civil to one another, I have offices and a residence at the cottage not too far from the estate. I have the freedom to do my work, see whomever I please, and so does he." Eveline listened, thinking that their relationship had not been built on togetherness, just like hers and Wallace's had been. She asked, "After the trip you mentioned, where will my residence be?" Eleanor explained that she had many accommodations for her staff within the confines of the cottage property. She assured Eveline they were more than adequate.

Before the meeting ended, Eleanor explained that arrangements were being made for Franklin and herself and ten individuals for the trip. Eveline was one of them and Jonathon would be the other. Eveline was not sure to what extent all this was true, she still had a difficult time understanding that all this could be happening. Eleanor said, "As for you and Jonathon, I felt it was vital you stay in his company. He is a strong and confident man. If I were not married, I might like him too. However, I have had enough with men, but you and he should be together. We will work on times for you and he to continue whatever activities you have encountered with each other in the past. By the looks of things, I think you and he have hit it off." Eveline blushed and said, "After what you know of my past life, you understand about me and Jonathon. He is the best man I've ever been with and the only person I have ever loved."

CHAPTER 59

T he staff received a directive about the trip to California. Until the itinerary had been posted, Eveline had no idea where she would be going. Eleanor had only mentioned going somewhere, but no more information had been discussed. Eveline had thought she should not ask too many questions and had not seen Jonathon to ask him. After she read the memo, she packed luggage to be ready for the next day, November 11. The limousines would be at the front entrance of the White House at 7AM. While Eveline got ready for the trip, she remembered the turmoil she had experienced on the last trip to California and tried to put those events out of her mind.

The next morning everyone assembled, awaiting for the transportation to the airport. Jonathon was dressed in a suit that gave the impression he was there to maintain a secure atmosphere. Eleanor appeared with Franklin and greeted everyone as they entered the limousine. While going to the airport, Franklin explained that a select few had been chosen to accompany he and Eleanor to the opening of the Golden Gate Bridge in San Francisco. Jonathon winked at Eveline. Eleanor saw this and smiled at her. Eleanor discussed how important the Golden Gate Bridge was because it represented progress and had given thousands of people jobs during its construction. There had been many fatalities during those times and Franklin would be there to dedicate the bridge to those who lost their lives and those who helped complete it. President Roosevelt explained that he would be giving a dedication speech and Eleanor would be cutting the ribbon to open the 8 ½ mile bridge. The Claremont Hotel overlooking San Francisco Bay would be where they were staying for the night.

When they arrived at the airport, instead of going to the American Airlines terminal, they were taken to a government terminal. Any dignitary from foreign countries would come through the highly secured terminal.

Eveline had not expected such official treatment, and then realized this was how government officials live. When they entered the airplane it looked like a living room with large chairs, tables, and office equipment. This was better than the first class they had flown on from Miami. Eleanor had the women at one end of the seating area and Franklin had the men on the opposite side. Eveline thought it looked like they were not to speak to one another by the looks of the separated groups. Once the airplane reached the required altitude, the ride was smoother than commercial airplanes. Franklin informed everyone that the government airplanes were designed for comfort and longer distances.

During the flight, a meal was served with all the frills. Eleanor discussed her plans for the future with the women. Eveline wondered, as Eleanor spoke, if Franklin had given any ideas for his men. All they seemed to be doing was smoking cigars, which created a choking atmosphere. Eleanor apologized for such crude aromas but said, "Men have a way of being enthralled with the effects of that nauseous smell." It had not taken Eveline very long to understand the relationship between Eleanor and Franklin, professional but distant. Eleanor explained that she had a great input into Franklin's government affairs and that they respected their personal endeavors. Eveline wanted to ask what this meant but she decided to remain quiet and listen. Eleanor said, "I have been accused of being outspoken and a radical most of my life. One of my hopes is to expand the roles for women in the workplace, especially newspaper journalism and the media industry. I have been successful in writing my articles in "My Day" illustrating what is going on in the country. I have attempted to focus on giving hope to the women of our world. I would like to create a department for child welfare that would oversee the care and well-being for children that have been affected by the Depression, abuse, lack of housing, and education."

While the men smoked their cigars and enjoyed cocktails, they listened to Franklin discuss what he hoped for in the coming months. The unrest in Europe had become a growing concern for the United States.

He reviewed the need to be extra vigilant when it came to involvement outside of the United States. He mentioned this to warn the security men and staff that some folks did not like the philosophy of the government regarding international affairs. When Eveline heard this she understood what Jonathon meant about possibilities of assault on anyone connected to the Roosevelt administration. Franklin continued speaking about the Second New Deal and how it had affected the workforce. The opening of the Golden Gate Bridge was an example of the revival of the economy. Economic indicators had shown a rising economy but it had been slow in improving.

Eleanor and her staff listened to Franklin's ideas and she asked, "Franklin, what are your views on what I have explained to my staff?" All eyes were on the President who hesitated. He said, "All you have in mind is very good for women to work on. I think these are good ideas and should be developed. The men have a greater responsibility to the security and improvement of the economy." Eleanor gave Franklin a writhing look saying, "So, what you are saying is that your work is more important than ours. I suppose you haven't given any thought to the civil rights issues concerning the conditions for the Black Americans." Franklin paused as he glanced at the group and said, "I believe that is your business to attend to. You have been given the nickname of "Lady Bountiful" and you have a capable group of women working with you. I don't see any reason for further discussion or involvement on my part. I believe we all have enough to do to get this country back on track. The women have their goals and so do the men in our administration." Eleanor said nothing more as she looked at the women with a raised eyebrow. Eveline glanced at Jonathon, both expressionless, and wondered how this would all work out.

The pilot announced the time of arrival into San Francisco and advised to prepare for landing. Franklin said, "This has been the fastest flight to California I can remember." Eleanor responded in a sarcastic way saying, "Probably with all the hot conversation, the plane flew faster." Everyone laughed as they approached the terminal. Once they disembarked from the airplane, the government limousine was ready to go to the Claremont Hotel. They were told they would have a brief time to freshen up and settle into their rooms. The ribbon cutting ceremony at the bridge would be in 2 hours. This would be a short trip; they were departing in the morning to Washington. Eveline thought that this must be the life of high government officials.

The Claremont was an exquisite hotel that had been built in 1916. It had all the conveniences one could wish for. The Presidential suites were in a separate area on the top floor. This reminded Eveline of her life at the Biltmore. While they were escorted to their rooms, Eveline wondered what the room arrangements might be. She was surprised when Jonathon was to be in an adjoining room with Eleanor on one side and she on the other. The other guards were placed, one for the President, and the others for the remaining staff. Eleanor took Jonathon and Eveline aside and said, "I thought you might need some relaxation activities after we return from the ceremony." Jonathon said, "I am at your service and whatever you tell me, I will do." Eleanor replied, "I knew you would be a perfect match for what I want to establish." She winked at Eveline as she entered her suite.

During the Golden Gate ceremony, many dignitaries were present and there were armed service men on duty for the ribbon cutting and dedication. An Army marching band played music as the ceremony began. While this was happening, Eveline stood next to Jonathon with Eleanor on the other side. She thought about Patrick and Andrew the day she saw them in New York City in the West Point Marching Band. She wished they had remained at West Point and thought that she would not have had to work for Eleanor Roosevelt to pay their debt. She still was not certain this was the best way to have satisfied the financial commitment. After listening to the conversation on the airplane, her view of people in high places had been shocking to her. Never did she think there was so much divisiveness between the people who ran the United States. Jonathon sensed there might be something the matter as he noticed a dazed look on Eveline's face. He nudged her and she shook her head and smiled. She said,

"I was thinking of the time in New York when Patrick and Andrew were marching and playing in the band. I wonder how things might have turned out if they remained at West Point." Jonathon shook his head saying, "You will never know."

When they returned from the ceremony, dinner was served in a private dining room much like the Biltmore had been. After the meal and discussion of the day's events, everyone went to their respective rooms. The morning would come soon and the flight to Washington left mid-morning. After all was quiet, Eveline heard a knock on the door. She had just finished dressing in her silk negligee and opened the adjoining door. Jonathon stood at attention. Eveline nearly screamed with excitement as Jonathon came in and said. "I am here to investigate this room. Everyone in here needs to take their clothes off for inspection." Eveline giggled as she nearly tore her gown off. She had not been this excited since the last time they were together. Eveline mounted Jonathon's waist as he threw her on the bed. Eveline could not get enough of Jonathon's powerful body. They attempted to be quiet so as not to disturb Eleanor, but when they were in the heat of arousal, Eveline moaned, "Oh. I want more. Do it again." Jonathon did as he was told and they went well into the night.

The next morning, Eveline had to work at looking rested and refreshed. As she looked in the mirror, she saw marks on her neck and cheeks. She covered them up with her makeup and wondered what Jonathon might be showing. Probably nothing on his face, she thought. Jonathon could cover up from his neck to his ankles. Eveline had gone wild on him and could not remember all the things she had done to him. When she left the room and entered the hallway, Eleanor appeared at the same time. She looked Eveline up and down saying in her smooth way, "I heard you had a wild night. I sensed Jonathon might be good, but you made it sound like he enjoyed his work."

CHAPTER 60

B ohemia 825 had become a popular place for discrete travelers and after a few months in operation, there had been very few vacancies. Patrick and Andrew found themselves busier than expected. When they told Winston this, he suggested that they could send extra money to help pay off their debt to the Roosevelts since neither of them had thought of those possibilities. After discussing the matter, they made a commitment to send a portion of the profits each month to help lower the debt owed to the Roosevelts. When they told Winston about their decision he said, "Who knows, if the debt gets paid sooner, maybe your mother will want to come back to Miami." Andrew told Patrick it would be great to have their mother back home. Patrick sensed that Andrew missed having their mother nearer to them than he did and wondered why.

On one of the busier days at 825, both Patrick and Andrew had been serving meals, cleaning, and answering the telephone for reservations. While in a busy moment, the telephone rang and Patrick answered it hearing Sable's voice saying, "Is dat you Patrick? Iz been meaning to call use. How business goin? Iz be wonderin if me and my Big Bunny could come to see use?" Patrick's mind began to race when he thought about what Sable had in mind. He asked, "When were you thinking of visiting? We are very busy." Sable in a nervous way said, "Wez dooz not want to stay overnight. Iz wanted to have my Bunny give it all to me in the backyard. Iz been told it like a wild jungle and peoples can do whatever theys pleases." Patrick's eyes went up when he listened to Sable's request and knew that Winston had been the one to tell about the atmosphere at 825. Sable cut in saying, "Iz be wantin to get my Bunny neked in the outdoors and wez can't do it where wez living." Patrick knew he might be making a mistake but told Sable they could come over anytime they

249

pleased. When he hung up the telephone, Andrew entered the office and asked who he had been speaking to. Patrick explained about what Sable had requested. When Andrew heard the request he said, "Oh Patrick, I hope they do not come over when we have all types of people relaxing and enjoying themselves. I'm not sure I want to see Sable and her Bunny doing what mother and Jonathon have done in the backyard." Patrick made a face and said, "Maybe they will be here on a slow day. I'm not going to be around for what that might turn into."

Andrew had gone to the store, leaving Patrick to manage the property. The bell rang and Patrick went to see who it might be. Two men stood peering through the gate as Patrick walked toward them. They held a brochure of places to stay in Miami Beach. Patrick opened the gate and invited them in. They explained that they had been staying at a hotel closer to the beach but saw the brochure for Bohemia. Patrick asked them how long they were in town. One was a white haired classy Frenchman. You could tell he had come from a charmed environment and enjoyed the finer things life had to offer. Patrick noticed the style of clothing the French man wore, with jewelry of the highest quality. Patrick asked what his name was. He said, "I am Francois and this is my German companion, Max. We are looking for an accommodation for a week." Patrick looked at the German and wondered what he might be like. He had been smoking a cigarette and spoke very little and had a similar style in his appearance as the Frenchman. Patrick told them that he had an apartment available on the first floor. It was obvious that Francois had been the one looking for a different place to stay when he said, "So, Max, what do you think?" Max asked to see what the rest of the property looked like. His response was firm when he said, "We are looking for a place that we can do as we please." Patrick assured them that this would be exactly what they wanted. When they saw what was happening in the backyard, Max looked at Francois and said, "This will be perfect. Here I can train you the way I want." Patrick watched the German stare at Francois letting him know who was in charge. While Francois and Max were in the office settling the bill, Patrick asked what type of work they did. Francois told him that they were jewelry dealers from Paris. Max said, "We come to the United States to buy jewelry for our boutiques in Paris. Francois and I like to model the jewelry we find and we do not like to wear anything else while on vacation." Patrick smiled as he handed them the keys wondering what these two men were going to be like.

Later that day, the telephone rang, it was Sable. Patrick knew what she was about to ask. Without letting her speak, Patrick asked, "Are you calling about you and Big Bunny coming for a visit?" Sable yelled, "You bets. I be savin my sugars for my Big Bunny. He and Iz gone be chasin each others all round dat backyard like Miss Eveline dun do wit Mr. Jonathon. I bets my bunny be bigger than what I saw on Mr. Jonathon." Patrick shook his head wondering what 825 Michigan Avenue was going to turn into. Maybe he and Andrew could get Winston to advertise for contests with the guests for the best backyard demonstrations. He laughed when he thought that he and Andrew could be the judges and offer free accommodations to the winners. Patrick told Sable that they could come over the next day. He hoped they might not come until later in the morning when the guests usually went off to the beach.

Patrick telephoned Winston to explain about Sable and the European guests. Winston thought it was funny when he heard about Sable's request and the description Patrick gave of the jewelry dealers. Winston said, "Maybe I should invite Mitchell over to 825 to watch the live action." Patrick told him it did not matter because it seemed people were coming from everywhere for the atmosphere. Winston reminded him that "sex sells" and they were making money off of people's need to be discrete and be free in a naturist environment. Winston asked if they had heard from their mother. Patrick said they had not and he was not sure if they ever would. He told Winston he had a feeling his mother would always be on the run. Winston said, "You may be right. Eveline has had a tough time wherever she has been. Maybe she will never change. She wanted you guys to be in Miami and now she left. We know about the debt to the

Roosevelts, but she might have used that to subconsciously find a reason to leave. I think your mother will always be running away from herself." Before they ended the conversation, Patrick asked about offering naturist activity contests for the guests. Winston agreed it might be fun, but he discouraged the idea by explaining that when running a place for discrete travelers, the guests might not appreciate such publicity. Patrick thought about that and agreed. After, Patrick thought about how lucky he had been to have Winston, because he had been the father that Wallace never could have been.

A massage service had been popular at Bohemia. There was a secluded area for the massage table with a masseuse available 24 hours a day. Francois had scheduled a massage the next morning. When Patrick had explained to Andrew about Sable coming, they hoped the massage and her activities with her Big Bunny did not occur at the same time. After the morning meal had been cleared, Francois appeared in the office and asked where his massage was to take place. Andrew had not met him yet and was surprised at what he saw. Only wearing a leather lariat around his neck and a towel in his hand, Andrew escorted him to the waiting masseuse. As Andrew was going back to the office, he saw Sable and her Big Bunny getting ready to ring the bell. He thought, "oh no", but let them in and Sable and her Big Bunny chit chatted about things with Andrew. Sable inquired if they had heard from their mother. When she heard the answer, Sable did not think that was very good that Miss Eveline took off and had not let anyone know anything. While they were chatting, they walked to the jungle environment. Sable said, "This is better than when wes worked here fo Miss Eveline. Use could get lost in here." Andrew escorted Sable and Big Bunny to an area furthest from the massage area. He could see as he walked by that the masseuse was doing more than rubbing muscles. Sable had not noticed, nor had her Big Bunny, what was happening on the massage table. Without wasting any time, they went after one another like most had done in an environment that welcomed such activities.

Sable and her Big Bunny were fully engaged in their sensual delights. Winston and Mitchell had come over to visit and wanted to see what had been happening. Patrick and Andrew were in the office when they came in. Winston had keys and could come without notice. He and Mitchell asked how things were. Andrew said, "You should go out in the backyard." Instead, they went upstairs to the rooftop deck that over looked the property. There they could observe the action without being noticed. Winston reminded Patrick and Andrew that guests sometimes felt inhibited when the owners were around. Up there they saw Sable doing things they never thought she was capable of. At one point, she was leaning back on a palm tree with her Big Bunny wrapped around her waist making her scream with ecstasy. Andrew nudged Patrick and said, "I think that is where mother and Jonathon spent a lot of time. Then, Max could be seen coming from the building holding on to a cat-o-nine tail whip. He moved closer to the massage table and told the masseuse to stop and get off the table with Francois. Max did not like what he saw and proceeded to whip Francois' backside, there still had been oil on his body, making the whipping sting more. Max said, "This is the way I like to treat him when I find him doing bad things. He will not forget this feeling." Max moved away, Francois never moved. The masseuse went about his business as if this behavior was the usual. Andrew said, "This is quite a place and it looks ordinary until you get in here." Winston agreed saying, "That Max character reminds me of what Rex said to me." Patrick said, "This could be an outside Acey Doucey Club." Winston shook his head.

While all the action was being observed, Jerome, the proper British gentleman, had gotten out of his Buick and as he entered through the back gate, he heard sounds of people engaged in activities not likely to be heard in the street. When he saw what was happening, he cleared his throat saying, "I say, I heard things coming from the backyard when I was in the parking lot. Where is the whipping sound coming from?" He walked closer to see Max striking his hand, ever so slowly, with the cat-o-nine tail whip as if he were looking for another person to train. Jerome, who was fully dressed, said as he walked away, "I am too proper for this type of behavior. I like Negro people." Then he saw Sable and her Bunny at the peak of their physical encounter. Sable screamed out for more. Jerome shook his head, grumbled, and walked in to his apartment. Winston thought it was hilarious watching Jerome's reaction to those in the backyard. He said, "He is the guy I met here when he bought Eveline's Buick and made his reservation. I met him at the gate, naked."

CHAPTER 61

A fter working with Eleanor Roosevelt, Eveline began to understand what an enormous job being "First Lady" entailed. Because Eleanor chose to be an advocate to a multitude of issues that plagued the nation, she rarely had contact with Franklin. The relationship between the President and the "First Lady" was a unique combination of politeness and individual personal lives. Their marital relationship was nonexistent and had been driven further apart by Sarah, Franklin's mother, who had been meddlesome in all situations. Eleanor found it more advantageous to involve herself outside of the White House and Hyde Park.

Eleanor had arranged a conference to discuss things which Eveline did not realize or feel was her business. She was told that the government had been in an isolationist mode when dealing with the European crisis. The controversy over American athletes attending the 1936 Olympics in Berlin had been a heated debate with the decision to attend. After the games, it was realized that the atmosphere in Berlin had been a cover up for the terror being inflicted on the Jews. The American athlete, Jesse Owen, won three gold medals and had not been congratulated by Adolf Hitler because he was a Negro and he fell under Hitler's discrimination laws. Eleanor further told Eveline that Franklin never recognized Mr. Owen when he returned from the Berlin Olympics. Eleanor had been campaigning for human rights for all people whether they were colored or white, much to Franklin's disapproval. Eveline listened and wondered where her role in all of this was to be.

One of Eleanor's endeavors began when she toured the coal mining areas of South West Virginia. There she witnesses unexplainable poverty. Most of the miners had been fired from their mining jobs. As a result of this, there was horrific poverty, resulting in a lack of adequate housing, food, and clothing. The children had been affected the worst because they relied on the parents, who had nothing to offer. Eleanor said, "There were families living in huts and coal mines in the early spring with only a few carrots to eat. The schools were nearly nonexistent because funds to provide supplies and pay teachers had run out." When Eleanor returned from West Virginia, she instituted a planned community in that region called Arthurdale to help the victims recover and improve their living conditions. It was a community that would offer housing, schools, and relief. This program was designed to show that the government intended to assist the poverty stricken areas. After listening to the information, Eveline asked what her role would be. Eleanor explained that she had given her these examples of the need for child intervention and her job would be to coordinate the department for child welfare. Eleanor explained about orphan farms that had sprung up throughout the farm regions. Eveline asked what that meant. These were places that housed children that were abandoned by the parents, or who had run away. There were no regulations on their care or what happened to these children. Most were considered indentured servants and put out to farm fields to work long hours or in dangerous conditions, such as sweatshops, with no pay and no hope for the future. Some of these children were sold into prostitution and human trafficking. This conversation brought back memories for Eveline of what Wallace had been doing before his death. Eleanor told Eveline that she had been selected to be part of this project because of her past involvement with criminals who conducted such affairs. Eveline felt like crying when she listened to the very thing her husband had done and thought about what might have happened to Patrick and Andrew.

After what seemed to be more than Eveline expected to hear, Eleanor said, "Remember when we had lunch at the Biltmore? I mentioned my personal relationships. As you may have surmised, I have had a friend that I call "Hick". She is an Associated Press reporter and we have been very close friends for years. We travel together, spend holidays together, and are more than friends. Franklin understands my needs, as I do his, with his personal affairs in Warm Springs, Georgia. He has developed a rehabilitation center for himself and those who are disabled. He uses it for more than rehabilitation, more for a private pleasure retreat for his escapades. We have agreed to keep this among ourselves and close associates. So, if you hear me refer to "Hick", you will understand who this is and you may meet her someday." Eleanor discussed her childhood and how turbulent it had been with her father dying of alcoholism. She told Eveline she had always had difficulty with conflict and would run away from it, even as an adult. She explained that she suffers from depressive events whenever she is saddened by situations. She found the best way to remedy these things was to write. Eveline said, "I am amazed that a woman of your importance and public image would suffer from such things." Eveline thought about her situations and life. Eleanor told her a motto she liked and shared with women. She said, "A woman is like a tea bag. You never know how strong she is until she gets in hot water." They laughed and agreed they had been in loads of hot water in their lifetime.

Eveline asked about the United States' attitude about what had been happening in Europe. Eleanor paused and said, "The policy for non-intervention has been that Germany owes our government millions of dollars from World War I. It is feared that if we become involved in the current issues in Germany, we may never see the money. I think this is an excuse and have cautioned Franklin on being too evasive and slow to make decisions on intervention. Franklin had communication with Adolf Hitler regarding the policies being instituted in Germany. Mr. Hitler would not listen because he compared the discrimination against Negroes in the United States with that of his policies concerning the Jews, Negroes, Homosexuals and other degenerates of society. He felt that the United States should not intervene or make attempts to negotiate when Negroes have been treated unjustly or worse. The Jesse Owen case was an example of the problems here as in Europe. Franklin did not have the courtesy to congratulate Jesse Owen when he returned from the Olympics. Franklin has been overly concerned about keeping the voters satisfied, so avoiding heated issues has been his way of dealing with things. We have known for a long time what has been occurring in Hitler's regime and I fear a war is coming very soon that will involve everyone. The Japanese are invading China, torturing, and killing people as in Germany." Eveline shook her head and wondered if she wanted to be part of this horrific state of affairs, but she was trapped because of the debt she owed the Roosevelts.

Eveline understood the importance of confidentiality when Eleanor had divulged so much information to her about her personal life and that of government affairs. She had been advised by others in her work group to stay abreast of all current happenings between the First Lady and the President. The other woman who were in office were older and had more experience with the atmosphere created by the adversity in the White House. During one of Eleanor's conferences, the topic of lynching had been on the docket. Eleanor had been advocating that a law be passed forbidding such torturous activities. There had been over 50 Negro lynchings in recent years. The Ku Klux Klan had been involved and when one of these occurred, all nearby Negroes were expected to witness it to the end, usually in burning of the body as it hung from a tree. Franklin avoided discussions to outlaw this activity. Eleanor and he had many heated conversations about how unlawful it was and how it caused terror among the Negro citizens. Franklin wanted nothing to do with the issue because he was more concerned with his reputation among the white folks in the country. All of these discriminatory practices gave Adolf Hitler the ammunition to disregard any commentary from the United States and continue on his path of genocide of the Jewish people in Europe. The conference ended with assignments given to each group for their department they would be working in. Eveline had been assigned to Eleanor's staff that would focus on child and women's welfare.

The next morning, Eleanor met with her staff to discuss the strong need to infiltrate in cities where women and children had been subjected to unsafe conditions. The employment opportunities had not improved as much as the Second New Deal had been designed to accomplish. Eveline was in charge of the children and another staff member would oversee the women. The first job was to visit cities that had been identified as places where there had been more abuse and lack of welfare for children and women. Newspaper reports gave examples of New York, Chicago, Washington, the southern parts of Pennsylvania, and the Virginias. Gang style shootings were common in these areas to scare any intervention away. Eleanor had assigned Jonathon to be in charge of ten men that would be covering the security of the women when they traveled to these dangerous environments. She took Eveline aside after the conference and said, "I did not necessarily assign Jonathon to our group. However, he is the most qualified for training men in espionage and security. Franklin has also informed me that he had been planning to send Jonathon to the West Coast to train officers. There is a fear we will be at war in the next few years and well trained officers will be extremely helpful to protect our country. You might want to enjoy him as long as you are able. No telling when he will be reassigned." Eveline said nothing as her mind began to race about all that might come.

CHAPTER 62

1938 had become a crucial year for the United States' and its influences on world affairs. The government maintained an isolationism policy with the European turmoil created by Adolf Hitler's determination to take over countries that bordered Germany. Newspapers would feature articles about the current happenings in Europe, the latest news item on March 22, attracted Mitchell when he read that Hitler's men had invaded Sigmund Freud's home. They confiscated his works, leaving his home in shambles. They destroyed his belongings, smashed the windows, and disconnected his utilities. Elderly Freud, having been ill, became overtaken by fear and his inability to help himself, was left near death. During the attack, the men kept yelling at Freud that "The Fuhrer" did not believe in his work in the mental examination of people and that he needed to be eliminated from society.

Winston had been conducting business at the Tropical Gardens with the help of Olitha and Sable. Even though he had become friends with Mitchell, he did not have the same feelings like he had had for Jason. Winston had conceded to the idea that he would be alone forever. After Sable's escapades at the Bohemia with her Bunny, Winston had a discussion with her about that. He told her he hoped she had enjoyed herself. She said, "Oh, Winston wez had the best times in the Bohemian backyard. Wez never dun sex in the open air. Wez hoping for another time at the Bohemia." Winston knew he needed to set limits on the visitations saying, "Sable, I know you have been a friend of ours for many years. I appreciate all you have been through and done for me and Eveline. Now, we need to leave Patrick and Andrew to their work. I have advised them that the only people allowed at the Bohemia are to be paying customers. We cannot have friends using the guest facilities." Sable stared at Winston saying, "It becuz we Negroes? We be forbidden everywhere in Miami. The only place

260

wez can go for fun is Virginia Key. That beach open to Negroes. Now you tells me wez can't come to visit Patrick and Andrew. I helped Miss Eveline raise doz boys." Winston knew he had hurt Sable's feelings and said, "You understand that the Bohemia is a business that attracts a special type of customer. They may not want to have the owner's friends mingling with them when they are on vacation." Sable shook her and said, I understands. Wez won't calls again."

A few days later, in the Miami Herald's headlines: "Adolf Hitler Wins Elections by a Landslide". April had been the month for the elections for top leaders in Germany. Pressure put on the citizens had been extreme. Everyone had been strongly encouraged to vote for Hitler. All votes would be checked to make sure a vote was given for Adolf Hitler. Most people had feared for their lives if they did not vote as directed, especially the Jews. It had not been publicized but many people had been rounded up and taken away to work camps, for no apparent reason. Accurate information had been difficult to receive because of the attitude of the United States government. It had been reported that shortly after the elections, Austria had been invaded and annexed into Hitler's Germany. "The German Armed Forces Were the Likes the World Had Never Seen". It was beginning to appear that Europe was on the brink of war. What would be the attitude of the United States if this were to occur, according to the newspapers. The United States decreed that all Americans were to leave Austria and Czechoslovakia. The government did not want to be responsible for Americans caught in the European conflicts. President Roosevelt had sent a letter to Adolf Hitler attempting to discuss a more reasonable approach to his invasive plans in Europe. Adolf Hitler had responded unfavorably to any United States involvement. Roosevelt had hoped for compromise, not war.

The United States Post Office had sent a registered letter addressed to Patrick Paine and Andrew Paine. The letter had been sent from the courts in Rochester, New York. When they looked at the envelope, they had no idea why they would be receiving a court registered letter. Andrew said, "I hope this is not more trouble for Mother." He opened the envelope to find

that their grandmother, Alice Paine, had died and her estate had been left
to them. A handwritten letter from Alice had been included in her will.

It read:

Dear Patrick and Andrew,

I have written this letter while I am of sound mind and good will. I
have named you both in my estate. The reason I am doing this is because
neither of you have ever had a decent father. Wallace, my first and favorite
son disappointed me when I found out how corrupt and criminal he had
been all of his short adult life. Since you are the only blood relation left from
Wallace, I want you both to have whatever remains in my estate. I hope you
will use it wisely. I remember how I loved you both when most of the family
did not and could not understand why your mother behaved the way she
had. Your mother and I always had a wonderful relationship and how I had
wished she had been my daughter. Please let your mother know what has
happened. I did see her before Frank died. I have never heard from her again.

Love, Grandma Alice

After Patrick finished reading the letter he looked at Andrew and said,
"Now what." A certified check had been enclosed. Andrew said, "I did not
think our grandparents had been so rich." Patrick shrugged his shoulders
and said, "We need to tell Winston. Mother should know, but we have
no way of getting in touch with her." Patrick telephoned Winston and
told him the news. Winston had forgotten about Alice, since he had been
in Florida and agreed that Eveline needed to know about her death. He
suggested that they call the White House in hopes the message would get
to Eveline. Winston asked, "What will you do with the money?" Neither
of them had thought about that. Patrick said, "We are earning so much
money with our business. I suppose we could save it." Winston replied,
"You guys could pay off your debt to the Roosevelts. Your mother had
no alternative but to work for them to pay back the debt because of your
resignation from West Point."

CHAPTER 63

After some discussion of what to do with the estate check from their grandmother, Patrick and Andrew decided to pay off the debt to the Roosevelts. They had been sending money to the treasury department that handled the financing of the West Point business for the Roosevelts and had been receiving a quarterly statement that listed the amounts that had been deducted from the balance due. Andrew asked how much was still owed to the government; the balance due was a bit more than the check from Alice's estate. They would need to send an additional thousand dollars to satisfy the indebtedness to the Roosevelts. How would their mother react when she found out that she did not need to work for Mrs. Roosevelt anymore? Andrew had telephoned the White House and was able to leave a message for Eveline because they had not yet heard anything from her.

Patrick telephoned Winston to explain what they had decided to do with the estate check. Sable answered the telephone and when she heard who it was said, "Patrick, Iz be talked to by Winston. He telld me wez not welcome anymo to you Bohemia. He tells me only paying peoples can have fun in the Bohemian backyard. Iz sorry wez embarrassed youz." Patrick had not expected such a conversation saying, "I'm sorry Winston said that to you but you do understand about the business and vacation folks." Sable told him that she did and would not ask to visit again. After, Winston was called to the telephone. When he heard Patrick's voice he asked if Sable had spoken to him. Patrick told him that she had and that he and Andrew had made a decision about the estate check. Winston complimented him on the decision and said the same thing Patrick and Andrew had, wondering what Eveline would think when she found out the debt had been satisfied.

Every day, newspapers featured world events that did not predict a calm future. On October 1, the Bohemian Forest that bordered Austria had been overtaken by the Germans for a 100 kilometer stretch, closing off vital routes to that country. It would not be long before there would be a takeover of that region. Slowly, Germany had expanded in every direction. The United States maintained its "long armed" involvement with much unrest in the country, due to conditions created by the Depression. The world was in a critical state, according to reporters, and no one seemed to do much about it, except Adolf Hitler.

Eveline had been sent to the depressed regions of the coal mining areas of West Virginia and Kentucky. Jonathon had been reassigned to be in charge of recruiting and training men in California. Eveline had not expected this to happen so soon. When Eleanor told her to enjoy Jonathon, they had spent one night together, then he was gone. If Eveline had not thought better of the Roosevelts, she could have wondered if this had been a set up. This way, the Roosevelts would be certain of getting Jonathon for the work he was good at and Eveline could pay them back for the debt from West Point. When she thought of this, she felt "had" and angry that her sons had not stepped up to be responsible for their debt. While she thought of these things, she and her group of women had been working in one of the most impoverished areas. Eveline never thought people could survive in such squalor and in less than human conditions. Whenever they went into a town with the supplies, undernourished children would come to them as if they were saviors. Eveline continued to wonder if this type of work was for her. Whenever she and Eleanor would have conversations, Eleanor complimented her on the superb job she was doing with the staff and those being assisted. Eleanor suggested that Eveline consider moving into a departmentalized position, being the head of the office of Child Welfare in Washington. When Eveline heard this, she wondered if she would ever see Jonathon again. Somehow, this had not turned out as Eveline had once thought and hoped for. She was beginning to feel helpless and trapped in a system that was government controlled. She had begun to lose hope of ever marrying Jonathon. All of these situations were beginning to make Eveline want to leave, never to return to anything from her past.

As 1938 was nearing its end, significant events had occurred in Europe. Ernst Von Roth, a German diplomat, had been slain in Paris by a Jewish dissident. After hearing the news, Adolf Hitler made a decree against all Jews. As a punishment, or an excuse to terrorize and eliminate the Jewish population, sanctions had been imposed against the Jews in Germany and Austria. In November, Jews were forced to close their shops, synagogues, businesses, and were forbidden services other citizens had. There were only a few places that Jews could do business and find services with limited hours to be seen on the streets. Slowly, Jews were being rounded up and transported to work camps by railroad cattle cars. As part of the punishment for the assassination, Nazis raided the homes of Jews, looting, raping, stealing, and destroying everything the Jews possessed. It became known as "Kristallnacht", or "The Night of Broken Glass". Every newspaper in the world had reports of the torturous and deadly actions against the Jews in Europe. An all-out attack on the Jews in Europe had begun. By the end of 1938, Finland had been the only European country to repay the United States for the war debt of World War I. Adolf Hitler made it clear that he would never repay the United States the money that Germany owed. When that became public in the United States, many questioned if it had been worth being so isolated from Europe in the hopes of repayment. Now, there was not much left to wait for.

During a return visit to Washington for further work directives, Eveline had been notified of an important meeting with President and Eleanor Roosevelt. She had no idea of why they had requested a meeting. The longer she worked in the capacity she had been assigned, she had little freedom. Eveline wondered if this was all it had been made out to be. As she waited to be called in to the meeting, she thought of Jonathon. Since he had been gone for a few weeks and had not made an effort to notify her. There she sat, not much further ahead than before when she worked at the department store in Miami. At least there, she had freedom and was in charge, for the first time in her life. The President's secretary invited Eveline into the office. She had never witnessed both Franklin and Eleanor together. They appeared more like one might expect the Presidential couple to be. None of this was making sense to Eveline. She sat as Eleanor commented on the good work being done for children. Franklin appeared disinterested, acting fidgety. He, in a curt way, said, "Mrs. Paine, I have here a document that states your indebtedness to us has been satisfied." We thank you for making that final, in such a short time, considering the amount of money." Eleanor reviewed about how disappointed they had been when they were told her sons had resigned from West Point. During their discussion, Eveline wondered how this sum of money had been paid off. She asked the question. Franklin shook his head saying, "If you would have dealt with your messages that have been coming to the White House you would have found out how all this came to be." Eveline, embarrassed, apologized for not knowing what had been happening, as Eleanor handed her the messages. The first was from her sons, wondering why she never called them. Eleanor said, "I recall you feeling bad when they never called you. Now, you have done the same thing to them. I hope this was not a punishment." The second note was regarding the death of Patrick and Andrew's grandmother, Alice Paine. Franklin asked how well Eveline knew the deceased. Eveline explained the family history and how she and Alice had been on good terms. After, Franklin showed Eveline the statement of payment that had been sent by Patrick and Andrew. Eveline was shocked when she saw that they had paid off their debt. Eleanor then said, "Eveline, you have a choice now. You may stay and work as a paid employee for the government or you can be free to go." Eveline was thanked and given a week to make her decision about working in Washington.

After the meeting, Eveline made a telephone call to Miami. Patrick answered saying, "Bohemia, may I help you." Eveline said, "Yes, you may help me be a better mother to you and Andrew." Patrick, sounding adversarial said, "Well mother it is about time you gave us a call. You never told us if you got to Washington with Jonathon. It was like you wanted to escape again. We left many messages for you. It's a good thing we did not need you. You seem to be that way whenever you get a chance to get away." Eveline listened and knew she had been wrong. She apologized and thanked them for paying off the debt. Having thought about all she had been doing to pay off the Roosevelts, she wanted to lecture Patrick on that. She decided not to because she understood Patrick's dissatisfaction with her, after many months of no communication. After asking about Alice's death, Patrick read the letter from Alice. He explained about the decision he and Andrew had made about the estate money. Now, all had been paid for, Eveline told Patrick what Eleanor said about making a choice now that the debt had been satisfied. Patrick asked, "So, mother what are going to do? Will you stay in Washington or will you return to an ordinary life? Sounds like Jonathon has gone off again just like you have done in the past." Eveline explained what her work had been and what it might turn into if she stayed in Washington. Whatever she decided, she would no longer be under the direct scrutiny of the Roosevelts. When the telephone call ended, Eveline felt guilty and regretted having been so unreliable to her sons. She had an inner sense that she wanted to return to an ordinary life as Patrick had said. What sounded like a glamorous job had turned in to working in a depressed environment. Eveline knew this might not be good for her well-being, especially now that Jonathon had been transferred to California. Maybe, she needed to be honest with herself and realize the relationship with Jonathon might never be any more than it had been. Eveline could no longer wait on hope and this may be another step in ending things of the past and taking care of herself.

CHAPTER 64

E veline had not made a decision about her future. She had hoped
something would occur making it easier for her to decide on
her next step. Her responsibilities had changed now that she
had not been under the jurisdiction of the Roosevelts. She had more
freedom to organize her work and the effects of the Depression and world
issues had occupied both the President and Mrs. Roosevelt. After much
debate and coaxing, on the part of Eleanor, lynching became unlawful
and severe disciplinary measures had been put in place. There were many
situations that the President had chosen to ignore, giving the reason of
non-involvement, the voters had become his main concern. His primary
concern had been to be reelected for an unprecedented third term. While
the world read about Hitler's takeovers in Europe, demonstrations of an
anti-Nazi coalition had been organized in the United States. These groups
had been rallying against Nazi Germany's acquisition of the surrounding
European countries. March 15, 1939 marked an invasion of the countries of
Bohemia and Moravia. Shortly after these occupations, a rally of over a half
a million people had been scheduled in New York City at Madison Square
Garden to show disapproval of Adolf Hitler's activities and philosophy. The
rally and a visit from Franklin Roosevelt to New York City had coincided
with no comment from the President, as if the event had not happened.

The United States government had attempted to remain focused on
its economic issues and recovery from the Depression, instead of the
European unrest. In an effort to lift the spirits of the country, the New
York City World's Fair opened on May 1, 1939. The theme, "The Dawn of
a New Day", would demonstrate for thousands of visitors, new inventions,
improved communications, faster transportation, and entertainment in
movies, and television. President Roosevelt had been the first person to
give an opening speech at the World's Fair, which was aired on television,

one of the newest forms of communication, while King George and Queen Elizabeth visited the Canadian exhibit. Because of unrest in Europe, many countries did not participate in the fair. Germany had never agreed to be part of the fair, with Poland and Czechoslovakia closing their pavilions shortly after the opening of the fair. An additional theme came about after the world's fair committee decided on the "Dawn of a New Day" theme, that being "America's Friendship and Peace", in the hopes of creating the image of fellowship in a world where war seemed inevitable.

While the World's Fair had been receiving favorable publicity, Nazi Germany had embarked on a refugee program. Over 900 Jews were given the chance to flee Germany or annihilation. A German owned ocean liner, the St. Louis, had been scheduled to depart for Cuba on May 13. After getting the necessary paperwork and payments for the trip, the passengers boarded the opulent ship and were treated with the highest respect, which seemed too good compared to the way the Jews had been treated. Throughout the voyage, problems presented themselves with fear of being misled and with the rumor that the Jews would not be allowed to disembark the St. Louis, upon arriving into Havana. The newspapers too reported about the voyage and the possibility of being turned away. The rumor became true when Havana rejected the ocean liner's passengers and held the ship in the harbor for a week before it was sent elsewhere. The St. Louis left and went north, close enough to see Miami, to New York where it was not allowed to dock. Newspapers had conflicting reports, some about the beauty of the World's Fair and the opposite was the discouraging voyage of the St. Louis. President Roosevelt would not accept the Jews either, reasoning that the country had been under enough strain and could not accept nearly a thousand refugees. The ship, with barely no supplies or food, returned to the Netherlands and docked at Antwerp where people were randomly put off the ship to survive on their own with nothing except their personal belongings. There had never been a commitment from Germany about the ship or its passengers, all had been a trick to let the world think the Nazis were compassionate to the Jews.

Throughout the time the World's Fair had been opened, the inventions shown had been in operation. The Age of Aviation had made advances with long distant travel. Eleanor Roosevelt had been invited to christen the "Yankee Clipper" on its survey flight for transatlantic service. On June 28, because of the success of the "Yankee Clipper", Pan American Airlines began transatlantic service on the "Flying Clipper". According to reports, similar services had begun from California to Hong Kong. What was seen at the World's Fair had become a reality for worldwide air travel. The movie industry had expanded to, "talkies", movies with sound and voices. Moviegoers had the privilege to see and hear movies, no more piano playing to enhance the action on the silent screen. On August 25, The Wizard of Oz came to the big screen. It starred Judy Garland as Dorothy. It became an immediate hit and filled the theaters. It had been the dream of Mr. Baum when he wrote the story for it to one day be a movie. It featured fantasy, surprise, music, dancing, and hope. All this came at a time when the country needed this on the movie screen.

On September 3, conditions in Europe had continued to decline. The United Kingdom, France, New Zealand, Australia, and India declared war on Germany because of mass destruction and the invasion of Poland by Nazi Germany. President Roosevelt continued advocating for neutrality in the European matter on a radio broadcast. Part of his speech included that all travel and communication with Europe had been stopped. Later in the week, Nepal, South Africa, and Canada joined in the declaration of war. The armed forces of the countries at war in Europe were no match to the Luftwaffe and land forces of the Germans. England, in order to fight the war, had ordered the Navy to mobilize and factories went on overtime building wartime equipment, as did all other countries at war with Germany. In October, Franklin Roosevelt had attempted to be a mediator for world peace. A conference with world leaders had been organized with Adolf Hitler to negotiate an agreement on the issues that created the war. The attempt for a plan had failed when Adolf Hitler rejected the proposed rules of war. The governmental climate in Washington had continued to be strained because there had been groups in Washington that found it necessary to consider intervention in Europe. The President maintained a strong foothold in neutrality, at Eleanor's disapproval. He would not consider any further involvement, after the discouraging attempt with the mediation conference

CHAPTER 65

Bohemia, at 825 Michigan Avenue, continued to be a profitable business for the traveler that enjoyed the freedom of a naturist environment. Patrick and Andrew maintained a high quality business that gained the reputation of an intriguing vacation playground, that no other guest facility could match. It had been rare that a vacancy had been available, even in the low season from May to November. Low season rates had been discounted to an amount that made travel to Miami attractive, especially in the economic climate due to the Depression. Many travelers enjoyed the sultry climate that the summer season offered, making a naturist environment more exciting. One of the guests told Andrew that the heat and humidity made the jungle-like environment more authentic when he and his vacation mate would enjoy all that the Bohemia offered. These had been the guests that checked in, and never left the property. For some of the guests, this seemed confining and limited the possibilities of seeing more of Miami. Whenever Winston visited, he would act as the travel guide, giving ideas to guests about what to enjoy around Miami, especially a visit to the Spaulding Tropical Gardens. Patrick had become the chauffeur whenever trips had been scheduled. A situation occurred when a couple arrived at the Tropical Gardens and proceeded to disrobe, thinking this would be a naturist center just like the Bohemia. Winston and an aghast group of visitors on a buggy ride came upon a nude man and woman strolling hand in hand in the gardens. He took the couple aside and admitted to them that he would rather be like they were, but the property had not been advertised as a naturist center.

One of the most interesting and startling groups of guests had reserved a room overlooking the back of the property, where all the action occurred. As Patrick was registering the guests, he was asked what the regulations for pleasurable activities were for the property. Patrick, who had thought he had witnessed everything, explained that there were no rules except to respect the rights of whatever others enjoyed doing. Shortly after the guests left the office and had unpacked, one man had returned to schedule a massage. Patrick had witnessed most all types of behaviors and levels of attire but when he saw the man's lack of attire, he blinked his eyes seeing only a leather flap that covered him. He carried a paddle. He had placed a handcuff on one of his wrists with the other part dangling. Patrick, attempting to be suave about what he was witnessing, asked, "Who are you expecting or what are you planning to do to the masseuse?" The man said, "As you can see on my registration form that my name is Buddy but I prefer to be addressed as "Sir". I am waiting for my partner who enjoys being punished. He especially likes paddling." Patrick said, "We have other guests who come from Europe that enjoy those activities. They are jewelry dealers but Francois enjoys being under the jurisdiction of the whip from Max." As Buddy left the office, he gave Patrick a devilish smile and said, "We should schedule a visit together so we can have a disciplinary training party." Patrick could not wait to telephone Winston to tell him what he had just heard. Winston answered the telephone and without much being said, Patrick told Winston about his day at Bohemia. Winston found the conversation funny saying, "It sounds like Rex has returned. When your guests get into their activities, call me and I'll be over to give some pointers. Rex had been a good teacher."

The longer Bohemia had been open for business, the more unusual some of the guests had become. When Patrick and Andrew thought they had witnessed it all, two women arrived. One was voluptuous and the other proper acting and well taken care of. Andrew had been working the day they arrived. It became clear who the "in charge" person was. The petite and classy lady baffled Andrew. The well-endowed woman could not wait to unfasten her brassiere, in front of him. He, attempting to be calm with his registration work, found this to be distracting and accidently double charged their account, the error had not been noticed. Later, the quick to disrobe woman, came back to the office with the receipt placed between her breasts saying, "Hey big boy, I think there is a problem with my bill. Did you double charge me because of my size or were you hoping I would come over here alone so you could appreciate me, without my girlfriend." Never had anyone said such a thing or come onto Andrew like this because he was shy and not the least bit attracted to her. He stood nervously waiting for her to take the bill from between her breasts. After what seemed like an hour, she said, "Well, aren't you going to take the bill and change it?" Andrew realized that she did not intend to hand it to him. Just as he had his hand on the bill, Patrick arrived. He did not expect to see Andrew with his hand on a bare chested woman. He cleared his throat, the woman released Andrew's hand and handed the bill to him. Andrew explained the mix up while Patrick had a look of disbelief. After, it was a joke when they discussed the two woman and Andrew's description became more hilarious as he told Patrick. They wondered what the week was to offer after registering the newest guests with their fantasy activities.

The next morning, during breakfast, set the stage for what the week to come might turn into, with the addition of the men and women that enjoyed disciplinary activities. While breakfast had been served, guests enjoyed conversation, food, and where they had come from. Some had arranged day trips around Miami by boat to see the mansions and homes of movie stars and entertainers. They were advised and understood the requirement for clothing after the story of the guests that had visited Winston's Tropical Gardens. Everyone found it amusing to hear about the two walking around as if they had been "Adam and Eve". While this happened, in walked Buddy, with less than his leather pouch and a person following with a dog collar around his neck, on his hands and knees. Everyone in the dining room froze, not knowing what might happen. Buddy, having a perfect physique, was lusted after by the women, and he proceeded to paddle his travel mate as if he were in a dog training situation. The look of uncertainty appeared on everyone's face, wondering if they were to be the next victims of such training. The dog collared person appeared to enjoy the treatment, especially having an audience. While this display had been going on, the two women came into the dining room. The atmosphere for the "ordinary guests" had now become two shows. The women proceeded to parade around the dining room with tassels attached to their pert cleavage. When they finally sat at the table, the woman, that had the bill between her breasts, positioned herself so that the table supported the weight of her cleavage. No one knew what to do or say.

When Winston heard about the activities at Bohemia, he told Patrick and Andrew that they might consider changing jobs with him. He said, "I think I would have a better time working at 825 than in the Tropical Gardens". Patrick told him that Bohemia was becoming better than the Acey Doucey Club. Andrew suggested that Winston consider turning his business in to "Pleasure Gardens" and allow naturist activities on the property. Then, guests could have acres of places to be free. Winston declined the offer because much of his business came from the Chamber of Commerce of Coral Gables. Winston offered to come to 825 to be around to supervise, if they needed extra help during busy times. Patrick gave Winston the date when Bohemia had been scheduled for a naturist fantasy festival with the theme, "Bare as You Dare". Winston could not wait.

CHAPTER 66

1940, the Burke-Wadsworth Act, more commonly known as the Selective Service Act had been ratified. The United States government had been lax in recruiting and training military personnel since World War I. Having been aware of the magnitude of the war in Europe, this created the need to increase the numbers of military in the armed services. Men between the ages of 21-35 were to be drafted into military service. When Eveline heard about this new law, she worried about the possibilities that Patrick and Andrew might be called into service, especially having been at West Point. It had been a high topic of conversation in Washington and the worry of war with Europe had been endless. President Roosevelt continued to maintain the "Hands off Europe" policy. He remained focused on domestic affairs and his campaign for re-election to the presidency.

Fashion designers had taken a more positive approach to encourage women to buy new clothing and accessories. Because of the Depression, only the well-to- do had been able to maintain a higher style of attire. It was hoped that a more reasonable pricing campaign would stimulate a wider range of buyers. Ida Lupino, a movie star, enjoyed great publicity when she had been featured in magazines wearing the newest in nylon stockings, dresses that had a flare, shoes with higher heels, holding a cigarette holder. After the Lupino look became so popular, every woman in the Washington circle of employees made a point of being seen in the latest styles. Eveline, having been accustomed to the latest styles, bought whatever she could find that matched the Lupino image. Since she had been earning more money, she had no problem making fashionable improvements to her wardrobe. While shopping in Washington's best department stores and boutiques, Eveline realized how much she missed her work at Burdines fashion office, remembering that her dresses and accessories would have been offered to her as part of the job. She had been giving serious thought about how much more time she wanted to spend working in Washington. She had received a letter from Jonathon that did not bring happy news to her. He had written to explain that he had been transferred from California and would be stationed in Hawaii. When Eveline read the letter she knew that she had been correct in telling herself that she needed to put Jonathon out of her mind and take care of herself. After rereading the letter, she convinced herself that she did not feel the same as she once had when he gave her news of being apart. Whenever issues like these arose, Eveline would remind herself of how much she had learned from Dr. Kane. She would never forget Jonathon for convincing her to go for counseling and him paying for it.

After Patrick had lectured Eveline on her evasive and run away behavior, she wrote a letter to her sons. She intended to explain her feelings for Jonathon and his whereabouts, her work, and concern about the Selective Service Act. While she wrote the letter, her mind kept taking her to thoughts of Jonathon, not their personal relationship, but his generosity in paying for her counseling. How could she ever repay him, now that she may never see him again? It became clear, as she wrote the letter, that Jonathon's presence had seemed to make working in Washington a good idea. That situation had changed, leaving her alone again and she was not happy with the job in Washington. She wanted to return to Miami. After being close to the Roosevelts and government operations, Eveline wanted no more of the high handed controls and game playing she had witnessed. The general public had no knowledge of government policy making and the American citizens were usually the last to be considered in the welfare of the country or economy. Eveline explained that she would be returning to Miami, but was not certain when this might happen. After sealing the letter, she wondered how the news would be received by all she had left behind in Miami.

The presidential election campaign had been taking precedents in the recent months. Franklin Roosevelt had been in office for two terms and because he had been given the credit for pulling the country out of the worst part of the Depression, the Democratic Party nominated him to be the presidential candidate. Since there continued to be much controversy over world policies and war possibilities, it appeared like a runaway election might happen. Wendell Willkie had been nominated as the Republican opponent to Roosevelt. Franklin Roosevelt had always been more concerned about his voter reputation than other pressing matters, but Eleanor had continued working on her social and equality issues. Their marital relationship had deepened into a mutual understanding of making things look good and publicly supporting one another. Eveline had been close enough to their relationship to see that it was similar to her life and marriage to Wallace, making her feel the need to get away from it. What had begun as a way to escape her past, had put Eveline in the viewer's seat, but had reminded her of her past life. All these situations had played heavy on her mind and she decided to submit her letter of resignation after the New Year.

News from Europe continued to plague the world. The countries that had declared war on Germany were fighting hard to overtake the strong German military forces. England had been bombed continually by the Luftwaffe in what had become known as the "Blitzkrieg". London had suffered enormous devastation but had maintained life with the threat of bombings and hearing the sirens warning of surprise attacks. Patrick and Andrew had been hearing the news of the war on the radio and from guests at Bohemia who had relatives that had been affected by the war. Some of the guests had sons that had been the first to be drafted in to military service. Most felt the Selective Service Act had been enacted to prepare the United States for war with Germany. Andrew and Patrick were the perfect age to be drafted into service, since they were soon to be 23 years old. The fact that they had been in officer training at West Point might be a reason for them to be drafted. Patrick had not thought of this and said, "Andrew, you have always been the worrier for both of us." Andrew replied, "I have a premonition of things to come. I have always had vivid thoughts about the future but have never spoke about it. I feared being thought of as crazy."

News of the elections had been broadcast over the radio and new technology made it possible to view a televised news report of the election for President. Most folks listened intently as they had many times when Franklin Roosevelt could be heard giving his "Fireside Chats", believing what the President had said on those occasions. This time, the news had eagerly reported that Franklin Roosevelt had been reelected to an unprecedented third term as President of the United States. There remained a terrifying fear of war with Europe, no matter who became the leader.

CHAPTER 67

The United States had been recovering from the Depression in the agricultural areas helping to improve the economic situation. Still suffering from economic hardships and unemployment, were workers in companies that had not been part of the government funded programs. Rumors circulated that the only way to end economic despair would be the countries' involvement in a war. Because of the European war, the possibilities of American involvement had seemed like a way to end all the effects of the Depression. When this topic would arise, anyone that had sons in the military feared the possibilities of a war. Advertisements were seen everywhere encouraging young men to join the military. A picture of men in uniform had become part of the campaign to enlist before being drafted. Every time Andrew saw a poster, he had a premonition of him and his brother in a place of war.

Winston had been visiting the Bohemia more than usual. Patrick thought the visits were to check out how the business had been operating. After a few weeks of more than usual visits, Patrick asked Winston if there had been a reason for his frequent visits. Patrick admitted that he felt like Winston did not feel things were going as well as possible. When Winston heard these things he said, "I am amazed at how well you guys have made this place a success. You have earned lots of money and have a full schedule of guests." Patrick asked, "Why are you here so often if you find everything in good order?" Winston admitted he was unhappy and lonely at the Tropical Gardens. Sable and Olitha had resigned and had found work nearer to their homes in Overton. Patrick had no idea that all these things had happened and asked, "Who is helping you with the business?" Winston explained that he had changed how things operate. He no longer had a tram service around the gardens and he ran the office and gift shop. He explained that he could do it all that way, but things were showing the need for improvement. He admitted that he did not have the energy to run the place anymore. Ever since Jason had died, he had never recovered, even with trying to create a relationship with Rex or Mitchell. Patrick asked why he and Mitchell had not maintained a friendship. Winston told him that Mitchell was too good for him. Patrick shook his head saying, "You must be kidding. You are every much a man as he." Winston admitted that he had never been able to get Jason out of his mind whenever he tried to get to know other people. Patrick looked at Winston and said, "Isn't life funny. You have always been like a father to me and been my idol. Now, I feel like things have reversed." Winston spoke, at great length, about all that had happened to him since Jason's death. While Patrick listened he thought about Winston's near death experiences with the crazy neighbor, who attempted to poison him and then the crazy behaviors with Rex. Patrick sympathizing with Winston, asked what he could do.

Patrick suggested they go to lunch on the beach. While they were at a restaurant, Winston told Patrick that he had written a will and his estate would be left to him and Andrew. The Tropical Gardens were to be given to Coral Gables to be established as a forever park. While Patrick listened he understood the need for such a document but asked, "Do you have any plans?" Winston finally got to the point of his frequent visits. He liked being around the atmosphere of the Bohemia better than the gardens. The clientele at Bohemia was more to his liking. Patrick explained that he would be welcome anytime, but they had been able to handle everything on their own. When Winston heard this, in those words, he knew that he would be in the way. Patrick jokingly said, "When Andrew and I are drafted in to military service, you can run Bohemia on your own terms." Winston had no response and only stared at Patrick. This had not been the usual reaction Winston would have given in the past.

After the lunch, when Winston went back to the Tropical Gardens, Patrick could not stop thinking about how depressed Winston appeared. Winston had been correct when he told Patrick he had not been happy since Jason's death but what could be done to help him feel better about his life? He spoke to Andrew about what had happened. Andrew listened intently and after a few minutes said, "I am not surprised. Winston has had life experiences that most have not or may never have. He is a devoted person and has shown us that most of our lives. He is deeply sad and unhappy without Jason. No one has realized how much he has suffered alone. Everyone thinks Winston is strong and can overcome anything. He has been hurt by many people, your father for one. I have had visions of Winston going off and never being found again. I wish I did not have these thoughts, because they might happen." Patrick became angry with Andrew saying, "You have always been afraid and acted scared of things. You probably have mistaken your fears for visions." Andrew said nothing, only shook his head, while Patrick walked away with a disgusted look on his face. He could not help wondering if his brother did have some ability to predict the future.

Every day at Bohemia brought new experiences. Just when things were uneventful, someone or thing would change the atmosphere. The doorbell rang and Andrew went to see who was there. He knew there were no available accommodations so who could this be? The mailman stood next to a woman who was over six feet tall. The mailman, being short, admitted he lost his key to enter the property to deliver the mail. The tall "woman" said in a deep voice, "You say that to all your tricks. I know you want me in the worst way." Andrew stood watching the show, now, not sure if the mailman was actually their mail carrier. He did not recognize him, but knew there had been substitutes for mail deliveries. Andrew watched as the pushy woman began to touch the mailman. Andrew opened the gate explaining there were no available rooms or apartments. This did not seem to matter and by this time, the supposed woman had her hands down the mailman's shirt. Andrew asked the mailman if he was for real. The mailman admitted he liked men in uniforms who worked for the United States Post Office and always wanted to dress up like one. Andrew had all he could do not to laugh, until the woman lowered her dress and exposed a muscular chest. Andrew, still trying not to laugh at seeing a man with a dress below his waist who was wearing a wig, was more than he could handle. While this was happening, Andrew had escorted the two to the back of the property. They only wanted to enjoy one another for an hour but paid for a full day. Just as this was happening, the real mailman came into the property and saw his imposter. He laughed and could barely hand Andrew the day's mail. He said, "This is one crazy place. Maybe I should dress up and deliver mail like the woman in the wig." He left Bohemia shaking his head and laughing, while Andrew looked at the mail and saw a letter from Eveline.

CHAPTER 68

————⟨⟩————

A ndrew looked at the envelope with a sense of suspicion. This
had been the first time his mother had written a letter to Patrick
and him. Andrew had not been aware that Patrick had lectured
Eveline on her lax attitude and runaway behavior. Andrew opened the
letter and it read:

Dearest Sons,

I have taken time to think about what you said to me, Patrick, about my
behavior. I realized I have not been as good to you about communicating
as a mother should have been. After you were found and reunited with
me, you both made a life for yourselves. I thought I could do the same.
After the turmoil of my financial downfall, because of issues I had been
unaware of, I wanted to escape. Even though I loved my job at Burdines,
and being on my own for the first time in my life, I am finding out that
I miss being near my family and friends. When I had no choice but to
accept employment from the Roosevelts to repay the West Point debt, I
did not think I would resent having to correct a mistake that had not been
created by me. After a while, I became angry that you boys did not take
full responsibility for the debt. It was only because of your grandmother's
estate and some repayment by you that the debt got repaid. I must admit I
became less angry with you after that. Even though most of my life I have
been forced to clean up situations and make good on things others had not
completed, leaving me responsible in one way or another.

My work here in Washington has been an experience, one that I did
not expect to have with so many diverse responsibilities. Since the debt
to the Roosevelt's has been satisfied, I am no longer as involved with
Mrs. Roosevelt as I once had been. My work has taken me to places that
I did not expect, like the severe poverty stricken areas of West Virginia.

The part of government that the ordinary citizens of our country never see, are not as glamourous as they are made out to be in the newspapers. I have witnessed many occasions where the general public is the last to be considered, especially after the effects of the Depression on the poor. The upper class folks in this country have never been as exposed to the severity of the last 10 years and the struggles of the poor to survive, due to the Depression and limited opportunities. My assignments have taken me to the people who have witnessed these difficult times. I am frustrated, lonely, and tired of living on the road and reporting to the office in Washington. I have received a letter from Jonathon that did not bring good news to me. After thinking and being convinced that he would be with me in Washington, he has been transferred. When I received the first communication, he had been transferred to California and recently he has been sent to Hawaii. The tone of the letter was more to inform me that he would not be returning and that I was on my own, once again!

I am sorry to pour out all this news and I apologize to you both. I have made a decision to resign from my work here in Washington. My responsibility to the debt to the Roosevelts is what made me take on this work. Now that I have had a chance to decide if I like my work, I do not, and want to return to Miami. I have submitted my resignation effective January 1 and will be back in Miami. I hope I can find a place to live when I return. I suppose that 825 Michigan Avenue is in full operation so there would not be a place for me. I am hoping to re-apply for a job at Burdines and maybe I can stay at Winston's Tropical Gardens. Could you please let him know of my intentions?

Love, Mother Eveline

After Andrew finished the letter, he sensed a difference in Eveline's letter with the strange closing, Mother Eveline. If he did not know better, he might have thought she was a friend, not his mother, in the tone of her writing. He would be interested in what Patrick might think when he read it. Andrew had not forgotten all that Winston had told Patrick and him about his loneliness and that maybe if their mother lived with him, he might feel better. Andrew knew that Winston had deeper issues than Eveline could handle. In Andrew's view of what he was sensing, he tried to forget about his being tormented about what might be about to happen. He could not pin point anything, except it had to do with them and Winston.

When Patrick arrived at 825, he asked how the day had gone. After a laugh about the episode with the mailman and his "Women", Andrew handed Eveline's letter to him. Patrick looked at it and said, "I guess my lecture to Mother made a difference. I wonder what she wants now?" Andrew did not respond, only watched as Patrick read. A lowering of Patrick's eyebrow let Andrew know the letter had had an effect on him. He began shaking his head when he reached the part about the money and their lax attitude toward payment. He sighed toward the end about the request that they intervene on her behalf to Winston about her living at his place. Patrick said, "If I did not know better, I would have thought our mother was an acquaintance and not our mother." Andrew agreed and admitted that is what he had sensed. He did not dare bring up his premonitions because Patrick already thought he was a worrier and might be crazy. Neither one thought it was their business to convey her request about living at the gardens. They decided to telephone Winston and read him the letter.

Winston answered the telephone with a somber tone. Patrick told him that he needed to use a perkier tone if he expected to get any business. Winston responded, "I do not want any business. I like it quiet and to be left alone." Patrick shook his head and explained about the letter. Winston sounded better when he heard that they had received a letter from Eveline. Patrick read the letter and made an effort not to use any tone that would suggest his discomfort with Eveline's attitude and desire to live at the Tropical Gardens. When Patrick finished reading the letter, Winston said, "Your mother always had a way with words. She never thinks before she says things. The best part about her is that she is usually right, even though she can have a big mouth." Patrick laughed when he heard Winston's description of Eveline. Winston asked if he was supposed to write and invite her or was she just going to show up at the Tropical Garden gate? Andrew said, "It is my thought that we should do nothing and see how things work out. I have a feeling we may have no choice in these matters." Winston could hear Patrick when he told Andrew, "There goes the worrier again. I think he needs a crystal ball."

CHAPTER 69

The Bohemia "Bare as You Dare" festival was soon approaching. Patrick and Andrew, with the help of Winston, sent out invitations to previous guests inviting them to make reservations for the event that was to be held in early October. It was hoped that guests would reserve all the accommodations and then the general public would be notified. While making plans for the weekend, Winston suggested contests for both men and women and some combined events that might create a more festive environment. His favorite was to be a game that would require the men and women to use anything but their hands, feet, and heads to hit a beach ball around and through the vegetation. If a contestant used any of these body parts to hit the ball, they would be eliminated. The last person standing would be a winner of a free week at Bohemia. Winston had volunteered to be the judge of the event. He told Andrew and Patrick that he had lots of experience with how creative people can be, he referred to it as volleyball without hands, feet, and heads. Patrick said, "Yes Winston, we remember how much you taught us as kids about being free with our bodies and swimming in the lake." Winston smiled, for the first time in a long time, when he realized what fun he had been missing by being at the Tropical Gardens. As part of the weekend, the invitation called for another contest for creative ways to be a naturist. They laughed when they included that in the invitation, wondering what types of gadgets might be used during the weekend. Andrew said, "I guess we will not be needing much except towels. Our jobs will be easy. All we will need to do is watch naturists having fun." Patrick could not believe he had heard such things coming from Andrew, who had the reputation for being the "Shy Worrier".

Early in spring of 1941, in the height of the tourist season, a technicolor movie musical had been released entitled "Moon Over Miami". It featured

Walter Lanz, Betty Grable, Don Ameche, and Bob Cummings. It had been advertised as "The Best Way to Get Over the Depression". It was a bright and bubbling movie that took place at The Flamingo Hotel. The story line depicted three women and their trials and tribulations while in Miami. Humorous and having lots of music made it a smash hit. As a promotion, Patrick purchased complimentary tickets for the paying guests during the week the movie debuted. These perks were good advertising and helped to encourage guests to return and tell others about the Bohemia. There had been no other place like it in Miami; one guest had been heard saying. When Winston asked why Patrick and Andrew came up with that idea, they told him that since the movie had been about staying at the hotel, they thought free tickets for their hotel guests would make a good impression. Winston complimented them for their good sense for business promotions.

The Miami Herald had continued to report about events in Europe. As months went by, Germany continued to invade countries and had intensified a campaign of targeting the Jewish populations in the countries that had been annexed to Germany. They had been rounded up and taken away, but now there had been news of further elimination of the Jews. On Memorial Day weekend, May 27, President Roosevelt made news when he proclaimed that the United States was entering into an "Unlimited National Emergency". It was beginning to be more difficult now with the Japanese at war in Asia, with the United States geographically between two continents at war. In order to prepare, the United States government escalated the military forces by raising the number of draftees necessary to build a larger military. When Andrew read this, his premonition of Patrick and he being drafted became a close reality. He wondered what would become of the Bohemia if they went off to serve in the military?

Eveline had sent her letter of resignation to Eleanor Roosevelt and had heard nothing. She wondered if she had received it or had ignored it. Having worked for months beyond the date of her resignation, Eveline attempted to contact Eleanor. While at the Office for Child and Women's

Welfare, she made a stop to see Eleanor's secretary. When Eveline explained her concern, the secretary gave her a piece of information that helped her understand the lack of response about her resignation. She was told that many people were, as she put it, "Bailing Out". Eveline asked why. Many employees feared that the country might be at war soon and wanted to escape any possibility of being pulled into the war effort from a government stand point. Eveline did not yet understand why she had not been given her resignation acceptance. The secretary explained that she had been told to hold her off for as long as possible. There had been a new organization formed that might be to her liking. The secretary admitted she had told her more than she should have but would let Mrs. Roosevelt know she had inquired about her resignation letter.

The "Bare as You Dare" festival had been receiving many reservations. The hotel sold out within a week by former guests. The general public had been reserving and paying the required fee which left only a few spaces available. The guest list was nearing 200, Patrick, Andrew, and Winston feared a possible crowd control situation. After discussing their concern with the Miami Beach police, Winston was told that there would be a few officers assigned to the event with no worry of arrests for lewd and lascivious behavior. One of the officers, who volunteered for the event, asked if he could come to the festival with only his hat and carry a night stick. Winston found that to be an exciting thought, but the Chief of Police recommended a casual uniform and no equipment to be used.

A week before the festival, two official letters, that Andrew hoped might never arrive, came in the mail. They had been sent from the Selective Service Department in Washington. He stared at the envelopes and knew that he and his brother were being notified of the time and place to report for physicals and the possibilities of being drafted into military service. He decided to wait until Patrick arrived before opening the letters. Because of his ability to sense things before they happened, he felt he had read the words before he opened the mail. Patrick came into the office, Andrew handed him the letters and said, "Do you want to read them or do you want me to tell you what they say?" Patrick shook his head, opened his letter and it read exactly as Andrew thought, except the date of October 12, 1941, to report for physicals. They looked at one another as Patrick said, "Now, what are we going to do with the Bohemia?" Andrew suggested they call Winston to explain the news and hope he would have a solution.

Andrew decided it was not a good idea to remind Patrick about his premonition of what had just happened. While Patrick telephoned Winston, he waited and knew the outcome of the conversation. After telling Winston that they might be drafted into military service, there was no conversation. Patrick held the receiver with a confused look. He asked, "Winston did you hear what I told you?" Winston could be heard, with the receiver away from Patrick's ear, that he had heard and had to think. He, in a cheerful tone, said, "I will move in to the Bohemia. I am tired of working the Tropical Gardens and will donate them to Coral Gables as I had intended in my estate. When you guys are finished in the service, you can return. This helps me and I hope for the best for you." Andrew knew that was how it was to happen, but Patrick asked, "Are you sure? You owned this place once when Mother transferred it to you and Jason before running off to California." Winston explained that was what he had hoped for and that had been why he spent so much time at 825. Now, he could continue with the dream he and Jason once had.

After everything had been decided, Patrick and Andrew thought that they had been put on the draft list because of their West Point affiliation. They had no choice but to accept the idea about going back to a military environment. Maybe, they would be given officer's jobs after their West Point training. Andrew had a gnawing feeling about their mother returning to Miami. While things were being planned for the festival, the weather forecasted a possibility of bad storms. Patrick worried that it would hinder the "Bare as You Dare" festival. A hurricane had struck in the Bahamas and was nearing the coast of South Florida. Winston telephoned them to report that he had been told by the Coral Gables officials to close the gardens and prepare for a hurricane. He suggested they do the same for Bohemia.

The media had begun to announce the emergency closing of all businesses. Patrick hung up the telephone and said, "I guess the festival will have to be cancelled. A hurricane is due to hit the day our festival begins." Andrew knew again this was to happen. He made no reference to his premonitions and said, "We will have to refund all the money we have received."

CHAPTER 70

Winston went to the Coral Gables town offices to discuss the transfer of the Spaulding Tropical Gardens. He had made the legal agreement that the gardens would become part of the parks department. He readjusted his will that eliminated the gardens from his estate. The officials at the town office were delighted to have been gifted such a noted landmark to be enjoyed forever. The city agreed to leave everything in place and never change the original contents or configuration of the gardens. The Coral Gables officials directed the overseeing of the operation and staffing of the gardens to the Coral Gables Historical Society and Garden Club. When Winston concluded his meeting, he left feeling like a weight had been lifted from his shoulders. What had begun as a gift from Eveline for the many years of friendship, to a sorrowful life after Jason's death, was over. He looked forward to new adventures.

The following week, Patrick and Andrew began preparations for leaving 825 Michigan Avenue for wherever their military experiences might lead. For them, it seemed like they had completed West Point and were moving into what they had been trained to do. It would have been about three years since they left West Point and would be graduated officers if they had remained there. Patrick, Andrew, and Winston agreed to meet at 825 the day before leaving, giving Winston time to become familiar with the property again. For him, he felt like he was returning to something he had never been able to experience or complete life in a guest facility. While the three were discussing the operations, the telephone rang. Andrew answered saying, "Good Morning, Bohemia, may I help you?" Eveline replied, "Yes, dear how are you?" Andrew paused, since he had not expected his mother's voice, because it had been many months since they spoke. Eveline, in a cheerful tone, told Andrew to let everyone know that she would be returning to Miami next week. Andrew's eyes went up upon hearing this news and said, "Well, Mother, Patrick and I have been drafted into the military. Winston has donated the Spaulding Tropical Gardens to the Coral Gable Historical Society and he will be living here and running Bohemia." There was no sound from the other end of the line until Andrew asked if Eveline had understood the news. She replied, "I did and am upset there will be no place for me." She hung up.

After the conversation, Eveline felt alone again. In the hopes of possibly getting her job at Burdines, she made a call to the fashion office. The woman Eveline spoke to had replaced the person that had taken over when Eveline left. After a few minutes of discussion, Eveline was told the only positions available might be in the restaurant or the stock room. Burdines had reduced the number of employees in the hopes of saving money because sales had dipped. Eveline, disappointed again, told herself that going back to Miami may not be a good idea. As she thought about the situation, she came to realize how alone she was. There was no more Jonathon. Her sons were leaving for places unknown, with war looming. Winston was overseeing 825. She had been left to survive on her own power. While she contemplated what to do, she remembered what Eleanor's secretary had mentioned about a reason why there had been no acknowledgement of her letter of resignation.

Eveline went to Eleanor Roosevelt's office to inquire about her letter. When she entered the office, Eleanor stood by the desk and said, "Eveline, we were just getting ready to contact you. Please step into my office." The three women sat in a circle, Eleanor not behind her desk. She began, "Eveline, you must think I was remiss in not responding to your letter. There has been reason for such delays. The first being that we knew your sons were to be drafted because they had some training at West Point. When I read your letter, I had a feeling you were planning to go back to Miami. However, since there are few reason for you to go back, there is a new organization that was established last February. It is called the United Service Organization. I believe this will be a positive move for you. Bob

Hope will be the main attraction who will be traveling around the country and to various parts of the world to entertain the military troops. I know how eager you have been to be in the spotlight and I have recommended you to be on staff and travel with the USO." Eveline sat stunned at such an offer. Her first inclination was to refuse and go back to Miami and be on her own. After a moment, she heard the voice telling her to get going and get away. She thought it was Catherine coming back to terrorize her once again. Without any hesitation, Eveline accepted.

She would be departing to meet Bob Hope and the staff that would be on their way to California. All the expenses were being paid by the USO. Eveline found no reason to notify anyone in Miami of her new endeavor or whereabouts. While packing, she wondered if she might run into Jonathon at one of the programs in Hawaii. Then, she thought about Patrick and Andrew being in training somewhere. It was the holiday season coming up and she wondered how they would make out alone on Christmas. Who knows, she might see Jonathon, Patrick, and Andrew. Eveline thought that would be a strange way to celebrate the holidays. Before Eveline could think about what might happen, she found herself seated on a government airplane heading for California. Never did she think she would be returning to California.

Things began taking a strange turn of events. Andrew had been exceptionally bombarded with premonitions. He knew their mother had new responsibilities that had taken her far away from Miami. He also visualized Patrick and himself seeing her in that faraway place. Patrick and Andrew had been stationed in a California Officer Training School. So far, everything Andrew sensed had come true, even though he feared what he sensed, he did not admit to anything. World events had become more intense with war almost a certainty for a United States intervention.

Patrick and Andrew received certificates for completing the officer training course and were given orders to go to Hawaii. They remembered their mother mentioning that Jonathon had been sent there. Patrick said, "Who knows, maybe we will see Mr. Bingham in Hawaii. Mother would be jealous," They laughed as they boarded an Air Force plane headed to Hawaii. When Eveline arrived in Los Angeles, she was greeted by staff members of the USO. They were delighted to meet her and mentioned that they had been briefed by Mrs. Roosevelt about the newest member of the entertainment committee. Eveline was told that there would be a dinner held that evening for a briefing at the USO planning office. Bob Hope would be there to meet everyone and discuss the itinerary. Eveline felt like she had arrived in Hollywood again, when she heard about show plans with Bob Hope. The itinerary had been published and their first stop would be Hawaii. Eveline had no idea that her sons had been deployed there. She only knew about Jonathon being there.

After having breakfast, the staff prepared to go to the Air Force Base and would fly to Hawaii. Just as they entered the airport, there was a news bulletin on the radio. There had been an attack on Pearl Harbor by the Japanese. On December 7, 1941, President Roosevelt could be heard saying, "This Day Would Go Down in Infamy. The United States was now at War." The trip to Hawaii had been cancelled. Everyone felt blessed they were not in Hawaii a day earlier. The radio continued announcing about the devastation and that the most recent count had been over 2300 people killed, with many ships sunk in the harbor. Eveline felt alone and panicked with the news and wondered if Jonathon had been near the attack and if he was still alive. As she stood in the panic of a terrified crowd, little did she know that her sons might have been in the attack on Pearl Harbor. She stood in a daze, alone, wondering what to do next.

AFTERMATH

After a few days, Eveline received a letter from the President's office. Before she opened it, she had a premonition of what it might say. She and many others had been waiting and worrying that their loved ones may not have survived the Japanese attack on Pearl Harbor. The USO travels had been suspended to Hawaii and the staff remained in California until further assignments. Eveline took a deep breath as she opened the letter which explained what she had feared most. Patrick and Andrew had arrived hours before the attack and had been among those killed on December 7. Eveline's reaction to this news made her feel more alone than ever. She did not think that could be possible, but now realized she had lost her entire family over the years. Eveline now knew that she could not return anywhere because her past experiences had eliminated all possibilities of "going home". According to the letter, all arrangements were to be taken care of for Patrick and Andrew's burials and a plaque honoring her sons would be sent to her.

While Eveline and others received similar letters, the USO office provided the necessary accommodations for the comfort of the people involved in the harsh news. As the days passed, Eveline met an officer who had been trained by Jonathon. She felt a sense of relief when speaking to this man. During the conversation, Eveline learned that Jonathon had seen Patrick and Andrew in Hawaii. The officer knew this information because he had been one of the fortunate people to have left Hawaii hours before the attack. When the officer explained this to her, this sent Eveline into a state of hysteria. The officer helped her to the medical office for a tranquilizer to calm her down. Eveline remained there until she was able to deal with the tragedy of her sons and her true love, Jonathon. She had convinced herself that her life was over because there was no one left and no place to return to. Eveline had been encouraged to remain on the staff of the USO to help honor and entertain the soldiers and to honor those who had lost their lives. She decided that was the only way to continue because she would always remember Patrick and Andrew when she saw young men that reminded her of her deceased sons. Whenever she saw security men, she remembered how much she loved Jonathon and had always hoped they would be together. Eveline Paine continued working and traveling with the USO until her death in 1957 in California, never fully recovering from the events of her tragic life.

SOURCES

_____, Geneva Daily Times 1932-1941

Wiesen, Blanche C. Eleanor Roosevelt, 1933-1938

Witts, Max, &Thoreau, Gordon, Voyage of the Damned

Ask.com/ Wikipedia

The 1930's- www.history.com/topics/ 1930s

Miami Beach Archives.com

ACKNOWLEDGEMENTS

Thanks to Marsha Houser for assisting in the reading and editing of this manuscript. Special gratitude goes to Vivian Dwyer, Donna Gibbs, and Shirley Wharton for accepting the challenge to read the drafts and offer feedback as the book was being developed. Special thanks to Steven Kane for assisting me in the accuracy of the counseling sessions referred to in the book.

Printed in the United States
By Bookmasters